THE EXODUS OF CHARLIE LORD

By

Bill Wetmore

Table of Contents

Dedication

To my father, who gave me a love of books, and my mother, who gave me the gift of laughter.

Acknowledgments:

I wish to thank Cynthia Tyler, Alister Reeds, Gayle Shunway, and all those who played a role in the creation of this book. No matter how large or small, your contribution to this work and your role in my life is cherished deeply. Most of all, I wish to thank Ms Karma Lavelle Hamsoak for her patience, love, laughter, and her refusal to let me publish this in its original form.

Prologue

My childhood friend, Willy Wetmore, wrote about me in his book, *The Autobiography of Charlie Lord*. I read it, and it was mostly true, but he put in a lot of poetic language that wasn't really necessary. Also, some of the stuff in the book never really happened the way he said it did, although he claims it's true in some mystical, deep, symbolic sense, whatever that means. Anyway, that's why I decided to write my own book. I don't necessarily want to set the record straight. I just want to tell my own story in my own words, without a lot of flowery language or symbolic meanings, just a fairly straightforward narrative about my exodus from Mythic, Connecticut, the town of my childhood, and my journey to discover that America I had loved so fervently, no matter how many times she ignored or turned her back on me.

Anyway, if you want to learn more about America Lightshadow, my Uncle Isamu, and the tornado that carried him off during my high school graduation, I recommend you read Wetmore's book, *The Autobiography of Charlie Lord*. It might not be 100% true in all the particulars, but it makes a good starting point for my journey to find the heart of America. If you've already read that book, then you can skip the first chapter of this one, which I basically plagiarized from Wetmore, but the rest of the book is all my own, for the most part, except a couple of chapters that Willy slipped in while the book was getting uploaded to the publisher. I have my doubts about how much of Willy's chapters actually happened, but he says even if the events in his narrative didn't happen exactly the way he claims they did, they're all just honest lies through which truth is revealed. I don't know if I agree with him. The truth is always the truth, even if it never happened.

So, I've divided the book into two parts. The first part is mostly my experiences in college, which some of you may find boring and irrelevant. If you're that kind of reader, then feel free to skip directly to Part II, which details how I set out from Mythic, Connecticut, in search of an America who turned out to be nothing more than the ghost in the mirror haunting herself as much, if not more, than she haunted me. Instead of America, I found Karma. Karma gets us all in the end.

3

PART 1

Institutions

Chapter 1 Dreams

My uncle, Isamu Kawabata, and I both loved America. He loved America as the land of opportunity, as the place where hard work paid off and dreams came true. He'd followed my mother from Japan to the US in the early 1960s and originally came with the idea of becoming a successful jazz musician. He played the saxophone and gave me my first lessons on the instrument when I was six or seven. He loved everything about America and Americans—the food, the music, the fast cars, the whiskey, and—most of all—the women. He seemed to entertain a new one every night, to the dismay and envy of my father, down in the basement of our house, where he stayed after his arrival from Japan.

Isamu got a job as a cook at The Lobster Pot, a restaurant near the lighthouse in Mythic, Connecticut. He worked there for a year, and after each shift, he'd come home and tell us all how busy the restaurant was and how easy it would be to open his own restaurant.

"Ah, I have idea for own prace. Make rot of money! Become rich guy!"

My father laughed at my uncle. After seeing combat in Germany during WWII and getting wounded in the Korean War, my father had opened a diaper service with a friend of his who'd invented the first waterproof coverings for cloth diapers. He'd worked long hours to make the business profitable and was convinced that his brother-in-law, the guy who spoke broken English, would never become a successful restaurateur. I heard him talking about it with my mother one night.

"Your brother's a fool if he thinks he'll ever become rich owning a restaurant. There are already millions of restaurants all over the country. If you're gonna start a business, you need to find a need and fill it! 'To be the man who does succeed, you must be he who fills a need!' I think Robert Frost or Emily Dickinson said that. I don't believe either of them ever ran a business, but it's true! Fill the need after you've found it!"

That's what my father did. There was a baby boom when my father opened The Diaper King. He was the right man in the right place at the right time. He had clients all over Connecticut and parts of Rhode Island and Massachusetts.

"I'm known as The Diaper King of New England for a reason, Charlie. Someday you, too, might be known as The Diaper King of New England. It's a legacy!"

In spite of my father's best, or worst, efforts to ridicule Isamu's dream of opening his own restaurant, my uncle was undeterred. He showed me some sketches he'd made of the restaurant he planned to open. It would be a seafood place, and he was going to have it built to resemble the lighthouse on Mythic Point. I was excited for him, but also incredibly sad the day he left with a woman named Cherry.

"I go west. Find good spot for restaurant. You keep saxophone!"

I kept the saxophone for ten years. During that time, I would listen to records by Charlie Parker, Ornette Coleman, Stan Getz, John Coltrane, Lester Young, and other jazz greats in my room late at night. I tried playing the way they did, which was impossible, but I started playing like me, which, as it turned out, was pretty good.

My uncle ended up opening The Mythic Lighthouse Seafood Restaurant on the south rim of the Grand Canyon. The restaurant proved wildly successful, and he opened another one, then another. We didn't hear from him for ten years, but when we did, he'd become massively successful and incredibly wealthy. He had about thirty restaurants in a dozen different states. He traveled around the country giving speeches about how America, his adopted country, was the great shining beacon of opportunity for anyone with a dream who was willing to work hard. That's how he ended up the keynote speaker at my graduation from high school.

Graduation for the 1973 class of Mythic High was held at the school's football stadium on a hot and overcast June day. While our parents and other family members were seated in the stands, we lined up outside the stadium and prepared to march ceremonially out to the seats set up for us in the middle of the field. Joey Shapp, the local mortician's son, came up to me while I was standing in line. Joey had cheated off me on nearly all our quizzes and exams since the second or third grade, not that I was all that great a student, and somehow he'd managed to do just enough to graduate. He was at the absolute bottom of the class, but that didn't matter to him. He made plenty of money selling drugs. He wore a pair of mirrored sunglasses everywhere and called himself 'Midnight.'

"Hey, Charlie, wanna buy some pot? Acid? I dropped a couple tabs an hour ago, and everyone's starting to turn into lizards."

"Jesus, Joey, my parents are in the stands! I can't be watching people turn into reptiles during graduation!"

"Everyone's already a lizard, Charlie! They just don't know it yet! Anyway, Midnight bids you adieu!"

Joey wandered down to the end of the line. I watched him stop and talk to Willy Wetmore. Willy had wrestled the weight class just above mine all through high school and had been my main wrestling partner for the past four years. We were both going to Renfield College in the fall and would be wrestling for the Renfield Fighting Quakers.

I watched Willy hand Joey some money, and then Joey reached under his mortarboard and grabbed one of the little dime bags of pot he'd hidden there. Willy took the bag and stuffed it under his gown, then our high school band started a lousy rendition of "Pomp and Circumstance," and my classmates and I began marching toward our futures.

Since we were arranged in alphabetical order, I was seated between Jennifer Losel and America Lightshadow. Jennifer's goal in life was to become a cosmetologist. America, on the other hand, had a dream of swimming in the 1976 Olympic Games in Montreal. She had a legit shot, too. She had already set national high school records in four or five events and had won six or seven gold medals at the National High School Championships a few weeks earlier. Her success was partially due to her powerful six-foot-five frame to which fate had appended a pair of webbed feet, but she also worked at her events with a passion that I found incomprehensible. I'd been a decent wrestler in high school. I'd even placed in the regionals my junior year and had gone undefeated my senior year, but America was on a whole different level. She swam five to six hours per day, including weekends, and after

7

wrestling practice, I sometimes went down to the pool in the high school basement and watched her preparing to swim herself into the history books. I was amazed by her energy and by the apparent ease with which she pulled herself, lap after innumerable lap, across the surface of the pool. Amazing, too, was the sight of America emerging from the water, her nylon swimsuit wet and stretched across the vast muscular continent of her body. Pallas Americana: The Great Sea Goddess, with webbed feet, swim goggles, and chlorine-green hair.

She'd been my lab partner in biology class, and once, while we were dissecting a fetal pig, America told me about her future goals.

"After I win gold in Montreal, I'm gonna make bank with endorsements, Charlie."

I picked up a scalpel and made some incisions on the pig's chest and abdomen. I pulled the chest plate away to expose the pig's internal organs.

"Everyone's gonna see my picture on boxes of cereal! I'll be in commercials for everything from motor oil to credit cards!"

"Oh, beautiful for spacious skies, for amber waves of sugar-coated grain!" I laughed.

"Go ahead, laugh all you want. Just remember, he who laughs last is the one left standing with stacks of cash!"

"I want you to win medals at the Olympics," I said.

"Gold medals," America said.

"I want you to win gold in Montreal, but I don't think success can be measured in dollars and cents, America. Not that I have anything against making money. I mean, I'm going to major in business at Renfield College. Then I'm going to help my father streamline his diaper service."

"I can smell the future, Lord, and it smells like gold."

I thought of my father's diaper service.

"I'm not so sure I want to smell my future," I said.

"It can't smell any worse than this pig," said America. "Anyway, who needs biology when your face is on a thousand billboards across the nation advertising insurance?"

I stared down at the dissected pig in front of me. I cut away some veins and arteries in the pig's chest and pulled its heart out with a pair of forceps. How had this little muscular organ been turned into a symbol of enduring love? I put the heart down in the dissecting pan and looked at America. She was spectacularly beautiful. I loved her with all of my heart; that much I knew to be true. And although I'd never said anything to her about it, I just knew, in the deepest recesses of my soul, that America and I were destined to find love with each other. First, I had to convince her there was more to life than commercial success.

Now, however, we were sitting in the sweltering heat out on the football field while the principal, Mr Doolittle, was standing at the podium. He'd prepared a few remarks, which he prefaced by reading a speech given by John F. Kennedy back in 1960. Then he launched into a rambling soliloquy about the need for young people to be fearless and dedicated.

"We must take the time to be fearless, dedicated, and self-reflective," he said.

I looked at Jennifer Losel. She was self-reflecting in a compact mirror she'd kept in her purse. She would be attending cosmetology school in Mianus and then spend the rest of her life cutting hair while fighting carpal tunnel. I looked up in the bleachers and could see my parents. My father appeared to be arguing with someone sitting in front of him who'd brought an umbrella to ward off the sun. The heat was oppressive. A lone cicada droned in the distance. I looked to the east. Dark clouds were gathering swiftly above the ocean. Mr Doolittle concluded his remarks to polite applause. One of the graduates set off a string of firecrackers. Someone set free a bouquet of helium balloons. I watched the balloons ascend until they disappeared into the darkness out over the Atlantic.

The valedictorian, Labiana West, took the podium. She and April Tyler had gotten straight A's all through high school, but April was selected as the salutatorian, and Labiana was selected as the valedictorian due to the additional struggles she'd seen, or hadn't seen, depending on how you looked at it.

Labiana was one of those rare students who actually lived up to her potential. She was captain of the girl's track team, the homecoming queen, and the prom queen. She was funny and animated. She was also the only person I'd ever met who'd been born without eyes. Unbroken flesh covered the spots where her eyes should have been. Her lack of eyes was occasionally a problem during track meets when she'd run out of her lane and knock some of the other runners off the track, but for the most part it wasn't an issue. I listened to her speak for a little bit. She told a funny story about falling off stage during the senior class production of Romeo and Juliet because she'd wandered too close to the front of it. Everyone in the bleachers laughed. I laughed, too. I'd been at that performance. Fortunately, she hadn't been hurt. Her eyes had been painted on for the play and looked pretty real from a distance except for the not-blinking part. She was going to Harvard in the fall, and I was genuinely happy for her. When she was done speaking, there was enthusiastic applause from the bleachers. Everybody loves a good story about individuals who overcome enormous obstacles to succeed; they just don't want to take the time or expend the energy to do it themselves. It's easier to drift from circumstance to circumstance and end up at some point in the future and look back and think you've overcome obstacles when all you did was just end up at a different point from where you started through nothing more than incomprehensible, random dumb luck. I looked back at the clouds. They were darker and thicker. It looked almost like the sky to the east was boiling, and the darkness seemed to be headed our way.

The keynote speaker came up to the podium. He was a short man in a three-piece suit and cowboy boots, which made him seem taller. It took me a few seconds to recognize him, but as soon as he started to speak, it was obvious that it was my uncle, Isamu Kawabata.

"Good afternoon, graduates of Mythic High School," he said. "Isn't it wonderful thing to be American right here, right now? I love America! When I first come to this country I had not two pennies! Now I am a multimillionaire!"

10

For the next twenty minutes, Isamu shared how after the war, he had come to Mythic with nothing and then had left to find his fortune. He had traveled all over the country for a year and moved from job to job, earning just enough money to stay broke until one day he'd come across a man who owned a piece of property on the southern rim of the Grand Canyon. Isamu had purchased the property with a handshake and a small down payment with money he'd saved working as a cook on a cattle ranch in Abilene.

"But I always remember my time in Mythic. The foghorn and the righthouse stay burned in my memories. So for two years I have vision to build restaurant resemble righthouse and serve delicious fresh seafood to America! Now I have many many restaurants all across this most wonderful country!"

In some ways, I was disappointed that my uncle had become an extraordinarily wealthy businessman. I wanted to remember Isamu as the playboy saxophone player who'd passed on his love of jazz to me. I had thought of him nearly every day for the past ten years, and the last thing I'd imagined him becoming was a millionaire restaurant owner. It was far more appealing to me to imagine him adrift somewhere out west, living a life of poetic poverty. It was confusing to me.

"My fellow Mythic Americans, as you go into wide world it is not so important what you do, how much money you make, what you accomprish. What is most important you have dream vision that pull you to your future. America is not nation. America is righthouse of shining opportunity."

Isamu ended his speech and was given a standing ovation for the simple fact that he was the keynote speaker, and it was the expected thing for everyone to do. I clapped, but I wasn't sure if I agreed that America was the lighthouse of shining opportunity. I thought about my own experiences with racism, ignorance, and downright stupidity, and it seemed to me that there were opportunities for some but not for others based on their color, ethnicity, and connections. Yet, here was my Japanese Uncle Isamu, who had left Mythic with nothing only to return, ten years later, a very wealthy man. My mind was like a rat searching its way out of this labyrinth of conflicting ideas all jumbled

11

up in my head, but these thoughts were interrupted by the band. They were starting to play "Pomp and Circumstance" again, and students were being called alphabetically to walk up to the platform. The first few students who were called received their diplomas from the principal. They shook his hand and then shook the hands of several teachers and my uncle, who'd remained on the platform. I looked up into the bleachers and noticed that about a third of the people were standing and pointing at the sky behind me. The graduation ceremony came to a sudden halt. I looked behind me and watched a finger-like whip of swirling darkness descend from the boiling mass of clouds above it. All the graduates and everyone in the bleachers stood and watched the tornado touch down on a hill in the distance and obliterate a barn in just a few seconds. Boards flew from the hillside in all directions, and the whip moved down the hill with astonishing speed. It was heading toward the stadium.

People began running from the field and bleachers to the parking lot. Hailstones the size of golf balls started raining down on us. I grabbed America's hand, and together we ran toward the school. Fortunately, the doors had been left unlocked, and we were able to make our way inside with about fifty or sixty other students, parents, and teachers, most of whom made their way down to the basement. I stayed behind a minute to watch the tornado rip across the football field and turn the platform and chairs into a swirling mass of rotating debris. The sound was deafening. It was like a freight train rumbling by so close that the ground shook. The tornado was no more than 150 yards away when I decided to head to the basement. I took one last look out the window and froze. There was a man about 100 yards away running toward the school in a suit and cowboy boots. It was my uncle. I pushed the door to open it, and it nearly flew off its hinges. He raced towards me and got about 75 feet away when he was suddenly lifted off the ground and disappeared into the whirling vortex of boiling madness. The door slammed shut, and with a great roar, the tornado smashed into the side of the school. The doors and windows exploded, and knives of glass flashed about me.

I awoke in a hospital bed wrapped in gauze. I'd been cut up pretty badly. One of the shards of glass had sliced through my left wrist to the bone and had severed muscles and tendons. They had stopped the bleeding in time to save me, but it had taken 160 stitches to repair my damaged

"...he was suddenly lifted off the ground and disappeared into the whirling vortex..."

wrist. As a result of the injury, I would never wrestle again. As for my uncle, his body was never found. The tornado veered back to the ocean after slamming into the school, and I assume that my uncle was flung into the water to be carried by the tides far away from the America that he loved—the Great Right House of Opportunity.

Chapter 2 Recovery

I was released from the hospital after a couple of days. Other than the cut on my wrist, most of the wounds were fairly superficial. There was a laceration on my neck that had just missed one of the carotid arteries, but most of the cuts hadn't required stitches and would disappear entirely in time. I had hoped that America would come and visit me, too, but other than my parents, the only other person to visit me was Willy. I told him what the doctor had told me, that it would probably be a year or two, if ever, before my wrist healed well enough for me to wrestle again. Willy looked annoyed.

"Crap, Charlie, now I'm gonna have to find another wrestling partner," he said.

"Gee, Willy, sorry for the inconvenience."

A pretty blonde nurse entered the room, and Willy eyeballed her pretty shamelessly. The nurse took my temperature, blood pressure, and pulse while Willy stood behind her, pantomiming what he wished to do to her by reaching his hands toward her hips and thrusting his pelvis back and forth with slow, rhythmic movements. When the nurse was done checking my vitals, she wrote some things on the chart hanging on the end of the bed.

"Okay, Charlie, you're good to go. We'll have someone call your parents and let them know they can pick you up."

The nurse left the room, and Willy started to follow her. When he reached the door, he turned and looked at me with wide eyes.

"I'm going to hit that, Charlie," he said.

After Willy left, I got out of bed, dressed myself as well as I could with one hand, and waited for my parents to show up. It occurred to me that "Shambala" by Three Dog Night was playing on the radio sitting on the table next to my bed. I turned the radio on and listened to the song spill into the room.

Ah-ooh-ooh-ooh, ooh-ooh, yeah

Yeah, yeah, yeah, yeah, yeah

Ah-ooh-ooh-ooh, ooh-ooh, yeah

Yeah, yeah, yeah, yeah, yeah

My parents came into the room just as the song was ending. My mother looked like she'd spent most of the past two days in tears, which was expected. I'd cried some, too. My dad gave me the news about the damage the tornado had inflicted on Mythic. The lighthouse out on Mythic Point had been damaged. Dozens had been injured, but my Uncle Isamu had been the only fatality. Several witnesses who'd fled to the parking lot had seen him get sucked into the whirlwind. They saw him circle once slowly about the outside of the swirling greenish-black funnel, and then he was gone. We drove home in silence.

I spent the rest of the summer mourning my uncle. I tried playing the saxophone a few times but would end up sobbing after a couple of minutes, so I hid the saxophone in the closet, where it gathered dust until the summer ended. I spent most of my time alone in my room clipping out newspaper articles about fatal car accidents, plane crashes, train derailments, and homicides, which I pasted into the disaster notebook I'd started my freshman or sophomore year in high school when I'd been going through a particularly dark spell of adolescence. I had stuffed the notebook in my backpack, and for three or four years I had carried it with me wherever I went. It was also during that time that I stopped eating solid food and drank nothing but Tang and fruit juice for unfathomable reasons. After a couple of weeks of fasting, I discovered that I could predict what song would be playing on the radio before I turned it on. I was able to do this only if I didn't think about it. The gift vanished when I tried to abuse it. As long as I left this ability alone, it stayed with me—just around the corner, just out of earshot.

About a month after the tornado had carried off Isamu, my father came into my room one night while I was lying on the floor in the dark. The radio was off, but The Who was just about to start playing "Baba O'Riley." My father turned on the light. He stood in the doorway with his hands in his pockets.

"Charlie, what the hell are you doing?"

"Nothing," I said.

"Exactly," my father said. "Listen, I know your uncle's death has been hard on you. It's been hard on all of us. Your mother's beside herself, but you can't just lie around doing nothing for the rest of the summer. You're starting college in a couple of months. It's time to move on, Charlie. You need to pull yourself up by your bootstraps. When the going gets tough, the tough get going. I believe that's a direct quote from Winnie the Pooh to Eeyore. Are you hearing me?"

"When the going gets tough, the tough get going," I said.

"I need you to dig deep and pull your head out of your ass, Charlie. I'm serious! Am I making sense here, or am I just talking to myself?"

"I need to dig deep and pull my head out of my ass," I said.

"Good! I'm glad we understand each other!"

"I appreciate the pep talk, Dad. Really."

My father turned off the light and closed the door on his way out. I turned on the radio and listened to "Baba O'Riley" play for a few minutes. The exodus was here. The happy ones were near. When the song ended, I turned the radio off and listened to the darkness around and inside of me. It occurred to me that nothing in my life had any meaning outside of America Lightshadow. I decided to pull my head out of my ass for her and her alone.

I got out of bed and showered for the first time in about a week. I dressed and went downtown to see if any businesses were hiring summer help. I probably went to a dozen places, but no one was hiring. I was about to give up and go home, but I decided to try the Rialto Movie Theater. There was a large older woman in the box office. She had sparse white hair through which you could see an excessive amount of pink scalp. She looked at me like I asked her to eat a turd when I asked if they needed any help.

"I've wanted to work in a movie theater my whole life," I lied.

"The last kid we hired was unreliable," she said. "I fired that Joey Shapp kid last week. He was worthless! You're not friends with him, are you?"

"No, ma'am," I said. "Never heard of him."

16

"Well, okay. I need an usher for the afternoons. You start at noon and work until the theater closes after the last show. We pay $1.60 per hour."

"Do I get overtime?" I asked.

The woman stared at me over the tops of her glasses. "We pay $1.60 per hour. Take it or leave it."

"Okay," I said. "When do I start?"

"Your shift starts at noon today. Come back at quarter to twelve, and I'll give you an usher's uniform."

I looked at the clock on the wall behind her. It was 11:11. For some reason the fact that it was 11:11 seemed auspicious. I went across the street to a deli and had a sandwich. Then I went back to the Rialto. The woman handed me a pair of black pants, a white shirt, and a red velvet jacket.

"Put it on," she said.

"What? Right here?"

"You ain't got nothing I ain't seen before," she said.

I got changed in the lobby. The pants were too tight. The shirt was too big, and the jacket smelled

like vomit.

"You'll get used to the smell," she said. "Everybody does."

She handed me a short-handled broom, a long-handled dustpan, and a putty knife. I looked at the putty knife.

"What's this for?"

"You'll find out soon enough," she said. "You need to clean up the theater. You gotta be done by 12:30. That's when the theater opens for the one o'clock show. When you're done sweeping, you'll find a mop and bucket in the closet between the restrooms. Don't use too much bleach. People complain about the smell."

I went into the theater with my broom and dustpan to clean up from last night's show. It was pretty gross. People had spilled popcorn and soda all over the place. There was chewing gum stuck on the back of the seats and wads of it all over the floor, hence the putty knife. I had to sweep up a used condom. It was fairly disgusting. Plus, I had to work essentially one-handed while my wrist healed. Sweeping up wasn't that bad, but mopping with one hand was virtually impossible. Anyway, I got it done in time. Then I stood in the lobby and took tickets from the four people who wanted to see a movie at one o'clock on a Tuesday afternoon. All in all, it was good to be gainfully employed.

I worked until about ten o'clock that night and for the rest of the summer. Other than cleaning up the theater before it opened and taking tickets, there wasn't a lot for me to do except stand around and look hospitable. I got the jacket cleaned, but it still smelled like vomit, but I got used to it, just like the woman said I would. Her name, I discovered, was Mrs Madrigal. Once I got to know her well, she was just as awful as when I didn't know her much at all, which is kind of how it is with most people. People don't become better humans once you get to know them. You just get better at working around them in such a way as to make them more tolerable for your own sanity.

"I got changed in the lobby."

On my days off, I usually got high and walked along the beach from the lighthouse on Mythic Point down to where the dunes gave way to rocks and cliffs. The lighthouse had been repaired pretty quickly after the tornado damaged it. Sometimes I'd stay out on the beach until the sun set and the stars came out. I loved walking back along the shore while the waves crashed and the foghorn sounded. The Fresnel lens in the lighthouse would rotate, and a great swath of light would sweep overhead, illuminating the cliff walls, then arc out over the water. It was all pretty great, and after a month or so passed, I didn't feel so sad about my uncle. By the end of the summer, I hardly thought about Isamu at all, which was all in all a pretty good thing, but then I'd feel bad that I wasn't thinking much about him. Then I'd spent the next fifteen or twenty minutes berating myself for not feeling sad enough about my uncle's death until something else came along that required my attention. Then I wouldn't feel so bad about Isamu's death until I realized, once again, that I wasn't sad, which would make me sad all over again for another fifteen or twenty minutes.

My eighteenth birthday came and went without fanfare. There had been no cake, no presents, nothing to mark my passage into legal adulthood. I picked up some morning shifts at The Lobster Pot restaurant washing dishes, and between working there and at the Rialto, I managed to save seven or eight hundred dollars by the end of the summer. I began looking forward to attending Renfield and taking classes in business management. Every so often I'd sit down with my father and talk about future plans for his diaper service. I can't say I was thrilled to have a future in his business, but I was happy to be part of his dream. He had customers all across Connecticut, Massachusetts, and parts of Rhode Island. He was the Diaper King of New England with plans on becoming the Diaper King of the entire Eastern Seaboard, and I was to be an important cog in the machinery that made his business run.

Chapter 3 Party

About ten days before leaving for college, I went to an end-of-the-summer party. I had called America to tell her about the party, but she'd already left for the University of Miami, where she'd swim for the Hurricanes and train for the Olympic trials. I hadn't seen her all summer and wondered if she missed me, too. It kind of bugged me that she'd left without saying 'goodbye.'

Willy Wetmore gave me a ride to the party in a Fiat that his father had purchased for himself on the upslope of a midlife crisis. Willy was a natural athlete. Besides wrestling, he'd run the quarter mile in under 49 seconds in high school. The first time he'd tried pole vaulting, he'd cleared 12 feet. He wanted to go to Hollywood after college and write for television. While we drove, Willy told me about his love for Mo Summer. She had been my first wrestling partner when I started the sport eight or nine years earlier. Her father had wrestled at Penn State and had started coaching her before she could even walk. She'd routinely kicked my ass until puberty hit me, and testosterone, the wonder hormone, had increased my muscle mass and strength. Personally, I could see the attraction. She was a tall, attractive redhead with long hair that completely hid the cauliflower ears she'd gained from all her years of wrestling. She was tough and smart. Right after graduation, she'd signed a contract with a roller derby team out of Hartford.

"I've called her a few times since graduation, but she hasn't answered any of my calls." Willy said.

"She's probably been busy with roller derby, Willy. America hasn't returned any of my calls either."

"Listen, Charlie, if Mo's at the party, give her this for me." Willy handed me an envelope with her name written on it.

"Why don't you give her this yourself?" I asked.

"I'm not staying," he said. "I'm heading to Renfield tonight. Pre-pre-season wrestling starts tomorrow morning."

"Pre-pre-season?"

"Yep. Apparently, the NCAA has rules about when you can start pre-season training, so in order to be in compliance we can't really wrestle, but we can watch films and look at training manuals. Coach wants us in full wrestling gear while we're studying film. He says it helps develop the proper mindset."

Willy pulled into the driveway of a big brick house. "Don't forget to give Mo that letter," he said.

"No problem, Willy. I'll see you at Renfield next week."

I got out of the car, and Willy backed out of the driveway. I watched him drive off to develop his mindset. I was sorry I wasn't going with him. Wrestling had been one of the few things that had held any meaning for me in high school.

The party was at Mason Mason IV's house. His parents were gone for the weekend. They had a really great place. It was built on a hill that sloped gently down to the beach. You could stand on the back deck where the keg was and watch the waves crash on the rocks and sand. Mason Mason IV came from a long line of bricklayers going back to the sixteenth century. Altogether, Mason Mason IV was actually like the nineteenth son who'd been named Mason and had become a bricklayer. The Roman numerals at the end of his name had been a recent addition to the Mason line. The oldest child in each generation would inherit the name 'Mason' and be expected to become a bricklayer, too. It was an honorable profession. Neither his father, grandfather, nor great-grandfather had gone to college after high school. All of their siblings, on the other hand, had been given names like 'James,' 'Thomas,' and 'Benjamin' and had been permitted to go to college and become doctors, lawyers, and engineers. I had to admit his family's stand on tradition and heritage was truly admirable. He came up to me while I was standing on the deck. He poured himself a beer, and we spent a couple of minutes discussing the fire-resistant properties of masonry along with the hydration characteristics of clay that the Egyptians may have used for the mortar while building the pyramids. The breeze from the ocean was cool and warm at the same time. The conversation kept flowing like beer from the keg.

"There's a very good theoretical work on this by a PhD out of Germany. He did some modeling of the firebombing of Dresden and the atomic bombing of Nagasaki and discovered that a ten percent increase in brick structures would have probably led to a two percent reduction in fatalities."

Mason Mason IV took a sip of his beer and looked out over the waves at some point in the unseeable distance. When he looked back at me, his eyes were red and watery.

"I'm jealous of you," he said. "I wish I was going to college, too, Charlie, but I can't break tradition. It would kill my dad."

"I'm not sure I really want to go to college now that I can't wrestle," I said. "I don't think it would kill him if I didn't go, but he'd definitely be pissed."

Joey Shapp came over and handed Mason a plastic bag full of pre-rolled joints.

"Party favors," said Joey.

"I don't want these!" said Mason. He tossed the bag onto a glass-topped patio table.

"Sure you do, Mason; you just don't know it yet."

Joey left Mason with the bag of joints and went over to talk to Gil Mosely and Danny Hepatario.

I grabbed one of the joints out of the bag, poured myself another beer, then went down the steps from the deck to the backyard. Someone had lit a fire in a 55-gallon drum. I drank the beer down in about fifteen seconds, then lit the joint. The pot was full of stems and seeds, and the smoke was harsh and burned my throat. Still, I'd managed to smoke about half of it when someone tapped me on the shoulder. It was Mo Summer.

"I just wanted to tell you how much I wanted to say 'hello,'" she said.

"Tell away."

"I'm not saying 'hello,'" she said. "I'm just telling you I wanted to say 'hello.'"

"Let me know when you want to tell me 'goodbye,' Mo. Anyway, Willy wanted me to give this to you."

I handed her the letter, and Mo wrinkled her nose.

"He's been calling me," she said, "and he's been writing. I've got a stack of letters from him that I haven't opened."

"Wait a second. You haven't opened his letters? Why not?"

"I'm trying to avoid the consequences of a response," she said. "On the roller derby rink, everything you do has a consequence. People get hurt—yourself and others. Sometimes it's better not to know what others are thinking or doing, so you can avoid the consequences of life."

"Ignorance is bliss," I said. "Wetmore's in love with you. You're all he talks about other than wrestling, becoming a writer, chasing women, and getting stoned."

"Yes, it's flattering, but I'm just not interested," she said. She leaned close to me and whispered. "I'm playing for the other team."

"What do you mean, 'the other team'?" I asked.

"Jesus, Charlie! Do I have to spell it out for you? I like girls!" she said.

I looked at Mo. Her head was cocked over to the side, and she wore a half smile on her lips. She raised her hands palms up toward the ceiling as though letting me know that she hadn't chosen her sexuality. It had chosen her, and she wasn't about to hide who she was anymore. Mo hugged me. She went up the stairs to the deck and disappeared into the kitchen. I went up the stairs, too, and had another beer. Then another. By the time eleven o'clock rolled around, I'd probably had eight or nine beers and was midway through my second joint. I was pretty fucked up. Not so fucked up that I felt I had to crawl to the bathroom and puke, but the kind of fucked up that makes you think you're perfectly okay to drive a vehicle full of passengers who are liable to get killed. That kind of fucked up. Danny Hepatario came outside and stood next to me. We both stared into the 55-gallon drum of fire.

"I just looked at the clock, Charlie. It's 11:11. Do you know what that means?"

"I'm fucking wasted, Danny. I don't know what shit means right now."

"I've been seeing 1111 everywhere, man. It's some kind of a code."

"Fuck, dude. If twenty people look at the clock over the course of an hour, there's a pretty good chance that someone's going to see 11:11."

"Geez, Charlie, why do you want to take the mysteriousness out of 1111? Why do you want to kill the mysteriousness and mystique of 1111?"

"It's the same forwards and backwards, Danny."

"That's more like it, Charlie! That speaks to its mythicality!" he said.

Danny spit into the 55-gallon drum and watched the spit bubble on a piece of burning wood.

"It's 11:13 now, Danny. Is there any mysteriousness in that?"

"In an infinite universe, I'm sure 1113 is mythic, somewhere."

"Thank you for introducing me to the concept of omni-mythicality," I said.

"Fortunately, I'm so high I won't possibly be able to remember any of this tomorrow," Danny replied.

Danny reached into the fire barrel and pulled out a burning piece of wood. "I dropped a shit ton of Sunshine with Joey about an hour and a half ago," he said. "I'm tripping balls pretty heavy now."

I knocked the wood out of Danny's hand and looked at his palm. It was pretty badly burned. Mason Mason IV came over and looked at Danny's hand.

"Put some butter on it," Mason said. "Someone get some butter and mercurochrome."

"Put some ice on it," said Gil Mosely. "Ice is a universal remedy for everything, including frostbite!"

"Wow! My fucking hand actually hurts," Danny said.

Mo came outside. Danny had given Mo a titty twister in high school during wrestling practice, and Mo had kicked his ass. She looked at Danny's hand.

"He needs to go to the ER," Mo said.

"He dropped acid an hour ago. The ER's not the best place for him," I said.

"Mason, you have any aloe vera lotion?" Mo asked.

"What the fuck's that?" asked Mason.

"Get me some petroleum jelly, some gauze, and some aspirin," said Mo. "You fucking guys are worthless."

Mason went into the house to gather what medical supplies he could find. Mo took Danny into the kitchen to run cool water over the burn for a few minutes. I followed them and watched Mo spread a thin layer of petroleum jelly on Danny's burn and wrap it in gauze. Danny held an ibuprofen in his non-burned hand and stared at it suspiciously.

"These fuck up your liver," Danny said. "They're not good for your kidneys."

Mo's jaw dropped. She put a hand on her hip and brought her face to within an inch of Danny's.

"You just dropped Orange Sunshine made God knows where from God knows what, and you're worried about 200 milligrams of ibuprofen?" she shouted.

"It was 11:11," said Danny. "It's 11:11 somewhere out there."

I looked at the clock. It was close to 11:30 now. I felt oddly sober and clear-headed.

"I feel oddly sober and clear-headed now," I said to Mo. Mo looked at me.

"You're completely wasted, Charlie." Mo grabbed Danny by the collar and shook him. "You're not as fucked up as this jerk, but don't be driving anywhere."

I went back outside and stood by the fire barrel. Someone had put on a Pink Floyd album and had cranked up the volume. The stereo speakers were being used as stools in the living room, and the entire house reverberated with the sound of clocks ticking, bells chiming, and alarms ringing. Then it was all epic, timeless rock. I looked down into the 55-gallon drum at the flames. I wondered if America missed me.

25

April Tyler came outside and stood next to me. Her long auburn hair cascaded over her shoulders and down her back. Her bright green eyes peered at me intently, as though she were looking into some part of me that I didn't even know existed. It was a bit unnerving to be X-rayed by another human this way. She was so smart her IQ couldn't be measured. April would be attending Rutgers University, where she'd be studying the intersection of post-postmodernism with theoretical number theory as it applied to Heisenberg's Uncertainty Principle.

"I'm solving the paradox of Schrödinger's cat," April said. "Where will you be going, Charlie?"

"Renfield," I said. "Business."

"Renfield," she said. "That was the name of the lunatic in Dracula, by Bram Stoker. Are you sure that's where you should be for the next four years?"

"I'm not sure I want to be anywhere," I said.

"She was so smart her IQ couldn't be measured."

April took one of my hands in hers and turned it over. She pretended to be reading my palm. "You complicate things," she said. "You're smart enough to do that. Just not smart enough to uncomplicate them."

She traced my lifeline.

"You're ridiculously creative, will age well, are terrible with money, and that mess you call hair speaks volumes about your organizational skills," she said. "You're also good in bed."

"I sleep well," I said.

"No doubt," said April. "Kiss me."

"I have a girlfriend," I said.

"I have a girlfriend, too," said April. "Kiss me."

We kissed. She had soft lips. Her tongue made little darting forays into my mouth. Pink Floyd sang about Us and Them. I kissed April again. She put her tongue into my mouth. I put my tongue into hers. Pink Floyd played a song without lyrics. If there was any moment in the entire evening that one could describe as being post-postmodern, this was it.

"This is a post-postmodern moment," I said.

"Don't be an idiot, Charlie. It's nothing of the sort," said April. "Now you've gone and ruined the moment."

April gathered her tongue and went into the house. Pink Floyd began singing a song about the dark side of the moon. In a little while I left the fire and went into the house, too. Mo and Danny were in the kitchen making out. I wasn't sure what to make of my earlier conversation with her. It was disconcerting when people slipped outside the parameters and perimeters of my expectations. I looked at the clock. It was 12:12, which may or may not have been omni-mythical. I couldn't decide. I decided to walk home. I'd walked about a quarter mile when a Malibu pulled up beside me. The driver-side window rolled down, and April stuck her head out and smiled.

"Get in the car, idiot," she said.

An idiot got in her car. Then we drove out towards the lighthouse on Point Mythic. The lighthouse beam swept the sky above us as we made love twice. We snuggled together under a wool blanket that April kept in the backseat.

"Summer ends with a bang," I said.

"Oh, please, Charlie. You are so much more attractive when you keep your mouth shut."

"I have an IQ above 130," I said.

"You may as well be a Neanderthal," said April. "Do you know I was born without a set of adult teeth?"

"Really?" I asked.

"I wouldn't have said it if it weren't the truth. I never say anything that isn't the truth. I'm the next step in human evolution."

"You're the next step in human evolution?" I said.

"You really need to pay better attention, Lord. I can't repeat myself forever! Now, come fuck me again!"

April pressed a note into my hand when she'd dropped me off at my parents' house at about 2:30 in the morning. I looked up at the night sky. A waxing crescent moon hung in the leafy branches of a maple tree in the front yard. I closed my eyes. I could hear the ocean's surge and the waves crashing against the Mythic shore and cliffs. I could still smell April's perfume on my clothing and taste her lipstick. All in all, the evening had been omni-mythical.

I awoke the next morning dressed in my clothes. I had a hangover, and I vaguely remembered having had sex with April in her Malibu. The note she'd given me was still in my hand. I looked at it. It was her phone number. I told myself I wouldn't call her. Technically, I hadn't cheated on America since America and I had never been on a single date, and I hadn't seen her since graduation day. She hadn't called or visited me while I was in the hospital, but I still felt guilty and ashamed of myself. I hid my head under my pillow and vowed that I would never, ever, be unfaithful to America again.

28

Chapter 4 Saxophone

I wrote to America every day after the party before leaving for college. I called and left messages for her, too, but she never returned any of my calls. I checked the mail every evening after getting home from the Rialto to see if there was a letter from her, but I never received so much as a postcard. A day before leaving for Renfield, I'd begun to lose hope that America and I would ever be more than high school friends.

I'd quit my jobs a few days after the party and spent the better part of the week watching TV and reading a couple of books by my favorite author, Gordon Gordon Gordon. I really liked his collection of short stories. My favorite story of his was "The House of Happy Snows." It's about a soldier in occupied Japan who falls in love with a geisha who's forbidden to see him. The soldier is so sad that a soft blue light starts to emanate from his body. At first the soldier's annoyed because the blue light attracts moths, but then he discovers the light is just bright enough to allow him to write down these amazingly sad love poems, which he ends up publishing. The book of sad love poems sells like a million copies, and the soldier gets rich, but once he's a success, the soft blue light disappears, and he never writes another poem again. I must've read that story about twenty times. Sometimes I'd read it two or three times a day.

A couple of days before I left for Renfield, I walked down to the Rialto to pick up my final paycheck. Mrs Madrigal was sitting in the box office when I arrived. It was a warm day, and her thin white hair was plastered to her pink scalp by a thin sheen of sweat.

"I came to pick up my final check," I said.

"What?"

"My final check," I said, "for working."

"You don't get paid until you turn in your uniform," she said.

"I turned it in the night I left," I said.

"You did?"

"Yes."

29

Mrs Madrigal opened her cash register and took out fifty dollars in ten-dollar bills that she passed to me through the opening at the bottom of the box office window.

"This isn't enough," I said. "I worked sixty hours that week."

"Taxes and deductions," she said. "Plus, your jacket needed cleaning. It smelled like puke."

"It smelled like puke when I got it!"

"Take it or leave it," she said. She reached up and pulled a shade down in the box office window so I couldn't see her.

I thought about throwing a rock through the glass or even lighting the place on fire. While I stood there wondering what act of vandalism I could commit without getting arrested, a car pulled up alongside the curb. It was April Tyler. She leaned across to the passenger door and rolled down the window.

"Charles," she said, "why haven't you called me?"

"I've been busy," I said.

"Oh, seriously? You are such a liar! Get in the car, moron, before I lose my patience!"

Against my better judgment, I opened the door and slid into the passenger seat. April pulled away from the curb and began driving out of town. I glanced at her, and she smiled.

"I thoroughly enjoyed having sex with you," she said. "With a little practice you might become very good at it, even great! Not that there's anything wrong with your technique now. You even managed to give me an orgasm, which isn't something that normally happens the first time I have sex with someone."

"Well, thanks, I guess. But I don't think you and I should do it again. I mean, I do have a girlfriend."

"So you've said. Who is she?"

"America," I said. "America Lightshadow."

"Oh, that Amazonian swimmer," she said. "How long have you two been an item?"

30

"Well, we haven't had sex if that's what you're asking."

"Why not? You're both of legal age in the great state of Connecticut."

"I want to," I said.

"What does she want?"

"I'm not sure," I answered. "We haven't discussed it."

"So let me see if I understand this. You want to have sex with her, but you don't know if she wants you in the same way. Have you groped each other while in the throes of passion?"

"Well, no."

"Have you kissed her?"

"No. In fact, she's not answering my phone calls or letters."

"Then I fail to see how she's your girlfriend, Charles. Critical thinking is not one of your strong suits, is it?"

I looked out the window. We were driving along a road with a view of the ocean. The water looked gray and was full of foaming whitecaps.

"Where are we going?" I asked.

"My bedroom," April said. "Where else?"

April pulled into the driveway of a two-story house built of granite and concrete. It had large glass windows all around the bottom floor and looked like something you'd see in an architectural magazine. The house was full of people milling about with drinks in their hands. We got out of the car, but before going into the house, April gave me a warning.

"My mother's like me. She's so smart that her IQ is unmeasurable. She teaches at Llyll College and publishes papers on chaos theory and non-linearity that only people whose IQs can't be measured actually understand. Just know, you are going to make my mother sick," she said.

"Why? Is it because I'm not smart enough?"

"No. She has a physical condition. She literally vomits whenever she meets someone new. We're all used to it, of course, but I thought it better to advise you of her condition prior to meeting her. It can be a bit startling to watch someone vomit while they're shaking your hand. I wouldn't worry about your lack of intellect, though. My father's IQ is only one standard deviation above yours. He can relate to anyone with an IQ above 130 in the same way that you relate to people whose IQs are between 115 and 175."

"What about you?" I asked.

"What about me, what?"

"You're so smart; your IQ is unmeasurable. Who do you relate to? Isn't it lonely being so smart?"

"That's the beauty of it, Charlie! I'm an outlier. I am so smart I can relate to anyone and everyone! Brilliant, isn't it? Someone with an IQ of 185 would be completely bored by you! They'd literally have almost nothing to say to you. It would be painful to watch. My mother and I are fairly remarkable in our ability to meet people on whatever intellectual level they happen to be on. Did you know that those with IQs between 85 and 115 are the most likely to express affection with baked goods?"

April's mother came out of the house and walked over to us. She was tall and angular, with an unruly shock of reddish blonde hair—attractive in that waspy way of the New England patrician class. Her eyes were bright blue and filled with laughter, as though she had just solved a riddle that no one had ever asked.

"Janice, this is Charles Lord. The boy I was telling you about," April said.

April's mother looked at me keenly. She reached into a pocket of her jeans and pulled out a plastic bag that she vomited into. She knotted the top of the bag and held it in her left hand. Then she extended her free hand to me so that we could shake.

"Oh, so this is the young man you're having sex with," Janice said. I looked at April.

"We discuss everything," she said.

"Well, once," I said.

"April told me twice," said Janice. "No need for modesty here. She said you gave her the second or third best orgasm she'd ever had!"

"He has great enthusiasm," said April. "With the right coaching, he could become quite good at it."

"Are you two in love yet?" Janice asked.

"We're getting to know each other," I said.

"He thinks he has a girlfriend," April said. "In Miami."

"She reached into a pocket of her jeans and pulled out a plastic bag that she vomited into."

"Your father thinks he has a girlfriend in Miami, too, if I recall correctly," Janice said. "She teaches an undergraduate class in Statistical Improbability and a graduate seminar in Impossibility. Your father was always attracted to women he had no hope of ever understanding."

April's mother looked into my face again. "You haven't told him? Have you?"

"I wanted to have sex with him again, Mother. Then I was going to tell him."

"Tell me what?" I asked.

"Full disclosure, Charles. I'm dying," April said. "I have recently been diagnosed with non-Wernicke's encephalopathy, a neurological condition that occasionally afflicts members of my family. The disease robs us of our intellect over a period of eight or nine months. We regress approximately one to two standard IQ deviations every month. I'm already down to nearly a measurable range of intellect. In another two months I'll be as intelligent as you. A few months later, and I won't be able to read or write my name. From six months on, I'll be able to do little more than suck my thumb and breathe. Isn't that exciting?!"

"All of us will miss her terribly, though she's treating it like a vacation across Long Island Sound. Well, I suppose you two better go in the house and have sex. April has already lost one IQ point while you've been standing here." Janice looked at me and smiled.

"It was a pleasure meeting you, Charles, in spite of the vomit," she said. "That's not something I say casually, either. I do hope you continue to visit while my daughter is dying. The more of her intellect she loses, the less she'll be interested in ideas and the more she'll want to be around people she recognizes."

Janice smiled warmly and began walking towards the house. I looked at April. I had no idea what to say to her. April grabbed my face with both her hands and pulled me towards her.

"You heard my mother," she said. "Let's go fuck."

We had sex in April's room. She could have an orgasm and carry on a conversation about statistical improbability at one and the same time. It was like her mind and her body functioned completely separate from each other, though April claimed this wasn't true.

"I'm multi-orgasmic," she said. "But the best sex takes place between my ears, Charlie."

"Is that good for me or bad?" I asked.

"It's neither good for you nor bad," April said. "I will say that you're somewhat of a sexual anomaly for me. I like guys who are truly exceptionally smart or exceptionally dumb. You're the only guy I've enjoyed being with who's had an IQ above 85 or below 190."

"How many guys have IQs above 190?" I asked.

"You'd be surprised," April said. "The sex is usually lousy. The men are generally socially inept, but it's incredibly hot between my ears."

"You're into aural sex," I said.

"Not bad for a pun. I find most wordplay incredibly boring. It relies on false assumptions about language and ridiculous connections between objects that don't really exist. Shakespeare wasn't really fit to carry Sir Isaac Newton's apple."

I looked around April's bedroom. Everything in the room, with the exception of the floor, was completely white: walls, bedspread, blankets, sheets, dresser, desk, nightstand, lamp. There was even a three-panel white painting on the wall. April noticed me staring at it.

"It's a Rauschenberg," she said. "If you know how to look at them, you can study the change of seasons in the canvases, in how the light from outside falls across their surfaces, in how the hours proceed across them with their shadows. When you strip away everything, you can actually begin to see everything."

April tossed aside the white sheet and blankets and walked across the bare wooden floor to the bedroom window. She pulled open the white drapes and let the long evening light into the room through the window stretching from the ceiling to the floor. From the bed, you could see the entire valley beyond the red oak close to the house. Sunlight filtered through the leaves and branches, and dark shadows fell across the three white panels of the Rauschenberg.

"Promise that you'll come visit me in this room as I'm dying," she said. She came back to the bed, climbed in next to me, and together we watched the slight, nearly imperceptible motion of the shadow branches and leaves etched across the white canvases on the wall. The sun was beginning to set behind a rise of stony hills across a broad valley of green fields, orchards, and little farmsteads. I watched the sun disappear. The shadows moving slowly across the paintings vanished, and the room was bathed in semi-darkness.

"Fuck me, again, Charles. If you'd like, you can imagine you're fucking America. I won't mind."

"I don't think I can do that," I said.

"Fuck me," she said. "Please."

It was completely dark by the time we finished. I got out of bed and got dressed in the darkness, then I went to the window and looked out at the stars hanging in the sky above the valley and the distant hills. I hadn't really wanted to have sex with April again, but I suppose I hadn't really not wanted to, either. A door opened in one of the farmhouses down below, and a rectangle of light was reflected in the wind-rippled surface of a small pond set between the farmhouse and the road that ran past it.

"I should get going," I said.

"Would you like me to give you a ride?" April asked.

"That's okay. It's only a couple of miles. I think I'll walk."

I left the bedroom and closed the door behind me. Then I went downstairs and walked outside. It was a warm evening full of cricket song and the distant crash of waves. As I walked, I thought about my Uncle Isamu, alone in the depths of the ocean. I thought about April. She would be dead sometime in the spring while the earth woke from winter, and the fields and meadows were reborn in the bloom of flowers and the budding of leaves. I thought about the notebook I'd filled with images of death and destruction. In spite of the warm night air, a cold shiver ran down my spine. I began walking faster, as though I could outwalk my thoughts. I decided that I needed to exorcise these morbid thoughts and ideas that had been weighing on my mind since my uncle's death.

The house was empty when I got home. The next morning, I would be leaving behind my hometown and moving on into the great unknown. It was as though I was being born into adulthood, and the idea both excited and terrified me. I went upstairs and grabbed my saxophone. I stuffed my tape recorder into my backpack, and then I got on my bicycle and rode out into the night.

A big crescent moon hung in the sky like a giant slice of ripe melon. The streets were deserted, so I rode down the middle of the road, my bike's headlamp and the moon illuminating the road's centerline. In

36

the distance, I could hear the rhythmic pulse of the ocean and the moaning cry of the foghorn, sounds that had been woven throughout the fabric of my life as much as my own heartbeat.

I rode out to a cliff overlooking Mythic Point. I looked out over the edge of the cliff. Waves crashed on a rocky beach down below and rolled up to the base of the cliff, then receded. I turned on my tape recorder and put the saxophone to my mouth and began playing just as the foghorn sounded. I shut my eyes and let the music pulse through me, let myself give birth to it, and in turn let it give birth to me, the sound of the foghorn like the moaning cry of a woman in labor, the night sky alive with stars and planets in the warm, clear darkness, dim candles burning out above the horizon and overarching body of sky. Melody after melody spun out of the saxophone's brass bell and disappeared into the darkness. I was musician and music, creator and creation, crafting the universe out of a pure embryonic jazz of saxophone, foghorn, and amniotic ocean, the world unborn into sound and sound remade into music.

"Melody after melody spun out of the saxophone's brass bell and disappeared into the darkness."

For the better part of an hour, I poured everything that I was into the saxophone. Then, when there was nothing left in me to play, I blew the last few notes of "Happy Birthday to You." When the last note tumbled from the saxophone and vanished into the night air, I lowered the sax and turned off the tape recorder. Then I just stood in the darkness. God was nowhere and everywhere. I reached into my backpack and grabbed my disaster notebook. I had no use for it anymore. I threw it over the edge of the cliff. I peered out at the waves and thought of my uncle lost and alone somewhere in the depths of the sea. I took the saxophone strap from around my neck and flung Isamu's saxophone as far as I could out over the cliff edge to the surging tide below. I was Charlie Lord, and as perfectly imperfect as it was, I loved America.

Chapter 5 Renfield

Renfield College in Stoker, Connecticut, was founded in 1881 by a Quaker woman, Prudence Renfield. She'd helped fugitive slaves escape captivity in the 1850s. She believed in freedom, and she believed in the power of money to transform lives. Immediately after the Civil War, she purchased a hat factory in Danbury that only employed former slaves. Unfortunately, the chemical solution the hatters used to wash the rabbit and beaver pelts contained significant quantities of mercury nitrate, and many of the freedmen suffered kidney damage, brain damage, and untimely deaths. There was a life-size painting of her in the dorm lounge. She wore men's clothing in the portrait. She was a Hicksite Quaker—a freethinker—and bore a striking resemblance to the Quaker Oats man. I liked looking at her picture. A student from a previous semester had written on the wall under the painting: "Nothing is better for thee than me," which, as far as the college was concerned, was certainly the truth.

"She was a Hicksite Quaker–a freethinker–and bore a striking resemblance to the Quaker Oats man."

Renfield had endowments in the billions, thanks to the donations of wealthy alumni. One of them, Emodium Goodfellow, had been the heir to the Goodfellow Tire fortune. One of the conditions Emodium required in exchange for his money was that Renfield open up a business school, so there were a lot of students there, like me, working on degrees in finance, marketing, business analytics, accounting, and operations management.

Emodium had lived in the Philippines as a child, where he'd learned to play the game of 'takraw,' which was a sport like volleyball, only the ball was made of rattan, and you couldn't touch the ball with your hands unless you were serving. After that you just had to use your feet, knees, chest, and head. It was a great passion of his. While other colleges had impressive football, basketball, or baseball facilities, the Renfield Fighting Quakers had the finest takraw facilities in the country. He'd built a 15,000-seat takraw arena. The university hired a coach from Malaysia who'd recruited a few of the best young players in all of Southeast Asia.

My roommate, Daeng Phibunsongkhram, was one of the takraw players who'd been recruited from Thailand. Since he didn't speak English and I didn't speak Thai, we got along perfectly. Neither of us could understand a word of what the other was saying, but as long as we each cleaned up after ourselves, nothing that either of us had to say was liable to irritate the other. Ignorance was complete bliss. If you want to make the entire world happy, it's best not to know what others are saying or thinking.

"While other colleges had impressive football, basketball, or baseball facilities, the Renfield Fighting Quakers had the finest takraw facilities in the country."

40

Unfortunately, there were no other college takraw teams in the country. Occasionally a match would be arranged against some team from Southeast Asia, but these were few and far between. When they did take place, they'd be attended by about a dozen fans. I went to one of the matches once. It was actually pretty exciting. The players on both teams had tremendous leaping ability and would often spike the ball over the net with their foot, then fall back down to the court. Sometimes they'd twist midair after kicking the ball and land on their feet, but most of the time they'd just land on their backs or on all fours and then scramble upright. It might not have been football, but it seemed as exciting, if not more so, than volleyball.

After the match I went down to the court to see my roommate. We stared dumbly at each other for a few seconds, then he did a funny thing. He touched his index fingers to his thumbs and held his hands up so that the palms faced me. I returned the gesture. Both of us laughed, though maybe we shouldn't have. Once you go down that road toward understanding another human, you open the door to all sorts of problems.

I left the takraw arena and went to find Willy Wetmore. He lived in an apartment on the other side of a man-made lake in the middle of campus, about a five-minute walk from my dorm. He'd just gotten back from wrestling practice and looked thrashed. There were two other wrestlers at his weight. One of them was Canaan Able, a wrestler from Greenwich Vocational that Willy had beaten in high school.

"He's kind of weird," said Willy. "He's from this religious family that has these dietary restrictions. Some days he can't eat vegetables that begin with certain letters. He can eat fish so long as it was caught in moving water like the ocean or a river. Anything from a pond or a lake is what his people call 'Hechem' and must be taken to a priest for a blessing before it can be cooked and eaten, so long as no woman in the household has had sexual relations in the past 36 hours. Apparently, it takes years for someone to learn all the rules about food as well as which cousins or aunts you may or may not sleep with. Personally, I find it pretty exhausting."

"It probably made sense when his people put those rules in place," I said. Willy eyeballed me.

"The problem with you, Charlie, is you're an innocent in a world of wolves, sharks, and ospreys."

"Well, that covers earth, water, and air," I said. "Any predators you can think of that live in fire?"

Willy grunted and pulled a rock out of his back pocket. He set it down on the table in front of him.

"I'm thinking about becoming an animist," he said. "I met a girl in LA who sorta turned me on to the whole animism thing. It's big in California and has roots in Asia, where people are much more spiritual than in the West. Do you have any thoughts or considerations about the wholesale worshiping of material objects and natural phenomena like climate patterns and ocean currents?

"I don't have any answers, Willy," I said. "Is there a practicing animist anywhere who you can talk to about your concerns?"

"Naw. They all live in California," he said. "It's easier to worship stuff out West than it is here. There's too many layers of tradition to break through on the East Coast. California's more of a free-for-all."

I left Willy staring at his rock on the table in front of him and went back to my dorm. The door to the resident advisor's room was open when I entered the lounge. The RA, Derrick Calibanos, was a tall, melancholic twenty-year-old with premature male pattern baldness. Derrick wanted to be a cartoonist and spent his free time reading DC Comics books and studying how the artists had drawn Batman or Superman. He would take pictures of himself without his shirt in the mirror and then use the photos as studies for his own superheroes he was creating, albeit with heavily padded chest, arm, and leg muscles. Also, Derrick possessed a bizarre pair of scrawny, useless wings that sprouted pathetically from his shoulders. The wings were covered with weird chicken-leg-like scales, but in his drawings they'd be transformed into a majestic set of fully functional superhero wings. They spanned at least ten feet in width and were covered in beautiful feathers of silver and gold.

"My family's originally from a small village on the isle of Crete," Derrick said. "Supposedly, the myth about Icarus has its roots in the actual historicity of my ancestor's unexceptional scapular appendages."

"That's quite a mouthful," I said.

"I wrote a paper about it in third grade," Derrick said. "I researched it semi-religiously for two or three entire days. To this day, I can remember everything I wrote."

In addition to having scraggly wings, which did absolutely nothing, Derrick was also born with an extra set of adult teeth which had begun replacing his first set in the past year or so. Every so often we'd be in the dorm dining room, and Derrick would bite into something, then suddenly swear and spit a tooth into his hand. Nearly all of his teeth had replaced themselves except for the wisdom teeth, which had gotten impacted. He'd had to go to an oral surgeon and have the extra wisdom teeth removed.

"It's hereditary," Derrick said. "Normally it skips a generation. Normally, you either get the wings or the extra set of teeth and premature male pattern baldness. I was supposed to just get the teeth and the male pattern baldness, but I got the fucking wings, too. It's quite a burden to be on the cusp of evolution, Charlie. I would say the cuspid or bicuspid of evolution if I wanted to engage in wordplay, but I'm not the type who normally does that. I shouldn't have these wings, man. I should just have the teeth and the baldness. These wings are kind of a cancer. I hate these fucking things. Plus, women are a bit freaked out by them. I can't even make them flap for Chrissakes. Fortunately, there are a lot of women who think bald guys are hot. Audrey thinks I'm hot."

Audrey Stone was a woman of incredible beauty. She had long, dark hair and breathtaking, silvery-green eyes. She was majoring in early childhood education. She was also deaf. She couldn't hear herself when she spoke, and her voice was hoarse and hard to understand. Audrey also had a severe stutter that not only affected her speech but also extended to her ability to communicate via sign language. It was weird. She would generally sign while she was speaking, and whenever the stutter showed up in her speech, it would simultaneously

43

show up in the movement of her hands. It wasn't pretty. There was a lot of spitting involved with her stutter, and her hands would just start waving spasmodically at the same time. It was quite a spectacle, though Derrick didn't seem to mind or even notice.

"Yes," he said one Sunday evening while we were playing cribbage in the dorm lounge, "she's got a pretty good case of Derrick-itis."

"Derrick-itis?"

"Yeah," he said. "She's got a case of Calibanos fever."

"Calibanos fever?"

"Is there an echo in here or what?"

"Or what?" I asked.

"Nyah! Fa!" Derrick said.

Derrick got up and walked to his room. It was right off of the lounge. When he returned, he was holding a canvas that was about four feet high and three feet wide. It was a big caricature drawing of Derrick and Audrey driving somewhere in a tiny sports car. Their cartoon heads were about twice as large as the car. They were driving and waving to me and anyone else who might look at the drawing. They looked happy. A big red cartoon heart surrounded their gigantic cartoon heads.

"It's a gift for Audrey," Derrick said. "She's gonna love it!"

Derrick was always getting Audrey gifts. He had taken a couple of his extra wisdom teeth to a jeweler's shop and had them fitted with gold posts and hooks so that Audrey could wear them as earrings. They were a gift for her birthday. He showed them to me before he gave them to her. They were pretty ugly. The roots of the wisdom teeth were twisted and gnarled. There was a cavity in one of them that the jeweler had filled with gold.

"Maybe you should just take her to dinner for her birthday," I said.

"I put a lot of thought into this, Charlie," Derrick said. "Love is the giving of one's self to another."

"Maybe write her a poem," I said.

44

"Love is a thing with teeth," he said. "Teeth and wings. I've both. By the time Christmas rolls around, I should have enough teeth to make her a necklace. Maybe even a bandolier with teeth in place of the bullets."

"Lucky girl," I said.

Probably the thing I missed most my freshman year was wrestling. Even though my arm had physically healed, I still had only limited strength in my left hand, and when anyone actually grabbed my arm where it had been cut, the pain was excruciating. It would be a long time before I gained anything like full use of that arm. In order to fill the time that I had devoted to wrestling in high school, I joined the rugby team. One of the guys in my dorm was on the team, and he'd seen me playing in a pickup football game outside the dorm between classes. His name was Domingas Cabral. He was a business major. His family had been fishermen and sailors for generations out of Cape Verde. He was the scrum half and was the only Black player on the Renfield Rugby Team. When I asked him how it felt to be the only Black player on the team, he looked at me like I had two heads.

"I'm not Black," he said. "I'm Cape Verdean." I looked at Domingas's face. There was no trace of irony in it. He wasn't one of the darkest-skinned humans I'd ever seen, but there was no mistaking his African ancestry.

"Cape Verdean?" I asked.

"Portuguese mostly, with a little African in the mix."

"Isn't the African responsible for your skin color?" I asked.

"We're Portuguese with some African. We're not black. We're Cape Verdean."

"That's a nationality!" I said. "That's not a race."

"Please, Charlie. Just refer to me as Cape Verdean from now on. I'm not Black."

"Ok," I said. "Suit yourself."

"Come out for the rugby team, Charlie. I've seen you play football in the quad. You've speed. You'd make a good wing."

"I'd make a wing?" I asked. "If I'm going to be making anything, I'd rather make one of the girls in Delta Chi."

"There are groupies," said Domingas.

"Groupies?"

"One of them even had sex with everyone on the team last year."

"Gee, I can't wait," I said.

"Plus, we've got really cool jerseys. They're marooned."

"Marooned?"

"Why do you always repeat everything anyone says?" Domingas asked. "It's exhausting."

"Isn't the rugby team already playing games?" I asked. "I don't know any of the rules. I've never even watched a game. How am I supposed to play if I don't know what the hell I'm doing?"

"No worries," said Domingas. "The wing just pretty much runs up and down the field. If someone pitches you the ball, you run down the sideline until you either score or get tackled. If someone on the other team runs down your sideline, you tackle him. Simple."

"Okay," I said. "I'll do it because I feel like there's a lifetime of trust between us, even though I've only known you for a month."

"The team'll be happy, Charlie."

"The Lord is with you," I said. "By the way, what happened to the old wing?"

"Timmy? He broke his collarbone last game. He's out for the season. It's a tough game. Quint Jones, the loosehead prop, got his eye gouged out last year. He finished the game, though. Strafe, the blindside flanker, has already gotten three or four concussions this year, and we still have four games to go. I keep telling him to stop leading with his head when he tackles, but he won't listen to anyone. Other than that, we haven't had a whole lot of injuries other than some sprained or torn knee ligaments and a bunch of separated shoulders. A couple of broken collarbones. If you're going to get injured, Charlie, chances are it'll be

46

a sprained or torn knee ligament, a separated shoulder, or a broken collarbone."

"Well, that's quite a relief," I said. "I can't tell you how grateful I am for the opportunity to injure myself for the glory of Renfield."

"That's the spirit!" said Domingas. "You'd make a good Cape Verdean, Charlie."

"We few, we happy few, we band of brothers!" I said.

"Wow, that's great, Charlie. Has anyone ever told you before you have a way with words?"

"Why, back home I'm known as the Shakespeare of Mythic, Connecticut."

"No, I'm serious," said Domingas. "You've got a gift. With your language skills, you should go into industrial sales or something. You'd make a fortune. When I'm a marketing executive at some Fortune 500 company, I'm going to make sure to hire you."

"Wow, first an opportunity to injure myself. Then a future full of cold-calling businesses in Cleveland. I don't know how I can ever rethank you."

"You're welcome, Charlie. Like you said, 'We're the brothers in the band'"

"M-I-C-K-E-Y M-O-U-S-E!" I said. "Just called me 'Goofy.'"

Domingas left, and I put away my books. I looked at the clock. It was almost nine pm. I was done studying for the day. I wandered down the second-floor hallway to the stairwell and went down to the lounge. The room was dark when I entered it. I was about to turn on the TV when a deep voice called out to me from the shadows.

"Lord," the voice called. "Come sit and talk."

I recognized the voice; it belonged to Marco Bocce. Marco was a freshman, like me, but he happened to be a full year younger. He was super smart. He'd skipped a couple of grades in high school and then spent a year traveling throughout Europe before enrolling at Renfield. I liked him. He was bright and perceptive. He was a psychology major. It suited him. I peered into the darkness and could just make him out sitting in an armchair. He was smoking a pipe that glowed and illuminated his face when he drew on it. I sat down on the sofa beside him.

"What are you doing up?" I asked.

"Paying attention," Marco said. "It's what I do."

"That's probably why I like talking to you," I said.

"It's not really me you're talking to, Charlie," Marco said. "You're really just talking to yourself."

"I'm fairly certain I'm talking to you right now," I said.

"It wasn't a criticism," said Marco. "It's what everyone does. When we find someone who lets us hear ourselves more clearly than other people do, we build friendships or fall in love with them."

"Interesting theory," I said.

"It was put together by Piaget's younger sister. Her name was Imogene, I believe. Maybe Esther. I'm not sure it matters. Besides, I've been drinking since 6:30."

"Maybe you should call it a night," I said.

Marco took a deep draw on his pipe. The tobacco in the pipe's bowl glowed bright orange, and Marco's face was illuminated. Blood ran down from his forehead.

"What the hell, Marco! You're bleeding."

"Just before you came in, I was trying to get my molecules vibrating at the same frequency as the dorm wall," said Marco calmly. "If I get them vibrating at the same frequency, I can pass through the wall."

Marco stood up and walked to the wall. He faced it and made a slight bow, then he leapt at it with astonishing speed. He smashed into it with his chest and face, then fell to the floor with a heavy thud. He rolled over onto his back and lay there without moving. His breathing was deep and peaceful. The floor was the best place for him. I left the lounge and went to the staircase. As I was going upstairs, Diekman and Bogie were coming down. Both were completely naked.

"We're going streaking, Lord. You wanna come with us?" Diekman asked.

"Why?" I asked.

"UConn had 250 streakers last night," said Bogie. "UMass had over 400 tonight. We wanna get in on the action."

"Just the two of you?"

"We're not queer if that's what you're thinking," said Diekman. Both Bogie and Diekman had erections.

"Why would I think that?" I asked.

"Everyone thinks that," said Bogie. "Sure you don't want to streak with us?"

"Another time," I said. "Streak hard and fast, deep into the dark."

I watched them exit the stairwell and enter the dark lounge. The door opened then closed behind them with an audible whoosh. The dorm was enveloped in a deep, humming silence. I appreciated it. I moved up the stairwell with as little noise as possible, got to my room, and put on a jazz record. The sound of Charlie Parker's "Yardbird Suite" filled the room. I lay down on my bed and let the music curl around my edges. No matter how many times I heard that song, it always amazed me. It was like stumbling across a meteor containing emeralds, rubies, sapphires, diamonds, and every time you looked at it, you saw another flash of brilliance as the light caught another precious gem and refracted otherworldly prisms of sound across the inner walls and dome of my skull. As I listened to the music, I realized, for the first time since returning my saxophone to Isamu, that I regretted throwing the instrument into the ocean. Had I done that out of my love for him? Or had I thrown my saxophone into the ocean out of the guilt I felt? He had reached his hand toward me as the tornado had lifted him off his feet, and I'd been unable to save him. I closed my eyes and let the music deflect me from the shame of being an innocent bystander. I fell asleep while the music was still playing.

When I awoke it was morning. Sunlight poured through the only window in the room. The needle of the record player still tracked the empty grooves at the end of the album as it spun round and round on the turntable, repeating the same sizzles and pops as the needle skipped across scratches in the vinyl. It was, I decided, an apt metaphor for my life. I listened to the sound emanating from the tinny speakers for ten or fifteen minutes before getting out of bed and lifting the stylus from the record. Then I went down the hall and showered, shaved, and brushed my teeth while the crackling silence continued to repeat itself in me like a mantra built out of shame and guilt.

Chapter 6 Games

I went to a few rugby practices before playing in my first game. Unlike my high school wrestling practices, rugby practice was a joke. We jogged around the field for a few minutes and then did some stretching exercises. When the stretching exercises were over, most of the team crowded around a keg of beer on the sidelines and spent the remainder of practice getting drunk. Following practice, we normally went to the campus pub and held competitions to see who could drink the most beer or drink beer the fastest, even though everyone knew the winner in both these contests would be Quint Jones. He was our loosehead prop and the largest player on the team. He'd lost an eye the previous season and had a glass one put in. After a few beers, he liked to take it out. If he liked you, he'd put his eye in your glass of beer.

"If he liked you he'd put his eye in your glass of beer."

"Here's looking at you!" he'd say.

Then he'd slam his eye into your drink. Anyone on the team who objected to having Quint's eyeball in his beer would have to fight him. Since Quint was six inches taller than me and outweighed me by seventy-five pounds, I said nothing and just drank my beer when his eyeball ended up in my glass. The only one who refused to drink with Quint's eyeball staring at him was the flanker, Strafe. Whenever Quint's eyeball ended up in his beer, Strafe would launch himself like a missile at Quint, though it usually ended badly for him. Quint would hit him three or four times in the head, and Strafe would slump, unconscious, to the floor. When he awoke a minute or two later, he and Quint would shake hands as though nothing had happened, then they'd be the best of friends until the next time Quint's eye landed in his drink.

I played my first rugby game at 8:30 am on a rainy Saturday morning in mid-November. The field was a swampy mess. After a few minutes, everyone was so covered with mud you could barely tell which team they were on. Quint Jones got his fake eye knocked out, and it got lost in the mud. Every so often the ball would get tossed out to me. I'd grab it and run downfield until I got tackled. When the other team's wing grabbed the ball and ran toward me, I'd tackle him. We may have won the game, but we just as easily may have lost. No one seemed to care. After the game, both teams gathered around a keg set up under one of the goalposts and drank until the keg was empty. When the beer was gone, all the players trudged off with their arms about each other as they sang and shouted obscenities at anyone who had the misfortune to wander across their paths.

I was one of the last to leave. I looked out at the field where Quint was wandering around it looking for his eye. Strafe came over to me.

"No concussion today?" I asked.

"Minor one, right near the end of the game. I couldn't remember my name for a minute, but I'm okay now."

Strafe looked at Quint feeling around in the mud for his eye. "Serves that prick right," he said.

"I take it you're not going to help him look for his eye," I said.

"Sure I am!" Strafe said. "He's a teammate."

Strafe wandered over to Quint to help search for the lost eye. As for me, I hadn't drunk too much. It was a good day for me to head over to the library and search for news of America. On the way to the library I felt depressed, which wasn't unusual. I'd been in college for a couple of months and was beginning to wonder what I was doing there. The parties were fun, and I'd made friends with some interesting characters, but there was nothing in my life that was particularly meaningful. In the past I'd filled the void by going to wrestling practice and working on takedowns and escapes for hours. Since the injury to my arm, which had cut through muscle and tendon down to the bone, I hadn't found anything to take the place of wrestling in my life. I'd thought that playing rugby might have filled that emptiness, but that hadn't happened. My classes were uninspiring, to say the least, and on more than one occasion I thought about leaving school and joining the Army, but the thought of choosing the same route that my father had taken kept me from going down to the recruiting office. There was no escape or even momentum in my life, although I wasn't even sure that's what I wanted.

The periodical room was on the library's main floor, but there weren't any new stories about America. The spring nationals wouldn't be held for another six months, and until then I probably wouldn't read much about her march toward the Olympics. I wandered around the library for a while and checked out some of the women studying in the carrels on the second floor, but I didn't talk to any of them. The effort seemed beyond me. Finally, I went into one of the special collections rooms. It was devoted to books by and about Gordon Gordon Gordon. He was a native son of the Nutmeg State and had grown up no more than half an hour from my hometown.

I'd read all his books and liked them. He'd had an interesting career. As a soldier during WWII, he'd written poems about his experience fighting in the Ardennes. He'd gotten wounded during the last days of the war and had spent nearly two years in a hospital in Switzerland where the long-term ramifications of his wounds were treated along with his symptoms of shell shock. He wrote about his time in Switzerland in *A Death Forestalled*, an autobiographical novel about an American soldier who recuperates in Zurich, falls in love with the mistress of a world-renowned psychologist who is treating him for shell shock, then goes home to his family's farm in Oklahoma, where he meets and marries a blind school teacher. The book is notable in that it's written completely in one-syllable words, as was his second book, the Pulitzer Prize-winning *A Bowl of Dust*, which is probably the definitive work about the Dust Bowl and the plight of the migrants from Oklahoma and Texas as they traveled to California.

Following that novel, Gordon G. Gordon wrote two slim comic works about a soldier who returns from the war and becomes a teacher. He educates the children of field hands at a fictional winery in the Napa

Valley. They were both works of lyrical beauty with tremendous insight into the absurdity of life. I must've read those books about three or four times each, and with each reading I gleaned some nugget that I'd previously overlooked. While I was studying the text of Gordon G. Gordon's acceptance speech when he was awarded the Nobel Prize in Literature, a librarian came over to where I was sitting.

"Did you know that Mr. Gordon will be visiting Renfield next month?" she said. "He'll be reading excerpts from his most recent book and talking about his work, in general."

She handed me a flier with Gordon's picture on it. Beneath his photo was information about the date, time, and location of the reading. I studied the flier for a minute, then folded it up and stuck it in my pocket. I couldn't wait for his visit. Maybe he'd even sign a copy of one of his books for me.

It was nearly noon when I left the library and decided to visit Willy. I walked across campus to his apartment. The temperature had dropped, and a few big flakes of snow were falling from leaden skies. It was a short walk, but by the time I reached Willy's place, the snow had stopped. The clouds were moving rapidly to the south, and it was getting noticeably colder.

Willy was dressed in his wrestling gear. He was weighing food on the kitchen table with an old-fashioned scale. He had a raw steak and a potato on one side of the balance and several balance weights on the other side.

"He was weighing food on the kitchen table with an old-fashioned scale."

54

".3629 kilos," Willy said. "I'm safe."

"Safe?" I asked.

"Got a match this afternoon," he said. "I can go .42 kilos."

Wetmore grabbed the potato like it was an apple and took a bite out of it. "It's not as bad as you'd think," he said.

"Hey," I said. "Gordon G. Gordon is coming to Renfield next month. He's going to be reading from a new book and talking about his work."

Wetmore took another bite of his raw potato.

"That guy? He's a hack! I don't know what you see in him. All those one-syllable words. What the hell's that about? It's like reading Dr. Seuss."

"I thought you'd be interested in going since you want to be a writer, Willy."

"I can write rings around that guy," said Willy. "Pulitzer, Schmulitzer."

The front door opened, and Willy's roommate entered the room. His name was Dan Butler, but everyone called him 'Chinaman.' Chinaman had blue eyes, blond hair, and fair skin. He was wearing a green parka with some type of fur around the hood, which was up, and Chinaman's face was lost in its shadows. He was a pharmacy major. He closed the door and locked it behind him. Then he went to the window and drew the blinds and closed the drapes, even though we were on the fourth floor, and there was no possible way that anyone could see in through the window. He peeked through the blinds for a minute. Satisfied that no one was spying on him, he put his hood down.

"Dudes," he said. "Salutations! Salutations and whatnot!"

He had an unusual way of talking. His mouth seemed to move independently of the words coming out of his mouth. It almost looked like his mouth belonged to a dummy that some unseen and unknown ventriloquist was filling with words.

"Whatnot," I answered.

I looked at Wetmore. He was holding the steak in both hands and yanking on it with his teeth. It looked like Goya's painting of Saturn devouring his children.

"He's all savage and whatnot," said Chinaman. "I wouldn't want to wrestle him, even with this."

Chinaman pulled a .38 from the waistband of his pants. He laid it on the table next to the scale. He unzipped a pocket on the inside left breast of the parka and unloaded three plastic baggies full of pot and tossed them on the table. He unzipped several more pockets around the parka and tossed baggie after baggie onto the table until the entire table was covered.

"Twenty–two lids," said Chinaman. He put one on the scale and put a number of weights on the other side. It looked to be a little over 20 grams.

"Fifteen bucks," said Chinaman. "How many you want, Lord?"

"None," I said. "I'm broke."

Wetmore reached into his wrestling singlet and pulled a wad of bills from somewhere near his jockstrap. He tossed $30 onto the table.

"Take one, Charlie."

Willy got up from the table and disappeared from the room. Chinaman put his hood back up. His face was lost amid fur and shadows. Only his mouth was visible. It moved oddly, and the room filled with language.

"My father imports these parkas from China, Charlie. This is a combination of real fur and fake fur. The fake fur keeps the costs down. The real fur gives him the opportunity to sell it at a higher price. I mix just enough stems and seeds and oregano leaf into the kief to keep my costs down. I put just enough primo Acapulco Gold into the blend to get prime dollar for it. I hope you enjoy it. Vale and farewell! Now if you'll excuse me, I need to make my rounds."

He opened the door and disappeared. Willy came back into the room with rolling papers and a lighter. "You need to get high with me," he

56

said. "Just don't let me eat anything when I get the munchies. I have to make weight."

"You're gonna get high before a wrestling match?" I asked.

"Helps me focus, Charlie. Plus, I've got a bad rotator cuff. The pot makes it so I can still feel the pain, only it doesn't bother me. Same with my knee. The only thing the pot doesn't do is help with the pain in my ankle. It still bothers me, no matter how much I smoke. Weird..., huh?"

I hung around for about half an hour and left when 'Chinaman' returned and nearly cut his finger off while showing us his collection of tactical knives. I had only smoked a little with Willy, just enough to be polite. Willy had smoked nearly the whole joint by himself. He was pretty relaxed when I left him seated on his sofa, staring at some old Godzilla movie on his black-and-white television, not that the movie was important in and of itself. I just tended to notice details like that. Or, at least, there was a part of myself that tended to notice details, and an internal monologue would take place inside me assessing and cataloging whatever it was that part of me had just noticed, independent of whatever it was the rest of me might have been doing and thinking.

It was early afternoon when I got back to my dorm. Strafe was in the lounge playing chess with Jonah Klonowicz, aka Klondike. Klondike was six-foot-eight and was genuinely smart. He was majoring in mathematics and had already authored a paper on string theory that had been published in some academic journal. He was only a junior but had already been recruited by some New York-based hedge fund where he'd work as a quantitative analyst. He was a brilliant chess player and beat just about everyone in the dorm with ease, with the exception of Strafe. I sat down and watched the game for a few minutes. Strafe was already down a rook, a bishop, and a pawn to Klondike. Klondike moved his queen and captured another bishop.

"Check," he said.

I looked at the board. From what I saw, Strafe's best move was to resign. Strafe moved his knight in front of the king. Klondike pushed a pawn forward. Strafe pushed his own pawn forward to check the queen. Klondike moved his queen to safety, then all hell broke loose.

Once Klondike's queen was out of the way, Strafe's knight took over. In three moves he managed to capture Klondike's queen and a rook. In five moves it was checkmate. Klondike swept the pieces from the board in anger.

"You brain-damaged moron," he shouted. "I can't believe how lucky you are!"

"Relax," said Strafe. "You still beat me three out of four games!"

"I should beat you a hundred percent of the time!" he said.

Strafe shrugged.

"You care too much," he said.

"Fuck yourself," said Klondike.

Strafe set the chess pieces back up on the board, and they began another game. This time Klondike checkmated Strafe in three or four moves. Klondike looked happy. Strafe looked the way he always looked, like a man who'd had a concussion earlier in the day. It was as though he was both there but not there. I envied him that trait, to be present and absent at the same time, unlike myself. I was always present, always hanging around the periphery checking things out: the perfect narrator of my life, but seldom its author. I looked at the clock. It was 1:11, a meaningless rendezvous with time that meant nothing. I looked at the chessboard. Klondike was smashing Strafe again. That, too, meant nothing. I stood up and went into the dining room. Domingas was sitting at a table reading a book about short selling on the stock exchange. Domingas looked up at me.

"Did you know, Charlie, that you can make more money betting a company will fail than you can betting that the price of the stock will go up?" he said.

"I don't know anything about the stock market," I said, "but why would anyone bet that a company will fail?"

"Money!" said Domingas. "Say there's a company that has invested in outdated technology or has lost ground to a competitor who has a similar product with more features. You can actually make a ton of money borrowing shares of the stock you're betting against. When the price of the stock drops, you purchase the shares you borrowed at a lower price and collect the difference between the price you borrowed the shares at and the price you actually paid for them."

"What happens if the stock price rises?" I asked.

"Well, basically you're fucked. There's no limit to how much money you can lose if that happens. Fortunately, there are ways to make sure that doesn't happen."

"Like what?"

"Well, naked short selling. You borrow shares that may or may not exist. You sell them, then sell them again, then sell them again and again and again. You dilute the value of the stock! People who've bought the stock think they hold real shares, but in reality those shares are fake, but no one can tell the difference between real shares and fake ones."

"Aren't there laws against this kind of crap?" I asked.

"Sort of, but no one really keeps tabs on this shit. The stock market is self-regulated by the largest banks and investment companies in the world. You think they give a fuck if your grandmother loses money? Hell no! There are all sorts of ways to manipulate stock prices so companies go bankrupt. That's how I plan on making a billion dollars! Even if you do get caught, you might be fined a couple million dollars by the Securities Exchange Commission, but if you make five hundred million, that's just the cost of doing business, Charlie. Shit! Stick with me, and there will be yachts and private islands and private jets! Basically, it's risk-free. No one ever goes to jail over shit like this! It's not like you're robbing people with a gun!"

"It sounds horrible," I said. "It sounds worse." Domingas put down his book and stared at me.

"Why are you majoring in business if you don't want to make money?' he asked.

"That's a question I've been asking myself," I said.

I left the dining room to go upstairs to the second floor. The door to Mark Wacyshyn's room was open. Mark was inside smoking a joint. I entered the room and sat down on a red velvet armchair that smelled exactly like the jacket I'd worn at the Rialto. Mark passed the joint to me. It was full of stems and seeds that would pop and crackle whenever you took a hit. Flaming seeds and twigs fell out and burned a hole in my shirt. There was a record playing on Mark's turntable: a lady was sure all that glittered was gold, and I had no doubt that lady was America.

Chapter 7 Calibanos

Paul Tsoukias came into the room without knocking and watched us without saying anything. He was odd. He wore the same shirt and pants just about every day and rarely washed them. Mark did his best to ignore him, which was difficult given that Paul was six-foot-five and did nothing but lift weights when he wasn't going to classes. He was gigantic and had enormous deposits of fat on top of his musculature. He looked cartoonish, almost as if you could stick a pin in him and he'd deflate. He was the only one in the dorm without a roommate. His had moved out a few weeks into the semester, citing Tsoukias's less than exemplary personal hygiene habits. Mark looked at Tsoukias.

"You stink," said Mark. "Why don't you take a shower?"

"I have phobias," said Paul. "I can't take a shower in the presence of circumcised males."

"As opposed to circumcised females," I said.

"Clitorectomies are endemic in Islamic nations," Paul said. "Not that I've been within three feet of a clitoris, either intact or ectomized."

"Any other phobias besides circumcision?" I asked.

"Just your basic ones. Spiders. Fear of heights. The number eleven. I have a recurring dream that I'm having a recurring dream. It freaks me out."

"Are you a psych major?" I asked.

"Absolutely," said Tsoukias. "Bingo."

"Why can't you be a bit more like Marco Bocce?" I asked. "He's pretty normal for a psych major."

Tsoukias shrugged.

"I could go into my relationship with my mother if you'd like," he said. "It's pretty scary if you're outside of my meat suit. Inside of my meat suit, though, it all seems perfectly normal and justifiable. It's the kind of stuff that happens in the lives of serial killers."

"Should I be concerned?" I asked.

"Wrong gender," said Paul. "I have enormous respect for humans with penises, either circumcised or not."

I felt myself sliding away into the music. I looked at my legs. They seemed far away, as though I were looking at them through the wrong end of a pair of binoculars. Tsoukias grabbed the joint out of my hand. He extinguished it, then put the roach in his shirt pocket. He walked to the door and opened it.

"Hey!" said Wacyshyn, "What the fuck!"

Tsoukias left, and Wacyshyn rolled another joint and lit it.

Marco came into the room a few minutes after Tsoukias left. He had a gauze bandage roll wrapped around his head all the way down to his right ear. He was wearing a fake leather and rabbit fur hat on top of it. He looked like a Van Gogh self-portrait.

"He looked like a Van Gogh self-portrait."

"What's going on with your ear, Marco?"

"It's not really my ear," Marco said. "I use acupressure in my ear as a treatment for bedwetting. Over the break, I had an electrical device implanted in my ear. It stimulates the nerves automatically so I don't have to wake up every hour and give myself acupressure treatments."

"So it's a bladder problem," Wacyshyn said.

"Negatory," said Marco. "It's neurological. I'm attempting to use electrical stimulation to re-route certain neural pathways associated with bedwetting. At the same time, I repeat certain affirmations designed to subconsciously reinforce the idea that I am as dry at night as you are. You might say it's an attempt at reprogramming myself through electro-neurolinguistics. I've basically taken classic psychotherapy anchoring techniques and overlaid them with practical applications from the work that Bandler and Grinder are doing in California. The west coast is pretty much where all the breakthroughs are taking place."

"That's amazing!" I said. "So you've been cured of bedwetting."

"Not really," said Marco, "but at least this technique hasn't made my bedwetting worse, unlike my last few attempts. Over the summer I tried a hybrid approach to nocturnal enuresis by fusing Mowrer's work on sphincter contraction and alarm systems with Freudian analysis. I had dreams of urinating on both of my parents."

"Marco, you're a mess," I said. I handed him the joint. "Smoke some of this. Maybe it'll cure your bedwetting."

Marco stared at the joint for a few seconds.

"I'm not sure that cannabis is recognized by the AMA as an approved treatment for bedwetting, Charlie."

"What about recreational use?" Wacyshyn asked.

"Just so long as it isn't used for medicinal purposes, I have no problem with getting high," Marco answered.

We smoked pot until I closed my eyes and went away for a bit, down into that little cocoon of blissful silence, which was as good a substitute for myself as anything else. It was like climbing into a warm, me-shaped coffin lined with wool and cotton. The thought occurred to me that this was what death must be like, and the idea both comforted and saddened me. I swam back up to the surface and opened my eyes. Marco was still rooted to his spot on the sofa. He was completely motionless except for his eyes. He looked at me and blinked both eyes at the same time. He'd blink three or four times, pause, then blink another three or four times, pause, then repeat the blinks. After a while, Wacyshyn sat up and studied Marco's face.

"I think he's sending us a message in Morse code," Wacyshyn said.

"Marco, I don't understand Morse code," I said. "I don't know what you're trying to tell us."

"I'm communicating with my soul. I'm sending soul semaphore to my eyes, which are translating it to Morse code."

Marco fell silent and began blinking again.

"Why don't you just tell me what you want to tell me?" I said. "I'm sure your mouth knows Morse code or semaphore or whatever other cryptic code is contained in your pancreas or liver."

"My heart knows sign language," he said. "The heart is a lonely signer, Charlie."

The door to the room opened and Paul Tsoukias came back in. He wore a dingy white t-shirt with a spray of red droplets across the front.

"Is that blood?" I asked. "That's blood, isn't it?"

I was pretty seriously high and was fairly convinced that Tsoukias had slit someone's throat.

"I wish," said Tsoukias. "Spandana accident. Maybe Mateus. I would've preferred spilling Mateus on myself. I like the way it sounds."

He pulled out one of the joints he'd rolled earlier from Wacyshyn's stash and lit it with the candle stuck in an empty brown Lancer's bottle. He smoked it entirely by himself in about three or four minutes, then put it out on his tongue. He put the roach into the pocket of his t-shirt and then pulled out the second joint and lit that, too.

"Did you hear about Calibanos?" he asked.

"Derrick? The RA?"

"The self-same."

"What about him?" I asked.

"He's in the hospital," Tsoukias said. "I hear it's cancer. That's what's going around, anyways. I've heard from some very reliable sources that it's cancer."

There was a knock on the door. Before any of us had the chance to ask who it was, the door swung open and Stan Melmac stepped into the room. Stan was a journalism major and wanted to go into sports broadcasting after college.

"Mind if I come in?" Stan asked. Without waiting for an answer, Stan sat down in a desk chair, backwards. He laid his arms on the back of the chair and rested his chin on the back of his hands.

"Did you hear about Derrick Calibanos?" asked Tsoukias. "The scuttlebutt is that he's in the hospital with the big 'C.'".

Stan put his hand up to his mouth as though he were holding a microphone and began speaking into it. He did this often.

"You heard it here first, ladies and gentlemen! The courage of this young man, Donald Caliban."

"Derrick," I said. "Calibanos."

"Facing the heartbreaking outbreak of cancer in his person."

"It's a rumor," I said.

"Rumors of tumors," said Stan. "Facing the unknown of potential inoperability."

"Hey," said Bocce. "Let's go to the hospital and visit him."

"Sounds great!" I said. "Who has a car?"

None of us had a car. We ended up borrowing Zooey Madrigal's Karmann Ghia by giving her some weed and promising to find a date for her roommate, Terry Washburn, a dietary sciences major who stood five-foot-three and weighed 280 pounds.

Zooey gave us the keys, and Marco, Tsoukias, and I went down to the parking lot to find the Karmann Ghia. It was parked under an oak tree at the far end of the lot. It was a convertible, and the top was down. As a matter of fact, the top was broken and had been down since the past summer. Icy water, branches, and dead leaves filled the front and back seats. It took us about twenty minutes to clear enough of the debris out of it so that it was drivable. Me and Tsoukias had to push it up and down the road for about ten minutes before Bocce managed to start the damn thing by popping the clutch.

"Marco, are you sure you're okay to drive?" I asked.

"Not really," he said, "but if anything happens, my father will get it taken care of. He's a judge in Fairfield County, so if anything happens short of us killing someone, we should be good."

It was about twenty-eight degrees when we left Renfield for St Gregory's Hospital in Hartford. The trip took about forty minutes, and we were completely frozen by the time we got there. To warm up before visiting Calibanos, we stopped at a package store a few blocks from the hospital and bought a pint flask of blackberry brandy. We passed the flask around in the parking garage under the hospital.

When it was empty, Tsoukias threw it against the wall next to the elevator. The sound of the breaking glass echoed and sounded oddly muffled but somehow resonant in the cavernous garage. The sound was satisfying.

"BOOM!" I shouted. The word flung itself away from me, crashed soberly against the walls of the parking structure, echoed, and faded. The elevator arrived, and we rode up to the fifth floor. The brandy had done its job. I was still half frozen, but for the most part, I no longer cared. Other than some vague feelings of drug-and-alcohol-fueled anxiety and paranoia, I felt completely relaxed.

Derrick Calibanos was sitting up in the hospital bed when we entered his room. He had a drawing board across his knees and was drawing another picture of a superhero with a pair of gigantic wings. His own wings stuck out of the back of his hospital gown. They didn't look as scraggly as they usually did. They seemed to have grown, and the white, black, and gray scales that covered them had also grown. They looked like something you'd see on a pine cone when it opened during dry weather. Calibanos noticed me looking at them.

"I've had a couple rounds of radiation," he said dispassionately. He pointed a thumb over his shoulder.

"I've had some chemo, too. The doctors think the radiation has been making these things grow," he said. "They suspect it, but they don't know. It might be the chemo. They have their suspicions, as do I, though I'd rather not get into it in case I'm wrong about it. Even if I

66

was right about it, I still probably wouldn't want to get into it. Some things I just can't talk about."

Marco sat down in a chair facing away from the bed and stared at the wall. He often did this when he spoke with people. He was planning on going to med school to become a psychiatrist, and he liked practicing his bedside manner, which involved not looking at the person he was speaking to. The afternoon sunlight filtered through the window blinds and cast a striped pattern across the blankets on Derrick's bed. I thought of April's room and the blank white canvas on the wall.

"So," Marco said, "how do you feel about this?" he asked.

"The doctors aren't very optimistic," said Derrick. "I heard one of them speaking with my parents when they thought I was sleeping. Three months, he said. Maybe six."

I listened without saying anything. There was nothing to say.

"So, how do you feel about this?" Marco asked again.

"I don't know yet," he said. "I'm not sure. Every so often I find myself kind of hoping that my charts and files have gotten mixed up with someone else's charts and files. Or maybe this is a dream and I'll wake up. That this isn't my life. That I don't have cancer, or a fucking pair of worthless wings, or a second set of adult teeth. That nature hadn't played some kind of sick joke when I was conceived and set in motion all the events and circumstances that have led me to this moment, in this room, talking to a man who is talking to the shadows on the wall."

Marco said nothing but nodded his head sagely and stroked his chin. Tsoukias stood on the other side of the bed from Marco. His face had an expression of indifference. I watched as he reached up to his face and squeezed a pimple until the pus oozed over his fingers. He looked at the pus and then wiped his hand on his pants. I went to the window and looked outside. The sun was going down behind the office and government buildings to the west. There was a building with a gold dome in the distance. Cold rays from the setting sun flared off the gold with such intensity that it was impossible to stare at it for more than a few seconds. That's the way it is when you're faced with too much reality.

On the drive back from the hospital, it was so bitterly cold in the open-air Karmann Ghia that we'd had to stop every ten or fifteen miles at some roadside bar or tavern to warm up. I'd probably had four or five beers or shots on top of the brandy I'd drunk earlier in the day. I wasn't falling-down-drunk drunk, just numb and somewhat stupid drunk. The edges between me and the world were slightly blurred. Mark Wacyshyn was sitting in the lounge when we got back to the dorm.

"Where you guys been?" he asked.

"Derrick has cancer," I said. "His doctors have given him three to six months."

"That's terrible, man!"

"His wings look better, though."

"Is that good?" asked Mark. "Do you think it's good that his wings look better?"

"I'm not sure, maybe. Maybe not. The doctors aren't hopeful."

I went up to my room, put on a Dave Brubeck album, and lay down on my bed. Paul Desmond was playing the coolest of cool alto sax laid over the piano's 5/4 rhythm and syncopated vamp. The door to the room suddenly opened, and Willy Wetmore came into my room. He had a duffle bag slung over his shoulder. On his head, he wore padded black and white foam and velour wrestling headgear as if it were a pair of earmuffs. He was just getting back from his wrestling match.

"Jesus, it's cold as fuck out there!"

"Hey, what are you doing here?" I asked. "You've got a great apartment."

"Fucking Chinaman," he said. "He's making butane hash oil in the kitchen. I left before he blew up the place."

"How'd you do today?"

"We wrestled North Coventry College for the Deaf," he said. "They were pretty good for being deaf. I barely beat my guy, and they pretty much kicked the snot out of the rest of the team."

"That sucks," I said.

"I don't feel too bad," Wetmore said. "They had these deaf and dumb cheerleaders who were pretty hot. They jumped around in these short outfits and did their cheers in sign language. After the match, I made out with one of them. She was my first deaf and dumb girl. Have you ever been with someone who can't hear or speak? It's pretty intense. There was a lot of eye contact and lip reading on her part. It may have been a little too intimate. I'm not a big fan of intimacy. That's how you lose yourself. Who wants that? I think I'd rather be with someone who was blind. I don't think there's as much intimacy when someone can't see. Ever been with a blind girl?"

"April wears glasses," I said. "Both of us are essentially blind when we take our glasses off."

"April Tyler? That really smart girl? She's way out of your league, Charlie. She's hot; she's got money and brains," Wetmore said. "I thought you were in love with America."

"Yeah, well…," I said. A long silence punctuated the air. "Anyway, Calibanos has the big C. We went to see him at St Gregory's in Hartford. The doctors told his parents he's dying. They've been giving him radiation treatments, which haven't done anything but make his wings grow. They think it's the radiation, but it could be the chemo."

"Jesus!" exclaimed Willy. "I wish I'd been there to see his wings. That kinda stuff is right up my alley! Wow! What about the nurses? Were there any hot nurses? I wouldn't mind getting a sponge bath from a hot nurse every now and then. A blind nurse would be particularly hot."

"Jesus, Willy! Don't you think of anything but chasing women?"

"Of course I think about other things, but who wants to hear my thoughts on spirituality or reality or language? No one wants to hear or talk about monotheistic dualism except you, which is why you never get laid."

"I get laid," I said.

"Seldom," said Willy. "Anyway, I think about a great many things just like everyone else on the planet, Charlie, things that are mostly inexpressible, unutterable, and non-communicable."

"April's dying," I said. "She has a disease that is making her lose her ability to think."

"Sorry to hear it," Willy said. "Is it communicable as well?"

"I don't think so," I said.

"Who knows?" said Willy. "Maybe death is the only thing that's truly communicable." Willy went over to my stereo and lifted the needle off the record.

"I'm turning this crap off," he said.

He took the record off the stereo and searched through my vinyl collection. He found an album by the Grateful Dead, put it on the turntable, dropped the needle on "Ripple," and then he pulled out a little bag of weed and rolled a joint. The song ended, and the silence rippled through us. We sat in my dimly lit dorm room and passed the joint back and forth in a stillness broken only by the pop and crackle of stems and seeds. Domingas knocked on the door and then opened it without waiting for a response. He sat down on Daeng's bed and got high with us. After about twenty minutes Willy stood up.

"I'll be back if Chinaman's blown up the apartment," he said.

Willy left. He was still wearing his wrestling shoes. They made a slight squeaking noise as he made his way down the hallway to the stairwell. After Willy left, I told Domingas about the trip to Hartford to see Derrick.

"That's rough," he said. "Three to six months? Fuck."

"Yeah. It's brutal. I don't even want to think about it," I said, "but at least his wings look better."

"Moço. Sta sab. That's good, man." Domingas took one last hit of the joint and stood up. He needed to find Strafe. Rugby season was almost over, and Domingas wanted to start an intramural ice hockey team.

"Do you even skate?" I asked.

"No, why?"

"It seems like one of the major prerequisites for playing hockey."

"Just so long as they let us fight, who cares about skating?"

70

Domingas left the room. He was a big guy, about six-foot-two, but his feet made no noise as he walked down the hall. For the next hour or so, I hung out in my room listening to the sound of footsteps out in the hallway. It was pretty interesting how it seemed like the people who made the most noise were the smallest people in the dorm. The big guys, like Tsoukias and Domingas, hardly made any noise when they walked. It was like everyone wanted to be, consciously or subconsciously, something they were not. I thought about Calibanos. He hated his baldness, his second set of adult teeth, his scraggly wings, his cancer. April was the only person I knew who was at peace with who she was and with her impending death, not that it made it any easier for me. I put the Brubeck album back on the turntable and listened to the calm, melancholic beauty of "Strange Meadow Lark." When the song ended, I felt a slight chill go down my spine, activating the muscles in my scrotum so that my testicles pulled up taut against my body. I'd had that reaction before when walking over bridges, only now my body was reacting, not to some vague fear of heights or fear of falling, but to thoughts of death. I hated thinking that neither Derrick nor April would live out the year, for my sake as much as for theirs. I didn't want to think about my mortality, but at the same time, there was a certain inexplicable thrill I felt when I thought about my own life ending. Perhaps that's why I'd kept that disaster notebook in high school, the one that contained pictures of car wrecks, plane crashes, fires, floods, atomic bomb blasts, and homicides. Perhaps by filling my mind with myriad images of death, destruction, and mass casualties, I was attempting to come to terms with the end of my own life, no matter how near or far in the future that event occurred. The music ended, and I got up and put the album by the Grateful Dead back on the turntable. It was just a box of rain, anyway, and when death came for me, would I hear his footsteps echo down the hallway, or would he arrive, voluminous but unannounced, on silent feet?

Chapter 8 Toad

I went to a lecture hall on the other side of campus the Friday night Gordon Gordon Gordon was supposed to come and read to us from his latest book, *Hall of Hail*. I'd bought a copy of the book in advance. I was hoping that I'd get to meet him, and if I did, I was going to ask him to autograph my book, but when I got to the lecture hall, the doors were locked. A hand-lettered sign on the door served notice that the reading by my favorite author had been canceled due to a conflict in Gordon Gordon Gordon's schedule.

I walked back to my dorm beneath a clear, crisp night sky illuminated by a full moon. My shadow reached the dorm before I did. The dorm lounge was crowded. Gerald Jacobs and Domingas Cabral were having a slapfight in the middle of the lounge. Stan Melmac sidled up alongside me. He held a spoon in his hand that he held to his mouth and spoke into while the two men slapped each other.

"Ladies and gentlemen, children, and people of all citizenry. We are in the midst of witnessing one of the indubitable scenes of modern sporting nomenclature! Unheralded Gerald Jacobs heaves a slap upon the savage visage of one Domingas Cabral, much to the chagrinful delight of the assembled multitudes!"

"How long they been going at this?" I asked Stan.

"It's a story as old as the anals of humanness!" Stan shouted into his spoon.

I watched Domingas reach his right arm back like he was going to throw a fastball. Then he launched his entire body forward, pivoted his hips, and rotated his upper body with incredible speed. The open-handed slap lifted Gerald off his feet and knocked him back about four feet.

"Game, set, match!" shouted Domingas. "That'll teach you to call me Black when I'm plainly Cape Verdean!"

Gerald sat on the ground rubbing his jaw. Unlike the Cape Verdean, Gerald Jacobs actively promoted himself as Black. He was the tighthead prop on the rugby team and was big and solid. He had dark olive skin and kinky hair that he'd let grow into long, tangled dreadlocks. He'd been bar mitzvahed and had gotten accepted at Yale but had decided to go to Renfield instead.

"Oh, ya mon, I'm escapin' mi Judah-ness…," Gerald said after practice one day. We were in his dorm room smoking a joint.

"Mi papi is lawyer. Mi papi's papi is lawyer. Mi two old'n bruddahs is lawyers for Gawd's sake, Charlie. Does you know what it's like to live up to da destiny of dis entire race of peoples?"

"Judaism is a race?" I asked.

"No bodies be 'spectin' any little t'ing from de Jamaicans, mon."

"Isn't that being pretty stereotypical?" I asked. "I mean, what does escaping your Jewishness have to do with being Jamaican?"

"Not one bless'd t'ing," Gerald said. "Not a bless'd t'ing."

In a lot of ways, I could relate to Gerald. I, too, had escaped various aspects of my personal history. Although my mother was Japanese, I felt zero affinity with that part of my heritage. I neither spoke Japanese nor had I been raised with any traditions that one could point to as being specifically Asian in origin. Like the stories my mother had told me of Noppera-bo when I was a child, the Japanese demons without eyes, mouths, or noses, my Japanese half was faceless. Escaping that part of my background was relatively easy. It would've been more difficult to acknowledge my Japanese-ness. On the other hand, escaping that waspy Teuton that had been passed down from my father and who held sway over the greater part of my soul was a larger challenge. For the most part, my Anglo-Saxonness was invisible to me. It was like water to fish or air to birds. Besides, I wasn't sure I could escape (or even wanted to escape) my deep-seated Lord-ness, though that didn't prevent me from trying with stupendous quantities of alcohol and pot.

There were keg parties just about every weekend at Renfield, held on campus in an old Quonset hut that had once been used as an airplane hangar for the Air Force ROTC. They had moved into a new facility a few years earlier, and the hut was made available to campus organizations for dances and parties. For two or three dollars you'd gain admission to the hangar, where a live band was usually playing, and you'd be able to drink beer for free all evening. The next day you'd wake up with a hangover. Sometimes you'd wake up with a hangover and a black eye whose origins were a mystery.

Those evenings when I didn't feel like waking up the next day with a hangover or a black eye were devoted to getting stoned. You could walk down the hallway on any dorm floor on a Friday or Saturday night, and the air would be thick with the skunky scent of weed.

After watching the end of the slapfight, I went up to the fourth floor to see if anyone was getting high. There were a couple of people hanging around outside Strafe's room. The guys waiting outside his door weren't rugby players, and neither of them even lived in our dorm. I stopped to talk with them.

"Why're you waiting outside Strafe's room?" I asked.

"We're waiting our turn to lick the toad," one of them answered. He was a scroungy-looking guy with bad skin and wispy sideburns.

"Lick the toad? What are you talking about?"

"This Strafe dude's got one of them bufo toads," the other guys answered. "If you lick it, it's like taking an acid trip for like five or ten minutes."

"You see God!" the first guy said.

Strafe's door opened and a girl stumbled out. I recognized her. She lived in one of the women's dorms directly across the quadrangle.

"Wow!" was all she said as she was leaving.

The two guys disappeared into Strafe's room. I decided to sit on the floor and wait around for them to come back out. After about fifteen minutes the door opened.

"Did you see God?" I asked.

"I am God!" one of them answered.

When I entered Strafe's room, it was completely dark except for the light from a terrarium on his desk. A large toad was sitting impassively in the terrarium's purple light. Strafe was sitting in an easy chair in the corner of the room. He was shrouded entirely in darkness.

"A large toad was sitting impassively in the terrarium's purple light."

"Are you here to lick my toad?" he asked.

"I don't know," I said. "I'm intrigued."

"Five dollars," said Strafe.

"Is it worth it?" I asked.

"I don't know," Strafe said. "I've never licked her myself. It's dangerous. People can die from the toxins. If you'd like, you can smoke some of the secretions. It's safer that way."

"Have you ever smoked your toad?" I asked.

"Me? No way."

I looked at him. He was dressed in a pair of checked white and brown bell-bottom jeans, a pair of cheap plastic cowboy boots, and a polyester lime green crew neck shirt. It was a ridiculous outfit that somehow looked good on him. Even in the room's darkness, I could tell he was staring at some spot far away, as though he were present and not present at the same time. I reached into my back pocket and pulled out my wallet. I had seven dollars. I handed Strafe a five-dollar bill, which he stuffed into the pocket of his bell bottoms. Then he stood up and grabbed a piece of paper from his desk. He thrust it at me.

"Sign this," he said. "Finucan in pre-law drew it up. It's a waiver that says licking or smoking the secretions of my toad has inherent risks, including death."

"Like rugby," I said.

Strafe looked at me.

"Oh, yeah," he said. "I thought I recognized you. You're the new wing, right?"

"Yeah, I'm the new wing. I don't know any of the rules."

"No one understands the rules," said Strafe. "That's the beauty of the sport. It's orchestrated chaos. When the ball comes your way, run with it. When an opposing ball carrier comes your way, tackle him. What's there to understand?"

"You missed it," I said. "Jacobs and Cabral were having a slapfight in the lounge."

"I didn't miss it," Strafe said. "Sooner or later they'll have to face me. I'm the undisputed champion of slapfighting at Renfield."

Strafe opened his desk drawer and pulled out a little jar. There were a bunch of whitish crystals on the bottom of it. Strafe opened the jar and pulled out a crystal about the size of a matchhead. He put it into a glass pipe and handed it to me. Then he had me sit down in his easy chair.

"Ready?" he asked.

"Let's do it," I said.

"Okay, just inhale once or twice. That's all you need."

Strafe lit a match and held it over the pipe while I inhaled once. A few seconds passed, then the entire universe squeezed through me in a fraction of a second. I was no longer Charlie Lord. I was no longer anything. I was no longer anywhere. I was everything and everywhere, all at once, but at the same time I was vaguely aware that I was still seated in Strafe's armchair, then even that dissolved. I was light, a burning star in the heavens. I had dropped acid a few times in high school, and this was a better experience than my best acid trip had been. After a few minutes, I became aware that my hands were on my knees, and then I became aware of the rest of my body. My experience of myself as a bright star slowly vanished, and I was sitting in Strafe's chair with a smile on my face.

"Holy fuck," I said.

"Alright," said Strafe. "Get out. See you at rugby practice on Monday."

I opened the door to leave Strafe's room. The light in the hallway was bright and harsh, a cheap imitation of the light I'd just experienced in Strafe's armchair. A girl stood waiting to enter.

"How was it?" she asked. "Did you see God?"

"One of them," I said.

"What's he look like?" she asked.

"Everything," I said. "Everything and nothing, wearing both our faces."

I left and went downstairs to my room, put on a record by The Who, and listened to the opening ostinato of "Baba O'Riley." The music swirled and eddied about the room like a rotating tornado that lifted me and flung me out into the dark, dream-tossed ocean of sleep where I sank into the nothing within and beyond myself.

Chapter 9 X-rays

I hitchhiked home for the Christmas holiday. I got picked up right outside of Renfield in Stoker by a Volkswagen bus full of Dead Heads who were on their way to a Grateful Dead concert in Tampa. They had a stash of Panama Red that they were very generous in sharing. They rolled joints and passed them around the bus all the way from Stoker down to New London. By the time I got to Mythic, I was so high that I had them drop me off downtown so I could wander around for a couple of hours before going to my parents'.

I walked down to the old harbor and sat outside the Lobster Pot Bar 'n' Grill and watched the boats come in on the afternoon tide. It felt strange being back in Mythic. It was almost like I didn't belong there anymore. In a certain way, I felt like I didn't belong anywhere, neither in Mythic nor in Renfield. It was as though I was a tribe of one in search of a nation. I'd enjoyed driving down Route 32 with the hippies in the VW bus, and I could see myself doing that for a little while, but there was just something about it that wasn't entirely me. I didn't mind visiting hippie land frequently, but I only wanted to be a tourist, not a native. I looked across the channel that ran past the Lobster Pot. On the far side was the cliff that overlooked the harbor, Mythic Point, and the lighthouse. It was the site of my last act before leaving for Renfield. I had thrown my disaster notebook over that cliff edge, just before heaving the saxophone after it. The disaster notebook and the saxophone had been different sides of the same coin. I had used both of them to escape the circumstances of my life, growing up in Mythic, and had tossed them off the cliff my last night there.

As I sat there pondering my life, I felt a hand on my shoulder. It was Joey Shapp. He was dressed in black pants, a white shirt, and a red jacket, the uniform of the ushers at the Rialto Theater in downtown Mythic.

"Welcome home, Charlie!" Joey said. "Midnight bids you all manner of pleasantries!"

"Still going by Midnight?" I asked. "And why are you wearing that uniform? Mrs Madrigal wasn't your biggest fan. How'd you manage to get rehired?"

"I'm still going by Midnight. It satisfies a certain void in my personality, Charlie. I can tell you this because you know me better than just about anyone, with the possible exception of Darryl Board, who I utterly detest. As for the movie theater uniform, I just wear it so I can lurk outside the theater and sell drugs to high school kids without arousing suspicion."

"Figures," I said. But you really detest Darryl?" I asked.

"That's not a word I'd use," Joey said. "It's just not a word that fleshes out the poverty of my vocabulary."

"What are you talking about, Joey? I distinctly heard you use the word 'detest'! You said that you utterly detested Darryl Board."

"The problem with you, Charlie, is that you've always heard exactly what you wanted to hear, whether anyone said it or not. Plus, you're completely stoned."

"Well, true on both accounts."

"I have acid and pot to get you through the New Year, Charlie. Come over to my dad's mortuary tomorrow. I'll give you the friends and family discount."

Joey's father owned the only mortuary in Mythic. When we were in elementary school, Joey would steal body parts off the corpses, bring them to class, and show them to the other kids. By the time we'd gotten to high school, Joey and I would get stoned in the basement of the mortuary. I had done acid with him a few times there, too. The last time I'd taken about 4 or 5 blotters and had a bad trip that lasted three-quarters of the day. I had no desire to do acid again, though. Plus I had enough of the Chinaman's lousy pot to get me through the holidays so long as I didn't go wild with it.

"Naw," I said. "I'm good, Joey."

"Call me 'Midnight,' Lord! Only my parents call me 'Joey' anymore. Only my parents and my pastor."

79

"You going to church these days?" I asked. "Really?"

"I do at least a third of my deals out of my trunk in the parking lot there," Midnight said. "They have an AA group that meets there Monday, Wednesday, and Friday. The ex-drinkers are some of my best customers. Gotta get your serenity on somehow, Charlie."

Joey spotted a teenager crossing the street. "Gotta go, man, show time!"

I watched Joey walk away and marveled at his brazenness. I wondered what it was like to be so unburdened of guilt, remorse, shame, morals, conscience, self-awareness, or any other internal or external regulators of behavior that you could just do whatever you wanted, no matter who you hurt or offended.

I sat outside The Lobster Pot until the tide slackened and then turned. The pot was wearing off, and it was time to go home.

My father was on the roof stringing lights on the TV antenna when I got to the house. I could tell he'd been drinking. I wasn't so high anymore, and it made me nervous to watch him. The roof slope was steep, and he held onto the antenna with one hand and was wrapping a strand of lights around it with the other. A couple of times his feet were close to slipping out from under him, but he managed to recover his footing just in time, or else he would've rolled down over the roof edge.

"Dad...," I hollered up to him. "Come on down. Let me finish doing the lights for you." My father waved his hand at me.

"Don't worry about it, Charlie. I'm 'bout done, anyhow."

My father wrapped the lights around the antenna two or three times and then disappeared to the other side of the roof where the ladder was. I held my breath until I saw him appear around the side of the house. He was pretty drunk. He shook my hand and then did something that he'd never done before. He put his arms around me and hugged me. It was weird. My entire body tensed up. I didn't know what to do, so I just stood there with my arms at my side. When he was done hugging me, he whispered in my ear:

"I love you, Charlie. Welcome home."

"You okay, Dad?" I asked.

"Never better," my father said. "Never better!"

My father walked over to the front porch. I followed him. He fiddled with a string of lights around the handrail, then he opened the front door, and we went into the living room. My mother was sitting on the sofa watching reruns of some soap opera involving vampires. It was one of her favorite shows. She had a big smile on her face.

"Oh, Charrie!" my mother exclaimed. "This such interesting show. The one on left is werewolf. The other one is vampire. His name Barnabas!"

"I know, Ma. You've been watching this show for the past seven years." My father sat down on the sofa next to my mother.

"Turn this crap off," he said to my mother. "Let's watch something a little more Christmassy."

"Dark Shadows is fine," I said. "Really."

My father got up and went to the TV. He started flipping through the channels. There wasn't a whole lot playing. Art Fleming was asking a game show contestant to name a president who didn't really chop down a cherry tree, but their response had to be given in the form of a question. It seemed completely stupid and random. On another channel, there was a show where three celebrities were being asked questions. They wrote down the answers on a piece of cardboard.

"Name a fruit," the host said, "that you find in a can."

A movie was playing on Channel 9 out of New York. It was Pork Chop Hill starring Gregory Peck.

My father watched it for a little bit.

"That fucking piece of shit hill wasn't worth the fucking shit it was made of. Not a goddamn GI should have died on that worthless motherfucker," my father said. He'd been wounded in 1950 during the breakout from Pusan. Pork Chop Hill had taken place nearly three years after my father had been shipped stateside to heal his shattered leg. I had never heard him talk about anything having to do with Korea before. That, combined with his earlier hug and his whispered "I love you, Charlie," had me a bit spooked.

My father turned off the TV, and a glowing white dot appeared in the center of the blank screen. It shrank and disappeared after a few seconds. We all looked at each other in silence. I looked at the Christmas tree next to the sofa. It was fake and reached nearly to the ceiling. The ornaments were all gold and glittered. I looked at the ornaments closely. They were all made of brass bullet casings. My father noticed me looking at the ornaments.

"I know the range officer at the base," my father said. "He gave me these casings. Browning M1917 mostly."

My father had taken the casings to his workshop in the garage and drilled holes through them. He'd strung fishing line through the holes and tied the ends of the line together so he could hang them on the tree. He'd welded a dozen or so brass shell casings together to make a five-pointed star that he'd stuck at the top of the tree. Like much of what my father did, this didn't make a lot of sense to me. It somehow seemed out of character for him, as though he were expressing something going on deep in his soul. It was as though the shell casing ornaments had been elevated to the realm of art. I had no idea what to make of it other than to simply acknowledge that my father was different now, and I had no idea why.

While I thought about my father, the door to the basement opened, and a short, dark-skinned man in his mid-thirties walked through the kitchen and dining room and entered the living room. Since neither of my parents seemed startled by his presence, I assumed they knew him. He sat down on the sofa next to me and stared at the blank TV screen along with the rest of us. I got up and turned the TV back on.

"I looked at the ornaments closely. They were all made of brass bullet casings."

Dozens of dead Korean, Chinese, and US soldiers littered a hillside. Gregory Peck got on the phone and was given orders to hold a flank position on the hill with men he didn't have.

"None of Korea was worth a fuck," my father said.

The little dark-skinned man looked at me and stuck out his hand.

"You are Mr Charlie, I am thinking?" he said. "I am Vasu Kumar. It is my great pleasure to meet you, Mr Charlie."

Vasu, I discovered, lived down in the basement. He was a civilian radiologist working at the submarine base in Groton. My parents had rented out the basement room to him to help make ends meet. People were switching over to disposable diapers, so my father's business had dropped by a third. My parents had paid most of my tuition for college, so money was tight.

In any event, I liked Vasu. He was happy and friendly and exceedingly polite. He insisted on calling me 'Mr Charlie' no matter how many times I told him to just call me 'Charlie.'

Vasu had been born in Mumbai when it was still called Bombay. He had completely redone the basement to suit his tastes. He had removed the bar, hung different colored silks on the wall, and put brightly colored rugs on the floor to create an ethereal quality in the room. This quality was heightened by the sitar music that he chose to play on the stereo virtually twenty-four hours a day. Vasu's only nod to modernity were the lightboxes that he'd hung on the wall above his bed. The first time I went down to the basement after coming home for the holidays was on Christmas Eve. Vasu had asked me to help him move an armoire out to the garage and replace it with a bookcase loaded with copies of the Bhagavad Gita, the Upanishads, the Vedas, ancient yoga texts, and biographies of yogis, fakirs, and gurus stretching back to the dawn of time. After the bookshelf had been moved and the books all placed on the shelves, with great care as to their order of importance in Vasu's eyes, I noticed the lightboxes on the wall. Vasu smiled shyly when he saw that I'd noticed them.

"They are for my vocation and my hobby, Mr Charlie," he said. "I would be most honored for you to see my collection."

"Sure," I said.

Vasu took a manila folder off the nightstand next to his bed and pulled a stack of X-ray photos out of it. He put a couple on the front panel of the lightbox and turned it on. The first one was an X-ray of a man's chest. The ribs and spine were visible, but the heart was a spectral outline. It was lower down in the chest cavity than I'd thought it would be. Five or six round objects were embedded in and around the ghostly heart.

"Shotgun pellets, Mr Charlie."

The picture beside it was of a man's head. The eye sockets, nasal cavity, and teeth were sharply defined, as was the knife blade that had entered the man's skull through the temporal bone and reached to the middle of his cranium. I looked at Vasu. He had an enormous smile on his face.

"All beings are unmanifest, or invisible to our physical eyes, before birth and after death. They manifest between the birth and the death only. What is there to grieve about?" Vasu said.

"I kept a disaster notebook in high school," I said.

"That does not surprise me, Mr Charlie. You are an old soul."

Vasu put up a couple more pictures. The first one appeared to be of a mouse stuck in someone's rectum. The second appeared to be a vibrator lost deep in a woman's vagina.

"We are not saints, Mr. Charlie."

For the next ten minutes, Vasu put up pictures of items that people had inserted into themselves for sexual stimulation but had failed to retrieve. Mostly they were simple sex toys, but there was one picture of a clear glass bottle of holy water in the shape of the Virgin Mary.

"She was most devout, Mr Charlie."

Vasu pulled one of the X-ray pictures from the stack and gave it to me. It was the shadowy photograph of a man who'd been stabbed in the chest. The point of the blade had penetrated all the way to his heart. I left the basement shortly thereafter and went upstairs. *It's a Wonderful Life* was on the TV. Jimmy Stewart was talking to an angel who had not yet received his wings. It was Christmas Eve. A virgin would give birth to a son who would save the world from its sins, and he would be called Immanuel: The Lord is with us. I went into the kitchen and dialed the number for America's house in the hope that she'd come home for the holidays.

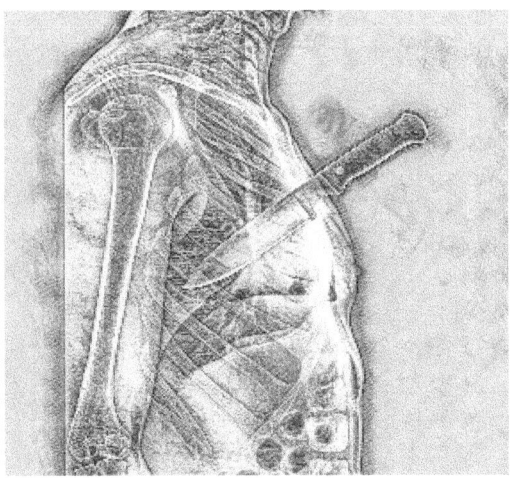

"Vasu pulled one of the X-ray pictures from the stack and gave it to me."

"We're sorry; you have reached a number that has been disconnected or is no longer in service. If you feel you have reached this recording in error, please check the number, and try your call again."

I hung up the phone. From the living room, I could hear the townspeople flooding into George Bailey's house and throwing money at him. It was a Christmas miracle! An angel got his wings! The Lord was with us! Us! US! U.S.! But America was not with Charlie Lord. I went up to my room and spent the rest of Christmas Eve studying the X-ray photo of the man who'd been stabbed and wondered if his wound, like mine, had been self-inflicted.

Chapter 10 April

I saw April several times over the Christmas break. It had been three months since I'd last seen her. She'd lost interest in theoretical math and physics and laughed at my jokes. We went to the movies and watched a romantic comedy, something she'd had no interest in doing a few months earlier. I noticed that she made more eye contact with me and seemed to enjoy kissing more. We spent more time in bed.

I made love to her one afternoon in late March while the rain beat against the roof and windows. April spent several minutes looking into my face after we had finished, then got out of bed and put on a bathrobe. She went to the window and looked out over the valley.

"It's beautiful," she said. "I'm surprised I've never really noticed how beautiful it is or how much I love the rain."

I got out of bed and looked out the window with her. She suddenly shuddered and grabbed my hand. "Tell me you love me," she said. "I need to hear that from you."

"I love you," I said. This was mostly true. There was part of me that was still in love with America; although I knew she would probably never love me back. There was also part of me that I kept in reserve. In another few months, as her intellect deteriorated, April would forget I even existed. She would forget her name and even how to feed herself. When that happened, I wanted to be able to retreat to some part of myself that was untouchable and inviolate.

"I love you, Charlie," April said. "I don't think I fell in love with you when I was brilliant, when my mind was a churning bowl of incandescence, but I love you now that I'm rapidly approaching mediocrity. I think it's fascinating that this is what slightly above-average people spend their time thinking about."

April looked into my eyes deeply, as though she were seeing me for the first time.

"I'm sorry I can't stay as intelligent as you for very long," she said, "but on the plus side, the sex seems better the dumber I get. In another month or two I'll probably want to stay in bed with you all day."

"Lucky me," I said. I looked out the window at the flooded fields and the barren orchards. In a couple of months the trees would be green and the fields would be a riot of corn and cabbage. April would slip into a coma and die sometime in the fall when the apples and the pumpkins were ready for harvest.

I also visited Derrick several times while he was dying. Mostly I'd tell him about what was happening back at Renfield. I'd read him short stories by Gabriel García Márquez and other writers he liked. I even brought him some copies of Playboy and a Hustler magazine. His wings were larger and more beautiful every time I saw him. They were now completely white with circular blue spots similar to those you might see on peacock feathers. The spots looked like eyes. While looking at the centerfolds, his wings suddenly flared out dramatically, but I pretended not to notice. I mean, I didn't want to ask if the sudden spread of his wings meant he was getting sexually aroused. I figured that everyone was entitled to a certain amount of respect and privacy, especially if they're dying.

"His wings were larger and more beautiful every time I saw him."

Once, when I went to visit, a researcher from some medical journal or university was there taking measurements of Derrick's wings and photographing them. Derrick seemed to enjoy the attention. It seemed to take his mind off the fact that he was dying. The Hartford Courant ran a full-page story about him, complete with photos. That story got picked up by a wire service and got republished in newspapers all over the world. A TV crew came to the hospital, and Derrick appeared on the evening news. He was weak, but he was able to spread his beautiful wings for the camera. Visitors from all over the world began showing up at the hospital to see him. Most of those who came believed that Derrick was an angel who'd been sent to earth by God as a message for humanity to repent of its sin and wickedness. It got so bad that the hospital banned all visitors with the exception of family and a few friends. I was fortunate enough to make the list of those approved to enter his room. The last time I saw him, he was propped up in his bed. His massive wings were spread open. They fanned the air slightly and kept a cool breeze circulating through the room. We didn't speak much, but before I left he reached out and took hold of my hand.

"I don't think I'll make it much longer, Charlie."

"Is there anything I can do?"

"Audrey hasn't visited me. Can you tell her that I love her?"

"Sure," I said. "I'll do that for you."

"Thanks," he said.

He folded his wings and shut his eyes. I left the room quietly and took the elevator to the lobby.

There was a cluster of people gathered in the waiting room trying to see Derrick. Many of them were carrying Bibles. Several had signs with writing on them proclaiming, 'The End is Nigh,' 'Repent and be Saved,' stuff like that. I wondered what they'd do if they'd found out their angel of God liked pornography, like just about everyone else, but I kept my mouth shut. I didn't want to shatter anyone's illusions, not that I could anyway. People believe the stuff they believe no matter how much evidence you provide contradicting them. They just end up getting pissed off and want to waste your time arguing with you. It's better to allow people the freedom to be complete morons just so long as you've got the freedom to be a complete moron in your own particular way. I've yet to meet the person who wasn't a moron in some particular aspect of their life. We've all got our blind spots. For those who don't believe me, try asking your spouse, kids, or friends if there's an area in your life ruled by your own personal inner idiot. They'll let you know. If they don't or won't, that means you're a bigger idiot than about ninety-five percent of every other idiot out there. Anyway, I left the hospital and spent a couple hours wandering aimlessly around Hartford. I didn't really want to go back to Renfield. I was spending less and less time attending my business classes and more time rereading all of Gordon Gordon Gordon's books. I loved the comfort that *A Death Forestalled* and *A Bowl of Dust* offered. All those one-syllable words created a sense of peace and calm in me: stone, sky, tree, house, love, moon, hate, fork, spoon, knife, plate, cup, food, death. I visited April a couple more times in the spring.

Her intellect had declined fairly rapidly. By the beginning of May it was pretty obvious that she was no smarter than the average high school cheerleader. We no longer talked about ideas but about shows she'd seen on TV or about other people.

"Charlie, do you remember Judy McNamara?" April asked while I was visiting in her bedroom.

"From high school? Yeah, she was in my English class."

"Do you think I'm prettier than she is?"

"Yes," I lied. God had blessed Judy with beauty and brains in inverse proportionality.

"I think she's really pretty," said April.

"She's really stupid," I said.

I grabbed a piece of paper and drew a graph on it. On the x-axis I wrote 'Beauty.' On the y-axis I wrote 'Intelligence..' Then I graphed Judy McNamara and April on it. Even in her debilitated intellectual state, April still scored higher on the Beauty/Intelligence graph than Judy did. I showed the graph to April. She furrowed her brow.

"This means I'm better, right?"

"Obviously," I said.

"Can I keep this paper, Charlie? I want to look at it some more."

I gave April the graph, and she folded it up and put it under her pillow. When she was done, she reached over the edge of the bed and undid my belt and unzipped my pants. I moved closer to her and let her pull

90

my underwear down and take me into her mouth. After a couple of minutes she pulled me onto the bed. My penis was still in her mouth. She pushed me onto my back, then straddled my face. I pulled her hips to me and traced my lips and tongue over her sex. Neither of us spoke. She ground herself into my face, and I could feel the head of my penis slip down into her throat. The word was made flesh and came into the world. April shuddered and came in my mouth, and I in hers.

When we had finished, I lay down on the bed next to her. She reached under the pillow and pulled out the graph paper and unfolded it.

"Will you still do this with me when I am stupider than Judy?" she asked.

"Yes," I said, "of course."

"I don't think you will, Charlie." April folded the graph up and put it back under the pillow. Then she looked at me and continued her swift journey to death and dumb.

I'd like to say that I continued visiting April until she died, but that would be a lie. After giving her the Beauty/Intelligence graph, I only visited her once more. She barely remembered me, and given the circumstances, it didn't seem right to have sex with her. I stopped going to see her from that point forward until she died. I'm not proud that I took the cowardly route and just vanished entirely while she was dying, but that's what I did. It was just too painful to watch her lose herself piece by piece until there was nothing left. Plus, there were other issues for me to deal with.

My father had a heart attack that spring. He was 48. He was hospitalized for four days while they ran tests and assessed the damage. I hitchhiked home to see him while he was recovering at St Elmo's General Hospital in Mythic. When I got there, my father was asleep. My mother was standing beside his bed, fanning him with a towel like it was between rounds in a boxing match.

"Ma..., what are you doing?" I asked.

"Is too hot, Charrie," my mother said. Even though she'd been in America for over twenty years, she still hadn't lost her Japanese accent or learned any of the subtleties of the English language. "Your father's blood needs cool down."

I looked at the fan standing in a corner of the room. "Why don't you just turn that on?" I asked.

"I don't want touch hospital equipment," my mother said. "Maybe something happen."

"What could happen?" I asked. "It's not like the fan is connected to any of the other equipment in here."

"You don't know," my mother said. She handed me the towel. "You take over. Fan father."

I took the towel from my mother and began flapping it up and down like my mother had done. Unfortunately, I was too close to my father, and the towel flicked his face. He woke with a start and looked at me waving the towel at him.

"Jesus, Charlie! What the hell are you doing?" he asked.

"Hi, Dad," I said. "How you feeling?"

"How the hell do you think I'm feeling? I just had a heart attack," my father said. I handed the towel back to my mother and pulled a chair up to the side of the bed. "You know, I haven't had a cigarette in a few days," my father said.

"That's really good, Dad."

"What're you talking about, Charlie? It's terrible! Why don't you go down to the canteen in the lobby and buy me a pack? Benson and Hedges 100's."

"Eddie! Doctor say you can no smoke," my mother said.

My father ignored my mother and handed me fifty cents off the nightstand. I looked at the change in my hand. A quarter, two dimes, and an Indian head nickel dated 1937. Someone had taken the time to carve away parts of the Indian's face and turn it into a grinning skull. I turned the coin over in my hand. The buffalo on the reverse side had ribs, vertebrae, and jointed leg bones. The buffalo's bearded head had been transformed into a skull as well. The words printed on the coin hadn't been immune to the vandal's skill either. The artist had engraved a 'C' in front of the word 'UNITED' above the buffalo and carved away the 'I,' the 'E,' and the 'D.'

"How many times you gonna count that change?" my father asked. "Make sure you get me a hard pack."

In spite of the heart attack, it was kind of nice to see that my father was back to treating me with the usual amount of contempt after the weird serenity he'd exhibited over the holidays. I took the elevator down to the lobby and bought a pack of Benson and Hedges 100s from a vending machine outside a door with an 'ONCOLOGY' sign on it. The pack only cost forty-five cents, so I put the nickel in my pocket. I was about to head back to the elevator when someone called me from down the corridor. It was Janice Tyler, April's mother. April stood beside her with her thumb in her mouth. I walked down the hallway and spoke to April's mother while her daughter stared vacantly at me.

"Don't feel bad, Charles; she barely recognizes me, and I'm her mother!"

I took April's hand in mine and looked into her eyes. Whatever had been April was completely gone. I let go of her hand, and it dropped limply to her side.

"The doctors think she'll lose whatever intellect she has left fairly soon," Janice said breezily. "Then she'll go into a coma. It's almost certain that her involuntary nervous system will shut down fairly quickly after that. Isn't that amazing, Charles? One day she'll just stop breathing!"

"Yes…," I said. "Amazing."

"Well, we've got to get going," Janice said. "It's almost time for 'The Price is Right.' It's the only thing that April responds to! She just loves all the fuss people make over the opportunity to win a microwave oven!"

I said goodbye to Janice, and they started to leave, but after a few steps, April turned and ran to me. She threw her arms around my neck, and we held onto each other for the last time. After a few seconds, she dropped her arms to her sides and her mother led her away. I rode the elevator back up to the 8th floor. Before the elevator arrived, I pulled the nickel out of my pocket and looked at it. Whoever had vandalized the coin had left the word 'Liberty' untouched to the right of the skull. Liberty and death. The price was right.

Chapter 11 Willy Wetmore's Story

My friend, Charlie, told me he was writing a sequel to a book I wrote about him, *The Autobiography of Charlie Lord*, which was mostly factual, though it had a bunch of stuff in there that I made up for dramatic effect. Anyway, I asked him a bunch of times if I could write some chapters in his book, and after about the fifteenth time, he said it was okay if I wrote just one chapter, so this is it:

Charlie picked me up in his father's 1967 Bel-Air with a manual 3-speed transmission with the gearshift mounted on the steering column: three on the tree and no A/C. That's a pretty good line, I told myself. I wrote it down in the little notebook I carry around with me just in case a good line occurs to me. I was going to be a writer. The summer before I'd even gotten a job at a studio in Burbank where my uncle worked. Yeah, I was only sweeping floors and mopping stuff up, but everybody's got to start somewhere.

We were heading to New London to meet up with Charlie's buddies from his dorm in Renfield so we could go to Derrick's funeral. I didn't know Derrick all that well. He was the RA in the dorm Charlie lived in. I'd met him a couple of times before his wings had grown to an enormous size. I'd seen a picture of his wings in the newspaper, so of course I had invited myself along when Charlie told me he was planning to attend the funeral. If you're gonna be a writer, you need stuff to write about, and this seemed right up my alley. I couldn't wait to see Derrick's wings with my own eyes.

"Jesus, Charlie. Can you drive any slower?" I said. There was a Plymouth Fury in the fast lane that had passed us. If I were driving, that wouldn't have happened. I'm not gonna lose a race to some guy in a Plymouth Fury. If I were driving, I would've passed the slow guy in front of me on the shoulder and then passed the Fury just before the exit to New London. A lot of people don't understand that everything you do is a competition.

We met at Domingas Cabral's house. Cabral's family was from Cape Verde, and their house was the only one in New London painted coral pink and turquoise. It was hard to miss. I knew Domingas. He was cool. He played rugby with my buddy Strafe. He was wearing one of those shirts that was purple until he moved slightly; then the shirt looked green. I'm not sure how they make a shirt like that. I made a note in my little book: 'Research up color-changing shirt.'

The rest of Charlie's buddies from Renfield were already there. They looked like losers. Marco Bocce, some poser smoking a pipe, had come up from Bridgeport. Gerald Jacobs was a loser from New Haven. I didn't really know him, but everyone else did. Apparently he'd had dreadlocks that he cut off when his father told him he'd stop paying for college if he didn't. Mark Wacyshyn had driven all the way down from Worcester. He was already so high that the pupils of his eyes looked like steel BBs floating in red oil. I pulled out the little notebook and wrote down 'steel BBs floating in red oil.' That would be a good line in a book someday, I thought. I'm not sure why Charlie hung around with losers, though. I think it's important to hang around with winners because you become like the people you hang around. That was gonna be the hidden message in the first book I wrote, I told myself.

Gerald had brought some pot with him. He said he'd bought it from a dealer in New Haven, and it was pretty decent, much better than the seed- and stem-filled crap I bought from that loser roommate of mine, Chinaman. By the time we got to the funeral home, we were all fairly stoned. Fortunately, no one seemed to even look at us when we entered the funeral parlor. They were too busy catching up on family gossip and talking about their golf games to pay much attention to us. Just about everybody said, "Sorry for your loss," to just about everybody else and remarked to each other about what a wonderful job the mortician had done.

It was an open casket funeral, so we all lined up to view Derrick, but when we got up to the coffin, I saw that Derrick's wings were either hidden by the dark suit jacket the family had chosen for the burial or they'd had them removed and put in a closet or thrown out or something! I was a bit xxxxx (I wasn't sure whether it was better to use the word 'unhappy' or 'crestfallen' there, so I made a note in my little book to fix it later).

I went to find Charlie. As usual, he was standing in a corner of the room just watching things. It was what he did. Maybe that was what made him a really good wrestler in high school. He was always studying and analyzing things around him. Even back then I planned on making him the narrator of a book I was planning to write about myself. I mean, unlike me, Charlie's not all that interesting of a character. He's a good guy, but he's got some really annoying habits. For example, he's got this habit of repeating anything you say to him like he's rolling it over in his head to amuse himself. I mean, I don't like other people laughing at me, even if it's only in their head.

"Hey, Charlie. Let's get out of here," I said. "I'm kinda pissed I didn't get to see the wings."

"You're kinda pissed you didn't get to see the wings," he said.

"Jesus, man! Don't keep repeating everything anyone says! I'm not sure he even had wings. You're always seeing and hearing shit no one else does!"

I got a drink and shook the hands of Derrick's mother and father, his two younger brothers, and his older sister, and told them what a great guy Derrick was, even though I didn't know him from shit. Mark Wacyshyn came over to me. He nudged me with his elbow.

"I'm kinda freaking out here," he whispered.

"What's the matter?" I whispered back.

"There's a dead body here," he said. "Plus I'm high."

"We're all high," I said.

I looked at Gerald. He was stuffing a joint into the breast pocket of Derrick's suit. One of Derrick's cousins came over and introduced himself to us. He was in the dress uniform of a Marine corporal. You could tell he wasn't a loser. I looked at the red and yellow emblem on his left arm. Charlie, Domingas, Gerald, and Marco came over and introduced themselves to Derrick's cousin.

"I'm Derrick's cousin, Derrick," he said.

"Oh my God!" said Wacyshyn.

Derrick looked at him suspiciously.

"You're friends of Cousin Derrick from college?"

"Yes," all five of them said simultaneously.

"We're not high," said Wacyshyn.

"What?" asked Derrick.

"We're glad you said 'hi,'" I said. "Derrick spoke a lot about you," I lied.

"Thanks for coming," Lance Corporal Calibanos said.

"Sorry for your loss," I said. I pretty much meant it, too. I shook Cousin Derrick's hand. Out of the corner of my eye, I noticed a woman walk up to the casket and place something on Derrick's chest. It was a necklace made of teeth. I knew her. She was the deaf girl that Derrick had dated before he'd gotten sick. She was incredibly hot. Her name was Andy or something. I watched her remove a pair of earrings made out of teeth, too, and place them into the same pocket with the joint that Gerald had gifted him.

After the service there was a reception at Derrick's folks' place in West Hartford. I didn't want to go, but Charlie said we had to. He was driving, so I didn't have much choice in the matter. It was in a nice neighborhood, and the house was filled with white carpets and expensive sofas covered in clear plastic. I got some food and a drink in the kitchen and then wandered into the living room. Wacyshyn stood by the window and stared out into the backyard. The pot had worn off, and none of us were high anymore.

"We don't do this in my family," he said.

"Do what?"

"Funerals. The whole thing is depressing. The casket, the embalmed corpse, everybody crying. It's weird."

"What's your family do?" I asked.

"Well, the person who died is cremated. Then some of the larger pieces of the cremains get put into snow globes so the ashes can fall down around Snow White and the Seven Dwarves or the Statue of Liberty. All the immediate family gets one of the snow globes. It's a tradition that's been around since I was twelve or thirteen."

"That's what? Like five or six years."

"True, but as a percentage, six years represents nearly thirty-three percent of my entire life. That's fairly substantial when you think about it."

"Well, just how many snow globes have become part of this family tradition?" I asked.

"Oh, tons! Two or three, anyway. My aunt's ashes got put in a snow globe with a scene out of *Vertigo*. Jimmy Stewart is climbing the stairs in the mission while his wife is about to jump off the mission's roof. My aunt was a big Hitchcock fan. It was her favorite movie, although everyone else in the family is more partial to North by Northwest. When my dad died, his remains were put into a scene from the movie *From Here to Eternity*. Burt Lancaster is kissing Deborah Kerr on the beach while the tide rolls in. It's like my dad is the sand in the water when you shake the globe."

"'When my dad died his remains were put into a scene from Here to Eternity.'"

"Quite the memento," I said.

"I have the snowglobe on my desk," Wacyshyn said. "I probably shake up my dad a couple of times a day."

"Uh-huh," I said. His whole family was a bunch of losers.

I left Wacyshyn standing at the window. It was dusk, and lightning bugs were everywhere, signaling one another in the twilight. The beautiful woman came over to me. She had a drink in her hand, the kind that had a little paper umbrella on the end of a long stick stuck in it. She saw me looking at it.

"It's my th-th-third," she said. "I'm Au-Au-Au-Audrey."

Her words seem to come from somewhere deep in her head, not her mouth. I'd never known any women who'd stuttered before. It was kind of hot. Her hands also moved around when she stuttered. That was kind of hot, too.

"Di-di-did you know De-De-Derrick well?" she asked. Her stutter had caused her hands to shake, and her drink spilled on my shirt and pants.

"Oh, Derrick, yeah. He was one of my best buddies," I lied.

Audrey watched my face intently while I spoke, looking at every nuance of my lips as they moved. It was incredibly hot but a bit too intimate.

"He drew me like a superhero." Her voice sounded far away, like it was bouncing off a ledge somewhere in her head and coming out of her mouth as an echo. Her stutter was starting to drive me crazy, so I made a note in my little book: 'Don't try to reproduce her stutter too much..'

"He always drew me in skintight outfits with huge breasts."

I looked at Audrey's breasts. She had ample endowment. When I looked back at Audrey's face, one of her eyebrows was raised, and there was a smile on her lips.

"Why don't I give you a ride?" she said. She was still stuttering, but I'm just not gonna point it out anymore. A good writer needs to know when something is gratuitous. I made a note in my book to look up the word 'gratuitous.' I went over to tell Charlie that I was leaving with Audrey. He was talking to Domingas.

"Okay, guys. I'm leaving with Audrey. See you."

"Not if I see you first," said Domingas.

"Wait a second," I said. "I'm pretty sure that's not how that's supposed to go."

"What do you mean?" asked Domingas.

"When someone says, 'See you LATER,' that's when you respond, 'Not if I see you first.' If someone just says, 'See you,' you're just supposed to say, 'See you' or 'Bye' or something like that. Let's try that again."

"See you later," I said.

"Not if I see you first," said Domingas. I thought about it for a couple of seconds.

"I don't think that's right, either," I said. "It doesn't make sense. If I say, 'See you later,' and you say, 'Not if I see you first,' that actually means you'll see me first, so I would definitely see you later if you see me first. I think the correct response to 'See you later' should technically be 'Not if YOU see me first.' That way if I see you first, I won't be the one to see you later. Let's try that again. 'See you later, guys.'"

"Not if you see us first," said Domingas. Charlie just kept standing there with a smirk on his face. It was fricking annoying as hell. I went outside. Audrey was waiting for me in the parking lot.

"What took you so long?" she asked. There was a whole bunch of stuttering in there and arm and hand movements, which I'm going to pretend didn't happen. Too much reality bores most people when they're trying to read a story.

"I had to explain some important stuff to Charlie and Domingas," I said. It was important, too. Clarity of expression is one of the things that separates good writers from hacks. I had no intention of being a hack writer. I wanted to be one of those writers who wrote prose that was clean and clear. That's probably why it took me so long to write anything. I'd started writing a novel in high school, a thinly veiled autobiography, and a couple of years later I'd gotten maybe nine or ten pages written. It wasn't a lot, admittedly, but it was the cleanest, clearest writing anyone anywhere was likely to encounter.

Audrey drove us to her parents' place in Manchester. They were traveling in Europe. They were on some houseboat on the Seine having sex with a couple of friends.

"My parents are swingers," said Audrey. "I grew up with them hosting key parties. It seemed normal when I was growing up. I still don't understand why everyone gets so hung up about monogamy."

Audrey unlocked the front door and opened it. The house was modest. Her father sold insurance, and her mother taught home economics or chemistry or something. Losers! The living room was filled with inexpensive ceramic knickknacks, the kind you could purchase at any mall in any city in America. The walls were hung with cheap prints of mediocre art along with a picture of a soulful, backlit Jesus with long, flowing hair. I'd seen that picture in about half the houses I'd ever been in. I looked at the print closely and realized that Jesus looked exactly like Audrey if she'd grown a beard. I turned around to tell Audrey of the resemblance, but she had already taken her clothes off.

We had sex in the living room, on the sofa, under the watchful eyes of Audrey's twin brother, Jesus. Then we went upstairs and had sex in her parents' bedroom. Then we went down into the basement and had sex in her parents' makeshift orgy room. There were chains hanging from the ceiling and cases lining the walls filled with whips, handcuffs, and dildos, but one of the cases was full of religious stuff. After we'd finished, I went over to the case and looked at it closely. There were candles in it that looked like Mary and Jesus, rosary beads, and even a crown of thorns. Audrey came over and stood beside me.

"My parents have a fetish about using Catholic rosaries and candles as sex toys," she said. "Apparently, it's not all that uncommon."

"What about the crown of thorns?" I asked.

"I don't think you want to know," said Audrey.

On the wall above this case was a clock. The hands of the clock on the wall were two penises. The hour hand was a white penis, and the minute hand was a black penis. Even the numbers looked like curved and bent penises. According to the penises, it was 11:45 pm.

After we screwed for the fourth or fifth time, we fell asleep on the four-poster bed with bondage ropes and manacles attached to each of the posts. When I awoke the next morning, Audrey was gone. I looked at the cock clock. It was eight o'penis. I got dressed and went upstairs. Audrey was in the kitchen dressed in a flowered silk kimono.

"Good morning," I said.

"Good morning, Willy," she said. It took about a minute for her to get the words out. The stutter was really bad. Her hands waved spastically in the air. I put my finger to my lips.

"Don't talk," I said.

I kissed her lightly on the cheek. Whatever had passed between us the previous night was completely gone. She was still beautiful, but there wasn't much chemistry or mystery there, but even so we still had sex right there in the kitchen. Afterwards, I got dressed and left. I stood by the side of the road and stuck my thumb out. It was a hot morning in late June filled with the shrill cries of katydids and cicadas. I thought about the past twenty-four hours: the funeral, Audrey, Jesus, and the penis clock. I made a couple more notes in my little book. 'This would make a really good story someday,' I told myself. Only I'm gonna leave out some of the details, like how I handcuffed her to the bed, etc., etc., etc. I mean, I don't want people thinking I'm some kind of crass pervert. A car pulled up beside me. I opened the door and climbed in. The driver didn't even need to remind me to put on my seatbelt. I was just hoping he knew how to drive fast as hell.

Anyway, that's my chapter. I made the mistake of letting Charlie read it. He laughed and said it was hilarious, but it didn't quite fit in with the rest of the book, so he wouldn't publish it. Fortunately for me, Charlie let me upload this book to his publisher, and by some miracle my chapter got included after all. A man's got to know how to get around the limitations of others.

Chapter 12 Diamond

April died a few weeks after Calibanos. Her parents had her cremated and turned into a one-carat, gem-quality blue diamond in an experimental process developed by General Electric. April's mother sat on GE's Board of Directors and was able to pull whatever strings were necessary to get April's remains treated in a lab with enough heat and pressure to turn her into a cold, hard stone. They passed the diamond around at her memorial service. Then she was put in a little velvet box lined with silk.

"Her parents had her cremated and turned into a one carat gem quality blue diamond...."

The service was held at the Tylers' home on a hill overlooking the ocean on an overcast and hot summer afternoon. April's mother, she of the immeasurable IQ, stood before us on a raised platform. She was tall and lean, handsome in that waspy yankee fashion of classic pale skin and wild strawberry blonde hair. She looked out over the guests attending the service, then vomited quickly into a plastic bag that she tied shut.

"Thank you all for coming to this celebration of April's brief existence. I won't dwell on the circumstances of her death, unfortunate though they were, but would rather focus on the next stages of her journey through those dimensions beyond space and time. To this end I have asked Miles Verbal, the esteemed conductor for the New York Philharmonic, to grace us with his presence today!"

Mrs Tyler gestured out to the crowd, and a man seated near me moved from his spot up to the platform. He took his place next to Mrs Tyler.

"Mr Verbal will now conduct Mozart's Requiem, a work of genius that Mozart came to write for his own funeral."

April's mother stepped off the platform and stood next to her husband while the conductor's assistant set up a music stand and put a sheaf of papers on it. I looked around. There were no musicians to be seen anywhere. The conductor looked through the score quickly. When he was satisfied that all was in order, he raised his hands over his head. After a brief pause, Verbal began moving his arms slowly through the air, his maestro's baton like a wizard's wand casting a spell, conjuring silence in a minor key from an invisible orchestra of violins and violas, cellos, trumpets, bassoons, timpani, and trombones. The movement of his arms accelerated. He pointed his baton at the invisible orchestra scattered about the lawn and urged them to pick up tempo or play more forcefully; then the rhythm would change, and his hands became a flock of birds flying over the fields at dusk.

After nearly an hour, Verbal coaxed the last notes from the non-existent woodwinds, the brass, and the strings, then his hands fluttered limply to his sides. His face was flushed, wet with perspiration, and his clothing was disheveled. All of us rose from our seats and applauded enthusiastically for nearly a full minute while the conductor bowed several times in acknowledgment of our acknowledgment of his brilliance.

When the applause ended, April's mother came over to me. She put the velvet box into my hand and closed my fingers around it.

"She'd want you to keep her safe," she said.

I took her home and put her in a drawer full of socks and underwear. I spent the rest of the summer washing dishes at The Lobster Pot, a bar and restaurant down in the Mythic Harbor. It was mindless work, which appealed to me. I enjoyed the sheer tedium of the job, the simple routine of stacking dishes and glassware into plastic racks and sanitizing them in steam and bleach. After the death of April, I welcomed this respite from anything requiring thought.

I didn't have to be at work until the afternoon, so I had mornings to do whatever I wanted. Most days I went to the Mythic Library and wandered around the stacks, picking books out at random and reading them in the carrels on the second floor. I liked opening the books at the end and reading backward towards the beginning. I would whisper the backward syllables and reverse diphthongs softly to myself. The difficult part was training myself to ignore sentences and paragraphs and read the books backward word by word. My mind wanted to understand what I was reading, to piece together the words into meaningful ideas and patterns, but I had to resist the urge to comprehend. I was only interested in unmaking sense of my life.

I discovered that having conversations with my father was as good a way of disbanding reason and logic from my life as anything else. He'd recovered from his heart attack and wasn't working as much as he had been. He spent most of his days watching game shows and ball games on TV. I sat down with him one weekend and watched the Mets lose to Cincinnati with the sound turned down. We drank beer and listened to the Red Sox on the radio in the dining room while the living room TV flickered with ghostly images of the Metropolitans playing dismal ball. As an added bonus, my father had a transistor radio in his lap and listened to the Yankees with an earplug.

Joe Morgan for the Reds fielded a ball and began a double play to retire the Mets in the fifth. "I don't know why I watch the Mets," my father said. "They're terrible!"

"How're the Yankees doing?" I asked.

"They're losing, 5-0. I hate those cocksuckers!"

"Why are you listening to them?" I asked.

"I hate them," my father said. "Why else would I listen?" The TV cut away from the ballgame, and an image of President Nixon sitting at his desk in the Oval Office filled the screen.

"I hate that cocksucker, too," my father said.

From the dining room came the sound of Ned Martin announcing the ballgame in Fenway Park.

Nixon looked into the camera and opened his mouth.

"Tiant facing Hisle for the Twins here in the seventh. Runners at the corners. Tiant with the big leg kick. Hisle swings and sends a ball high and deep to left! Mercy! That's a three-run homer, and the wheels have come off here in the eighth for Luis Tiant! He entered the inning leading 9-0 and has given up six runs. Manager Darrell Johnson heads to the mound, and that'll be all for El Tiante!"

Nixon stopped speaking. He looked sad and defeated. The Mets game reappeared on the TV. A man named Bench hit a ball into the left center gap but was thrown out trying to take second. My father picked up the paper and pulled out the sports page. He tossed the rest of the newspaper on the floor. I looked at the headline on the front page.

"Hey, Did you know that Nixon resigned? It's in the paper!"

"Yeah, I saw that. I hate him as much as I hate the Yankees. Good riddance." From the radio, Curt Gowdy spoke to us soothingly.

"Hi, neighbor! Have a 'Gansett! It's light! It's dry! But it's never lost its flavor!" On the TV a man named Tug threw a ball past a man named Geronimo.

"The Yankees just scored a run," my father said. "Cocksuckers!"

My father tossed aside the sports page. I picked it up and went upstairs to my room with it. I liked looking at the box scores and breaking the blood and bones of games into numbers and statistics; the game played out on diamonds translated into decimal points and percentages, the flesh and muscle stripped away to reveal reality in all its cold perfection. Diamonds were forever.

Chapter 13 Semiotics

Summer ended, and I went back to Renfield. I spent my days going to about half of my classes. They were all fairly basic and boring: math, English, psychology, and economics. By the midterms I'd read just enough of the textbooks and turned in just enough of the assignments to get solid C's in about all of my courses. The only class I really enjoyed was an upper-level linguistics class in semiotics that I managed to get into because there were only two other students enrolled in it. The course was taught by Dr Ernst Friedman, a Holocaust survivor. American soldiers had liberated him from a death camp just as Dr Friedman was being marched to the gas chambers along with another thirteen hundred Jews, Poles, gypsies, Russian prisoners of war and other undesirables. The experience had been so traumatic for him that he spent the rest of his life attempting to describe, academically, the indescribable horror of those moments where he'd been facing certain death.

For some unfathomable reason, the class was held in the freight elevator of the Humanities building from 6-7:30 every Tuesday and Thursday evening. The elevator was large enough to hold us and our chairs as well as the occasional piece of office furniture or equipment that came in through the loading dock. We read no texts. There was no homework. We were only required to look at haunting photographs of Auschwitz, Treblinka, Chelmno, Dachau, Majdanek, and Buchenwald. The pictures were all horrific: gas chambers, bone-crushing machines, starving prisoners half-dressed in rags, mountains of corpses, lampshades made from the skin of the exterminated. For the midterm we were required to show our grasp of the material through some sign or symbol. One of the other students showed up the day of the midterm with a number tattooed on his left arm. The other student chose to wear a six-pointed star on her blouse. As for me, I had stopped eating food as soon as I discovered what the midterm entailed. For six weeks I lived on nothing but bread and water and lost 30 pounds. The day before the midterm, I shaved my head. The other two students received B+ grades on their midterms. I was the only one in class to receive an A.

When the midterm ended, I exited the elevator and stood on the loading dock. It was a cold, clear evening in late October. From the dock I could see long V's of geese overhead, heading south for the winter. Dr Friedman stepped out onto the loading dock and stood next to me. Neither of us spoke. After a minute of silence, he walked down the stairs leading from the dock and headed toward the parking lot where the light of a single lamppost flickered on and off. I watched him get into an expensive German-made vehicle and drive away. On my way back to my dorm, I stopped at the campus pub and ordered three hamburgers, an order of fries, and two large chocolate shakes. Forty-five minutes later I was in the pub's bathroom. I stuck my finger down my throat and puked up everything I'd eaten. I was already planning for the final exam.

My roommate, Daeng Phibunsongkhram, was asleep when I got back to the dorm. His takraw practices were grueling, even though no other colleges in the country had a takraw team, and he'd usually be in bed by 9:30. I went downstairs to the dorm lounge. Marco Bocce was sitting there in the dark, as usual. I dragged a chair over to him, and together we stared out of the lounge window into the silence of the empty quadrangle separating the dormitories. Marco spoke without looking at me.

"Word association," he said. "White."

"Gray."

"Suit."

"Funeral."

"Death."

"Nothing."

"Everything."

"Illusion."

Marco fell silent and pulled his pipe out from his pocket. He filled it with tobacco and lit it with a phosphorus-tipped match that he lit on the zipper of his jacket. Then he leaned back in his chair and sucked at his pipe. After a couple of minutes he took the pipe out of his mouth and held it in his hand while he spoke.

"First Calibanos, then April. How does it make you feel?

"How does that make me feel?"

"Their deaths," said Marco.

"Their deaths."

I looked out the window into the deserted quad. A little vortex of wind swirled a pile of leaves, twigs, and a sheet of paper around and around a lamppost. Marco watched me watching the pile of circling rubbish.

"And they became what they beheld," he said.

"But their idols are silver and gold, made by human hands," I answered. "Those who make them will be like them, and so will all who trust in them."

"Sooner or later you need to deal with their deaths," said Marco. "You can't hide from it forever."

"What do you want me to say, Marco? I'm sad? I feel terrible? I miss them? I don't know what I feel."

Marco put his pipe back in his mouth and sucked on it. His face glowed orange as the tobacco burned each time he drew on the pipe. I watched the wind whirl the rubbish around and around the lamppost, then the little wind died, and the leaves, twigs, and paper lay motionless on the pavement.

"I think you do know what you feel," he said. "I think that's why you've been starving yourself for the past month and a half."

"That was for my class," I said. "I got an A."

"That's just another way of punishing yourself for the deaths of Derrick and April."

"Can we change the subject?"

"Now you can add avoidance coping to the list," said Marco.

"What about you?" I asked. "How do you feel?"

"Well, on the one hand, I got Derrick's job as the dorm resident assistant, so I'm happy my room and board are now paid for completely. Plus, I never did like him all that much. I found him egotistical to the point of being narcissistic. I made my peace with my feelings about Derrick long ago."

"That seems a bit callous," I said.

"It's honest," said Marco. "I'm nothing if not honest. It's my best quality. I actually belong to The Washington Club, an organization that takes its name from those legends about George Washington's supposed inability to tell a lie. I went to their annual convention in Springfield last year. It was somewhat of an encounter session. For three days we sat in a ballroom and told uncomfortable truths about ourselves. The police came and arrested one member who confessed to pedophilia as well as a woman who confessed to embezzlement. Personally, I was hoping to hear someone confess to murder, but that didn't happen. Most of the other people who attended told garden-variety stories of adultery and drug or alcohol addiction. Honesty makes a fantastic therapeutic tool when used correctly, of course."

"I'm not so sure I want everyone knowing everything about me," I said. "I like keeping some parts of my life private."

Marco took another long drag on his pipe. In the glow of the burning tobacco, his face looked serene, but I noticed that he had a black eye that looked relatively new.

"In the glow of the burning tobacco his face looked serene, but I noticed that he had a black eye that looked relatively new."

110

"What happened to your eye?" I asked.

"I went to a party off campus last night," he said. "I got drunk and tried to put my penis on a woman who was passed out in a bedroom."

"What? That's crazy!"

"It's honest," said Marco. "Her boyfriend walked in on me and gave me a beating. I think he broke one of my ribs."

"Jesus!"

"I'm at peace with all of it," said Marco. "If you can face your past mistakes fearlessly, then they have no power over you in the present or the future."

"I'll remember that the next time I try raping someone," I said.

"I was completely flaccid during the entire incident," said Marco. "Not to minimize the situation, but the worst you can call it is sexual assault, not rape."

"Well, what would have happened if her boyfriend hadn't walked in on you?"

Marco paused and took a long draw on his pipe. He pondered the question with his eyes half closed. "I probably would've put my penis in her mouth," he said calmly. "I'm not proud of it. I'm just honest about it. That's what's important. It's why people trust me. Everyone makes mistakes. How you face your mistakes is the most important thing. Honesty is freedom."

"Maybe," I said. "But it's probably better if you don't commit sexual crimes to begin with."

"Well, I can't guarantee that something like that won't happen again, but I can guarantee that if it does happen, I'll be able to be truthful with myself and others about what happened."

"Maybe you should quit drinking," I said. "Then you might not have to be so honest."

"If alcohol ever gets in the way of my honesty, then I'll be the first to stop drinking. Until then I'll keep being responsible for telling the truth about my actions. Did I ever tell you about the time I found naked pictures of my mother?"

"No," I said. "You'll have to save that for another time. I'm going to bed."

I left the lounge and walked up the staircase to the second floor. Phil Rukowski, an engineering student, was drunk and passed out on the second-floor landing. An empty bottle of grain alcohol lay next to him. I stepped over his sprawled limbs and opened the door to the second-floor hallway. Through the hallway window next to the door, I could see a sliver of moon hanging in the night sky surrounded by stars and the dull orangish glow of a planet. My eyes were still looking at the moon when I punched the window. I felt only a tiny sting of pain around my knuckles. When I looked down, there was a large shard of glass embedded in the flesh between the third and fourth knuckles of my right hand. I pulled the glass out and tossed it on the floor. Then I put my hand to my mouth and sucked at the blood for a couple of minutes. I went to bed that night without bandaging the wound. When I woke in the morning, my sheets and blanket were covered in blood.

Chapter 14 Victory

After putting my hand through the hallway window, I stopped going to classes except for the one in semiotics. I hung around in the dorm lounge by day and played games of hearts, spades, or cribbage with other dorm members who were killing time before class or after class. They'd normally hang around for forty-five minutes to an hour then disappear and let the machinery of the university transform them into accountants, nurses, teachers, journalists, and other agents of Corporation America. I wouldn't play that game anymore, or maybe I couldn't: distinctions have a tendency to blur and dissolve into each other the more you look at them.

I'd made the decision to leave Renfield even before punching the window; before my conversation with Bocce; before starving myself for an A in a class held in a freight elevator with neither syllabus, texts, nor lectures; maybe even before the deaths of April and Derrick, though maybe it's easier to say that I didn't make the decision. The decision made me. There was an inevitability about leaving Renfield as soon as I'd enrolled there, given that Renfield and I had nothing to offer each other. I couldn't see myself being a doctor, lawyer, stockbroker, therapist, architect, or any of another million cogs in the machine. I wasn't sure what I wanted, but I was pretty sure that whatever I was looking for couldn't be found at Renfield.

I didn't see much of Willy. Wrestling season had started up again, and he was really working hard at improving himself. He'd placed third in the league championships the previous season and wanted to take first this year. He'd actually stopped smoking pot and drinking as a way of showing his dedication to getting better. I saw him just two or three times that semester. The first couple of times we'd run into each other on the way to classes and exchanged pleasantries. The last time I saw him was because he'd come to my dorm and sought me out.

"Hey, Charlie! How come you didn't tell me Mo Summer was a lesbian? I had to hear about it through the grapevine," he said. "I also heard, through the grapevine, that you've known about it for nearly a whole year. How come I had to learn this all through the grapevine when you could've just come right out and told me so I didn't have to hear all this through innuendo and rumor?"

"I figured she'd tell you herself if she wanted you to know," I said.

"That's a violation of the code," he said.

"Code? What code?"

"You know. The code! Pals before gals. Jimbos before bimbos."

"Jimbos before bimbos?"

"Don't pull that repeating stuff with me," he said. "I'm not particularly happy that you've violated one of the main tenets of the code."

"Okay, Willy, I'm sorry I didn't tell you about it earlier. To be honest, it just slipped my mind on account of Derrick and April. I guess I was preoccupied."

"Well, it's okay, anyway. I started seeing this art major named Victory Megiddo. She's a paleo-lithographer."

"What's that?" I asked.

"Well, it's kinda weird," he said. "It seems to involve the stealing of old headstones from graveyards.

She grinds one down until it's perfectly flat and smooth, then draws on it with oily pencils. Then she washes the stone with acid and gum arabic and rolls ink over it. Then she covers the stone with paper and runs it through a roller press, as in any old-style lithographic process, but the essential piece is the stone has to come from an old graveyard. Anything pre-Revolutionary War is best, but any headstone up to and including the Civil War period is acceptable. I actually helped her steal a couple of old headstones from the Renfield Memorial Cemetery. Some of them had been there since the 1600s. When I asked her about why they had to come from a graveyard, she looked at me like it was the stupidest question anyone had ever asked her. She tells me that the gravestones contain spirits. During the printing process, a little bit of the spirit body gets squeezed out of the stone onto the paper. Otherwise, what would be the point?"

"I don't know what to think about that," I said. "On the surface, it sounds crazy."

"'I happen to look back down the path toward the entrance to the cemetery and notice a young woman in a white dress staring after us.'"

"Yeah, but here's the thing. I think there's actually something to this whole paleo-lithography thing. For example, we're in the graveyard, and I find the perfect gravestone half hidden behind blackberry bushes and ivy. There's a name and some dates etched in the limestone. The gravestone belonged to a Mary Stratford, who was born February 17, 1653, and died March 21, 1681. I helped Victory carry the gravestone back to her car. As we near the end of the footpath, I happen to look back down the path toward the entrance to the cemetery and notice a young woman in a white dress staring after us. I grabbed Victory by the arm and pointed back to the cemetery gate, but the woman had disappeared. So, anyway, I load the grave marker into Victory's car, and we drive back to her dorm and set it in a corner of the room. Her roommate had gone home to Litchfield for the weekend, and Victory invited me to stay the night. I fall asleep but wake up a few hours later to see Victory moving about the room. I'm about to ask her what she's doing when suddenly I realize that Victory is still asleep in the bed next to me. The woman in the room stops moving and looks at me. It's the woman I saw in the cemetery. We stare at each other for five or six seconds before she begins moving towards me, but with each step she just becomes more and more transparent so that objects behind her start to become visible—a chair, a wall lamp, the limestone burial marker. She stretches out her arms as she approaches me and leans her face towards mine as though to kiss me, but before her lips reach mine, she has completely disappeared."

"No way!" I said. "That's really bizarre!"

"I got out of bed after that and got dressed. I mean, I was ready to walk away and to never look back, but I decided to stay."

"You stayed? Why?"

"Well, the sex is pretty phenomenal. Plus, I figure if I'm gonna be a writer, I need material. From that perspective, I figure it's worth staying with her for a while anyway. She's got an interesting background, too, for what it's worth."

For the next half hour or so, Willy told me as much of Victory's story as he could remember. She'd grown up in Danbury and had come from a long line of hatmakers. Her great-great-great-great-grandfather, Henri Pierre Dumont de Sainte Croix, had been a fur trader out of Quebec who'd bartered with native tribes for beaver pelts in the area to the west of Lake Michigan, an area that would one day become the state of Wisconsin. One afternoon, while snowshoeing across the frozen lowlands north of the La Baye des Pauns to negotiate with a tribe of Winnebago for their pelts, he came upon a beautiful woman who sat naked in the snow between two blooming rose bushes. At Dumont de Sainte Croix's approach, the woman stood and spoke to him.

"All my future…," she said. "I have waited for this moment." Although this woman had no recollection of her past, she had been gifted with a great and terrible clairvoyance that made events of the far future as clear as crystal to her while events of the near future were cloudy. When Henri Pierre Dumont de Sainte Croix had come across near the Baye des Pauns, which was an event that grew less certain to her the nearer he drew, she vaguely recognized him as the man with whom she would have children and grandchildren. Henri Pierre covered her with furs.

"Comment tu t'appelles?" he asked.

"You will name me 'Sibylle' on account of my great and terrible gift, and you shall never again do anything I won't already know. We shall have two sons and one daughter, a dozen grandchildren, and a great-great-great-great granddaughter who will also have the gift of clairvoyance."

Willy stopped speaking.

"Wow! That's an amazing story!" I said. "You need to write it down!"

"I'm planning on it," he said, "but she told me that she's the great-great-great-great granddaughter of Sibylle. Victory's the one who inherited the gift of clairvoyance, and when she looks out into the future, I'm not going to be a writer. I'm going to sell insurance and make a bunch of money. So I feel a bit stymied now. She told me that we're gonna have three kids together and that she already knows everything I'm gonna do before I do it. So I'm kinda spooked. What do you think?"

"I don't know," I said. "I mean, we're getting into the realm of the supernatural here. I'm not sure I believe in it, though my father did give me a Ouija board when I was a kid. I remember that the spirits in the board would tell me stories that I wrote down, though I'm not sure if there were actual spirits or whether I just made up the stories myself."

"Yeah," Willy said. "I'm not real happy about not being a writer, but the sex is really super incredible. I don't want to give that up, that's for certain. I mean, if it comes down to a choice between being an author or having great sex, I'm gonna pick sex every time. Anyway, I want you to meet her. There's a student art show in the Fine Arts building tonight that she wants me to go to. You should come with me and see what you think."

"Okay," I said.

Willy left, and I mulled over the conversation in my mind. I tried making sense of it rationally. It seemed like there should be a logical explanation for it. I was pretty sure ghosts didn't exist. Maybe Willy had hypnotized himself into believing that he'd seen a ghost and that the story of Victory's clairvoyance was true only because he believed it to be true. I kinda felt bad that he was gonna give up his future plan of being a writer, but maybe love was more important than making a mark on the world. When I thought about it, the people I knew who'd been really successful were mostly so driven to succeed that they'd lost some of their humanity along the way. I thought about my uncle, Isamu, and America Lightshadow. My uncle had been so focused on succeeding at business that he'd had no real life outside of opening restaurants and traveling around giving talks on how to achieve the Great American Dream. America Lightshadow had been so consumed with the possibility of winning gold medals at the Olympics that nothing else seemed to matter to her. Even though I hadn't seen or spoken to America in a year, I determined that somehow I would someday save her from herself. I wasn't exactly sure how I would do it, but I would do everything that I could to make her see that success was more than getting your face plastered on a million boxes of cereal. The real prize might just be the ring you found inside the box. Even if it was just a piece of plastic junk, it just might represent the most real thing you'd ever find, whether you knew it or not.

Chapter 15 Pyramid

After my conversation with Willy, I went up to my room. My roommate, Daeng, was lying on his bed reading one of those old primers they used in grade schools. Mary, Dick, Jane, and Spot were respectively running, jumping, hopping, and barking across the pages of his book. Daeng had picked up quite a few English words and phrases, which was disappointing to me. He put down his book when I entered the room.

"Hello, Charlie," he said. "How are you today?"

"Fine," I said. I flopped down on my bed and counted the holes in one of the perforated acoustic tiles in the ceiling. I liked it better when neither of us could understand anything the other was saying and wasn't sure I liked him, or anyone else, mounting any assaults against whatever barricades I'd thrown up to keep others at arm's length. It wasn't that people couldn't get to know me. It just had to be on my terms. It was difficult to maintain my self-imposed subjectivity about others when they insisted on violating the rules and customs of my interpersonal boundaries. Fortunately, Daeng had a takraw match that evening against a team visiting from East Germany. He left the room shortly after I lay down on my bed. When he was gone, I got up and turned on the radio. A commercial was on, but The Beach Boys were about to sing a song about a surfer girl. My gift of radio prophecy, the ability to know what song was about to play before it started playing, was still with me. That ability had been with me as long as I could remember, but I was only able to tell what song was about to play on the radio if I didn't think about it. The moment I tried harnessing the ability, the gift vanished only to reappear when my mind was relaxed and empty. The commercial ended and "Surfer Girl" began to play. Maybe my gift of radio prophecy sprung from the same source as Victory's clairvoyance, but who could tell? My gift wasn't really explainable. It was one of those things that stayed hidden in me when I searched for it and only showed up when I stopped searching. In that regard, it was a lot like love. I had fallen in love with America the moment I set eyes on her in high school, but it wasn't like I'd gone looking to fall in love. It had just appeared, like the ghost that Willy had seen: beautiful, strange, and somewhat scary, all at once.

The song ended, and I looked at the clock. I needed to go over to the Fine Arts building and meet up with Willy. I got up and put on my sports coat. It was a bit ratty, but it had patches on the elbows that gave me a professorial look, in my eyes, anyway. I went downstairs and walked outside. It was a foggy night, one of those evenings when all the streetlights seemed soft and fuzzy when you looked at them through the mist. I walked across the campus, and people came out of the fog suddenly, then passed and vanished into the mist like specters. It was like I was moving through some eerie dream where everything seemed familiar and unrecognizable at the same time. I remembered the Japanese stories my mother had told me when I was a child, the ones where the faceless ghosts, the noppera-bō, impersonated someone familiar to you, but when you drew close to them, they'd make their features disappear, and all that would be left was a smooth empty sheet where their face should be. The stories terrified me when I was a child. I remembered one story where a fisherman decides to fish in the imperial koi ponds. Despite his wife's warning that the pond is sacred and is near a graveyard, the fisherman goes there anyway. When he reaches the pond, he meets a beautiful young woman who begs him not to fish in the pond. When he ignores her, she wipes off her face. Terrified, the fisherman runs home, where his wife confronts him and reprimands him for his wicked behavior. Then she passes her hand over her face, and her mouth, nose, and eyes are wiped clean away. I tried thinking of something else. I thought about April, but I had difficulty recalling what she'd looked like. I saw her, in my mind, lying naked on her bed. I lay down beside her. We kissed and made love, and then when we were finished, she turned her face to me, and it was completely empty. When you gaze into the abyss, it gazes back into you, and it tells you who you are and what you are made of. I began to cry for the first time since April's death.

By the time I reached the Fine Arts building, I'd stopped crying. Willy was waiting for me on the steps. We went inside, and Willy brought me over to a woman standing in front of three framed lithographs.

"Victory, this is my friend, Charlie."

"Hello," I said.

She was not at all what I'd expected. Willy's previous girlfriends had generally been large and voluptuous, but Victory was tiny, no more than 5'2", with delicate hands and features. She was pretty, of course, as were all Willy's girlfriends, but there was something else about her, the way she held herself, that made her seem larger than she really was and also seemed to pull me into her the way those vague images and thoughts seem to pull you into another reality during those moments between waking and sleeping where everything is both familiar and unreal at the same time. It was that same thing I'd experienced just minutes before while I walked through the fog. She looked at me, just for an instant, her gray eyes piercing right through to the secret core of who and what I was, and suddenly it was as though I were a volunteer in a hypnosis act, the kind where everyone in the audience is laughing uproariously at you up on the stage, clucking or barking like a dog begging for a treat, and the only one who doesn't realize what's going on is you. I made a conscious effort to pull away. She was powerful, no doubt, and Willy had given himself over completely to Victory's psychic influence. I was convinced that the ghost Willy had seen existed nowhere but in his mind. I wondered if Willy would revert back to his brash egotism if he and Victory were ever separated for an extended period of time.

I excused myself and left them standing together while I walked around looking at the exhibits. I can't say with any certainty that I understood any of the art, but some of it I liked. One guy had painted some trout that looked pretty realistic, only they were swimming up in the air above the head of this fisherman who looked like Jesus. He was oblivious to the trout and just kept casting his line into the water. There was a woman performance artist who stood for 4 hours and let anyone do anything they wanted to her. People would go up to her and fondle her or spit on her. Someone took a pair of scissors and cut her dress to shreds. It was pretty disturbing. I actually tried to stop some guy from putting his hand down her blouse and up her skirt, but she chased me off.

"If you don't stop interfering with my process, I'll call security," she said. I stopped interfering with her process and ended up talking with Wilson McGregor, a senior art student. He was standing next to his art project and grabbed me by the arm as I was walking past.

"We were meant to have this interaction," he said. "It's happened infinite times before. We're reliving memories, some of which haven't yet occurred."

Wilson had built a big pyramid out of wood and iron. It was painted to resemble the pyramid on the back of a dollar bill. A big blue neon eye winked on and off at the top of the pyramid. You could walk inside it where there was stuff like a pair of pink plastic breasts that he'd turned into a table lamp. There was a Christmas tree in the corner that was hung with glass dildos instead of ornaments. A naked male angel sat at the top of the tree with a tree branch stuffed up his anus. Wilson had also taken apart a toaster and reassembled it so the hole for the bread looked like a vagina. There was even a rotary phone in there that worked. He'd replaced the mouthpiece and earpiece with parts that looked like rectums for reasons that only he understood. When I asked him about it, he straightened up and cleared his throat like he'd been waiting all night for someone to ask that question.

"Decommodification…," Wilson said. "The almighty dollar has made us indistinguishable from household appliances. Take my toaster, for instance. Not that I literally want you to take my toaster, but everything is for sale. Therefore, you could take it for the right price, which in this instance is $250."

"It looks like a vagina," I said.

"Absolutely," he said. He took a slice of white bread from his pocket and popped it into the vaginal opening at the top of the toaster.

"Now I could have used wheat bread. I could have used a jam-filled toaster pastry, which, frankly, is delicious. I could have eschewed bread and pastries altogether and used any number of luncheon meats, although thick-cut bologna is the one that immediately springs to mind. A nice slab of Canadian bacon would have had a certain cachet, too, don't you think? But I decided to go with my gut instincts on using white bread as a metaphor. Bread of life in a 'fucking appliance.' The ironies are too rich to ignore."

What Wilson had ignored, however, were certain fundamental elements of proper electrical installation. While building his pyramid, he'd left some bare wires in the walls, and a fire had begun smoldering behind the drywall as we spoke. A flame appeared in the wall by the outlet that the toaster was plugged into and quickly spread up the wall to some curtains that were covered with images of naked men and women engaged in sexual intercourse. By the time Wilson grabbed a fire extinguisher, it was too late. The mammary lamp caught fire, and bright yellow flame shot upwards towards the ceiling from the nipples. The fire tore through the inside of the pyramid so quickly that we were lucky to make it out. Everyone inside the gallery was evacuated, including the woman performance artist. Out of all the artists, she was the one who seemed to be the most upset even though she hadn't actually lost any physical pieces of artwork. She'd just had her performance cut short. She actually attacked Wilson and had to be pulled off him by a trio of women artists who'd illustrated every paragraph of a twelve-hundred-page edition of War and Peace with thousands of different images gleaned from Picasso's work.

Firefighters came and put out the fire before there was too much damage to the Fine Arts building, but the gallery, and all the pieces in it, were ruined. Willy, Victory, and I hung around and watched the firemen pump water into the gallery. It was quite exciting. Wilson got into a shouting match with the artist who'd painted Jesus fly fishing.

"Calm down for God's sake," yelled Wilson. "Don't you see this is just a memory we are reliving?"

Victory lost a couple pieces in the fire, but since she had printed about a dozen copies of each litho, it was no great loss. She could print more copies anytime she wanted, though she claimed, in my presence, that during the printing process she had probably squeezed out the last vestiges of those spirits that had inhabited the gravestones. I looked at Willy. He kept nodding his head while Victory spoke, but it wasn't my role to pull him aside and tell him that he'd allowed himself to submit to this insanity of his own free will, and that he would willingly give up any future career as a writer, mediocre though it might be, for a fistful of insurance contracts, a suburban tract home

"The fire tore through the inside of the pyramid so quickly that we were lucky to make it out."

in a nice section of town with an above-average school district, and the allure of quality sex–his drug of choice–with the hypnotically beautiful Victory. Many men have sold their souls for less.

Chapter 16 Satisfaction

After the fire in the Fine Arts building, I ended up going over to the takraw arena and watching the Renfield Fighting Quakers play a match against the East German National Takraw Team. Even though takraw had only been introduced into East Germany in the past two or three years, the Germans were absolutely dominant. They were all enormous, with cartoon-like muscles, but had the leaping ability of gazelles. They beat the Renfield team in three straight matches, but it was pretty obvious that their abilities on the court were less a function of training and more a function of performance-enhancing chemicals. After the match, I left before Daeng could come over and practice his English on me. I already knew myself well enough to admit that most of my relationships existed for the sole purpose of keeping me amused. Daeng's prowess on the takraw court kept me entertained, and that was enough. I didn't want him to get any closer to me than he already was. He was a nice guy and didn't particularly deserve to be dissected by the gleaming surgical steel implements that my mind wielded, with few exceptions, on just about everyone else who crossed my path.

I went back to my dorm and hung around with Marco. He was the Resident Assistant now and had moved into Derrick's old room between the lounge and the dining room. I told him about Victory and Willy's claim that he'd been visited by a ghost in Victory's presence.

"I think Willy's allowed himself to be hypnotized by her," I said. "He told me that he's not going to be a writer now because Victory claims to be clairvoyant. She told him that he was going to sell insurance instead of becoming an author."

"So what?" said Marco. "Let's talk about you for a little. Why is this any of your concern?"

"I believe in freedom, Marco. Willy giving up on his dream to sell insurance because he's having great sex with a woman seems the opposite of freedom."

"Charlie, did someone appoint you to be the freedom monitor for Willy or anyone else? Maybe you need to start looking at your own issues surrounding the deaths of April and Derrick. Willy will be fine. And you might be right. Willy's ghost might have its roots in autosuggestions planted in his subconscious mind. It's quite a gift she has, and it speaks volumes about his willingness to maintain a relationship with her. Many people might find that admirable. You, on the other hand, do everything you can to prevent people from getting too close to you. Do you think that's normal?"

"Well, for me it's normal. Sure."

"You may want to look at that, Charlie. I can give you some very powerful personality assessment tools that can help you on the journey of self-discovery, but you'll have to apply them."

"Thanks, but no thanks, Marco. Anyway, I wanted to tell you that this is probably my last year here. Everyone at Renfield seems to be taking classes to become something: doctor, teacher, engineer, computer programmer. I can't see myself being happy spending the next fifty years of my life sitting at a desk designing auto fenders or pulling teeth or teaching history to future generations of history teachers."

"What do you want to do with yourself then? You're a smart guy, Charlie, sometimes too smart for your own good. What will inspire you to be the best version of yourself?"

I thought about America Lightshadow and how I wanted to save her from herself.

"Maybe I'll go see America," I said.

"Good," said Marco. "I know from personal experience that travel broadens your mind and will definitely give you a greater appreciation for how your own gifts can benefit you as well as everyone around you."

Marco lit his pipe and leaned back in his chair with a smug look on his face. He'd made peace with his inner rapist and would have a long, prosperous career helping hundreds of people befriend their own personal demons so they could endure life as faceless cogs in their own ghost stories. That held no interest for me; although, to be honest, there was nothing I could think of that interested me with the exception of doing something to make America love me. I went up to my room and was about to climb into bed when it occurred to me that The Rolling Stones were about to sing a song on the radio about a man who wasn't a man because he didn't smoke the same cigarettes as the singer did. I turned on the radio and listened to the opening strains of "Satisfaction" and then put on my pajamas and spent the night in blissful, dreamless sleep.

I was awakened the next morning by Daeng. He was having sex with one of the members of the East German women's takraw team. I watched them for a few minutes. They had pretty good technique, but it was a bit formulaic: missionary, doggy, cowgirl, missionary, cowgirl, missionary, doggy. The woman was big and sturdy with arms as big around as Daeng's thighs. She noticed me watching them while she rode Daeng at full gallop. She had large cantaloupe-shaped breasts that looked like they had been surgically attached to her chest. She gestured for me to join the fun, but I turned away and put my head under the pillow so I didn't have to hear their guttural grunts and moans. They finished, and I waited until the woman got dressed and left. When I looked over at Daeng, he smiled sheepishly and shrugged his shoulders. I got out of bed and went down to the bathroom at the end of the hall and took a long shower. When I got back to the room, Daeng was gone. I opened one of my drawers, and while getting a pair of socks, I noticed the little velvet box containing the diamond that had once been April. I opened the box, took out the gem, and held it to the morning sunlight streaming in through the window. Particles of dust swirled in the light. Unlike April, the diamond hadn't lost any of its brilliance. It sparkled and flared with all the colors of the rainbow. Then I returned April to the silk-lined box and returned her to the drawer. In a couple hours, I was seated in a freight elevator on the ground floor of the Humanities building watching films about Nazis ripping gold teeth from the mouths of Holocaust victims and taking the rings from the fingers of the newly dead.

I decided to play the part of a death camp prison guard for the final exam. The thought of ushering people to meet death held a certain appeal to me metaphorically, no matter how disgusting and horrifying the reality behind the metaphor might be. It wasn't something I could talk to anyone about except Marco, but he seemed to be enjoying psychoanalyzing me just a little too much. Plus, I didn't really want to open up to him after he admitted to sexually assaulting a woman who'd had too much to drink. Honesty is a bit overrated when you just use it to justify how and why you're nothing more than a massive asshole. I bought a used Waffen-SS uniform with a Death's head cap at a junk store on the outskirts of Stoker and put it on at night when I was alone in my dorm room. I'd even purchased an actual Luger pistol complete with a belt and holster that I'd strap on. Then I'd march about my room in my uniform while listening to Wagner's *Der Ring des Nibelungen* and giving myself Nazi salutes in the mirror. My hair had grown out about an inch since the midterm, so I slicked it down with baby oil to make it look *richtig und authentisch.* On a couple occasions, I would stand in front of the mirror and let my reflection shake his fist at me.

"On a couple occasions I would stand in front of the mirror and let my reflection shake his fist at me."

"Fuck you, you motherfucking Nazi fuck!" my reflection would shout. "Fuck everything about you!"

Somehow I felt liberated by unleashing my inner fascist. By the time the final exam took place, I was so convincingly a Nazi that I received an A+ just by showing up to the freight elevator in my uniform and lighting a cigarette with Germanic superciliousness. I was so

Übermensch I didn't even have to pull out my Luger and wave it at my classmates. After class, Professor Friedman didn't look at any of us as the door to the freight elevator opened and let us all off at the loading dock. Outside of a couple of brief words spoken at the beginning of each class, he hadn't really addressed any of us. There wasn't a lot to say because there was too much to feel. There was too much to feel, so you became numb to it. Once you were sufficiently numb, you were able to ignore it. I watched Dr Friedman walk across the parking lot and get into his fancy black German car. Then he drove off into the frigid December landscape of leafless trees silhouetted against bleak skies. I went back to my dorm. I took off my Waffen uniform and hung it in the closet, then I went back to living my life as though nothing had happened.

I stayed around Renfield until the spring semester ended. I didn't go to any classes and just hung around getting high while everyone else moved on with their hopes, dreams, and plans of becoming cogs in the machinery of Corporation America.

I made a few half-hearted attempts to track down America. I'd heard from a friend of a friend of a high school acquaintance that America was living in a high-rise dorm in Miami while she continued training for the Olympic Trials. I called down to the dorm about a dozen times, but either no one picked up, or if anyone did pick up and take a message, I never got a callback. Oddly enough, this just made me want to save her more from living the life she wanted.

Most of the people I'd hung around with weren't graduating, but they'd landed jobs for the summer that would help them achieve their future goals. Domingas Cabral had gotten an unpaid intern position at some big hedge fund headquartered in New York. Marco had gotten an eight-week position with a state-funded pilot program out of Hartford that worked with inmates in the Connecticut penal system. He'd be going into various prisons and reading nursery rhymes to individuals convicted of violent crimes in an attempt to reduce recidivism.

Paul Tsoukias wasn't graduating, either, but he'd already been attending summer classes at Yale. He stopped by my room on my last day at Renfield while I was waiting for Willy to come and give me a ride back to Mythic. For some reason, Paul had shaved the hair off the left side of his face but had left all the hair intact on the right side except for his right eyebrow.

"You look ridiculous," I told him. "What's the point?"

"I enrolled in an advanced psych class called 'Thwarted Expectations,' Charlie. It's being held at the Yale Divinity School. Most of the discussion centers around coping mechanisms individuals would, could, or should use to deal with the failure of Christ's Second Coming to materialize, but we're free to examine thwarted expectations in the secular world, too. As long as I observe and measure the social implications of my behavior, I can do what I want. So far, ninety-five percent of the people I meet avoid eye contact with me."

"Do you blame them? You look crazy, Paul! I'm surprised that anyone makes eye contact with you at all."

Tsoukias lit a cigarette and stood in the doorway studying me. He blew a smoke ring into the air and disintegrated it with a quick swipe of his hand.

"In the land of the blind, the one-eyebrowed man is king, Charlie."

"I don't think that's how that expression actually goes," I said. "Anyway, you're starting to weird me out."

"Maybe that's the point," he said.

He opened his hand and crushed out the cigarette on his palm, then he put the extinguished butt in his shirt pocket. He turned to leave the room, then stopped and looked back at me.

"I'll be going to med school after I graduate next year," he said. "Brown. My dad's on the board of trustees. In a few years, I'll be a psychiatrist."

"Lucky for all of us," I said. "You and Marco."

Paul left, and his absence only made me think of his presence. It was unnerving. I went down into the lounge. Wacyshyn was there. He and Domingas were talking about yields on treasury bonds and small-cap stocks. Like me, Wacyshyn was a sophomore, but he was working toward a finance degree. In a couple of years, when he graduated, he would work for his stepfather. His stepdad was the head of some

130

Fortune 100 development company that made hundreds of millions by borrowing money for construction projects that they never completed. They would declare bankruptcy, reorganize, borrow money for another construction project, and declare bankruptcy once again. I don't know how the particulars of this scam worked, but according to Mark, it was lucrative.

The only one who wasn't planning on working for corporate America was Strafe. He was sitting by himself in the lounge, reading a book, while waiting for his father to come pick him up and drive him back home to Majestic, New Jersey. He'd been at Renfield for four years already and still had a year or two left before graduating with a degree in English that would be virtually useless. I went over and sat in a burnt-orange fake leather armchair across from him. He was wearing his ubiquitous sunglasses, a lemon yellow shirt, rust-colored velour bell bottoms, and a pair of black and white saddle shoes in desperate need of a good cleaning. When I asked him what he planned on doing during the summer break, Strafe put down his book and shrugged.

"Don't know. Don't care," he said. "I'm just trying to stay open to what the universe lays down before me. I'm thinking of becoming a Hindu."

I looked at the book he'd dropped into his lap. It was a picture book titled *The Golden Big Little Book of Karma, Dharma, and Samsara*. On the cover was a cartoon drawing of a wheel resembling a ship's helm. Knives were jutting out of the wheel where the helm's handles should have been. Beside the wheel were a little boy and girl holding their hands and crying. On the ground in front of the wheel were a pair of severed fingers.

"Wow, interesting book. Anyway, good luck with your future or lack thereof," I said.

Strafe ignored me, picked his book back up, and started reading again. He moved his lips while he read. I watched him for a bit. His lips squirmed around like a pair of leeches. It seemed therapeutic for both of us, though I can't explain why. It just was.

I went back upstairs to my room. Tsoukias' absence didn't remind me of him anymore. I smoked a whole joint by myself. It was really crappy stuff. Chinaman had taken leaves and seeds from some male plants and mixed them with just enough female buds to get me high. I put on a record and listened to Thelonious Monk thump out jazz piano improvisations full of dissonance and spectacular silences until the late afternoon. Sunlight slanted down through the blinds of my dorm room and fell in regimented stripes of brightness and shadow across my face and body as I lay on my bed for one last time. I looked at my clock. It was 3:33. Nothing meant anything. I left the room a few minutes later. The only thing I left behind was my SS uniform and my luger. In a couple of hours, I was in Willy's Fiat heading to Mythic. There was nothing left of or for me at Renfield but knives on a spinning wheel. I would not be returning.

Chapter 17 Carousel

I moved back home and got a job in my hometown of Mythic working swing shift in a warehouse for one of those stores that sold cigarettes, toys, pharmaceuticals, household goods, sporting equipment, and condoms, and spent the better part of the next seven or eight months loading and unloading box trucks with pallets full of soft drinks and cheap barbecue sets made somewhere in the Philippines.

My direct boss was a skinny Black man named Joe Hayes. Joe had played minor league ball in the Red Sox organization in the sixties. He played left field and was a great defensive ballplayer. He had speed and range and led the International League in assists two years in a row, but his defensive prowess did little to mitigate his anemic batting average. He couldn't hit a curve, and that effectively ended his baseball career.

Joe was also a deacon in his church, the Second Baptist Church of Mythic, and was always wandering around the warehouse with a little red leather-bound version of the New Testament in his back pocket. During lunch and breaks, Joe would either spout scripture at me or try to show me pictures from the gay pornography he kept in his desk drawer. For the most part, I just ignored Joe's attempts to convert or pervert me and mostly spent my breaks with Danny Sheaf, a forklift driver from Arkansas who, as a young man, had the misfortune to attend a Nascar race in which one of the cars had gone airborne during a three-car collision. Pieces of the car had ended up in the grandstands and injured about a dozen spectators, including Danny. Part of an axle stove in his head, and although he survived, his cranium looked like a misshapen melon. The entire top of Danny's head was concave, but despite his head's deformity, Danny seemed perfectly normal, for the most part. In some ways, he was better than normal. The trauma to his brain unlocked some musical ability he'd never had before the accident. He could pick up virtually any musical instrument and start playing it as though he'd played it his entire life. Someone would hand him a guitar, and he could play just about any song you could ask him to play.

It was pretty great, though the accident had also left him with an inability to remember lyrics or to recognize faces. Whenever I sat down across from him at the lunch table, I had to make sure to wear my name tag or tell him who I was; otherwise, he'd think some stranger had just sat down across from him. Danny would always apologize profusely for his inability to recognize me.

"Sorry, Charlie. I cain't tell you how awful I feel not reckonizin' you right off."

"No problem," I'd say. "Did you bring your guitar with you?"

"Yessir! Or would you druther hear me play the bagpipes, t'day? Got 'em in my car, and I could drag 'em in and play "'Mazing Grace" if'n you'd prefer."

"Maybe another time, Danny. Let's hear some rock 'n' roll."

Danny would wander off to the back of the warehouse and come back to the table with an old Martin in his hands. Then for the rest of the lunch hour, he'd play Led Zeppelin tunes or songs by the Beatles or Rolling Stones as though it was easy as breathing. Even Joe Hayes would put aside his gay porn and stroll over to our table. He'd stand there grinning with his hands in his pockets. Once, when Danny finished a song, Joe put his hand on his shoulder.

"That there's a gift from God," Joe said. "A gift like that should be used to glorify the Lord, Danny. My church could use a guitar player with your ability."

"Maybe that gay bar you go to in Middlesex might need a guitar player, too," Danny said drily.

"Judge not, and you will not be judged; condemn not, and you will not be condemned; forgive, and you will be forgiven," said Joe. "Besides, every man must know the darkness and wickedness that surrounds him."

While Danny and Joe stood around discussing the finer points of theology, I went back to work loading pallets with orders from the various stores. Altogether there were seven different stores, and it took me nearly all day to completely fill the orders and restock the seasonal items that the stores no longer needed. Basically, it was mindless work, but I didn't care. After two wasted years in Renfield, supplying

Connecticut with cosmetics, rubbers, Quaaludes, Christmas ornaments, and Easter decorations gave my life meaning and purpose.

My parents weren't particularly thrilled that I'd left college and moved back home. Vasu was still living down in the basement. Even though they'd recently inherited a ton of money from Uncle Isamu's estate and really didn't need another nickel for the rest of their lives, they still rented out my old room to a submarine line cook, Chad Wicker, who would stay there when his sub, the Corpus Christi, was docked in Groton. They'd met him through my high school friend Gil Mosely, a cook on board the SSBN St Mary. The only available space for me was the cramped confines of the attic. I put a mattress down in a corner where the roofline slanted down to nearly hit the floor, and that's where I slept for the next few months, surrounded by old toys, furniture, boxes full of cracked pottery, chipped dishware, and musty-smelling old *National Geographic* and *Life* magazines. In short, my parents used the attic to store everything in their lives that had been deemed worthless, which meant it was the perfect place for me. After April's death, everything in my life seemed futile and without value.

Chad wasn't there very much. He'd show up every two or three months when the Corpus Christi was back from shadowing Russian subs in Arctic waters. I only saw him a handful of times after moving back home. He was a short, pale young man with red hair, bad skin, and a mouthful of small, rodent-like teeth that were stained yellow by coffee and cigarettes. Curiously, when he spoke, his voice was mournful and oddly resonant. It was as though his voice belonged to someone much larger, as though he were the puppet of some unseen ventriloquist, or someone whose chest was completely hollow so that the sounds coming from his mouth were deep and sad, like a dirge played on a cello.

The attic hatch was just outside Chad's room. You pulled a rope, and a ladder dropped down. The only time I saw Chad was when I was going to or coming from the attic. Usually, he was seated cross-legged on the bed with his head bowed over some quasi-pornographic piece of pulpy fiction. Most of the time he ignored me, although one evening, as I was about to climb the ladder up to the attic, Chad put his book down and spoke to me in his deep, uncanny voice.

"You're the son," he said. I folded the ladder back up into the attic and entered my old room.

"As opposed to the man in the moon, yes," I said.

"I hear you walking around above me, "he said. His deep, sad voice echoed around the room. "You have light feet."

I nodded and looked down at my feet. All my years of wrestling had trained me to move quietly and swiftly with a minimum of wasted effort. I looked around the room. Unlike Vasu, Chad didn't collect X-ray images and display them on his walls. In fact, there was nothing on the walls. All my old blacklight posters had been taken down, and the walls were completely bare. The only evidence that anything had been on the walls previously was little bits of yellowing tape that clung perilously to the wall's flaking paint. The rest of the room was fairly spartan: bed, chair, empty bookcase, nightstand upon which he'd placed a shadeless lamp, an alarm clock, and a brass statue of some Hindu god dancing within a ring of fire. Chad noticed me looking at the statue.

"Shiva the Destroyer," he said. "I keep it to remind me of the impermanence of the world. Creation, destruction, transformation, extinction." Chad rubbed his hand over his short-cropped red hair and smiled. His rodent teeth gleamed yellow.

"You're a submariner," I said. "Isn't that enough destruction?"

"The *Corpus Christi*..., Body of Christ. Enough firepower on board to set the world on fire."

"I'm somewhat opposed to nuclear conflagrations," I said.

"I'm just a cook," Chad said. "I don't push the buttons that launch torpedoes or missiles."

"You just feed those who do," I said. Chad chuckled and looked back down at his book. I noticed that the cover featured a woman with her blouse half torn off while a house burned in the background.

"Well, it's been really great talking with you, Chad."

Chad ignored me, and I left the room. I pulled the ladder back down and went up into the attic with my feet of light to rejoin everything in my world that was broken and useless.

I spent the next few weeks avoiding my parents as much as possible and spent most of my free time in the attic getting high. When I ran out of pot, I paid Joey Shapp a visit. He had moved out of the mortuary and was living in a rundown motel full of drug addicts and prostitutes. When I asked him why he lived in such a place, Joey laughed.

"These are my best clients," he said. "They're paying my way through law school, Charlie."

"Law school?" I asked incredulously. "You were a terrible student, Joey. How did you get into law school?"

"I cheated," he said. "I plagiarize and pay others to do my work for me. I'll pay someone to pass the bar exam, too. Law is easy if you know how to navigate the system."

"What about when you're a lawyer? How will you represent clients if you don't know the first thing about law?"

Joey shook his head and laughed.

"I'm not going to practice law," he said. "I'm just using it as a springboard for a career in politics."

"Politics?"

"Yeah, Senate, I'm thinking. That's where the money is. Guys get elected by making bullshit promises. They enter Congress broke and wind up rich by taking money from lobbyists and special interest groups. Plus, there's insider trading. When you know in advance what companies will be getting government subsidies, you can make millions playing the stock market. Congress is full of hundreds of guys just like me."

"That's terrible," I said.

"It is what it is," said Joey. "Just vote the party line and pad your wallet. I can plagiarize a few speeches that make it look like I know what the hell I'm talking about, and I just might end up in the Oval Office."

"Wow! That's fucking horrible."

Joey looked at me and narrowed his eyes.

"The difference between you and me, Charlie, is that you're an idealist with some pretty naive ideas about how the world is supposed to work. Me? I'm a realist. I have zero illusions about the world. It's doggy dog...."

"Doggy dog?"

"Catshit wrapped in dogshit wrapped in bullshit. Tie a bow around it and sell it as fertilizer for the Great American Dream that anyone can succeed in life if they're willing to work hard and play by the rules. That's the great big lie that everyone believes. The truth is that everything important in this country is rigged by people with power."

"That's fucking depressing as hell," I said.

"It ain't depressing on the other side of the fence, Charlie. I guarantee you that. It's only depressing if you believe that everyone should be equal or that no one should be above the law. Power pays, Charlie. Power pays. Speaking of pay, gimme fifteen dollars, Charlie, and I'll give you an ounce of the finest New Jersey weed that money can buy. They don't call it The Garden State for nothing."

I gave Joey his money, and he reached into a duffel bag and pulled out a plastic bag full of pot. It looked pretty crappy, but as long as it got me high, who cared what it looked like?

"As always, Charlie, it's a pleasure doing business with you."

"Wish I could say the same," I said. Joey walked me to the door and held it open for me.

"C'mon man, I'm a necessary evil. Just remember that when I'm your senator."

"I can't wait," I said.

I walked outside and looked at the dusky sky. A cold wind off the ocean rattled the leaves of a sycamore tree above me. A crescent moon was caught fast in the tree's branches, and out over the ocean, Virgo, the constellation representing innocence and virtue, and Libra, the scales of justice, shone side by side in the gathering dark. I walked down to a little park nearby and sat down on one of those kids' carousels. I rolled a joint and smoked about half of it. Then I got up, grabbed one of the push bars on the carousel, and ran until the carousel was moving at a furious clip. I jumped on board, lay down on my back, and watched the moon and stars wheel and circle above me. I closed my eyes tight and watched the darkness on the inside of my eyelids. Life was a carousel. Power pays. The gods create, and the gods destroy, and all of us are caught in a circle of fire.

The carousel slowed and gradually came to a halt. I sat up and looked around me. A police car pulled up alongside a curb kitty-corner from the park. I got up and walked across the park to a low fence that I hopped over. Then I ran down some back alleys and side streets until I reached the bridge over the Mythic River. As I was crossing the bridge, I could see the shadowy silhouette of a submarine gliding beneath it as it headed to open water. It was the *Corpus Christi*. Chad would be on board preparing meals for those who answered the call of men like Joey Shapp: liars and thieves willing to bring the world to the brink of destruction while enriching themselves. I reached into my pocket and pulled out the joint. I lit it and took a few tokes, then I looked out over the mouth of the river and watched the *Corpus Christi* head darkly into the shimmering lights of Virgo and Libra.

"I looked out over the mouth of the river and watched the Corpus Christi head darkly into the shimmering lights of Virgo and Libra."

Chapter 18 Shrewsmberg

I went to see a counselor in the fall of 1975 right after the Red Sox lost the World Series to Cincinnati's Big Red Machine. After the Reds won game seven, I cried uncontrollably for several days. For some reason, Boston's loss hit me harder than Derrick's or April's deaths had. I called Marco Bocce one morning and asked if he could recommend a counselor near me.

"You probably need to see someone who specializes in grief, Charlie," Marco said. "I think you're still suffering from losing April, mostly, with some issues around Derrick's death, too."

Marco stopped talking, and I sat passively in the dim silence with the phone pressed to my ear. I looked at the clock on the wall. It was 11:11. I listened to Marco's breath on the phone. It was comforting in some omni-mythical way. Marco began speaking again after the clock hit 11:13.

"There's a counselor in New London who's done amazing work with Holocaust survivors and athletes who've struggled emotionally because they can't hit a curveball. I read a fascinating article in The Modern American Journal of Applied Linguistic Psychology about his work with the NBA on helping players overcome the guilt associated with being freakishly tall."

"That's a thing?" I asked.

"Charlie, you'd be surprised at how many things are actually things."

"I'd probably also be surprised by the number of things that aren't actually things."

"Everything's a thing, Charlie, if you believe it's a thing."

I mulled that over while Marco gave me the name and phone number of the psychologist in New London he'd thought could help me. After I hung up the phone, I called Dr Shrewmsberg's office and set up a consultation. I was surprised that they had an opening for the following day. The receptionist who scheduled my appointment had a great voice that seemed scented with the fragrance of jasmine and orange peel. I found it oddly arousing. That it was a thing that was a thing, there was no doubt. In my mind anyway.

Dr Shrewmsberg's office was in a strip mall near the Thames River. Unfortunately the receptionist, Afloria, with the voice made of jasmine and orange peel, looked nothing like those aromas. She was a short and thick-waisted woman in her fifties with a large mole on her chin from which sprouted several long black hairs. The thing I thought was a thing had turned out not to be a thing after all. Afloria had me fill out some paperwork and then had me sit in the waiting room while the doctor finished up with another client.

While I waited, I sat and stared at my hands. I remembered that April had read my palm the first night we'd met. The memory was sharp and bittersweet. I recalled that she'd told me I would age well, that I was terrible with money, and that I was good in bed. The memory made me happy and sad at the same time. I looked up from my hands and discovered that the receptionist was staring at me.

"What's wrong with you?" she asked. It was weird, but her voice still carried the scent of jasmine and orange peel with a subtle undercurrent of geranium.

"I'm not sure," I said. "I get sad."

"Did your wife kill herself?" Afloria asked. The geranium scent grew stronger now.

"No," I said. "I've never been married."

"My husband killed himself," she said. Now the aromas of jasmine and orange peel had completely vanished. The smell of geraniums with an undercurrent of garlic was nearly overwhelming. I grabbed the armrests of my chair and gripped them tight. "Blew his brains out when he found out I was having intercourse with his best friend. Fortunately, Dr Shrewmsberg helped me through the grieving process. Rest assured he'll help you, too."

Fortunately, I was spared any further conversation with Afloria when the door to the doctor's office opened and a tall, cadaverous-looking man in his seventies or eighties exited. A second man wearing a suit and two pairs of glasses exited the room, and the two shook hands.

"Thank you, doctor," said the tall, thin man in an accent that seemed to be German. I noticed that he had a number tattooed on his left forearm.

The man left, and the doctor looked at me and smiled. At least one of his mouths smiled. His other mouth opened, and some words fell out.

"You must be Mr Lord," he said.

"Charlie," I said.

Doctor Shrewmsberg looked at me over the tops of both sets of glasses. I noticed that his eyes were different colors. The eyes in one of his heads were brown and blue. The eyes in his other head were blue and brown and quite piercing. It was this head who was to be my therapist.

I had gone to Mythic High School with two sets of conjoined twins. Vijay and Ashneel Patel had been on the wrestling team with me in high school, and I'd even gone on a double date with Rebecca and Cheryl Sims, the discus thrower(s) on the Mythic track team with Willy Wetmore, so it wasn't particularly unsettling to have a set of conjoined twins as my therapist(s).

Dr Shrewmsberg ushered me into his office and gestured for me to have a seat in a leather chair facing his desk. While I was waiting for him/them to seat himself/themselves, I looked out his window. His office overlooked the Thames River, and I watched the ferries, barges, and Coast Guard vessels shuttle back and forth across the water. Dr Shrewmsberg cleared one of his throats.

"Well, Charlie, what brings you here today?" he asked. The other head just smiled at me pleasantly but said nothing. Dr Shrewmsberg noticed me looking at the other head and pointed to him with the hand attached to the arm that was closest to his head.

"My brother," he said. "I'm his legal guardian. I hope you don't mind him sitting in, Charlie."

"That's fine," I said. "I think I'm here because my girlfriend and a friend from college died, and the Red Sox lost the World Series to the Reds."

The doctor took his glasses off and wiped them with his brother's tie. He put his glasses back on and nodded his head sagely.

"Tell me about that," he said. His brother just sat there grinning at me.

For the next hour, I just sat and talked about April, Derrick, the Red Sox, Victory, Audrey,

"Dr Shrewmsberg cleared one of his throats."

America, and anything else I could think of. The doctor just sat and listened and nodded his head. Every so often he'd write something down on a notepad, but he didn't interrupt me or ask any questions. He just let me spill myself as the afternoon sun faded and long shadows began to cast themselves across the river.

I stopped talking near the end of the hour, and the doctor took his glasses off and rubbed his face. He put his glasses back on, shut his brown eye, and squinted at me with his blue eye.

"I think you've given me enough to work with today, Charlie," he said. "You're definitely dealing with issues of loss, which can be addressed with some common tools that I can teach you to apply practically as a method of coping with grief in a way that both honors and extinguishes it completely. But to be completely honest here, your story kind of bores me."

I looked across the desk at the doctor while his brother began drooling and shaking his head back and forth.

"I'm used to dealing with Holocaust survivors and world-class athletes, Charlie. People with really interesting stories. Your problems are really garden variety compared to the issues of loss and trauma that really get my juices flowing. But if you can live with the fact that I'm not all that inspired by your little tale of woe, then I'd be delighted to help you work through these issues for the next three or four years. What do you think?"

The doctor leaned back in his chair and reached into his jacket pocket for a handkerchief, which he used to wipe the drool from his brother's chin. They both sat staring at me with their blue and brown eyes.

Without saying a word, I stood up and walked out of the room. I walked through the geranium- and garlic-scented waiting room out into the shadow-darkened streets. I decided it was time to buy a saxophone. That was a thing that really was a thing. For me, anyway.

Chapter 19 Barky

The first and only saxophone I'd ever owned had been a gift from my mother's brother, Isamu Kawabata. I had played it for about ten years but had thrown it off a cliff into the ocean after Isamu had been swept up by a tornado during Mythic High School's graduation ceremonies. The tornado had disappeared over the water, and my uncle's body had never been recovered. I'd thrown the saxophone into the ocean as a way of honoring him, which, truth be told, pleased my father no end. He wasn't a fan of the instrument. He would've preferred that I'd spent more time helping him with his diaper service than listening to recordings by Charlie Parker, Ornette Coleman, and Paul Desmond and emulating the deep, rich sounds that came from their instruments. I had really missed playing the sax, but there was something comforting about knowing that I had helped reunite Isamu and the saxophone at the bottom of the ocean.

Following my encounter with Dr Shrewmsberg, I went to several different music stores and pawnshops in Mythic, Groton, Norwich, and New London, but the saxophones for sale were all in terrible shape and overpriced for the amount of money and effort needed to get them in playable condition. I even took the ferry over to Long Island and visited a pawnshop where a disheveled guy not much older than me was trying to build a banjo out of parts from a car transmission and a hockey stick. He smiled broadly when I asked if he had any saxophones.

"You're in luck," he said. He rummaged under a pile of scuba equipment until he located a black case that he placed on the glass counter holding broken watches and rusty pearl-handled handguns missing firing pins or triggers.

"I just got this baby in from a guy who played with Benny Goodman. He's going through a divorce, right, and he needs some dough, so that's how it come to me. It's like new! All original! The price is two seventy-five, but I can let it go today for one fifty."

I pulled the saxophone out of the case. It was a cheap Conn student saxophone that had been soldered together with parts from a vintage Buescher alto.

145

"I don't think so," I said. "That thing'll never be playable. You couldn't pay me to take it off your hands."

The manager put his hands on the glass counter and leaned across it.

"Your loss," he said. "But I can tell you're a man of particular tastes. Might I interest you in a tooth from the head of the man who shot Abraham Lincoln?"

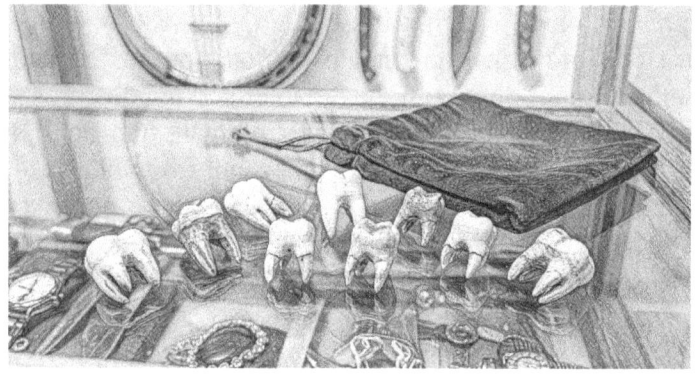

"'Might I interest you in a tooth from the head of the man who shot Abraham Lincoln?'"

"Seriously? You have one of John Wilkes Booth's teeth?"

"As sure as my name's Barky Peters! I even have two of his baby teeth. For seventeen dollars you can own a real piece of Americana." Barky unlocked the glass case and pulled out a little velvet bag. He emptied the bag's contents into his hand and held seven or eight teeth up to my face.

"Yep. Those are teeth," I said.

"Pure Americana!" said Barky. "What's more American than a tooth from one of the most famous incidents of gun violence in our nation's history?"

"They say that John Dillinger's penis is on display at the Smithsonian," I said.

"I wish I had John Wilkes Booth's dick in a jar. I'd travel around the country with the jar and a semi-naked woman with overly large breasts and charge everyone a dollar to look at it."

Barky held a hand up over his head and moved it from left to right. He looked up and spoke as though he were reading words written in the air.

"See the dick and teeth of the man who assassinated the president who freed the slaves!"

"Barky, you really have a gift," I said. "You ever think about going into marketing?"

Barky smiled and put the teeth back into the bag.

"Yeah," he said. "A man can make a metric fuck ton of money giving the American people what they really want."

"Bread and circuses."

"Teeth, chicks, guns, and dicks."

"You're a great American, Barky. The real McCoy."

"Live free or die!"

"Give me liberty or give me Liberty Valance's penis in a jar."

Barky opened his mouth and grinned. He looked like a hyena. He closed up the saxophone case and reburied it under the pile of scuba gear.

"I like you," he said. "I'm gonna to tell you something I hardly tell anyone. Barky's not my real name."

"No kidding."

"I kid you not. My real name is Peter Peters."

"I know a Mason Mason," I said. "My favorite author is Gordon Gordon Gordon."

Barky nodded and ran his hand through his disheveled hair.

"I hate the name 'Peter,'" he said. "Too many entendres surrounding that word. I call myself Barky cause I have the gift of gab. Anyone hearing my name immediately thinks of a carnival barker."

"Or a yapping dog," I said.

"People would just laugh at a man named Peter Peters displaying John Wilkes Booth's dick in a jar, but Barky Peters traveling cross country with the phallus of the most infamous assassin in all of Americana…, well, people would line up just to throw money at him."

"Tell me the truth, Barky. Were those really John Wilkes Booth's teeth in that bag?"

Barky put the palms of his hands back on the glass countertop and leaned across it toward me once again.

"No one knows if Jesus really existed or not, but half the world believes he did. It doesn't really matter whose teeth are in that bag, does it? Just like it doesn't really matter if I have the actual dick of John Wilkes Booth in a jar when I start traveling cross-country with an attractive, well-endowed woman dressed in a manner guaranteed to arouse the prurient interests of John Q Public."

"Barky, are you related to Joey Shapp, by any chance?"

"Never heard of him. He's not planning on traveling cross-country with anyone's dick, too, is he?"

"Not that I know of. The only penis he owns is his own."

Barky looked relieved.

"Thank God," he said. "I'm not sure a nation of two hundred million people can support two men traveling cross-country with another man's penis in a jar." Barky picked up the torque converter and squinted at it.

"Time to get back to work," he said. "I get $40 for each of these banjos I make. Pulled this Dynaflow from a '53 Cadillac."

"Do they actually play?" I asked.

"That's the wrong question," he said. "The right question is, do they sell? The answer to that question is not negative."

"But aren't you swindling people by selling them worthless shit?"

Barky flashed his hyena face at me again.

"I'm providing a service," he said. "Without people like me, how would half the people in this country learn not to be such fucking suckers?"

"Well, time for me to go, Barky," I said. "I have a saxophone to find. Plus I need to take a shower." I left Barky fitting the hockey stick into the torque converter.

It was raining outside. The rain fell gently across my face and hands, and after a few minutes, I felt clean and light. I could never be like Barky. Still, there was something about him that I admired. He was pure in his cynical pursuit of the great American grift, an embodiment of our fallen natures that both repulse and fascinate us, and in my secret heart of hearts, I hoped he did start traveling the country with a penis in a pickle jar. One man's dream is seldom understood by anyone else, but that doesn't mean you won't pay for a glimpse of it.

Chapter 20 Halloween

The following day I drove up to the town of Stoker. It was Halloween. I'd left Renfield College abruptly and hadn't really said goodbye to anyone there, so I wanted to close that chapter of my life. I stopped by my old dorm, but only a couple people were around. Everyone else was in class. I spoke with my old roommate, Daeng, the takraw player. I found him sitting at a table in the dorm cafeteria eyeballing a bowlful of cucumber-filled lime Jello. He was wearing a skull mask pushed up on top of his head and a long-sleeved T-shirt printed with skeletal bones and ribs that would've looked pretty cool under a black light.

"Charlie*! Goo dee jai tee dai jer mung wa*! I am so happy to see you! Many here have been worried about your welfare!"

His English had improved dramatically during his stay at Renfield.

"I'm fine," I said. "I just needed to get away and clear my head."

"Are you returning to the college?" Daeng asked.

"I don't think so," I said.

"What then will you do?"

"Not sure, Daeng. Maybe travel. Work a little. Right now I'm just trying to find a decent saxophone.

"Travel's good," said Daeng. He pushed his chair back and stood up. "I'm going to my home country of Thailand today for a takraw tournament, Charlie, but it was such wonderful to conversate you!"

Daeng left as Domingas Cabral and Strafe entered the cafeteria. They were wearing their game-day rugby jerseys.

"Charlie, hey!" said Domingas. "We're playing the Piscataqua Valley Bread Bakers today and could really use your speed at wing. Wanna play?"

"I'm not even a student here anymore," I said. "I didn't think non-students could play."

"Nobody cares about that," said Strafe. He was wearing a pair of sunglasses even though the cafeteria wasn't particularly well-lit. "It's not like anyone's gonna check, and even if they did, we can say you're Malbec O'Toole. He broke his neck last game and is questionable for today."

"Jesus! He broke his neck?"

"Only a hairline crack in what is essentially a non-essential vertebra," said Strafe. "It's not as bad as it sounds. He's got a little trouble moving one of his arms, and his doctor says he can't play anymore, or he could die or be completely paralyzed or some shit, but O'Toole's doc is a tool. Some duct tape, whiskey, ibuprofen, cannabis, and medical-grade amphetamine made by Paul Azimuth on the fourth floor should be able to get him up to speed."

"Nah, I don't think I'll play. I don't think Malbec should play either, but I'll come watch."

"Turkey," said Domingas. "You used to have the real fighting spirit of a true Fighting Quaker, but you've gone soft."

"Bitter, bitter, rugby quitter," chanted Strafe. "I've had five or six concussions this season, and I'm not a quitter."

"Well, we've gotta head over to the field for pre-postgame cocktails," said Domingas. "See you there."

"See ya, quitter," said Strafe.

They left, and I looked around the cafeteria. I didn't recognize anyone else there. I went out into the lobby and found Klondike watching Mark Wacyshyn and Paul Tsoukias play chess. Wacyshyn was in blackface, and Tsoukias had smeared himself with blood. A long-handled ax was propped up against the side of Paul's armchair. He'd lost about one hundred pounds since the last time I'd seen him, but I could smell, even from a distance, that he still wasn't showering. I looked at the chessboard. Wacyshyn was down to his king, and Tsoukias only had a king and a bishop left. There was no way either of them could win.

"I've been watching these morons play for the past two hours," said Klondike.

"We can hear you," said Wacyshyn.

"Why didn't you tell them the game is a draw?" I asked.

"What? And deprive myself of the contemptuous joy I've been experiencing? No way."

"I just wanted to say goodbye," I said.

"Nobody cares," said Klondike.

Wacyshyn looked up at me.

"You're leaving Renfield?" he asked.

"I left last June," I said.

"Huh…, I was wondering why you never stopped by to get high with me anymore. I just figured you were mad at me."

Tsoukias groaned suddenly. I looked at him. One of his hands was moving furiously under the table, then stopped.

"Are you masturbating?" I asked.

"Not anymore," he said.

"You're disgusting," said Wacyshyn. "You're half pig, half dog, and half ass."

"Wow!" I said. "You should switch your major over to Math."

Marco Bocce lumbered into the lobby. It looked like he'd gained the weight that Tsoukias had lost. He was dressed in a bald wig and white face paint with black crosses over his eyes. A pair of gigantic red shoes with blue laces were on his feet.

"Charlie! Are you back to stay?"

"No…, just saying goodbye."

Marco pulled me aside and spoke softly so the others couldn't hear.

"Did you go see Dr Shrewmsberg?" he asked.

"Yeah, but I decided to buy a saxophone instead," I answered.

152

"Hmmm. "Don't you think that's just another way for you to avoid examining the real issues in your life?"

"Maybe. I don't know."

"You can't run from those things forever, you know."

"I'm not really running," I said. "It's more like a casual stroll."

"More deflection," said Marco. "Don't you want to make peace with your inner demons?"

I looked at Marco and laughed.

"I'm not sure I should be taking life advice from any more Bozos today, Marco."

"Well, stick around tonight. We're having a Halloween party here."

"I'll do my best," I said.

I said goodbye and then walked across campus to the rugby field. It had rained the day before, and the field was a mess. Willy Wetmore was standing on the sidelines watching the teams warm up.

"Piscataqua looks tough," he said. He pointed over to one of their players. "Their tighthead prop is a fucking monster."

I looked at the player Willy had pointed out. He was big but wasn't even as large as our loosehead prop, Quint Jones.

"I wouldn't call him a monster," I said.

"I've seen him play before," said Willy. "He gets bigger as the game goes on."

"Probably from harnessing his inner demons," I said.

Willy looked at me and frowned.

"That's not funny," he said. "It's Halloween, Charlie. The veil between this world and the spirit world is stretched incredibly thin today. Things from the other side leak into our side."

"So long as their props don't turn into three-headed dogs, I think everything will be fine, Willy. Anyways, how's the animism going?"

"I gave it up," said Willy. "I found a group of practicing animists in Windsor Locks, but it was more a social club than anything else. I was hoping for a full-blown cult, not a coffee klatch."

"Still wrestling?" I asked.

"Yep. Kicking ass and taking names, though I've been questioning that, too. I've joined a group of disaffected Jesuits who've left the church but still believe in God and everything. They call themselves Roaming Catholics."

"Roaming Catholics? How come?"

"They, meaning we, believe that God's mysterious ways can only be made manifest by humans. We are the hands and feet of the Lord, Charlie. God bids us to wander through the world and perform good deeds as a sign to all of His love and grace, without which we are but clanging gongs."

"Interesting," I said. "Have you been performing good deeds?"

"Not really," Willy said, "but I'm working up to it."

The game started, and it was a muddy slog. No one could score. Strafe got another concussion when the Piscataqua hooker lowered his shoulder and drove it squarely into Strafe's forehead. Quint Jones lost his eye in the mud, again, and the Piscataqua fly-half had to be carried off the field after getting tackled by Malbec O'Toole. After the tackle, Malbec lay on his back in the mud with his arms outstretched.

"I think he's dead, Willy. I think he really broke his neck this time."

"Nah, his hand is twitching," said Willy. "He's still alive. He might not be able to walk again, but he did take out their fly-half. At least the teams will both be down a man until halftime when they can sub out the injured."

The game ended in a scoreless draw. An ambulance came and took away Malbec and the Piscataqua fly-half. Quint Jones found his eye, wiped the mud off it with his shirt, and popped it back into his head. A keg was set up in the middle of the field, and Domingas Cabral ran from the sidelines with a bottle of Irish whiskey in each hand. Both teams gathered and drank and talked until the beer and whiskey ran out. That's when a fight broke out. Mostly it was Renfield players fighting with Piscataqua players, but Strafe and Quint Jones were throwing punches at each other until Strafe clipped Quint in the temple with a wild right. Quint's good eye rolled back in his head, and Strafe stood over him shaking his fist.

"I got lightning in my left, thunder in my right, and hailstones in my heart!" he shouted. He helped Quint to his feet, and the two combatants limped off the field with their arms around each other's shoulders.

"This is all some Biblical shit," said Willy.

I looked up at the sky. It was getting on dusk, and the sun was setting red out over the rocky meadows and pastures of Connecticut. The clouds were tinged with streaky flames of orange and pink, and stars were beginning to show through the deepening purple above me. The veil between the worlds was stretching thin, and things were leaking back and forth between them. It was time to go back to the dorm and party.

Willy walked back to the dorm with me. He held a clear plastic cup that he spit into every thirty seconds or so. He had a match the following day and was wringing as much moisture from himself as possible in order to make weight. I'd done the same thing myself when Willy and I had been high school teammates for the Mythic Owls. In one of the intervals between expectorations, Willy asked me what I was going to do.

"I mean, I'd hate like hell for you to get stuck in Mythic for the next fifty years, Charlie. It's nice and all, but I'd die of boredom there."

"You've always been an adrenaline junkie, Willy. Live for the thrill! But I know what you're saying. I'm thinking about doing some traveling," I said. "I'm thinking about seeing America."

Willy spit into the plastic cup. It was about three-quarters full.

"See the USA in your Chevrolet," Willy crooned.

"Well, yeah, that, too," I said. "But I meant America Lightshadow. I'm thinking about going down to Florida and seeing her."

"Still in love with her?" asked Willy.

"Yes, but there's stuff about her that bothers me, Willy. She's a great swimmer, obviously, but I question whether she's doing it for the money and fame or because she loves doing it."

"Love is a thing that makes your life swing," said Willy. "I'm gonna use that line in a book someday." Willy pulled a little black notebook out of his back pocket and wrote the line he'd just spoken on a page full of such witticisms.

"That's a terrible line," I said.

"Not the way I'm gonna use it," Willy said. "Context is everything."

"I thought you were giving up on your dream of being a writer," I said.

"I've been reconsidering some of my goals lately," he said.

We stopped talking and walked in silence punctuated by the sound of Willy spitting into his cup. It was nearly full now. My old dorm came into view. The lights were on in the cafeteria, and I could see people decorating the windows for the party with cardboard skeletons, ghosts, witches, and black cats. As we got closer, I could see inside the cafeteria. The tables had all been folded up and stored away. A bar had been set up on a tall counter that contained a refrigerator and an adjacent spot that was the perfect size for storing a beer keg, and a record player sat on a low table set between the counter and the double doors leading from the cafeteria into the kitchen.

"Are you staying for the party, Willy?" I asked.

"Natch, Satch. I just can't drink. I should be right at weight now."

Even though Willy had lived in an apartment off campus while at Renfield, everyone in my old dorm knew him. He was a minor celebrity at the college, mainly due to his elevation of the sport of streaking to the realm of performance art. On Valentine's Day his sophomore year, he'd taken his clothes off in Victory's dorm room and had her paint hearts on his chest, back, and buttocks. She'd even sewn a pair of wings out of red cloth stuffed with cotton batting and stitched those to the side of Willy's Red Sox cap and attached a chin strap to the cap so it wouldn't blow off. Willy put on the cap and checked his appearance in the mirror. Satisfied, he crawled out Victory's second-floor window and climbed down the trellis. Then he set off across the snow-covered campus.

It was about 4:30 when Willy started his run. Dinner was just being served in the south campus dorms, and the cafeterias were full when he streaked past their windows. He ran naked from the south end of the campus around the duck pond to the east, looped around the Humanities building, circled the library, and then sprinted back down to south campus. He ran with a bag of candy kisses, which he threw to startled bystanders along the route. He'd run the quarter mile in high school and had blinding speed. It was like watching Mercury, the messenger god, delivering missives of love to the masses. By the time he'd burst back into view of south campus, word had spread. The residential halls had all emptied out, and students were lining the walkways around the quadrangle in the midst of the dorms.

The students erupted into frenzied cheers when Willy sprinted to the center of the quad, stopped, threw the remaining candy kisses to the crowd, then did a handstand. He walked fifty feet on his hands in the snow to Victory's dorm, climbed up the trellis, and disappeared through the open window of her room. The crowd clapped and cheered for him to reappear in the window and acknowledge their admiration of his performance, but the window remained empty. The gods may bring love and even answer mortal prayers, but they don't give encores.

The memory of Willy's epic Valentine's Day streak made me laugh out loud. He had that effect on just about everyone. He didn't always run deep, but he had a knack for bringing laughter and joy into every situation he found himself. It was his gift, and I envied him for it. He lived a lot closer to the surface of reality than I did. As for me, I resided a level or two deeper below the surface, in that area where distinctions like past, present, and future vanished and everything was nothing and nothing was everything, but it wasn't the kind of thing you could talk to anyone about without them being somewhat concerned about you.

Willy seemed to read my thoughts as we were about to enter the dorm.

"You would've been a prophet a thousand years ago, Charlie. One of those guys who spoke the truth as revealed by God, or the universe itself. The kind that sees clearly through dark glass or darkly through clear glass. The kind that no one listens to."

"I don't know that I'd look good in sackcloth, Willy."

"All prophets grow long beards, Charlie. Lots of women love long beards. I'm planning on growing one after wrestling season. Many of the Roaming Catholics I know are wearing them. It was one of the reasons I got involved with their movement to begin with."

Willy opened the door to the dorm, and we went in. The lobby was full of people dressed in costumes. I looked around the room. Bogie and Diekman were each wearing mini-skirts, wigs, and high heels. Both of them wore enormous fake breasts beneath silk shirts with high collars. Diekman noticed me staring at them and came over.

"We're not homos, Charlie, if that's what you're thinking."

Bogie came over and took Diekman's hand.

"We're twins," he said. "Sisters. We wanted to come to the party as Siamese twins, but we couldn't find a blouse that would fit both of us." He looked at Willy, and his eyes widened.

"Oh my God! You're him! We have a picture of you doing your naked handstand! Very manly, even though it was really cold that day."

"Very kind of you," said Willy.

I went into the cafeteria, and Richard Molten sidled up to me. He was tall and looked consumptive. He wore a long trench coat and had a guitar in his hand. A harmonica brace that held a beat-up Hohner was slung about his neck, but it wasn't a costume. He pretty much looked like that every day. He was a language major with an emphasis on Russian.

"*Zdravstvuy*, Charlie. I'm glad you're here. You're one of the few people I don't hate."

"I'm flattered," I said.

"I hate my mother," he said. "She's a bitch."

"Is misogyny a Russian trait?" I asked.

"I'm really a misanthrope," Molten said. "My father's a compulsive asshole. Most people are, as I'm sure you're aware."

"Compulsive? Have you been reading Dostoevsky again?"

"I just finished *The Brothers Karamazov* for the fifth time. The greatest novel ever written."

"Better than *War and Peace*?"

"Tolstoy? Seriously? *On bespolezny kusok der'ma*! Worthless shit!"

"Have you read anything by Gordon Gordon Gordon? He's my favorite author."

"That guy? He's a hack."

"So you've read him?"

"Hell no! Not planning to, either." Molten put the guitar strap around his neck and started strumming the strings. His fingernails were long and dirty. I recognized the song. It was "Dead Skunk" by Loudon Wainwright III.

"Mertvyy skuns posredi dorogi

Mertvyy skuns posredi dorogi

Mertvyy skuns posredi dorogi

vonyuchiy k vysokiye nebesa"

I took off when Molten started blowing into the harmonica. Some of the reeds were cracked, and it sounded pretty awful. I walked away and went over to the bar. The cafeteria was getting crowded now, and the line at the bar was long. I decided not to wait. I was about to go back into the lobby when someone tapped me on the shoulder. It was Audrey Stone. She was dressed as a vampire, but even with the fake fangs and blood on her mouth, she was still breathtakingly beautiful.

"I can hear," she said. "I had cochlear implants over the summer, and I can actually hear now."

"Really? That's amazing!"

"It really is," she said. "Plus my stutter disappeared as soon as I got the implants."

Audrey bit her lip with one of her fangs and looked away briefly. When she looked back at me, her eyes were glistening with tears.

"I should be happier," she said, "but sometimes I don't know who I am anymore. Sometimes I miss the deaf, stuttering girl I was. I still dream in sign language, Charlie. My hands still stutter in my dreams. There are times when I feel oppressed by my ability to hear. I'm just like everyone else now, and it's disconcerting."

"Give it time," I said. "One day you'll wake up and be really happy you can hear."

"That's what I'm afraid of," she said.

"Happiness is loss denied," I said. "That's a quote from The 'House of Happy Snows' by Gordon Gordon Gordon." I wasn't sure I actually believed it entirely, but it was the only thing that came to mind at that moment. Audrey threw her arms around my neck and kissed me on the lips.

"Would you like to go back to my dorm room and have sex, Charlie?"

"Sure," I said. "When the party's over, come get me."

Audrey grabbed my face with both hands and kissed me. Her tongue probed my incisors and cuspids while my own tongue flicked over her fangs. She dropped one of her hands to my crotch and squeezed gently before backing away and disappearing into the crowd. Someone turned off the cafeteria lights, and the room went dark briefly; then another switch was flipped, and the room was lit by the eerie glow from several long ultraviolet lamp strips that had been placed around the room. A song by the Grateful Dead began playing from the stereo speakers, and witches, vampires, and other assorted monsters began dancing. Actually, the cafeteria was so crowded that everyone just sort of stood in place and shimmied or bounced up and down with their arms in the air. I didn't feel like pretending to dance, so I decided to go out into the lobby. On the way out I saw Willy. He and Audrey were making out by the doorway. His hand was up her dress. She looked happy in spite of her ability to hear.

The lobby was crowded, too. Strafe and Domingas were in the center of the room having a slapfight. Domingas was dressed in his rugby uniform, and Strafe was wearing a kilt. A circle of warlocks and cross-dressers stood around them cheering. Then I saw it. Strafe had a saxophone under one of his arms. Flowers and butterflies were etched on the bell, and I recognized it right away. It was a Mark VI, one of the greatest saxophones made by the Selmer company in the sixties. Strafe took a hard slap to his left cheek and grimaced. Then he looked around, saw me, and extended the saxophone to me with his left hand.

"Hold this," he said. I took the saxophone from him and watched as he jumped in the air, raised his arm, and hit Domingas so hard with his open hand that the Cape Verdean was knocked off his feet.

"He jumped in the air, raised his arm, and hit Domingas so hard with his open hand that the Cape Verdean was knocked off his feet."

161

"Game, set, match, over, done, finished!" shouted Strafe. Someone handed him a bottle of beer, which he drained in three or four gulps. Then he threw the bottle against the wall and raised both arms over his head like he'd just won a heavyweight boxing title. Domingas had gotten back on his feet. The entire left side of his face was bruised and puffy, and his eye was bloodshot.

"Best two out of three," he shouted.

"Loser," sneered Strafe. "Loser, loser, chicken chooser!"

Strafe came over to me. I held the saxophone out to him.

"I don't want that thing," he said. "Some guy across campus gave it to me so he could lick my toad once a week for a whole semester, but I think he ended up in the infirmary before the midterms. That fucking toad is toxic as shit."

"I can keep it?" I asked. "You're sure?"

"Certainly! My generosity to others of the Asian persuasion is well known by all and sundry."

I looked at Strafe's face. If he hadn't said anything, I wouldn't have thought he was Asian, but now that he mentioned it, I could tell.

"My mom's Japanese," I said.

"So's mine," said Strafe. "That's why I can't date Asian women. I don't know any other Asian women besides my mom, so it would be like committing incest if I slept with any of them. No Chinese, Japanese, Korean, Filipino, Vietnamese, Cambodian, Thai, Laotian, Mongolian, Indonesian, Malaysian, or Eskimo women for me!"

"You do realize that 60% of the women in the world are Asian, right?"

"So what? I'm still not sleeping with anyone who looks like my mother. I probably will never have sex with anyone who has dark hair or speaks French, Spanish, Italian, Portuguese, Turkish, Greek, German, or Australian, either."

"They speak English in Australia," I said.

"Barely," Strafe said. "I'm pretty much committed to marrying someone from Sweden, Norway, Denmark, or Iceland, but screw the Dutch!"

"You mean don't screw the Dutch," I said.

"Exactly," said Strafe.

Strafe walked to the cafeteria to grab another beer, and Willy came over to me.

"I'm taking off," he said. "I'm taking Audrey back to her dorm."

"What about Victory?" I asked. Aren't you still seeing her?"

"She's in France for the semester," he said. "She won't be back until just before Christmas."

That explained why Willy was talking about becoming a writer again, I thought. Victory's absence had freed Willy from his self-imposed exile from himself. Strafe came back over with a bottle of beer in each hand. He drank one quickly and threw the empty bottle against the cement wall. The sound of tinkling glass was oddly satisfying. I'd been known to dispose of my empty beer bottles in similar fashion.

"Strafe and I are gonna be roommates next semester," said Willy. "I'm fed up with Chinaman's drug dealing."

"Just don't lick Strafe's toad," I said.

Willy nodded and headed back into the cafeteria to find Audrey, and Strafe walked off to get high with one of the last segments of a centipede. I took one last look around the dorm. Marco Bocce was still dressed in his clown costume and smoking his pipe. He stared wistfully at the wall as though he were still thinking about how he might get his molecules to vibrate with the same frequency as the molecules in the wall so that he could pass through to the other side, which, I suppose, was what I wanted, too. I looked at the saxophone in my hands. It was beautiful. I couldn't wait to put a new reed in its mouthpiece so that I could play and let the music transport me far away, to that place where all distinctions vanished and everything was nothing, and nothing was everything. I tucked the saxophone under my arm and walked out of the dorm into the chill, dark air sparkling with stars. A meteor streaked past overhead and disappeared swiftly to the west. I walked with measured steps to the parking lot behind the south campus dormitories and found my car. I wrapped the saxophone in a blanket from the trunk and laid it down like a sleeping child in the backseat. Then I drove back to Mythic, into the everything that was nothing and the nothing that was.

Chapter 21 Graveyard

I spent the next few months working. For the first time in my life, I actually had a plan. I was going to save enough money to travel to Miami, where America Light shadow was swimming for the Hurricanes and training for the Olympic trials. When I wasn't working, I spent most of my time in the attic listening to jazz records on an old Fisher cabinet stereo system stored there and playing the saxophone. The Mark VI was an incredible instrument. When I blew into it, the sound was like silky smoke, dark and smooth and sweet. Time seemed to dissolve when I played it, and I was always surprised when I stopped playing that a couple hours had passed when it seemed like twenty minutes. I bought a hard shell case for it at a music store in Norwich, then I pretty much carried it everywhere I went.

I took the instrument with me to work nearly every day, and during lunch break, I'd play wild bebop rhythms while Danny Sheaf grinned and played along, behind, around, and ahead of me with his beat-up 1966 Kay Speed Demon guitar. I had never played with anyone like him before. Joe Hayes would wander over with his Bible in one hand and a porno magazine in the other and nod his head appreciatively.

"It ain't Gospel music, but you boys can play," he'd say.

He'd always ask us to do a jazzy version of Amazing Grace, which we'd start slow and simple, then turn a corner and chase each other up and down the scales with frenetic arpeggios, then turn another corner and swing back home with buttery, soulful riffs. Then lunch would be over, and I'd go back to filling backorders for lawn darts and cheap costume jewelry.

For my efforts, I was paid two-fifty per hour, which wasn't a lot but was still forty cents above minimum wage. After taxes, I was lucky to take home seventy dollars a week, even with overtime. I picked up an extra $60 a week working under the table on weekends and two or three weeknights washing dishes at the Lobster Pot. By the end of May 1976, I'd managed to squirrel away nearly three thousand dollars even after spending a couple hundred having April's diamond set in an art deco engagement ring. I planned on giving it to America when I asked her to marry me. I'd given that decision a lot of thought over the past couple of weeks. Spending the rest of my life with her and helping her to see there was something more to life than crass materialism seemed to be the only thing that made any real sense. I wanted to show her that I was willing to part with one of the things in my life that was most valuable to me, and that if I could do that, she could, too.

I called America near the end of June, and she actually picked up the phone when I dialed her dorm! I was so shocked that she answered I forgot to ask why she hadn't responded to any of my earlier calls or the myriad letters I'd sent her. She'd placed first in the Olympic trials in the 100-meter butterfly, the 200 freestyle, and the 400 medley a week or so earlier and would be on her way to Montreal for a chance to win gold medals, etch her name into history books, see her photo on the cover of magazines, and her likeness on the front panel of cereal boxes. That had been her goal ever since I'd met her in high school. I called her on a Saturday morning from a pay phone outside the Lobster Pot. America answered the phone on the first ring.

"Good morning, America, how are you?" I said. America laughed.

"Charlie, if I had a nickel for every time someone's said that to me over the past few years, I'd be rich," she said. "Where are you?"

"Still in Mythic," I said. "I'm thinking about hitchhiking down to Florida to visit you before you leave for Montreal."

"Better hurry," she said. "I'm leaving for Canada in another week or so. I won't really have lots of free time to visit, but I can carve out a few hours."

I told her I'd call as soon as I got to Miami, then I hung up. The next few days flew by as I prepared for my trip. I sat down in the living room while my parents were watching All in the Family that evening. I told them about my plans and was surprised that they didn't try to talk me out of hitching fourteen hundred miles to Florida. They actually seemed relieved that I was going to do something besides hole up in the attic with my saxophone.

"Are you planning on coming back?' my father asked.

"I guess," I said, but secretly I hoped that America would say 'yes' when I asked her to marry me, and I would stay in Florida for the rest of my life.

My father frowned when I told him I might be coming back. If I left for good, he'd be able to rent out the attic for $40 or $50 a month. My mother, on the other hand, seemed happy that I'd be returning after my trip to Florida.

"Too hot Frorida. Prus bugs, Charrie," she said in her Japanese-accented English. "How come she don't live someprace crose? Merry land, huh?"

"Marry land," I said.

"Not so hot," she said. "Merry land."

"It's close to DC," my father said. "I hear you can go to the Smithsonian Museum and see John Dillinger's penis in a jar."

"Peanuts?" said my mother.

"I don't know that his nuts are in the jar, too," said my father. "I think it's just his Johnson." "Johnson not president now," my mother said. "Henry Ford."

"Jerry," said my father.

"Jury? What kind jury? Maybe Nixon go to trial."

I left my parents as they continued their discussion of America's political leadership and went through the kitchen and knocked on the basement door. Vasu came up the stairs and opened the door for me. He was wearing green hospital scrubs. I went down into his room and looked around. Shadowy X-ray photographs were still clipped onto the light boxes he'd mounted onto the basement walls. One of the X-ray images showed the bones of a woman's hand that had eight fingers and no thumbs. I recognized it right away as the hand of Diane Moleed. She'd been born with eight fingers and no thumbs on each hand. Diane and I had gone on a weird double date in high school one night along with Willy Wetmore and Rebecca and Cheryl Sims, the set of conjoined twins who threw the discus on the girls' high school track team.

"The world is filled with such wonders and amazements, Mr Charlie, yes?" Vasu's head bobbled to the right and left as he spoke.

"Yep," I said. "Wonders and amazements. Signs and signatures."

Vasu smiled beatifically and continued bobbling his head.

"I came to say 'goodbye.'" I said. "I'm going to Florida and might not be back for a long time. If everything goes well, the next time you see me, I'll be married."

Vasu smiled broadly.

"Marriage is such a sacred duty," he said. "May the gods bless your marriage with many children!"

Vasu went over to the shelf on the wall beside his bed and picked up a little metal figurine that he placed in my hand. It was a miniature brass statue of a woman. The third finger of her right hand was bent so that it touched her thumb.

"Parvati is Shiva's consort," he said. "She is the goddess of love and fertility, Mr Charlie. It is my gift to you. May she bless your union for the rest of your days."

I thanked Vasu and then went upstairs to pack. Chad was seated cross-legged on his bed, flipping through the pages of a *Hustler* magazine, when I went to pull down the ladder to the attic.

"Parvati is Shiva's consort," he said. "She is the goddess of love and fertility...."

168

"I'm leaving tomorrow," I told him. "I may or may not be back." Chad put down his magazine and looked at me.

"The only permanence is impermanence," he said. "Everything returns to its source. One day I might help destroy the world with nuclear Armageddon, but the world will not truly be destroyed."

"Thanks for your kind words, Chad."

I pulled the ladder down, went up into the attic, and packed a duffel bag with some clothes and toiletries, then climbed back down the ladder with my saxophone, grabbed my bicycle out of the garage, and rode across town to the old cemetery. From the hill at the top of the cemetery, you could see virtually all of Mythic. It seemed like a fitting place to spend some time if I was never coming back. I locked my bike to the iron fence surrounding the cemetery, then trudged up the hill past the granite crosses, obelisks, and mausoleums on either side of the path. At the top of the hill was a bench that I sat on, and I stared out over the scenery. Downtown Mythic was completely lit up, and the lights were reflected in the river where it flowed out to the sea. Beyond the town in the distance, I could see the screen of the Mythic Drive-In where adult movies played. I watched an orgy unfold before me with close-ups of random penises, breasts, and vaginas. The actors and the movie reached their respective climaxes, and the screen went dark.

"Beyond the town in the distance, I could see the screen of the Mythic Drive-In where adult movies played."

The June night air was thick with insects and moist air from the ocean. I pulled the saxophone out of its case and played for ten or fifteen minutes while the moonlight illuminated a marble angel standing nearby, with spread wings and a drawn sword, guarding the eternal resting place of one of the recently dead. Then it was time for me to stop playing and to leave the cemetery. Twelve hours later, I stood at the top of an entrance ramp to I-95 with my thumb pointed to the sky as the traffic surged past me. In a little while a car stopped. The passenger door opened, and I headed south to see America.

Part 2
The Road

Chapter 22 Elijah

The person who picked me up was in his early thirties. He was dressed in a gray double-breasted pinstripe suit with silver cufflinks and a red tie decorated with silver paisleys. He had thick, bushy hair, sideburns, and a mustache that vibrated when he spoke.

"Where you heading?" he asked after I'd stowed my duffel bag and saxophone case in the backseat and slid into the passenger seat.

"Miami," I said.

"I can take you as far as Washington. I've got a conference there starting tonight."

"Great."

"I'm Elijah," he said, extending his hand to me.

"Charlie," I said. I shook his hand and then looked out the window. The sky was overcast with low clouds. A few drops of rain spattered against the windshield. We drove for a couple of hours, making polite conversation over nothing. The rain stopped somewhere in New Jersey. I looked out the window at the refineries and chemical factories lining both sides of the highway. I remember Strafe telling me he'd grown up somewhere around here, which seemed to make sense. Like the area we were passing through, Strafe was a bit of a mess. I looked back over at Elijah and noticed that his jacket was unbuttoned. I could see that he had a gun holstered under the jacket. Elijah saw that I'd noticed his weapon and laughed.

"Don't worry, kid. Ex-military. I work for a think tank working on policy decisions around national security. Military preparedness. We advise the Pentagon regularly. That kind of stuff. I carry just in case."

"In case of what?" I asked.

"You never know," he said. "Why you heading down to Florida this time of the year? Vacation?"

I told Elijah about America Lightshadow and how I was going to see her before she left for the Montreal Olympics.

"Wow! I've read about her. You really know her?

172

"Yeah, I do!" I pulled the velvet jewelry box out of my pocket and showed Elijah the diamond ring. "I'm gonna ask her to marry me."

"Good for you!" he said. "Gotta back backup plan if she says 'no'?"

"I haven't really thought about that," I said.

"Always have contingencies in place, Charlie. If there was one thing the military taught me, it was to always have an exit strategy and an exit strategy for that exit strategy, which is kind of why I'm heading to DC. The Pentagon screwed the pooch pulling out of Saigon. Lots of good men died. Plus we fucked over virtually all our local intelligence assets there. It was a clusterfuck of epic proportions. The clusterfuck of all clusterfucks. My group wants to make sure the next shitstorm doesn't happen, which is exactly why the next shitstorm will happen. Most of these Pentagon assholes think they know everything because they read Clausewitz in some class at West Point. As soon as someone like me comes along who's had actual boots-on-the-ground experience, they dig their fucking heels in and double down on their stupidity. People die."

I nodded.

Elijah sighed, took a gold cigarette case out of a breast pocket in his jacket, and pulled out a cigarette. Before he put the cigarette case away, he offered one to me. I took one and he lit his, then handed me a battered lighter. There was a coat of arms embossed on the lighter: a gloved fist held an upraised sword inside a horseshoe. The tip of the sword reached up to a banner containing the words 'Garryowen.'

"I was a lieutenant," Elijah said. "1st Battalion, 7th Cavalry Regiment. Custer's regiment. My first action was Ia Drang. The Valley of Death. LZ X-Ray. Took a bullet in the ass on day two but fought through until evacuated the next day. Lieutenant Commander Moore is the greatest man I've ever served under. He should be head of the Joint Chiefs of Staff."

Once again, I didn't know what to say. I'd never heard of Ia Drang or Lieutenant Commander Moore. The best I could do was roll down my window and let the smoke escape. Elijah stubbed out his cigarette in the ashtray. I looked at the clock in the car's dashboard. It was 11:11 am. With a little luck, we'd be pulling into DC by 2 pm. I leaned back in my seat and shut my eyes. I went away for a little bit and dreamt of America. She was naked and dressed in green scrubs like the ones Vasu wore. I grabbed her face with my hands and tried to kiss her, but she turned away from me. I awoke with a start. I looked at the clock. It was after twelve. I looked over at Elijah. He was staring in the rearview mirror.

"Shit's about to get real," he said. "That black van's been following us for the past twenty minutes." He looked at me. "Good, your seat belt's on."

I was about to ask Elijah what was going on, but he braked suddenly, and I lurched forward. The car screeched to an abrupt halt in the middle of the interstate. My seat belt stopped me from hitting the windshield. Elijah reached into his jacket and drew his gun. He opened the car door, jumped out of the car, and pointed his gun at the car behind us.

"Get out of the fucking vehicle!" he shouted. I watched as a young man exited the driver's side of the black van and raised his hands above his head. A young woman exited from the passenger side, and a couple kids exited the van from a door on the side.

"NSA?" shouted Elijah. "NSA, CIA, or DOD? Who sent you motherfuckers?"

The young man looked terrified, and the kids were crying.

"Don't shoot! Don't shoot! We're on our way to Disney World!"

"Fuck you, you fucking motherfucking fuck! Who sent you!?"

"I work for General Electric!" the young man shouted. "I swear, we're heading to Disney World."

"On your fucking knees, asshole. I should put a fucking bullet through your head right now, motherfucker! Are you KGB? Stasi? Mossad? Who the fuck sent you?"

The young man knelt on the roadway with his hands over his head.

"We're nobody! the young man yelled. "I swear, we're just on our way to Orlando!"

Elijah pointed his pistol at the roadway and fired a shot into the asphalt.

"He opened the car door, jumped out of the car, and pointed his gun at the car behind us.

"Tell whoever sent you that you're dead if I ever see you again!" Elijah hollered. He jumped back into the car and slammed the car into gear. The car fishtailed across the road, straightened out, and Elijah began passing traffic on the right shoulder of the highway. He handed the gun to me.

"I don't want this!" I said.

"You're in the shit, now, soldier!" Elijah yelled. "If that fucking van pulls up alongside us, shoot the driver in the fucking head!"

I looked at the gun in my hand. I'd never held a loaded one before. If the van were actually full of KGB agents, I'd be the last person you'd want trying to protect your life.

"They're probably Stasi," Elijah said. "They've been shadowing me since Watergate with the help of the DNC. They'll do anything to put Carter in office."

Elijah looked in the rearview mirror again. He breathed a sigh of relief but didn't slow down.

"We're safe for now," he said, "but they'll be back."

I handed Elijah his gun, and he returned it to his holster. A roadway sign welcomed us to Baltimore. Washington, DC, was still about an hour away. Elijah continued driving like a madman. He pulled off the interstate and continued south on a two-lane road. Whenever a car appeared in front of us, he stepped on the gas and passed it. I watched in the side view mirror as a hubcap came off and spun out of sight into the weeds alongside the road.

"This isn't my first rodeo, kid," Elijah said.

We finally reached DC, and Elijah drove until the Washington Monument came into sight. He pulled over about a hundred yards from the monument near a complex of marble and brick buildings.

"Wait here," Elijah said. "I need to check in with my handler." He pointed over to a man in a yellow vest picking up trash on the National Mall with a set of litter prongs. Elijah got out of the car and walked over to the trash picker. While he was talking to the man in the yellow vest, I grabbed my duffel bag and saxophone from the back seat, opened the passenger door, and got out. I ran down a walkway and ducked into a building that looked like a brick castle. A Black security guard stopped me.

"Hey, there's no running in the Smithsonian, man."

I stopped running and bent over to catch my breath.

"Sorry," I said. "I was trying to get away from some crazy guy." The guard laughed.

"Washington's full of crazies," he said. "Some ain't even 'lected."

"So this is the Smithsonian," I said.

"Part of it. There's all sorts of buildings that make up the Smithsonian. Prolly take two hun'ed years to see it all."

"No kidding," I said.

"I kid you not!" The guard started walking away, but a thought occurred to me.

"Hey," I called. "Mind if I ask you a question?"

"No, man. Ask away."

"I hear John Dillinger's penis is in a jar on display somewhere here. Is that for real?" The guard laughed and took off his hat.

"Look here, ever'body wants to see that gangsta's dick, but the truth is it ain't on no display." The guard put his hat back on and began walking away again.

"Hang on," I said. "You said it's not on display. Does that mean it's here but not on display?"

"Oh, man. I really can't answer that question without getting in trouble."

"So it's here!" I said.

"I didn't say that."

"Have you seen it?" I asked. "Is it really as big as they say?"

The guard removed his hat again and looked at the brim.

"Well…, yeah. I done seen it. I don' know how big it is, but I'm a guess a good seventeen eighteen inches. They got it in a special collection an' only show it to congressmen an' presidents an' such.

Nixon used to come an' look at it five or six times a year. Craziest white man I ever met, an' that's sayin' a lot. There use to be a congresswoman would come by reg'lar. Ever'body had to vacate the room so she could stare at it private like. She always had the damn'dest smile on her lips when she left that room."

The guard returned the hat to his head and sauntered off into one of the exhibit rooms. I went to the exit and peered outside. Elijah was nowhere in sight. I stepped outside and looked at the gigantic phallic symbol of Washington's might and power a few hundred yards away. Elijah's car was gone. The man in the yellow vest was still picking up trash at the monument's base. I walked down to the roadway and stuck out my thumb. A few cars passed without stopping. Then a big rig pulled over, and I jumped into the cab. Ten hours later I was at a Waffle House outside Atlanta, Georgia, reading a menu and wondering what in the world grits were.

Chapter 23 Waffle House

The Waffle House was down the street from a bus station. The trucker who'd given me a ride told me there was a bus leaving for Miami at 2 am. When I walked into the restaurant, I looked at the clock on the wall behind the counter. It was 1:15. I sat down at the counter, and the waitress handed me a menu and placed silverware on a paper napkin beside the coffee cup in front of me. I was starving. I hadn't eaten anything since leaving Mythic nearly seventeen hours earlier.

The waitress was an attractive Black woman wearing silvery frosted lipstick that matched her eyeshadow and a Dolly Parton wig. She wasn't as well endowed as Dolly, but the Waffle House clientele seated at the counter at 1:00 am on a Saturday didn't seem to mind that one bit. She walked back and forth from the counter to the booths behind me with a coffee pot in her hand, refilling the cups of the truckers, travelers, and night owls while nineteen eyeballs watched her every move. The nineteenth eyeball belonged to the man seated at the counter a couple stools away from mine. He wore an eyepatch over his left eye under a pair of gold-rimmed aviator glasses. The waitress stepped back behind the counter and refilled his cup while he grinned and looked her up and down shamelessly.

"Damn, Louise, ain't you all that and then some." Louise smiled and patted him on the arm.

"Oh, you hush up now, Percy. I already done tol' you I ain't goin' home wid you no matter how many sweet things you say."

Louise came over to me to take my order.

"Waffle sandwich?" I asked. "Is that any good?"

"Oh, child, this is the Waffle House! Ever'thing is just fine an' dandy here!"

"Okay," I said. "I'll have that and a cup of coffee."

Louise wrote my order down and then walked over to a red tile surrounded by gray tiles in the floor behind the counter and called out my order to the 350-pound grill cook. The cook looked at Louise the way everyone else in the restaurant looked at her. Louise came back over to me and poured coffee into a large ceramic mug with the words "WAFFLE HOUSE COFFEE" printed on it in black letters surrounded by yellow squares.

"Y'all want some cream with dat, honey chil'?"

"Just some sugar," I said.

"Black as death an' sweet as love! Ain't that so?"

"Jest like you, Louise!" Percy said.

"You gon' be the death o' me yet, Percy. Bes' get on home to that woman o' yours!"

"She visitin' her sister in Athens," said Percy. He reached into his pocket and put $.25 on the counter for a tip. "I'll leave the door unlocked for you, Louise."

"Dat ain't happening, Mr Percy." Louise picked up the two dimes and nickel and put them in her apron pocket. After he left, a tall, thin guy with long blond hair, bushy sideburns, and a soul patch below his lower lip sat down to my left. He had a guitar case with him that he leaned up against the counter. He ordered a cup of coffee and lit a cigarette. He took two or three drags on the cigarette and then stubbed it out in the black plastic ashtray on the counter in front of him.

Louise brought my waffle sandwich. She hadn't lied. It was definitely fine and dandy, as was the coffee. When I was done with the sandwich, I ordered a slice of peach pie, which Louise served with a scoop of French vanilla ice cream on top of it.

"Dessert's on the house," said Louise, "on account of y'all had to sit an' listen to all Percy's tomfool'ry."

I thanked her, drained the last drops of coffee from my cup, then reached for my wallet. As I was pulling it out of my pocket, the box with America's ring fell out onto the floor. I bent down and grabbed it. When I stood up, I noticed that the long-haired man to my left had glanced over at me. He looked down at my saxophone case.

"You any good with that?" he asked. He had a soft, quiet drawl for a voice.

"I play jazz," I said.

"I like jazz," said Louise.

"Well, then, let's play." The man opened his guitar case and pulled out an acoustic Gibson. He dropped the sixth string down to a D and strummed a few chords while I took the Mark VI out of its case and swung the strap over my head and around my neck. When I was ready, the man nodded his head three times and began playing a bluesy song I knew. I'd heard "Midnight Rider" on the radio a thousand times and had often played along with it. He played the intro twice. The second time through, I played along. It wasn't a particularly difficult song to play. After a couple times through, I began improvising and embellishing around the notes from his Gibson. He closed his eyes and began to sing with a powerful, soulful voice that bore the stamp of a man who'd been marked by all of life's triumphs, failures, losses, and tragedies.

"'Well, then, let's play.'"

"But I'm not gonna let 'em catch me, no. Not gonna let 'em catch the Midnight Rider...."

While we played, a crowd gathered around us. We reached a bridge in the song where the man stopped singing. He nodded at me and just played a C major chord down to a B flat back to C major and back to B flat.

"Take it," he said softly.

I closed my eyes and let the saxophone cut loose, the notes flaring from the Mark VI like the rasping cry of uncaged birds soaring over the treeline beyond a meadow at twilight or sudden shafts of sunlight piercing through morning fog across the rippling waters of a lake. Then the Gibson's driving rhythm reasserted itself, and the man's soulful voice repeated the refrain over and over. We both stopped playing, but the voice continued, plaintive and defiant, filling the Waffle House and then dropping away to silence. The people standing in a half circle about us looked stunned. A few clapped. A middle-aged trucker wearing a baseball cap wiped tears from his eyes with a red bandana. The guitar player looked at me.

"That was better than alright," he said. I put my saxophone away and looked at the clock on the wall behind the counter. It was 1:50. I needed to get down to the bus station. I rose from my seat and reached for my wallet, but the long-haired musician stopped me.

"It's on me," he said. "You earned it."

"Thanks," I said. I reached my hand out to him. "I'm Charlie."

"My friends call me Coyotus." The man said. "Coyotus Maximus."

We shook hands, and I picked up my duffel bag and the saxophone case and walked outside. The air was warm and moist, and I wanted it to smell like honeysuckle and magnolia blossoms, but it smelled like city sewer and the astringent smell of chemicals from some nearby factory. I looked around at the deserted streets. In spite of the smell, I liked it. It felt vibrant and alive. I could see settling down in Georgia with America one day and raising a family in a farmhouse on some acres full of peach trees and pecans outside the city limits.

I got to the bus station and bought a ticket. The station was pretty well deserted except for a few exhausted-looking individuals waiting for their buses and one shady-looking character who wandered about the station. I watched him bend down and pick a cigarette butt off the floor. He made the sign of the cross over it, then put the cigarette in his pocket. Then he went over to the line of payphones and checked the coin returns to see if there was any change in them. When he was done checking the phones, he checked them again, and again, and again. After about the fourth or fifth time checking all the phones, he suddenly sank to his knees and put his hands on his head. Then he jumped to his feet and pointed a long, dirty finger at me.

"Fuck Jesus, Joseph, and Mary!" he yelled. "Fuck the Jews!"

Fortunately, I was rescued from any more of his insanity when the bus pulled up and I boarded with a couple of other passengers. I settled into a seat near the back of the bus and slept peacefully all the way to Florida. When I awoke, the bus was nearing Port St. Lucie. I'd be in Miami in a few hours. I patted my pants and felt the velvet jewelry box in the left pocket of my jeans. I thought about my late-night music session with Coyotus Maximus. The man could play guitar and sing. No doubt about it. He wasn't as good a guitar player as Danny Sheaf, but if you're gonna have your head caved in by the flying axle of a race car driven by Richard Petty, you might as well let God compensate you with a gift that few mortals have ever been given. But unlike Danny, the long-haired guy could sing better than just about anyone you might meet at a Waffle House at 1:00 am. A guy with that kind of talent could probably pick up a few extra bucks playing bars and nightclubs after working swing shift at the local lumber mill or factory canning peaches and sweet potatoes, though a few months later I saw his picture on the cover of *Rolling Stone* magazine. He and his deceased brother were super famous. His band had toured all around the world, spreading a bluesy southern rock gospel that paid homage to the common man, but I didn't know that the night I boarded that bus in Hot 'lanta. At that moment in time, I just looked out the window and thought about blue skies, sunny days, and the image of America sprawled naked across my bed as she turned her love my way.

Chapter 24 Homicide

It was nearly one in the afternoon when I got to Miami. After the bus pulled into the station, I got a cup of crappy coffee from a vending machine in the terminal. I called America from a pay phone on the wall and was pleasantly surprised that she answered.

"I'm here!" I said.

"Thank God!" said America. "I was afraid you weren't going to make it on time. It turns out we'll be leaving for Montreal sooner than I expected. We're going tonight. The coach wants us to get acclimatized to being there for two weeks. He says acclimatization is critical. The East Germans lead the world in performance-enhancing acclimatization. You wouldn't think there'd be an acclimatization gap, but apparently there is."

I patted my pocket. The ring was still there. "I can't wait to see you, America!"

"Me neither. I mean, I can wait to see me, of course, but I can't wait to see the best friend I ever had, other than some of my teammates and a couple people I've gotten real close to since being in college. But in the overall big picture of things and stuff, Charlie, you've always been on my list of the top seven or eight persons I think about when I think of random people I know!"

"You really mean that?" I asked.

"Verbatim!" America said. "Verbatim times two!"

I gave America the location of the bus station, and she said she'd pick me up.

"It's only a couple miles from here. We can have guisado in this Cuban restaurant I go to, or some fried pork dough. Maybe all three."

"You mean two," I said.

"Whatever," said America. "I'll be there in a few minutes."

I sat on one of the plastic seats that were bolted to the floor in the bus station and waited for America to pick me up. The seat was the most uncomfortable one I'd ever sat in. It was shaped in such a way that, the longer you sat, the more your body would slide down. After a couple minutes, I just stood up and read the news from a three-day-old newspaper that someone had left there. They must have left it on one of the plastic seats, and it had slid off onto the floor.

America showed up about forty-five minutes later. She was wearing flip-flops and a white cotton Cuban peasant blouse embroidered with palm trees and automatic rifles. Words were stitched in the cotton in red thread:

"Recuerda siempre la Bahía de Cochinos"

She was still Amazonian in stature. Blond, blue-eyed, statuesque. Strafe would've fallen hard for her had he ever met her. She grabbed me and squeezed me so hard I felt a rib pop. Then she kissed me on the cheek.

"You've gotten taller!" she said.

"Yeah! I'm almost six feet," I said. In reality, I was almost five-foot-ten, but since America was six-foot-four, saying that I was almost six-foot seemed better. I reached into my pocket that held the ring.

"I've got a question I want to ask you, America," I said. I was just about to pull out the velvet box when the glass door to the bus station swung open and this really tall guy with broad shoulders strode into the room. He came up alongside America and draped his arm around her shoulders. He was at least six-foot-six, was all tan and white teeth, and had the chiseled good looks of a movie star.

He was at least six-foot-six and was all tan and white teeth and had the chiseled good looks of a movie star.

"Charlie, this is my boyfriend Cooper. Cooper Bradley. That's not his real name, which, if you must know, is Rafael Santiago. Cooper is his stage name. He figured maybe he'd make more money with endorsements and maybe a movie deal and such with a legit American name."

Cooper extended his massive right hand to me. I took my hand out of my pocket and we shook. His fingers were so long that his middle finger and thumb met across the back of my hand. Our hands disengaged, and Cooper wiped his palm against his white cotton shirt.

"Don't worry. After a while you'll get used to the Miami heat and won't be so sweaty," Cooper said. "Anyway, I'm glad America's little friend from high school made the trip in person to wish her well in Montreal!"

"His father was one of the Escambray gorillas," America said.

"Gu-ree-yaas," said Cooper. "Brigade 2506."

"Whatever," said America. "Anyway, his dad spent nearly two years in jail after the revolution against the revolution until the US worked out a prisoner-for-baby-food exchange. And that's how Cooper came to Miami as an infant."

"I was nine," said Cooper. "Anyway, Charlie, we are glad you came to wish us luck!" Cooper reached into his shirt pocket and pulled out a little gift box made out of thick glossy paper. He handed it to America.

"Just a little something from me to you," Bradley said.

"Thank you, Coop!" She held the gift box in her hand. "He's always getting me presents, Charlie. Did you know that he invented the fourteen days of Valentine? Every day for the first two weeks of February, you exchange gifts, but if you don't like the gift the other person gives you, then you can just take the gift you gave him back. That's how I got this fingernail polish. I gave it to him; he didn't like it, so I took it back!"

The door to the bus terminal swung open, and a man walked into the station. He looked familiar. "Anyhow, Charlie, you had a question you wanted to ask," America said.

"Uh... yeah. I...uh... wanted to know how many medals you think you might win at the Olympics."

Before America could answer, the man who'd just entered the terminal began running toward us. He held a gun in his hand, which was leveled at Cooper. A shot rang out, and Rafael fell to the floor. Blood seeped from a bullet hole in the back of his head. There was another shot, and America fell, too. The man turned and raced out of the terminal. It had all happened so fast I hadn't had time to move. I knelt down beside America. She'd been shot in the back and was bleeding profusely but was still conscious. A security guard ran toward us and pushed me over.

"Call 911!" he shouted.

I ran over to the pay phone and dialed 911. A dispassionate voice asked what my emergency was. Curiously, I felt calm and focused. It was how I felt in high school during wrestling matches or while playing the saxophone. I gave the 911 operator the information and then hung up the phone. When I turned back to look at America, another man was staring down at the security guard who was applying pressure to America's gunshot wound. It was Elijah.

"They were DI," said Elijah. "Dirección de Inteligencia. Cuban secret police. This was probably ordered by Castro himself or the KGB, or it could be a Stasi hit to ensure the East German swimmers aren't challenged in Montreal." Elijah reached into his pocket and pulled out a business card, which he handed to me. I read the card:

US Department of Justice

Federal Bureau of Investigation

Elijah Vouvray, Agent

"FBI?" I said. "I thought you worked for a think tank."

"Cover identity. I initially thought I was the target, but a source in Havana informed me there'd be an attempt on Rafael's life." He gestured at America. "They tried to kill two birds with one stone."

"There were two bullets," I said.

"You should have stayed in the car, Charlie. I might have prevented this tragedy if I hadn't wasted time tracking you."

"I thought you were crazy."

An ambulance pulled up to the bus station doors, and two paramedics jumped out with a portable gurney, which they placed on the floor beside America. One of the EMTs covered Cooper with a sheet.

America was awake during my conversation with Elijah. "Is Rafael going to be okay?" she asked weakly.

"He's dead, Miss Lightshadow," Elijah said flatly. "Sorry for your loss."

"I can't feel my legs," said America.

"The bullet probably damaged your spine," one of the paramedics said. They rolled her onto the gurney, raised it, and then wheeled America out of the bus station and into the back of the ambulance. I felt shaky and lightheaded. A wave of nausea swept over me.

"I think I need to sit down," I said.

"The adrenaline's wearing off," said Elijah.

I sat down on one of the crappy chairs. Elijah sat down beside me and asked me questions about what I'd seen. He wrote down my answers in a little leather-bound notebook. Every so often one of us would slide down the chair and almost fall off. When he was done interviewing me, he put his notebook away and pulled out his cigarette case. He offered me one, and together we smoked in silence while we watched the police come and cordon off the area. A detective drew a chalk outline around Cooper's body while a police photographer took pictures with a camera that whirred before the automatic flash went off. The detective came over to us, and Elijah introduced himself and showed the detective his FBI shield. They talked for a few minutes, then Elijah left without saying goodbye. While a forensics team was putting Cooper into a body bag, the detective sat down and asked me the same questions that Elijah had asked. After a few minutes of slipping down the plastic seat, the detective stood up.

"I think we're done here," he said. He walked away to talk to the woman who'd been working in the ticket booth when the murder had happened.

I watched the police put the body bag on a gurney and wheel it away. The bus station was pretty quiet now. If there hadn't been a couple pools of blood in the center of the room, you'd think it was just another quiet afternoon at the station. I took several deep breaths. I wasn't feeling so shaky now. I went outside. A light summer rain was beginning to fall, and the tall palm trees outside the bus station swayed in the breeze. I watched an iguana climb halfway up one of the trees. It stopped and bobbed its head a few times. There was a sudden flash of lightning, and buckets of rain began falling from the sky. The iguana raced up the tree and hid in the palm fronds. A few seconds later, the sound of thunder cracked and boomed around me, and the hard rain continued to fall.

I hung around Miami for a few days after the shooting of America and the death of Cooper/Rafael. I got a dingy room in a motel near the hospital for two bucks a night and endured the couple in the room on one side arguing and swearing at each other at 3 am while the couple in the room on the other side spent most of their time listening to some country station out of Fort Meyers on a cheap transistor radio afflicted with severe speaker buzz. My room had a black-and-white TV that got about three stations that faded in and out depending on the wind conditions. The shooting was a big story, obviously. Journalists came from everywhere to write about it, and dozens of TV news teams set up their equipment to film.

Cooper's chalk outline was still on the bus station's bloodstained floor. Reporters even camped out at Diogenes of the Holy Lamp Hospital, where America underwent emergency surgery, but the hospital wouldn't let anyone in to see her except immediate family. I tried seeing her a couple times, but nurses sent me away as soon as I mentioned America's name. I finally just walked past the nurses' station during a shift change and wandered around the ICU until I found her room. She was asleep. She had a bunch of electrodes attached to her, and various colored liquids in plastic bags dripped into her through intravenous lines. I stood by her bedside for a couple of minutes. The gift box Cooper had given her was on the nightstand next to her bed. The glossy paper was stained with blood. I picked up the box and opened it. He'd given her a pair of half-inch colorful ceramic parrots that had been turned into earrings. All in all, maybe a pair of earrings made from a set of gnarled wisdom teeth would've been better. I shook the little parrots into my hand, laid them on the nightstand, and then threw the box in the wastebasket. I didn't want her to see the blood. Then I wrote her a short note:

America,

I will always love you.

Charlie

I put the note on a chair next to the bed and laid the little velvet box with the ring on top of the note.

As I was leaving America's room, a nurse spotted me. She was sitting at the nurses' station drinking coffee and eating a donut. She stood up as I approached and waved her arms to get my attention. She was short and stout, and her nose, cheeks, chin, and forehead were covered with patches of rosacea. "How'd you git in here?" she said. "You ain't s'posed to be in here."

"I'm leaving," I said.

"You cain't jest do whatsoever you want!"

"So I've been told."

"We got rules," she said. "You shouldn't be here breaking none of our rules!"

"You shouldn't be eating donuts," I said. "Your skin would probably clear up if you cut the sugar out of your diet."

She called a security guard to escort me out of the hospital. He was a nice guy. As he walked me toward the exit, he asked where I was from. I told him that I'd hitchhiked from Connecticut. He spoke an odd Appalachian dialect that I had difficulty deciphering.

"Yuins from Conne'tacut, huh? Ain' that somethin'? I'm from East Tennessee! My kin's all hill folk for the past two hunnert years, but I come down cuz my elder brother 'herited the farm when Pappy passed."

"I came down to see my friend, America. The girl who got shot. I saw it happen."

"'Merica, huh? Damn shame. Yuin done seen the shooting itself? Ain' that somethin'? Never know what kin' o' gom a body might traipse acrost! Nurse lady done tol' me that poor darlin' might'nt never walk a body like she useta could. The sweet milk has done turnt to blink an' clabber, ain' it?"

We got to the exit, and the security guard shook my hand.

"Well, this here's goodbye spring fella. Where yuin headin' nex'?"
"I'm not sure," I said.

"I don't think I'm going back to Connecticut."

"If'n I was fresh an' green I'd shake leg for Californy. They say it's the Golden State. A land drippin' with milk an' honey! Ever'thin' ripe, turnin', an' hummin' like bee gums in flowerin'! Anyhow, that's what this ol' boy might fix on doin' if'n I might could turn back the stars and pick jest one pair o' britches out'n the Sears wish book."

"Maybe I'll end up there," I said.

"Yuin got naught but time. Might could fiddle-foot an' such afore settin' down on t'other side o' the Jordan."

"Thanks for the advice," I said.

"I warn't much fer book larnin', but I a'ways had a passel of livin' wisdom."

The guard turned away and walked back down the corridor. I felt miserable and incomprehensibly hopeful at the same time. I walked back to the motel and grabbed my duffel bag and saxophone and headed over to the bus station. The blood of America and Cooper had been cleaned off the floor, but a small group of people stood around staring at the spot where the two had been gunned down as though they'd been somehow personally connected to the events that had transpired there. I went over to the ticket booth. The same woman who'd been there when Cooper and America were shot was behind the counter. I asked her when the next bus was leaving.

"We got a bus heading to Nawlins in seventeen minutes," she said.

I bought a ticket and then went out the side door where the bus for New Orleans was waiting. The driver was a sad-looking bespectacled older man with a long, bushy mustache that covered his mouth completely. He stowed my duffel bag and saxophone in the luggage compartment under the bus and took my ticket.

"What time do we get to New Orleans?" I asked.

"11:11," he said. I couldn't see his mouth, but his mustache trembled slightly when he spoke.

"Wow!" I said. "That's omni-mythical!"

The driver straightened up and stared at me with his sad, watery eyes. "Y'ain't gonna be a problem are you?"

"Problem? What? No."

"Good. Cause if you're gonna be a problem you can take the next bus to New Orleans at midnight. You can be that driver's problem."

I boarded and walked all the way down the aisle. A young woman about my age was seated a couple rows from the back. She was attractive, slender, and had long blonde hair and blue eyes. She glanced up at me and smiled as I passed her. I returned the smile and then moved past to the bench seat that stretched across the entire back of the bus. I caught myself thinking that had Strafe been there, he probably would've been smitten by the young blonde. He would've sat down next to her and spent the entire trip talking about himself. By the time the bus had reached The Big Easy, Strafe would've asked her for drinks, and they'd spend the night together in the French Quarter in a room overlooking Bourbon Street while I sat in the Cafe Du Monde at midnight drinking coffee with chicory and eating beignets, listening to Dixieland jazz bands out in the street playing "Sweet Georgia Brown," "Hello Dolly," and "I've Found a New Baby" until the sun came up over the Mississippi and flared the sky with a palette comprised of fire and blood.

Chapter 25 Karma

The bus trip to Miami had taken a full day. When the driver said we'd be arriving at 11:11, I assumed he meant 11:11 in the evening of the same day, not the next morning. I figured we'd head north and take 1-10 around Lake City to Tallahassee on through to Mobile on the way to New Orleans, but the bus kept traveling through Lake City into Georgia. I stood and walked up the aisle to where the young blonde woman was working a crossword puzzle in a copy of The Miami Herald.

"Excuse me, Miss, I thought this bus was going to New Orleans. Shouldn't we be heading west by now?"

The blonde put her newspaper down and looked at me with piercing blue eyes.

"You goober," she said. Her voice was like the scent of magnolia blossoms. "We're headin' to Atlanta first! Then we head down to Montgomery an' Mobile before gettin' to New Orleans. Didn't you check the schedule?"

Before I could answer, the bus lurched, and I stumbled and almost fell. The young woman moved over to the window and motioned for me to take the now-vacant seat next to her. I sat down, and the woman smiled and introduced herself.

"I'm Karma," she said. "Karma Lavelle Hamsoak."

Karma extended her right hand to me. I shook it.

"'I'm Karma," she said. "Karma Lavelle Hamsoak.'"

Her hand was surprisingly large. She had long fingers and a firm grip, but the palm was cool and dry.

"I hope I'm not too sweaty," I said.

"Well?"

"Well, what?" I asked.

"Well, silly, what's your name? Don't they teach y'all manners where you're from?" Her eyes sparkled with laughter while she spoke.

"Oh, yeah, sorry. I'm Charlie Lord. I'm from Connecticut."

"Connecticut! That's amazin'! My ex-husband was from Connecticut!"

I looked at her. She couldn't have been much older than me, and I was still a month shy of my twenty-first birthday, but she'd already been married and divorced. Karma glanced around, leaned over toward me, and whispered.

"He was the first man I ever, you know, went all the way with." She leaned back in her seat.

"We was married for four years. Can you believe it? We only did it like once ever' two weeks, and it wasn't all that great, to be honest, but I just thought that's the way sex was s'posed to be."

Karma leaned over toward me again and whispered to me in her magnolia-scented voice.

"He mostly just liked, you know, like oral stimulation. After a few years I kind of thought maybe he really didn't like girls all that much. After we divorced, I went to a bar an' asked a stranger to take me home and screw me, just to see what I'd been missin' all them years. After we did it an' he left, I just lay there a-smilin' and a-thinkin' how wonderful it was an' how really wonderful it might be to share somethin' that wonderful with someone I truly loved an' who loved me for who I truly was with all his heart an' soul an' body an' mind an' spirit with passion forever an' ever in breathless timeless eternal wonderment an' such."

Karma leaned back in her seat again. Her cheeks were flushed, and her eyes had a faraway look in them.

"Y'all like girls, Charlie? Or is every man from Connecticut like my ex?"

"I like girls," I said.

I thought of America and April. I'd loved both of them but in different ways. Maybe if I'd combined both into one person, maybe my feelings toward that one person might be like something Karma had described.

"I probably shared too much too soon, but life's too short to leave anything in the unsaid," she said. She reached into her purse and pulled out a deck of cards.

"You play gin?"

We moved to the back of the bus and played gin on the long bench seat, laying the cards down on the worn vinyl in the space between us. Karma kept score with a pencil and notepad she pulled out of her purse. It was pretty amazing. The purse wasn't particularly large, but it seemed to have anything you needed in it: books, granola bars, sunglasses, gum, tissues, lip balm, a pocket knife, a screwdriver, a pair of pliers, an orange, a camera, and several rolls of film. I wasn't carrying anything on me except my wallet and some pocket change. We played cards all the way to Macon. Karma pretty much won every game, but some of that was because her math skills were atrocious. I laughed and pointed out all her addition and subtraction mistakes on the notepad. Karma laughed, too. None of it mattered. It was just fun playing cards and laughing. We stopped playing cards when Karma shut her eyes suddenly and slumped back against the seat.

"Migraine," she said. She opened one eye, peered into her purse, and pulled out a little plastic bag with some pot and a half-smoked joint in it. She walked up a couple of rows to a seat with a window that she slid open sideways. She lit the joint and took two or three puffs, then extinguished it, returned to the back of the bus, and put the joint back in the plastic bag, which she returned to her purse.

"It's the only thing that works," she said. "I should be the poster child for the medicinal benefits o' cannabis. As soon as I feel a migraine coming on, I just smoke a tiny bit of pot, an' it goes away. My doctor wanted to use me for a study, but he's afraid we'll both get arrested."

"That's crazy," I said. "Everyone I know gets high."

"I know," Karma said. "The law is a bitch, unlike me."

"Karma's not a bitch," I said. We both laughed. Karma pulled a paperback book out of her bag, and I rested my head back against the seat. I was awakened by the sound of the bus slowly braking to a halt. I sat up and rubbed the sleep from my eyes.

"Well, look who's alive," said Karma.

The driver's voice came to us all cracked and tinny through the PA system. "'tlanta. All transfers north and west. Watch your step gettin' off the bus."

Karma and I stood up, and I followed her off the bus. She waited while the driver unloaded all the luggage from under the bus. After I'd grabbed my duffel bag and saxophone, she threw her arms around me and kissed me on the cheek.

"Goodbye, Charlie!" she said. "My auntie's picking me up here!" She turned and waved to an exceedingly stout woman standing next to a 1968 red and white Ford Falcon. I watched Karma run over to the car and embrace her aunt. They got in the car, and it wasn't until it drove away that I realized I hadn't asked Karma for her phone number or her address. I hadn't met anyone like her before, and I had been smitten by her in a way that was completely different than with America or April. I muttered several Anglo-Saxon swear words to myself as the bus driver climbed back up into his seat, put the bus in gear, and slowly pulled away. When the bus left, I wasn't particularly surprised to see I'd been dropped off at the exact same bus terminal down the street from the same Waffle House I'd been to just a few days earlier. I went into the bus station and found out that the transfer to New Orleans wouldn't be leaving for another hour or so, then I walked down the street and went into the restaurant. Louise was still serving coffee, and Percy was still seated at the counter leering at her. It was 1:15 am, and I wished Karma and I had stayed together for the rest of my journey.

Chapter 26 Faces

The night bus trip from Atlanta to New Orleans was interesting. A troupe of carny sideshow performers boarded because their own bus had broken down, and they needed to get to Montgomery for their next show. There was a strongman, a bearded lady, a couple pinheads, a drunk geek (who pretty much just slept and snored the whole way), and a man with two faces. This last performer looked normal from the front, but when he turned around, there was a face that stared at you with vacant, milky eyes that followed you around when you moved. The other performers didn't seem to like him much, and they sat together in a group near the front of the bus while he walked all the way down the aisle to where I was sitting in the back. He introduced himself to me with a pleasant smile on his front face, but when he turned to sit down, I caught a glimpse of the face on the back of his head by the dim amber light that shone from a plastic fixture mounted on the back wall above our heads. This second face had an unpleasant sneer on its lips, which twitched and quivered occasionally. If I had to put a name to the expression this second face wore, I'd have to say it was rage. After the performer sat down, his second face was hidden from my view for most of the trip, but every so often the man would turn his head to the side so that his main face could look at something, and the second face would stare at me contemptuously, as though the sight of me had unlocked some deep hatred in its soul. Then the man would turn his head to face the front or turn toward me and engage in pleasant, banal conversation about the weather, sports, or current events, and the sneering, rage-filled face would be hidden from my sight once again.

"Are you headed to Montgomery, too?" the man's front face asked me. "If you are, I can give you a free pass to one of our performances there."

"I'm headed to New Orleans," I said. "I won't be staying in Montgomery."

"Pity," said the first face. "I like making new friends. I like getting to know young men like you, having drinks with them, and learning all about their lives in this great big world of ours! I bet you have some wonderful stories to tell about your life, don't you?"

Something about the words coming from the mouth of the first face struck me as odd. I was glad that I wasn't going to Montgomery to see the carnival sideshow, although the idea of watching a man bite the head off a chicken, though horrifying, had a certain grotesque appeal for me.

"Have you ever been married?" the first face asked me in a polite, soft-spoken tone.

"No, I was going to ask a girl, but I found out she had a boyfriend. Then they both got shot," I said.

"Oh! So you do have an interesting story to tell!"

"She's a really good swimmer and was going to the Olympics to compete. Only now she can't. She may never swim or even walk again."

"It's so nice to speak with a young man who has such an interesting story! Most of the time I have to listen to him." The man gestured to the back of his head. "He whispers such terrible things to me. Dark things. Wicked things. He fills my mind with so much evil! You have no idea!"

"That's horrible," I said. I really didn't know what else to say. The man reached over and tugged on my shirt sleeve.

"Why don't you stop in Montgomery? Come to the show! I have an extra cot in my trailer you can sleep on. We can stay up all night and tell each other stories to pass the time! I'd like that, and I'm sure you'd like that, too!" The man turned away from me to open a beat-up leather bag he had on the seat beside him. When he turned, the second face glared at me with its horrid eyes and quivering lips, which opened suddenly. No words escaped, but I could plainly read the words that whispered over the lips of this face.

"Murder," it said. "Murder."

"'Murder,' it said. "Murder.'"

The man turned back to me with a ticket in his hand that he gave to me.

"It's for the show," he said with a polite smile. "Promise me you'll come. It'll be ever so much fun."

"I'll certainly think about it," I said.

"Oh, you must be my guest! I insist!"

"Well, maybe I'll come to the show," I said, "but I can't spend the night." Actually, I had no intention of going to the carnival or even getting off the bus in Montgomery. I just said that to the two-faced man to get him to stop pestering me. The front face smiled pleasantly. Then the man yawned and stretched.

"Oh my! I'm feeling a bit tired this evening. Please forgive me, my friend, but I must give in to the demands of the body for slumber!"

The man settled back in his sleep comfortably. After a few minutes, he began to snore. His head tilted over and rested against my shoulder. I pushed him away as quickly and gently as I could, and his head tilted away from me. When it did, the second face fixed me once more with its vacant stare. It opened its mouth again, and a silent whisper dropped from its quivering lips.

"Rape," it whispered. "Torture."

I stood up slowly and moved past the two-faced man as quietly as I could. I walked up the aisle and found an empty seat next to one of the pinheads. She was nice. She smiled when I approached her.

"I'm Rose," she said. "My name is Rose."

"Hello, Rose. Do you mind if I sit next to you?"

"My name is Rose," she said. She smiled and rocked back and forth and nodded her head over and over and over.

I sat down beside her. "I'm Rose," she said.

"I'm Charlie," I told her.

"My name is Rose!" She continued to smile and nod her head and rock herself back and forth and back and forth, but she only had one face. I closed my eyes, and all of my faces fell asleep.

I woke up and spent a couple of hours listening to Rose tell me her name. By the time we reached Montgomery, the sun was just beginning to rise, red and angry. The bus pulled into a rundown terminal, and the carnival folk disembarked, their long shadows dark against the white concrete sidewalks outside the terminal. The two-faced man was the last to get off the bus. He stopped by my seat and leaned over toward me.

"Well, are you coming to the show?" he asked.

I pulled the ticket out of my shirt pocket and handed it to him. "I don't think so," I said.

The two-faced man plucked the ticket from my hand, and the same rageful expression that his back face bore flickered across the face he now presented to me. Then, as swiftly as the expression had appeared, it vanished, and the man's front face was calm and full of polite smiles.

"Pity," he said. "I'll just have to give this ticket to another young man who has interesting stories to tell." The two-faced man turned away from me and headed to the exit. As he started walking down the bus steps, the terrible face on the back of his head fixed its eyes on me and whispered silently.

"America!" it said. Then they were down the steps.

I watched out the window as the two-faced man approached a young Black man about my age outside the bus terminal and began a conversation with him. He was standing in such a way that I could see the silhouette of both his faces outlined in his shadow on the concrete. I moved across the aisle to a pair of vacant seats and slid the window open.

"Don't take the ticket!" I shouted. The young man looked up at me while the two-faced man turned his front face at me and glared. The young Black man saw the face on the back of the other man's head and edged away quickly, his shadow moving swiftly behind him as though attempting to keep up.

"Don't go!" the two-faced man pleaded. "We have ever so much to talk about!"

I closed the window, and the bus pulled away from the station. I spent much of the trip from Montgomery to Mobile wondering what the sinister face had meant when it said 'America..' Was it referring to America Lightshadow, or was it referring to America, the country? And why had it said 'America' at all? I shivered in spite of the warm, humid air filling the bus. While the bus moved southwest, the sun continued to rise, and the air in the bus grew rank and stifling. A large woman wearing a hat covered with red silk flowers in the seat in front of me began fanning herself frantically with a copy of *The Montgomery Advertiser*. I leaned forward and caught some of the breeze from the newspaper. It didn't do much to cool me down, but she was wearing some jasmine-scented perfume that made the air in the bus smell a little less horrible. After a while, the woman slowed down her wild fanning, and I was able to discern the date on the newspaper's front page. It was Sunday, July 4th, 1976, the 200th year of the country's declaration of independence. In previous years I'd have celebrated the Fourth of July by watching fireworks in my hometown of Mythic, Connecticut. My father had actually put on a big display of illegal fireworks every Fourth of July until the year I was thirteen, when he tried launching a rocket ship that he had built out of sheet metal and filled with fireworks that were supposed to explode out over the mouth of the river. Unfortunately, the rocket had taken off and hit the clock tower of the First Baptist Church, which then burned to the ground. Fortunately, my father avoided doing any jail time, but he did have to make restitution to the church, which took years, and he had to promise the judge during his trial to never possess so much as a Chinese ladyfinger firecracker as long as he resided in Mythic. In spite of all that (or possibly because of all that), the Fourth of July had always been one of my favorite holidays. I began looking forward to seeing the Bicentennial of our nation's founding when I got to New Orleans.

We got to Mobile, Alabama, about twenty minutes ahead of schedule. I got off the bus and walked down to the end of the street to watch a parade go down one of the main streets. It was mostly a pretty conventional one with high school marching bands, fire trucks, and American flags, which were only outnumbered by flags of the Confederacy. There was a float depicting the ironclad Civil War ship, the CSS Tennessee, which was the last ship to surrender to Union forces during the Battle of Mobile Bay.

There was also a string band dressed in tuxedos in the morning heat and wearing blackface. I'd seen the same thing in Philadelphia at the Mummers' Parade on New Year's Day when my family visited one of my father's cousins there, but the string band in Mobile was unique in that there was a Black banjo player wearing whiteface. I didn't know whether it was a good thing or a bad thing or just a thing, but he looked happy. The band played "Bill Bailey," and it was one of the few times I could listen to the sound of the banjo without wanting to shoot the person playing it. The crowd loved it, too. Everyone waved their Confederate and American flags like crazy when the Black man in whiteface strutted by strumming a banjo. When the parade ended, I got back on the bus and continued my journey.

Chapter 27 Nawlins

The temperature was about 100 degrees with about 95 percent humidity when I got to New Orleans. I found a cheap hotel near Jackson Square where I rented a room. The room was on the fourth floor, and the wooden stairs leading from the lobby to the upper levels were rickety and coated in some greasy substance that stuck to the bottom of my shoes. I stashed my saxophone and duffel bag in my room. Then I went out to wander The Big Easy.

In spite of the heat, the city streets were full and bustling in celebration of the Bicentennial. It was all pretty crazy. It was before noon, but half the people seemed to be drunk already. Someone stopped me in the street and handed me a plastic cup filled with a green liquid.

"What is it?" I asked.

"Quinquina!" he said.

I took a sip of it. It was really bitter. "It's horrible," I said.

The man grinned.

"Pourquoi non? Why not? *Il est composé de quinine, d'eau de Chartreuse, et de grenadine*! No malaria, eh!"

He left, and I drank the rest of the quinquina, bitter though it was. Then I wandered over to a park with benches surrounding a statue of Andrew Jackson, the Hero of New Orleans, astride a horse and raising his hat in triumph. I sat on one of the benches and watched a toothless Creole man feeding pigeons. Every so often the man would throw his head back and laugh maniacally. After a few minutes of this, the man noticed me watching him.

"I come *chak jou* to feed *le pijon so yo* crap *on tèt la nan* Andrew Jackson! *Gate san*! He killed my *bon grand papa* in the *premye* war Seminole. My *grand-père* was Seminole et *nwa*. He become slave on account of *Misye* Jackson, *pa vre*?"

A pigeon landed on the head of Andrew Jackson and crapped on him unceremoniously. The man on the bench next to me shook his knees, bent over, and laughed so hard that tears streamed down his face.

Another pigeon crapped on Jackson's hat, which elicited the same response from the man next to me. I decided to get something to eat. I hadn't had any real food since about 1:30 am at the Atlanta Waffle House. I stood up and waved to the old man.

"See ya!" I said.

"*Bonjou!*"

I walked away from the park with the man's unrepressed laughter ringing in my ears. The Mississippi was only a couple hundred feet away, and there was a restaurant where I could sit and watch the river roll by. A waitress came and handed me a menu. I ordered some jambalaya, which was one of the best meals I'd ever had in my life. Then I ordered some coffee, which I drank while watching a steam paddleboat come down the river, pass me by, and dock about a hundred yards to the south of the restaurant. I watched the passengers embark and disembark from the paddleboat and thought about America. I wondered how she was doing and whether she'd gotten the ring and my note that said I'd love her forever. I thought of April and how much I missed her incandescent brilliance and those short winter afternoons while we lingered in bed and watched the shadows lengthen and deepen as the day turned to dusk. Then I thought of Karma Hamsoak and how it had been different with her than with any other woman I knew. She was attractive and smart and funny, and I cursed myself for not asking for a phone number or an address where she could be reached. *Zut alors! Modi lè sa a!*

I spent the rest of the afternoon wandering around and watching the Bicentennial celebrations. There seemed to be a band on every street corner playing jazz, ragtime, and Dixieland. It was a city unlike any I had ever been to in terms of food or language or music or smell or general overall attitude. I couldn't explain it, but everything seemed to move slower and faster at the same time, as though the city was as the river itself, only giving the appearance of moving slowly when in reality the city, like the river, reached some of its greatest depth and swiftness through the heart of the French Quarter. I walked down Bourbon Street, which smelled like fried pork, cigarette smoke, used cooking grease, stale beer, and sun-warmed piss, as the sun reached its zenith and began its slow descent out across the bends of the river as it curved from the west to writhe about the city like a giant serpent.

I went back to my hotel, lay down on my bed, and slept for an hour or two. Then I grabbed my saxophone and walked along the Mississippi and watched the moon rise up over the river in the late afternoon. I leaned up on a railing as the setting sun cast long rays of light interspersed with the shadows of buildings, docks, and boats upon the surface of the water. Everywhere I went, the air was fragrant with the scent of music drifting to me through the warm, moist air. Then it was twilight, and stars and planets came on out over the river and the city like jewels. I looked into the sky, and the first fireworks started to shoot up and explode out over the water and above me and all about the city, so that it was one continuous kaleidoscope of color and motion punctuated by the aerial explosions, the smell of gunpowder, cooling asphalt, decomposing river algae, and beneath, above it, and around it all there was the sound of jazz, like some crazy heartbeat pumping life through The Big Easy. I put the saxophone to my mouth and played "God Bless America" while fireworks went up in celebration of two hundred years for a nation born out of blood, faith, and slavery, as are all nations. Suddenly, dozens of rockets went up one after the

"I put the saxophone to my mouth and played "God Bless America" while fireworks went up in celebration of two hundred years for a nation born out of blood, faith, and slavery...."

other over the river in an orgasmic finale of exploding color and sound so loud and deep I could feel it in my chest while I spun out the final lines of the song on my sax. Then the fireworks over the river ceased except for some singular ones shot from boats out on the water or from the far shore while the half-moon rose up high over the Mississippi. I took the saxophone away from my mouth and tucked it under my arm. I thought about the events of the past week or so as I walked back to my hotel. For the first time in my life, I both loved and hated America.

I awoke the next morning about 5:30 and walked to a cafe nearby. I ordered a cup of chicory coffee, which I drank at a table still coated with powdered sugar and cocaine from the previous night's revelers.

"She put one hand on her hip while the other hand played with her bright red hair."

I got an order of beignets to eat later. While I was drinking my coffee, a young woman about my age came into the cafe. She wore heavy makeup, a short red dress, black fishnet stockings, and a pair of stiletto heels that were nearly worn out. The dress was stained, and you could see a tiny portion of bare leg through a cigarette hole in the fabric. She looked around the cafe, saw me, then came over to my table. She put one hand on her hip while the other hand played with her bright red hair. I could smell her perfume. It smelled like vinegar mixed with oranges that were starting to rot.

"I'm Jessie Belle," she said. "What's your name?"

"Charlie," I said. "Charlie Lord."

"Nice to meet you, Charlie Lord."

She extended the hand that had been buried in her red hair. Her fingers were dirty, and her nails were covered in chipped emerald green nail polish that looked like it was a month old.

"Buy me a coffee, hon?" "Okay," I said.

I got up and bought another cup of coffee. When I returned, Jessie Belle was sitting at my table. I set the coffee cup down in front of her, and she wrapped both hands around the cup. I looked at her face. She was beautiful, but a mess. Her mascara and lipstick were smeared. A single tear rolled down through the powdered makeup on her face and salted her coffee.

"Are you okay?" I asked.

"I'm fine," she said. "I truly am, hon. It's just that I got a phone call last night that my mother is really sick. She might be dying, hon, and I don't have the money for the bus ride to Omaha."

"That's terrible," I said. "I'm sorry to hear that."

"I haven't seen her in ages," the girl said. "I really want to see her before she dies. You wouldn't be able to help me out, would you, hon? I don't need much. Maybe $15. That's all, hon. I swear, just $15 so I can see my dying ma in Tulsa."

"I thought she lived in Omaha?" I said.

"She's in Tulsa right now," Jessie Belle said, "but they'll be moving her to Omaha soon so she can be next to kin."

Even though I knew I was being played, I felt sorry for her. I reached into my pocket for my wallet and fished out a ten-dollar bill and a five. Jessie Belle snatched the bills from my hand almost as soon as I'd gotten them out of my wallet and stuffed them down the front of her blouse.

"Oh, thank you so much, hon. You don't know how much your kindness means to me!"

"I'm sure your mom will be happy to see you," I said.

Jessie leaned across the table toward me. She put one of her dirty hands under her chin and parted her lips seductively.

"Can I ask you one more thing, hon? If I could ask one more teensy favor from you, I'd be ever so grateful."

"Okay," I said.

"I haven't eaten anything since yesterday at noon. You couldn't help a girl out with that, could you?"

"Sure," I said.

I opened my bag of beignets and offered one of the sugary pieces of fried dough to her, but Jessie Belle just wrinkled her nose and waved her hand.

"Not those, hon. I can get a good, solid breakfast down the street for two dollars and lunch later for another couple of bucks. Plus tips and all that comes to about ten or fifteen dollars. I just need fifteen dollars for breakfast and lunch and another five dollars for my room. If you want, I'll show you my room, hon. You're really cute. I'll show you my room and a good time, but you have to pay for my room and my breakfast and lunch first, including the tip. What do you say, hon? I'm not trying to be a pest, but you've already been so kind to me, and I'm just trying to do the right thing here. You don't want me spending the money you already gave me on breakfast and lunch, plus tips and my room, instead of going to see my dying ma in Kansas City."

I shook my head and sighed, but once again I reached into my wallet. This time I pulled out a twenty, and once again Jessie Belle snatched it and stuffed it in her bra.

"Thanks, hon, from the bottom of my heart. I don't know what I would've done if it weren't for you and your kindness! Now, I'm gonna use the lady's room and freshen up a bit before we go back to my room. It's got a nice big bed in it that don't hardly squeak at all!"

Jessie Belle stood up and walked toward the restroom. I watched her veer off before she got there and head out one of the open doors. One of her stiletto heels suddenly broke loose, and she nearly fell, but she caught herself, and without stopping to take her shoes off, she wobbled down the street strewn with the wrack and detritus of the New Orleans

Bicentennial festivities. She was as the city itself: beautiful, dirty, toxic, and full of false promise. Treacherous. Corrupt. Resilient. I watched her limp slowly east and disappear into the sun as it was rising out of the morning mist hanging over the Mississippi. It was time for me to go.

Chapter 28 Cajun Danse Macabre

I left the cafe and hitched a ride. A beat-up pickup truck pulled over, and I jumped in the cab and got a ride from a shrimper heading to Galveston for the summer season. His name was Pierre LaFleur. He was a Cajun and spoke sing-songy English sprinkled with patois French. He played fiddle at fais do-dos and had noticed my saxophone case, which is why he stopped and picked me up.

"I know de man who play de saxophone is *bon, n'est-ce pas?*" He grinned, and his face was all weather-beaten creases and gold teeth. He asked me where I was coming from, and I gave him a synopsis of my trip from Mythic to New Orleans.

"C'est incroyable!" he said. He was astonished that I'd witnessed a murder and the shooting of America, but his biggest reaction came when I told him about my visit to the Smithsonian.

"Monsieur Nixon, he liked to regard *le gros penis*, eh? *Putain de mère!"*

Pierre fell silent, and I leaned back in the seat and went away for a little bit, into that region of half-sleep where everyone and everything is jumbled together, where time and place are made of fluid shadow and the undercurrent of unremembered melodies. Then I woke, and for a brief instant, I glimpsed the entirety of that shadowy universe of my unconscious mind before it vanished entirely. I rubbed the sleep from my eyes and looked out the window at the road ahead. We were on a narrow one-lane road lined with black gum and oak trees covered with Spanish moss.

"Where are we?" I asked.

"Ah, Charles, you alive! *C'est bon*! I bring to de Beauxart. My home, *d'accord*. I want to see wife and daughter first. Then, to Galveston, *oui*."

Pierre began whistling a Cajun fiddle tune through his gold teeth as we drove down through pine thickets, cypress swamps, and bayous flowering with hibiscus, black-eyed Susans, and alligator weed. After about ten or fifteen minutes, Pierre turned down a dirt road and crossed a wooden bridge over a wide expanse of brackish bayou ringed with tall, reedy grasses and about a dozen cypress trees. I watched a fleet of pelicans launch from the trees and form a single line that dipped down toward the water, then they were behind us, and the truck slowed and rolled to a stop before a cabin in a broad meadow. To the side of the cabin was a boat dock jutting out from the bank into a slow-moving channel of dark water. On the other side of the channel, egrets and herons nested in a dense tangle of mangroves at the water's edge.

I had gotten out of the truck and looked beyond the mangroves to where the channel opened up to a sunlit crescent of still water. Pierre came and stood beside me.

"C'est bon! N'est-ce pas? Beautiful, eh?"

He walked a few dozen paces to the cabin. The door opened, and a short, stocky, brown woman with long dark hair, wide hips, bare feet, and a brilliant golden smile stood on the threshold for a moment, then stepped out onto the weathered porch. Next to her was a child of five or six holding a dirty rag doll with red hair, button eyes, and a painted smile.

Pierre ran up a pair of rickety steps and embraced his wife. Then he picked up his daughter and kissed her on the cheek. He set her back down on the porch, and she immediately tried to hide herself behind his leg. She peeked at me from behind it with a hazel eye flecked with gold.

"Charles, this is Izora, *ma belle épouse*."

"Hello," I said.

"*Bonjou*! *Bonjou*! Izora said. "You wan' du cafe?"

"C'est si bon!" Pierre responded enthusiastically.

Izora excused herself and went back into the house. Pierre bent down and picked his daughter back up. He hugged her tight to his chest.

"Fleur, say '*bonjour*' to Charles."

"*Bonjou, monsieur* Charles."

"Hello, Fleur," I said. "*Bonjour*, Fleur LaFleur."

I looked at the worn, ragged doll in her arms and realized, with a start, that the doll resembled Jessie Belle, the young woman who'd taken my money in New Orleans and had limped away with it down Bourbon Street.

"Your doll's pretty," I said. "Just don't let her near your pocketbook."

Pierre set Fleur back down on the porch, and she immediately ran into the house only to return a moment later with her mother. Izora bore a tray with a pair of bone china coffee cups filled with steaming black liquid. Pierre and I each took a cup. I took a sip of mine. It was the same delicious chicory coffee I'd had in New Orleans, but this cup was thick with molasses, too, and seasoned with nutmeg and a liberal dose of rum.

They threw a party for me that night. Even though most of their friends and neighbors were still hung over from the Fourth of July weekend, about thirty people showed up with steaming bowls of gumbo; chicken sautéed with peppers, tomatoes, garlic, and Tabasco; tureens full of stewed alligator; crawdad étouffée; shrimp creole; platters of rice filled with pork sausage, celery, paprika, and cayenne; and various moonshines distilled from rice, sorghum, molasses, condensed milk, and honey.

When everyone was done eating, the women retired to the kitchen to clean up after the meal, while the men stood around the yard talking to each other in their sing-song Cajun patois. Pierre pulled out his fiddle, another man hung a washboard about his neck, and someone else produced a pair of spoons that he began clacking between his open palm and one of his thighs. A toothless old man, about five feet tall, slid into the harness of an accordion that was nearly half his size. While they were preparing to play some Cajun tunes, a man limped over to me on a pair of crutches made from cypress branches. He extended his hand toward me. I shook it and looked at him. He was severely overweight and only had one leg. He had a bulbous nose, resembling a red roasting potato, and gin blossoms on his cheeks. He also had a chain, fastened to his waist, that was attached to the collar of a squat six-foot alligator that lumbered beside him.

"He also had a chain, fastened to his waist, that was attached to the collar of a squat six-foot alligator that lumbered beside him."

"Tiens! I am Monsieur Jacques Broussard. I got de diabetes," he said.

He offered me his hand, and I shook it, but I made sure to stay as far away from the alligator as possible. I didn't want to be walking around with one leg, or not walking around, as the case might be.

"When de wife disappeared wid de man from de agency o' de fish an' wildlife, well, dat's when de docs took my toes, den my foot, den de whole leg."

Jacques paused to mop the sweat from his forehead with a page of newspaper. Black ink from the newsprint smeared across his forehead. He took a swig from a mason jar full of a deep red liqueur full of cherries. The women came out of the house, and the band began playing a lively two-step. The women sought out their husbands, and everyone began dancing or clapping their hands to the rhythm of the music.

"De only t'ing dat stop me from de suicides was my good boy, Rollo."

Jacques pointed down to the alligator. Rollo crouched impassively by Jacques' side with his mouth wide open. An evil perfume, composed of the flesh of rotting chickens, crabs, and fish, emanated from Rollo's teeth.

"I raise Rollo from de egg. He t'inks I am his mamma. Dat's why he don't never try to take off de *autre* leg. *N'est pas vrai?*" he said, addressing Rollo.

In response, Rollo let out two bellowing coughs that echoed out over the channel of dark water. The music stopped playing, and all eyes turned to Rollo. He coughed violently one more time, and a giant ball of undigested wild pig and rodent hair, wrapped around a red plastic shoe, plopped out onto the ground in front of him. A length of half-digested bone attached to a half-digested foot poked up out of the red shoe. One of the women walked over and looked at the shoe. Her face turned white.

"*Qu'est que c'est, Jacques?*" she stammered. "I know dat shoe. It belong to Amelie! You tol' *tout le monde* she run off wid dat skinny fishery man!"

"She did!" Jacques cried. "She run off wid him!"

"Den how her shoe and bones be in Rollo's gullet, huh?"

Pierre had stopped playing fiddle and had walked over to the hairball. He poked around in it with a stick, then he reached into it. When he pulled his hand back, a gold ring with a sparkling stone gleamed between his fingers.

"Dat's Amelie's wedding ring!" said Izora.

Pierre went back into the house and brought back his shotgun. He shot Rollo in the head, then a half dozen men seized Jacques and marched the one-legged man to the house and sat him down on a woodpile on the porch. Rollo was turned over, and someone with a hunting knife sliced open his belly. A pile of half-digested bits of crab, turtle, marsh deer, rodents, and a human skull spilled out onto the ground. Then Pierre called the sheriff.

A couple of the men who had dragged Jacques to the woodpile stood on the porch with him. Every so often, one of the men would yell and point his fingers angrily at Jacques. Then the other man would slap

Jacques across his gin blossoms, then launch into a spectacular waterfall of French and English curse words. Then he'd stop swearing, and the other man would slap Jacques across his gin blossoms, too.

Before the sheriff arrived, six or seven of the men decided to take some lanterns and walk down the dirt road to Jacques's house. I went along with them. Jacques's place wasn't much more than a half mile from the LaFleur cabin. When we got there, one of the men kicked in the front door. A couple of the men ran from room to room until they found a locked freezer on the back porch. The old accordion player broke off the lock with a ball-peen hammer. Then he slowly lifted the freezer lid. I peeked over the edge of it, and the hair on my arms stood on end. A woman's head and naked torso, limbless, but for one bare leg outfitted with a red plastic shoe, lay at the bottom of the freezer. Next to her, the headless body of a man, dressed in a Department of Wildlife and Fisheries uniform, kept her frigid company.

They'd been shot numerous times, after which Jacques had taken the time to cut off the man's penis and stuff it into his faithless wife's mouth. No one spoke for several seconds. Then the accordion player closed the lid and ran a bony hand nervously through his hair.

"Sacre bleu," he whispered. *"Sacre bleu."*

It was after 2 am when the coroner finished fishing the bodies out of the freezer and the sheriff wrapped up his investigation into Amelie's death. The two men on the porch had already beaten a confession out of Jacques. He was hauled away to the parish jail in the back of an old black and white Chevy Nomad. The remaining guests departed shortly thereafter, and after the last guest was gone, I fell asleep in a chair out on the porch.

When I awoke, the sun was just rising out of the wide crescent of water beyond the mangrove trees. Someone had thrown a quilt over me while I slept, which kept some of the mosquitos off me, but I still had all sorts of bites on my face, my neck, and even my ears. Pierre was sitting cross-legged on the porch whittling a whistle from a little piece of bone he'd found in the hairball. I watched him put the whistle to his mouth and blow. It made a sound like the cooing of a mourning dove. Pierre turned to look at me.

"Maybe I t'ink dis is some of Amelie bone da way it sound so sweet an' lonesome."

"What do you think will happen to Jacques?" I asked.

"Oh, de diabetes will kill Jacques soon, *très bientôt.*"

I stood up and stretched. Down on the boat dock, Izora was just finishing up cutting thick slabs of meat from Rollo's tail. I watched her for a couple minutes and wondered whether any of the alligator stew I'd consumed the previous evening had come from one that had been fortunate enough to have been fed from Jacques' freezer. I shuddered and tried to push the idea from my mind. Pierre seemed to read my thoughts.

"You are Cajun now!" he said. "Cajun is *aujourd'hui,* right now. It is all de past and all de future rolled into dis!"

Pierre swept his hand toward Izora and Rollo's carcass. His hand kept moving, inviting me to take in the slough of dark water, the egrets nesting in the mangrove trees, the bright curve of the lagoon where the pelicans dove and rose and dove again. It was both what it was and what it was not. Pierre blew into the whistle once more, and the sweet, mournful note hung in the morning air briefly before dying out over the channel of slow-moving water.

In another hour or so, we were back in Pierre's truck heading west. We drove for a few hours or so, and then I shut my eyes and fell asleep. I was awakened sometime later when the pickup pulled onto the shoulder of the road. I looked over at Pierre, who was staring out the front window. His mouthful of gold teeth was open, and he was pointing to something up ahead. I followed his gaze and saw that a tornado was touching down in a field a few miles up ahead. It was a monster, about twice the size of the one that had carried off my Uncle Isamu. We watched it cross the freeway and move away from us at about 40 miles per hour. After about five minutes the tornado vanished beyond the flat horizon to the north.

"Ooh *la vache!*" Pierre said.

"Holy cow!"

"Mebbe you are de jinx!" he said. "I never seen a cyclone, ever, but today, ooh *la vache*!"

 "Holy cow!" I said.

We drove in silence for the next hour or so, and then Pierre pulled off the interstate in Beaumont, Texas, for gas. I tried to give Pierre a couple bucks, which he refused, so I went into the diner next to the gas station and bought coffee for both of us. There was a picnic table outside the diner where we sat and drank the coffee and ate the beignets I'd saved. Pierre had grabbed his fiddle case from the bed of the pickup and pulled the fiddle out after we'd finished eating and drinking. He spent a minute tuning it, then launched into a Cajun waltz. It was full of shuffling bow rhythms and droning strings that seemed both mournful and joyous at the same time. It was an anthem of the Cajun experience. I listened to Pierre play for a minute or two, and then I went to the pickup and brought my saxophone back to the picnic table. I had picked up enough of the melody to be able to do a serviceable job playing along, but the saxophone didn't seem to completely do justice to the tune, so I stopped playing and just listened. When Pierre was done with the tune, he put his fiddle down and grinned at me. His gold teeth flashed in the sunlight.

"Mebbe you stay, eh? You can play de fais do-do, too, huh? We find you *tres jolie* Cajun girl for make da babies, no? What you t'ink?"

I laughed and was about to answer when a scorpion with two black stripes down its back crawled up from the underside of the picnic table and scurried across it.

"Le scorpion!" said Pierre. "As I say, mebbe you are da jinx! Eh!" He flicked the scorpion off the table with the back of his hand, and I watched it hit the ground and scurry off to hide beneath some rocks at the edge of the parking lot. We packed up our instruments and loaded them in the back of the pickup. Then we headed down the road toward Galveston.

The trip west was uneventful. I was exhausted from the events of the last few days and slept for most of the trip until Pierre pulled the pickup truck into a truck stop in Houston before heading south to Galveston. I thanked him for his hospitality, and we shook hands. Then I took a cab downtown and wandered around for a few hours, but other than a couple of armadillos I saw digging up someone's front yard, the city wasn't all that interesting to me. It was hot and humid and full of all manner of stinging bugs. I ate dinner at a Tex-Mex barbecue joint, then found the interstate and hitched a ride to San Antonio, which was just as humid and full of insects as Houston, but it seemed to have a little more soul. I got a room for the night in a motel by the Alamo, which I visited the next day. It was a lot smaller than I expected. I wandered around the fort for a while and looked in some of the rooms. While I was poking around, a stocky man with Indian features stood near me, shaking his head.

"It's all a lie!" he said in Spanish-inflected English.

"What's a lie?" I asked.

"This!" he said. "This was a Mexican fort! The gringos come in and take over cause they don' wan' to follow Mexican laws and pay they taxes! It's always the same no matter where the gringos come! Such a big lie! If America invite people from other country to Nevada who don' wan' follow no rules, don't pay no taxes, then try to take over casinos and steal they money, keep slaves against the gover'ment wishes, what would you do? This is nothing but big lie! This not fight for independence! This only about most important thing for greedy gringos! Money!"

I listened to him rant for a couple more minutes then walked away. History was the lie told by those on the winning side, and most people on the side that wins don't want facts to get in the way of self-serving mythologies. I walked back to my motel and got my gear. In a few minutes, I was on the side of the road with my arm out and my thumb extended to the sky. Five hours later I was in Dealey Plaza in Dallas, standing on the spot where President Kennedy's head had been blown open like an overripe watermelon dropped onto the pavement.

Chapter 29 X

There was a white 'X' in the road that marked the spot where the assassination of one of America's presidents had taken place. While I stood staring at the 'X,' a disheveled-looking man in a grease-stained sports jacket and dirty white pants and scuffed white shoes stood on the sidewalk staring at me. He was balding, had bushy sideburns in need of a trim, and was smoking an unfiltered cigarette that he tossed into the street.

"While I stood staring at the 'X' a disheveled looking man in a grease stained sports jacket and dirty white pants and scuffed white shoes stood on the sidewalk staring at me."

"It was the CIA," he said to me and to no one in particular. "That thar 'X' markin' the spot o' Kennedy's quietus is the irony of all ironies, innit? 'X' from time outa mind has always been the symbol o' the unknown! But them motherfuckers want ever'body to think ever'thing is known about how the goddamn president of these United States was kilt. What I do know is them CIA boys done kilt him cuz he left Cuba in the lurch after they'd spent all them resources tryin' to get rid of

219

Castro, y'know. Them was the ones trained Lee Oswald to begin with an' put the second shooter on that knoll yonder."

The man pointed across the street to a little hill that had some trees and a low concrete wall attached to a pergola. I left the street and joined him on the sidewalk. The man stuck out his hand quickly and introduced himself.

"Maxwell Folger," he said, "which is funny since I never developed any taste for the stuff. Always seemed to be like drinkin' dishwater, y'know, but that's the moniker they done saddled me with."

"Charlie Lord," I said.

"That's a good name!" said Maxwell Folger. "Strong name! That's a name with character! It ain't no name that nobody can dismiss offhand, y'know. It ain't no monkey business name, that's for dang certain!"

Then for the next forty-five minutes, Maxwell Folger told me all about his 'research' into the Kennedy assassination that had led him to the inevitable conclusion that the CIA had had a hand in it.

"The first bullet missed. They say the second bullet hit the president in the back, exited his throat, went into Governor Connolly's chest, down through his right wrist, and finally ended up in the governor's thigh. Now I mighta been born at night, but I warn't born last night! Thar ain't no way in God's green creation that a bullet fired from the sixth floor o' that book depos'tory, which the Warren Commission done tol' us was traveling on an upward traject'ry, can pinball itself through fifteen layers of clothin', the president's back brace, seven layers of skin, fourteen to fifteen inches of muscle, the governor's rib, and shatter his wrist bone on the way to his thigh! Then there's the matter of the president's brain. It's disappeared! Don't nobody know where it is! Kinda convenient, don't you think? Ain't nobody nowhere can find an' do no proper f'rensics on it!"

Maxwell Folger lit a cigarette and inhaled deeply.

"Plus, them FBI marksman done tested Oswald's rifle, and they done proved, beyond a shadow of a shadow of a doubt, thar warn't no way, no how, no man, woman, nor child could've gotten off more'n two shots in 5.6 seconds, as that Zapruder film done clearly showed, with that single-shot bolt-action rifle, let alone three! Thar was three shots in 5.6 seconds! Count 'em! Thar had to be a second shooter! The laws of nature and logic dictate thar were at least one other shooter! He was up on that grassy knoll! The CIA done put him thar! An' that's why old Oswald was done for by that Ruby fella! Them CIA sons of bitches was afeared ol' Oswald would spill them beans so they hired that nightclub owner with all them ties to the Chicago mob who hated Kennedy cuz they lost all that money when the president done screwed them by backin' out on Cuba. They was gonna open up all them gamblin' casinos that was shut down after the revolution! So, it was the CIA workin' hand in glove with the Mafia to kill the president and cover it over with horseshit and murder! Everything we been told ain't nothin' but a lie! An' if'n they can kill the president of these United States of America right underneath our very nostrils and get clean away with it, well sir, we ain't no better than them Godless Russians, I tell you what!"

By this time, a middle-aged woman was standing in the street staring at the white 'X' on the pavement.

"It was the CIA done killed him," Maxwell Folger said to her and nobody in particular.

I figured it was as good a time as any to make my retreat, so I picked up my duffel bag and saxophone case and walked down the street until I found a restaurant that was open for dinner. There were about a dozen fly strips hanging from the ceiling, and you could hear the recent additions to the strips buzzing their wings as they tried to escape the glue holding them down. I ordered soup and a grilled cheese sandwich, which only had one or two hairs in it. While I was eating, a middle-aged couple came in and sat down in a booth behind me. I was midway through my meal when someone tapped me on the shoulder. It was the middle-aged man. I swiveled on my stool and looked at him.

"Say, young fella. I see by your bags you must be traveling. Am I correct in my assessment?"

"Yeah," I said. I've been traveling around for the past couple of weeks," I said.

"Well, son, I am Pastor Merlin Parson, Parson Parson, if you will, an' that there is my wife Delores, who was the one who noticed your bags. The Good Book tells us to treat strangers like they was our own kin, an' it would be an honor an' a privilege if'n you was to join us as we partake of our evenin' meal!"

I got up from my seat, went over to their booth, and sat down across from them. They seemed nice enough. They asked me questions about where I was from and how I'd come to be in Dallas and where I was heading next. I answered all their questions as best I could. Their meal came, and the pastor said a prayer. Parson Parson grabbed one of my hands, and his wife grabbed my other hand, and they asked God to bless the food and to bless me on my journeys and to bless the state of Texas and the whole of the United States and even the starving millions in China and the poor suffering souls in the Soviet Union. It was one of those prayers that went on for a couple of minutes. When the pastor was done praying, he let go of my hand, but his wife seemed a bit slow in letting go of mine. It even seemed to me that she'd intentionally slid the tips of her fingers slowly across my palm. I looked across the table at her, but her eyes were fixed on the pork chop and applesauce on her plate.

"Well, young man, what name do you go by?" Parson Parson asked me. He stuffed a healthy piece of sirloin in his mouth and moaned in satisfaction.

"I go by the name of Charlie," I said. "Charlie Lord."

"Why do you now? Isn't that somethin'. A young man named Lord! Course I know you know who the real Lord is, doncha son?"

"My father?" I said.

"That's right," the pastor said. "Your heavenly father! Our Lord an' Savior Jesus Christ, who died up on the cross for our sins, was laid in the ground for three days an' rose from the dead to redeem all mankind from sin an' folly! The everlastin' Word, who will come again on clouds o' power an' glory on the last day! That final Day of Judgment when every knee shall bend an' every head shall bow, an' every man shall proclaim him King of Kings an' Lord of Lords!"

"An' every woman, too," said Delores.

"As it is written!" said Parson Parson.

"Amen," said Delores.

"Amen to that," said the pastor. "Now what I want to know, son, is your name written in the Book o' Life so that you might spend eternity in Paradise? Or will you be cast down into the fiery pit of eternal damnation to suffer never-ending unspeakable degradations an' such until the end o' time?"

"What kind of unspeakable degradations?" I asked.

"Well, bein' as they're unspeakable, there ain't a whole lot to say on the matter," the pastor said. "Though I reckon there's sodomy with a red-hot poker."

The pastor's wife covered her ears.

"I can't bear the thought of eternal sodomy," Delores said, "'specially with no red-hot poker!"

"Mebbe havin' your guts twisted outa your belly an' eaten by all them demons down there forever an' ever!"

"I don't think I'd like that," I said.

"Course you don't, young man!" The pastor patted me on the arm, and his wife leaned across the table to me and took both my hands in hers. She wore a loose-fitting blouse that I could look down and see her ample, milky-white cleavage. I looked at the pastor.

"If'n you accept the Lord Jesus Christ into your heart this day, then when you leave behind this world o' sin, lust, greed, sloth, fornication, an' all the abominations o' the flesh upon the death and corruption of your mortal body, you shall not suffer the torments o' the eternal pit but shall be welcomed into the Kingdom o' God. A man would have to be some kind o' fool to pass up that deal!"

The pastor's wife leaned further across the table toward me. She wore a lacy bra, and the tops of her breasts were tinged with pink. She gripped my hands tightly and stared into my eyes the way April had on those long winter afternoons in her bed.

"No matter what manner o' sin or perversion you might commit for the rest o' your life, you will be forgiven, for there ain't nothin' you might do, no crime you might commit, no heinous atrocity you might perpetrate against your fellow man that can separate you from the love and saving grace o' Jesus Christ!"

Parson Parson leaned across the table toward me and whispered.

"Why, you might could even commit fornication with my wife in our sacred marriage bed while I watch from the shadows in the corner and take pictures with my Polaroid while I touch myself, but so long as you repent o' such behavior, and I repent o' mine, we shall both end up in Paradise. Ain't that right, Delores?"

"Oh, yes! Oh, yes! Yes! Yes! Yes!"

The pink flush had crept up the neck of Delores and had reached her cheeks. I would be lying if I said I hadn't found her attractive, but for some reason, I just couldn't bring myself to go home with them.

Maybe if the pastor hadn't talked about all that God and Jesus stuff and was just some regular guy who wanted me to screw his wife while he took pictures and masturbated, I might've said, "Sure," and gone on home with them, but the whole paradise and eternal damnation thing was just too far a bridge for me to cross.

"I appreciate the offer," I said, "but I just can't do that."

"Do what?" asked the pastor. "Ain't nobody asked you to do nothin'. Did they, Delores?"

Delores had let go of my hands as soon as I said I couldn't, and the pink flush slowly crept down her cheeks and neck and vanished into her blouse.

"You can't accept Jesus into your heart?" Delores asked.

"Not today," I said.

I stood up and grabbed my saxophone and bag and walked over to the register, where I paid for my meal. The girl at the cash register looked at me and then glanced over at the pastor and his wife.

"You ain't gonna screw his wife?" She covered her mouth with her hand and giggled.

"Not today," I said.

"Well, you do be one o' the first to turn them down," she said, "and they be comin' here like clockwork ev'ry week for the past year an' a half since I been workin' here."

I gave the waitress a big tip, left the restaurant, and made my way over to a freeway heading north. It was a fine afternoon. The sky was full of large, milky cumulus clouds tinged pink like the pastor's wife's breasts. I thought about walking back to the restaurant and taking them up on their offer, but a car pulled up. The passenger door opened, and a couple of attractive young women smiled at me. They looked like they could be twins even though one was white with black hair and one was Black with straight blonde hair.

"Where y'all headin'?" the driver asked.

"Paradise," I said. And that is how I ended up in Paradise Valley, Arizona, a wealthy suburb outside of Phoenix.

Chapter 30 Paradise

The girls, Kate and Cookie, were heading to Arizona State University in Tempe to begin summer cheerleading practice. It was a long trip. It took over sixteen hours to get there from Dallas. I helped pay for gas and bought a case of Lone Star beer in Fort Worth. I even drove for several hours after the girls shared a joint between them and fell asleep after giggling for about an hour. They were both tall with perfect legs and teeth, and both their fathers had good jobs. One of their dads was a lawyer who specialized in mergers and acquisitions, while the other was an executive for an oil company that drilled out in the Permian Basin. It was about six in the morning, and we'd made a pretty good dent in the case of beer. For the time being, Kate and Cookie were sitting in the front seat of the gigantic Lincoln Continental while I was seated in the back.

"My daddy says that oil is America's strength," said Kate. "We wouldn't have won World War II without all our drilling. He says we'd all be speaking German if it warn't for our precious oil."

"My daddy says that all the oil in the world's gonna run out in another 20 years," said Cookie, "and that's why we need to start producing cars that run on nucular energy, but if you ask me, I ain't driving nothing that's gonna blow up like Hiroshima."

Cookie turned around and looked at me. "How 'bout you, Mr Charlie?"

"How 'bout me what?" I asked.

"Would you drive a car that might blow up and kill you with gamma rays and plutonium and what have you?"

"I'd never drive something that might kill me with what have you," I said.

"You're funny," said Cookie. She rummaged around in her purse for a pack of Virginia Slims. "You wanna cigarette?" she asked. "I know they're girly cigarettes and all, but it's all I got."

"Sure," I said. Cookie handed me a cigarette and a book of matches.

"Every man I know smokes Marlboros," she said, "but I don't like 'em. They're too manly for me. Even the package looks masculine, don't it? All that red."

"Oh, Cookie! Don't be such a big fat liar! Everybody knows that after a couple of drinks, you'll smoke Marlboros, Winstons, Salems, Newports, anything a'tall. Heck, girl! Give you tequila, and you'll put just about anything in your mouth if you know what I mean," said Kate.

I finished my cigarette and stubbed it out in the ashtray set in the armrest on the passenger side. Then I stared out the window. We'd been on the road for about ten hours now, and the level of conversation hadn't changed all that much during the entire time we'd been driving. We were just outside of Las Cruces and still had another six hours to go. I stared out the window toward a mountain range in the distance.

Cookie turned around again and slapped me on my knee. "Them's the Organ Mountains," she said.

"You'll mount just about any ol' organ," said Kate.

"Ha-ha," said Cookie flatly. "She's just jealous, Mr Charlie, cause I'm head cheerleader."

"Giving head cheerleader," said Kate.

"Honestly," said Cookie. I don't know why I put up with you. Why do you think I put up with her, Mr Charlie? Maybe it's cuz I'm so gracious and all? My mama says that graciousness is next to godliness. Do you believe that?"

"Was that before or after your mama kicked your daddy out for sexing up the maid?" said Kate.

Cookie took off her black wig and threw it at Kate. Kate took off her blonde wig and threw it at Cookie.

"Well, she did take him back in but had to fire the maid, which was too bad. She was the only one who knew how to press pleats in any of my skirts without making a royal mess!"

I shut my eyes but wished I could shut my ears. I had nothing against Kate or Cookie, but they were products of wealth and status in a country where wealth and status were the twin currencies that bought privilege and access to power. If they continued to be lucky, they'd marry men with just enough brains and ambition to parlay the money they'd married into for successful careers in politics or finance where the rules no longer applied to them, just so long as they didn't screw over too many others who moved in the same spheres of power and influence. If Kate and Cookie's luck ran out, they'd marry some jocks without the necessary skill and/or drive to sign a contract with a major sports franchise, and the girls would live comfortable lives until the inherited money ran out. Then things would get ugly fast.

I went to sleep for a good while, into that realm of amorphic, fluid twilight where the real world unraveled into half remembrances becoming ideas becoming conversations becoming dreams becoming words becoming the idea of a car, the idea of a cactus, the idea of America, the idea of Karma. The world unmade by the word unmoored. I slept for a good couple of hours, every now and then rising near the surface, sinking back under, and waking suddenly somewhere around Willcox, about an hour and a half outside Tucson.

The girls were now wearing each other's wigs. They were giggling and drinking warm beer. It was only another couple of hours to Paradise Valley, where, truth be told, I was only going to complete the joke I'd made when Kate and Cookie had first picked me up in Dallas.

We stopped in Tucson for gas and then ate breakfast at a Waffle House just across from the gas station. I was foggy-headed from being awake most of the night, and even after sitting down at a booth in the restaurant, I felt like I was still in the back seat of the Lincoln, driving through the Texas night into the New Mexico and Arizona desert as the sun came up and baked everything outside the air-conditioned Lincoln to one thousand shades of brown while the arms of the saguaro were lifted as though in praise to Absurdity, the Lord God of all Creation.

I ordered pancakes and coffee while the girls just smoked and drank orange juice spiked with vodka from the little airline bottles they kept in their purses. When we were done, I paid the bill, and we walked outside. A lone tarantula moved slowly across the parking lot asphalt.

228

"They say they're harmless," said Cookie. "How 'bout you, Mr Charlie? Are you harmless like that tarantula over there? Just a-wanderin' 'round the highways and byways of these United States of America?"

There was a vacant lot full of fescue and wild grass adjacent to the restaurant. I watched a roadrunner emerge from beneath some mesquite and race across the parking lot. It grabbed the

"They were giggling and drinking warm beer."

tarantula in its beak, paused briefly, then raced back to the vacant lot.

"So are you the roadrunner or the tarantula?" asked Kate.

"I've never really thought about it," I said.

"Both, I guess. Both and neither. Just like everyone."

"Daddy says it's a dog-eat-dog world," said Cookie. "An' it's better to be the dog that does the eatin'."

229

We got back in the car and drove the rest of the way to Paradise Valley. The girls were about talked out now, and I felt drained and exhausted beyond words. I replayed the scene in my head of the man with the gun as he shot Cooper and America. It had happened so quickly that there was nothing I could do. It occurred to me that my life had always been one where I was neither victim nor victimizer. I had always been somewhat of an outsider, watching as life swirled about me like a cyclone, the bystander wracked by the knowledge and guilt of his innocence.

We reached Paradise Valley, and the girls dropped me off with few words. They were as exhausted as I was. It had been a long trip, and there were many more days of travel ahead.

I spent almost no time in Paradise Valley. It was probably the wealthiest town in Arizona. Fancy restaurants and hotels catered to golfers who came from all over the US to play on its courses while their spouses and children shopped in the upscale retail stores dotting the valley floor. Meanwhile, the locals, who'd made their fortunes in real estate or banking, shuttled back and forth between their offices in Scottsdale and Phoenix to their luxury homes between the Camelback and Mummy Mountains. I felt uncomfortable just being there.

I tried calling America from a phone booth outside a gas station, but the hospital said that she wasn't able to take calls, whatever that meant, so I hung up the phone and went into the gas station to use the restroom. The cashier eyeballed me seriously when I asked for the restroom key.

"Restroom's for customers only," he said.

I stepped away from the counter for a minute and looked at the magnificent selection of food items under a sign printed in an old English font: COMESTIBLE TREASURES. I decided to forgo the comestible treasure resembling a hot dog and bought a couple of candy bars and a pack of gum, the kind that had twin girls telling me to double my pleasure. Then I got the key to the restroom and read all the clever witticisms written there, which were pretty much the same content and quality as those scrawled upon the walls of public toilets today, the ones known as social media.

After that, I walked around for a bit and ate the candy bars. Then I sat on a bench outside one of those hotels that had a bunch of convention rooms that could hold several thousand people at once. I watched a police car drive past the hotel. The officer behind the wheel slowed down as he was passing and watched me through a pair of mirrored sunglasses. I decided to leave before I got a citation for loitering, trespassing, or some other violation of the local ordinances.

I slung my duffel bag over my shoulder and picked up my saxophone case, then I walked down the road through one of those neighborhoods with custom-built homes on huge lots with perfectly manicured lawns, neatly trimmed palm trees, and giant swimming pools. They were the type of homes serviced by a phalanx of underpaid maintenance men trained in the intricacies of HVAC, pool maintenance, landscaping, painting, roofing, and garage door repair. They were generally the same guys that screwed the bored wives of the men who worked in the oil, finance, tech, and pharmaceutical industries. The betrayed husbands were America's cuckolded power brokers, the ones whose self-worth dictated they work in big, phallic steel and glass office buildings where, if they were lucky, they got to screw their secretaries when they weren't screwing each other and the rest of the country.

But there was one thing I did appreciate about Paradise Valley. I had thought it was all white, but walking through that neighborhood dispelled that belief. The lawn maintenance guys all had brown skin, so I thought it was pretty great that even though the homeowners kept voting for politicians who made the most noise about kicking all the illegal immigrants out of the country, it was those very same homeowners who were so kind as to hire the illegals to keep their yards manicured and trees trimmed for wages that nearly allowed the recipients to feed, clothe, and shelter themselves and their children in some of the poorer sections of Phoenix while the homeowners and their spouses committed their rampant adulterous liaisons with their employees and their pool boys named Buffy and Chip.

I managed to get out of Paradise Valley without getting arrested or fined by catching a ride with a young couple, Benson and Artemis White, who were heading north to the Grand Canyon National Park. Like me, they'd been bouncing around the country. Mostly they'd been visiting tourist attractions like the world's largest ball of twine in

Cawker City, Kansas, that measured over eleven feet in diameter. They'd even been to my home state of Connecticut, where they spent several hours in the Cushing Brain Collection in New Haven, where over five hundred human brains filled with cancerous tumors and other diseases floated in jars. The collection had been donated to Yale by the doctor who had pioneered the field of neurosurgery. I told them about John Dillinger's humongous penis floating in a pickle jar at the Smithsonian, and like everyone else, they were fascinated by it and vowed to try to see it the next time they were in Washington.

"They don't let you see it unless you're a congressman or president or Supreme Court justice," I told them. "It's kind of sad that the common man is prohibited from looking at something that the leaders of the United States can gather round and gawk at, willy-nilly, whenever they want!"

"Maybe they'll let us in," Artemis said. "My dad is one of the biggest campaign donors to the Democrat Party, though if Jimmy Carter wins the election, we probably won't be able to see it. I don't think he's the type who would want anyone to look at someone else's penis in a jar."

"I heard that after fifty years or so, lots of things get declassified by the FBI," Benson said. "So maybe by the mid-1980s Dillinger's penis will no longer be considered a national security issue, and they'll put it on display for viewing by the average tax-paying citizen."

It was really nice talking with people who were interested in some of the same things that interested me. I told them about the murder of Cooper and the shooting of America, as well as the CIA's involvement in the assassination of John F. Kennedy, as it had been related to me by Maxwell Folger, and they listened with rapt attention.

"I knew it!" said Benson. "I bet that warmonger Lyndon Johnson was up to his eyeballs in it, too, as well as that prick, Dick Nixon."

"He visited Dillinger's penis every few months while he was president," I said.

"Tricky Dick liked looking at Dillinger's prick," said Artemis.

232

So the hours just seemed to fly by as we drove, and it seemed like we reached the Grand Canyon in no time at all. That's how it goes when the conversation is scintillating. They dropped me off by Desert View and then went off to get a campground nearby. They invited me to stay with them, but I declined the invitation. They were going to camp there that night, and then the next day they were heading to see the world's shortest highway east of Tuba City, AZ, but I wasn't planning on staying for more than the afternoon. After the Grand Canyon, I planned on getting a ride to Salt Lake City, then to Boise, then up over to Yellowstone Park. After Yellowstone, I wasn't sure where I'd go, maybe Alaska or California. I just wanted to experience as much of America as I could.

Chapter 31 The Cave and The Highway

After Benson and Artemis dropped me off, I wandered over to the Desert View Watchtower, a circular seventy-foot-tall building in stone that someone had built right on the edge of the canyon. I went up to the top floor, where a kind lady let me borrow her binoculars so I could peer out over the canyon walls. Then I walked up to the rim of the Canyon itself and gazed down into the abyss at the silver thread of the Colorado River as it serpentined its way at the bottom of the Canyon a mile beneath me.

After about ten minutes I'd seen about everything necessary to tell other people that I'd been to the Grand Canyon and had looked down at the mighty Colorado. Then I walked back to the parking lot. I was about to leave when I noticed a man standing and staring at a building a couple hundred feet or so away from the Watchtower. Part of the building was probably supposed to look like a replica of the stone watchtower, but in actuality, it looked more like the lighthouse that stood out on the point in Mythic. The man who stood there was bare-chested, had long, straggly black hair, a long, wispy beard, and wore something resembling a loincloth. Something about the man looked familiar. I stared at him for a long time, and after about a minute I realized with a start that I was looking at my Uncle Isamu, my mom's brother, who had been carried away by a tornado on my high school graduation day and presumed dead, since his body had never been recovered.

"Uncle Isamu!?" I shouted at him from across the parking lot. "Isamu, hey!"

The man in the loincloth turned and looked at me. His expression registered neither surprise, indifference, delight, nor anger. His face wore an expression of utter serenity and amused satisfaction, as though he'd known in advance that I would one day be shouting at him across a parking lot on the edge of a giant hole in the earth.

I ran across the parking lot to my uncle and hugged him. "I thought you were dead!" I said.

"Ah, nephew Charrie!" he said calmly in his heavily accented English. "How are you?"

"Everyone thinks you're dead!" I blurted.

Isamu ignored my comment and just pointed to my saxophone case. "You still have my old saxophone," he said. "So! You still pray!"

"I still play," I said, "but this is new. I threw the saxophone you gave me into the ocean after the tornado carried you off. As a gift. For you!"

Isamu seemed touched by the gesture I'd made after his disappearance. He closed his eyes and smiled.

"Where've you been all this time?" I asked. "What happened?"

Isamu opened his eyes and stared at me keenly.

"I will explain while driving to my home," he said.

He led me over to an old Chevy pickup truck from the 1950s that was blue and rust. It was missing its front hood, and the fenders were held on by machine screws, some two-by-fours, and about fifty feet of rope. He opened the passenger door for me and closed it after I got in. Then he went around to the driver's side, opened the door, and climbed in. He turned the key in the ignition, and the truck sputtered and coughed for a few seconds. Then the engine roared to life with a cloud of thick smoke. He put the machine in gear, and we drove east in silence for a few minutes. After we'd gone three or four miles, Isamu told me his story.

The tornado had picked him up and carried him away. He lost consciousness, and when he woke, he found himself in the ocean, attached by barbed wire to a wooden fence post, which kept him afloat.

Something must have hit him in the head, for he had no memory of who he was or how he'd come to find himself in the ocean. He drifted for two days and would be dead, but a fishing boat found him and brought him to a hospital on Long Island where he recuperated for several days.

"When they release me, I still not have memory. I have no money, but kind person gave me ride to New York City, where I got job as janitor in Grand Central Station. There I save money, and after nine or ten month I have enough money for truck. Then quit job and drive west.

Still no memory for long time, but slowly slowly I remember some thing. Remember restaurant by Grand Canyon. Maybe that a crue, I think. So I keep going west. Sometime stop week or two for job. Mop floor. Wash dish. Then I drive until finally I arrive here at Grand Canyon!"

"Wow," I said. "So you've been here nearly all this time?"

"When I see restaurant nearly two year ago something inside me say 'I know this place!' Then slowly memory begin return until many month pass and one day I know my name! Who I am! That is why I come back sometime to parking lot where you just find me. That was my restaurant. Mythic Righthouse!"

I stared out the window as my uncle spoke and looked at the arid landscape of the Coconino Plateau to the south of the canyon. There wasn't much vegetation, just some juniper, sagebrush, bitterbrush, and some scrubby-looking pine trees. A lone tumbleweed rolled across the road and vanished into an arroyo a couple hundred yards out on the plateau. I looked back at my uncle.

"This place where I find my old self, but I had lived for entire year as new self. It was too soon for me to return to old life of work, money, business, make deal, investment, open more franchise, speak attorney, fry jet, speak conference, and on and on like hamster wheel spin round and round and round faster, faster, faster for what? Put more money in bank? Feed ego? That is why I sometime come back to this spot to revisit old self with new eyes, new heart and mind."

By now we had driven for about forty-five minutes. The moon was already rising in the early evening sky. It was nearly full and resembled the acid-bleached skull that had come from the alligator's belly. We drove into the moon for several miles without speaking, and then Isamu turned off onto a dirt road and followed it for another couple of miles. This part of the plateau was about fifteen hundred feet above the Colorado River, and the area to the south was covered in stands of tall pine. Isamu pulled the truck over to the side of the dirt road and got out. I followed him as he walked toward the edge of the plateau. He looked down into the canyon.

"This my home!" he said.

"Where?" There weren't any buildings in sight.

Isamu said nothing, but he started walking. I grabbed my duffel bag and saxophone case and followed after him. There was a narrow path between a cluster of boulders that we squeezed between, then the path descended steeply down the side of the canyon for several hundred feet until we reached a three-foot opening in the rock wall. Isamu crawled into the hole in the wall, and I followed him, pushing my duffel bag and saxophone case ahead of me as I went. I crawled for about ten feet, and then the tunnel widened and I was able to stand. Isamu struck a match and lit a lantern that was hanging from a spike that had been hammered into the rock. When the lantern was lit, I gasped. We were in a cave about twenty feet long and fifteen feet wide. The ceiling was about a dozen feet over our heads. I looked around the cave. There was a bed made of colorful Native American blankets against the far wall behind a fire pit. To the left of the bed, a shelf, made from a couple of wooden planks and some rocks, held canned goods and some cooking utensils, beside several five-gallon buckets of water. There were a couple canisters of kerosene stashed in the cave as well as some three-gallon cans filled with gasoline by the cave entrance. Isamu lifted the lantern above his head, and the light from it shone against the wall to the right of his bed. There were pictures on the wall of bison and deer painted with charcoal and red ocher. A man with a bow ran toward them. I was astounded.

"We were in a cave about twenty feet long and fifteen feet wide."

237

"Welcome, Charrie, to my humble home!"

Isamu lit a fire in the pit. When the fire had burned down a bit, Isamu opened a can of condensed tomato soup, which he poured into a pot with some water from one of the buckets. He set the pot on the fire, and in about five minutes the soup was ready. He ladled the soup into bowls and threw a handful of crumbled crackers on top of it. Then he handed me a bowl and a spoon, and I wondered if Isamu had been the first person to stumble upon this cave since ancient Puebloans had inhabited it centuries earlier. and we ate while seated against the cave wall by the water buckets. I stared at the paintings on the opposite wall as I ate. They were probably ten thousand years old. I wondered if Isamu had been the first person to stumble upon this cave since ancient Puebloans had inhabited it centuries earlier.

After we ate, Isamu boiled some water. He washed the pot, dishes, and spoons with some of the water and used the rest to make coffee in an aluminum stovetop percolator that he put directly on the coals. We drank the coffee black with sugar that he spooned from one of several five-pound bags. Then he took a couple of rolling papers that he filled with tobacco from a leather pouch hanging from another spike. He handed one of the cigarettes to me, and we drank coffee and smoked as the light from outside the cave entrance dimmed by degrees and finally vanished.

When we had finished smoking and drinking coffee, I opened up the saxophone case and played a couple of songs to show Isamu how far I'd come since he'd first given me lessons thirteen years earlier. Isamu clapped his hands. Then I handed him the saxophone. He hadn't played since he'd given me his sax when he'd left Mythic, but he could still play well enough for me to marvel at his skill. He stopped playing after a few minutes and handed the saxophone back to me. I put the instrument back in its case and set it against the cave wall. Then I sat back. There was a flash of light that came from the cave entrance, followed ten or eleven seconds later by the sound of thunder. A couple minutes later, rain started to fall. After a while, I could tell from the noise that the rain was pouring down like crazy. The interval between the lightning and the sound of thunder was down to about four or five seconds now, but we were dry, and the cave was surprisingly warm.

Suddenly there was a flash of lightning followed immediately by the crash and boom of thunder. The sky must've opened up then, for the sound of rain was about as loud in the cave as it could be. Then there was another flash of lightning at the mouth of the cave, but this time the thunder took a couple of seconds to reach us. The sound of the rain diminished, and after a few more minutes the storm had moved on beyond us. The rain stopped, and the intervals between the lightning flashes and the thunder increased to eight or nine seconds before vanishing completely. I looked over at my uncle. He was seated cross-legged with his back against the rock wall and his eyes closed. All in all, I could see why he'd chosen this life for himself even though others, like my father, would've thought he'd gone mad. In certain ways, I envied my uncle for the life he was living.

"Do you ever think you'll find your way back to the life you left?" I asked.

Isamu opened his eyes and looked at me.

"One day," he said. "One day, I think. Maybe soon. Maybe not. For now is good to live this way. The ancient way where I can see my real self. Not the self the world tells me who I am or what I must be. This is the truth of my soul in harmony with the nature of all things."

We sat up for another hour or so talking. Then Isamu handed me a pile of blankets that were stacked up against the wall under the rock paintings. I spread them out on the floor about five feet away from the fire pit. Isamu put a couple of logs on the fire. Then he turned the wick down on the lantern so that the flame went out. I lay down on the blankets and fell asleep quickly and didn't awaken until the next morning when Isamu shook my shoulder and handed me a plate of eggs fried in lard that I ate with a couple of corn tortillas he'd heated over the fire. He'd made more coffee, which we drank while smoking another cigarette. When we were done, we rolled up our blankets and crawled out of the cave. The sun had risen above the plateau, and the river down below sparkled with mosaics of reflected light. We climbed up the path we'd taken the day before and walked between the boulders back to Isamu's truck. I got into the passenger side, and Isamu drove me back to Desert View. It was a cool, clear morning, and Isamu had put on a T-shirt above his loincloth. When we got to Desert View, a lot of people were walking to the rim of the canyon so they could take pictures. I got out of Isamu's pickup and gave him a hug. I told him I hoped to see him again, but I was just glad I got the opportunity to see him this one time.

"Maybe you find me again. Maybe not. More important, Charrie, find own self. Not one day wake up and you are who you are like house built of stick, but everyday wake up and continue be reborn each minute so that you always in present. That's what mean to find own self."

"Wait," I said.

"I don't understand!"

"Good," said Isamu. "Not understand something is better than know everything. Freedom come from not understand."

Isamu hopped back in his truck and drove away to go back to living after being dead for all those years, even those years before the tornado had carried him off. I watched him pull away in a cloud of exhaust and dust until he disappeared into the sagebrush and tumbleweeds of the Coconino Plateau. Then a car pulled up alongside me, and the passenger window rolled down. It was Artemis and Benson.

"You're still here," Artemis said.

"Yeah," I said. "I'm gonna head to Salt Lake City."

"We're going to Tuba City to see the world's shortest highway," said Benson. "Then we're headed to Kanab. We'll take you that far, anyway!"

"You bet," I said.

In a couple of hours, we hit Tuba City then wound our way east past sandstone arches, wind-sculpted buttes, and weird columns sticking up out of the desert floor like giant mittens.

"Those are called 'hoodoos,'" Benson said. "They've been shaped by wind and water for over fifty million years!"

We drove on until we came to a flat spot surrounded by buttes. A hand-painted sign informed us that the world's shortest highway was just one mile ahead. We drove on and came to an area fenced off by barbed wire. There was a sign on a locked metal gate that read, 'Honk for Admittance.' Benson honked the horn a couple times, and then we waited around. A few minutes passed, and we were about to drive away when a really old Jeep from the 1940s came around a column that had a big mushroom-shaped cap on top of it and drove up to the gate. A weather-beaten Native American dressed in dirty overalls and a New York Yankees cap got out of the Jeep and unlocked the gate for us.

"You want to see the highway?" he asked.

"Yes," Artemis answered.

"Follow me around the hoodoo," he said. He jumped back in his Jeep, and we followed him for a couple of minutes around the circular sandstone column and past an old wooden shack. Then the Jeep stopped by a butte that had a fissure carved through it by eons of wind, water, and ice. We pulled up alongside the Jeep, got out, and followed the man through the fissure. It was wide enough for Benson and Artemis to walk through side by side holding hands. I followed along behind them. From the bottom of the fissure, you could look up and see clear, bright blue sky above us. We walked for about a quarter mile or so, and when we came out the other side, we were on a wide plateau. The old man walked to the edge of the plateau and motioned us over with a hand that was even more weather-beaten than his face. We walked to the edge of the plateau and looked down, and there it was: The World's Shortest Highway.

It was down below us about seven or eight hundred feet and appeared to be made of concrete. From where we stood, it looked like a cross or an 'X' on the desert floor. The main section of the highway ran about a half mile, while the shorter section ran maybe two-thirds that distance. There was an on-ramp that started a couple hundred feet from the main portion of the road and an off-ramp that ended a couple hundred feet away from the highway, too. A traffic light had been placed where the main section of the road intersected with the shorter section. I watched the light change from green to yellow to red a couple of times. The old man crouched down and watched the lights change with us.

"From where we stood it looked like a cross or an 'X' on the desert floor.

After a couple of minutes, he stood up and motioned for us to follow him again. He led us to the east side of the plateau, where the ground sloped down gradually so that we could easily descend to the desert floor. Then we spent the next half hour or so walking up and down the highway. It was both astounding and absurd. After I'd walked both sections of the highway as well as the on and off ramps, I went up to the old man who was standing on the highway with his hands in his pockets, staring up at the traffic light.

"You built this by yourself?" I asked.

"I did," he answered.

"Why?" I asked.

"Because I could," he said. "I worked for the road department for 30 years. After I retired, I built this as a hobby. At first, it had no meaning beyond the road itself. I was doing it to occupy myself. But as the years passed and I built more of the road, I thought about the insanity of a nation that prizes possessions over people and over the natural order of things. I built this monument to absurdity on reservation land as a reminder and a warning. All of America's great endeavors have been as meaningless as this highway. We think we are moving forward as a nation, but we are only building highways that go nowhere with no real entrances or exits, only laws that tell us when we can stop or go. I'm ashamed that I worked thirty years for the road department without realizing that I was only contributing to the insanity of America."

The old man stopped talking and motioned for us to follow him again. We walked back up to the plateau and then followed him once more through the fissure in the butte. When we got to our car, Benson pulled out his wallet and asked how much our visit to the world's shortest highway had cost. The old man seemed amused by the offer.

"Why, nothing, of course. May all your travels be safe," he said. Then he climbed back into his Jeep, and we followed him around the hoodoo on out to the gate. No one spoke for ten or fifteen minutes. It was Artemis who finally broke the silence.

"Wow," she said quietly. I looked out the window and watched a plane fly over the buttes and hoodoos about thirty thousand feet above us heading west. Sunlight glinted off the fuselage, and the plane left a long streaking contrail that intersected with the contrail of another plane that had passed overhead earlier. I wondered if the passengers in the plane could look out the window and see the highway down below them in the middle of nowhere, going nowhere, just as we all are.

Chapter 32 Into the Unknown

I was standin' on the back porch o' my Uncle Newton an' Auntie Mercy's place up on top o' that ridge in DeKalb County, watchin' the sunset an' thinkin' them colors was just like a bunch o' roses all yella an' red an' pink an' or'nge an' I thought why I might could put together a collage of all them diff'rent color rose petals arranged on canvas to look jus' like that particular sunset so I jus' planned it all out in my head 'zactly how many petals I'd need on what size canvas etc etc wishin' I had my Polaroid so I could capture it but then I says well Karma y'all are just gonna have to mark it with your mind an' that's what I did I done marked it with my mind so that I might always remember how it was the same as I did with that young man Charlie Lord on the bus to Atlanta him askin' me how come the bus wasn't headin' to New Orleans when we was headin' to Atlanta first who does that who doesn't check the bus schedule before buyin' a ticket somewhere I wondered but I noticed him settin' in the back o' the bus under that tear drop shaped amber lamp on the back wall above him the light surrounding him as he looked out the window handsome I thought but maybe a bit lost there as though he was an' angel that God tol' go on back to Earth cause it ain't your time an' so he was settin' there with the light all 'round him then he was standin' alongside me in the bus askin' how come we wasn't heading west who does that an' the bus lurchin' an' that young man nearly fell so I moved on over an' motioned for him to set down beside me I could tell he was kind but lived a lot inside his head the way he would look away an' think a bit then turn 'round back to look at me before answerin' questions that light still shinin' 'round him even though he weren't sitting under no light no more I tol' him 'bout my divorce an' how my ex husband weren't no good in bed prolly cause he really didn't like girls an' after my divorce went through I went to a bar an' talked to that handsome young Black man studyin' to be a doctor at Morehouse he was a bit full of hisself cause he was gonna be a doctor like I'm s'posed to be really impressed but I asked him to take me home anyway cause I wanted to see what it was like with someone other than my ex an' didn't care if'n he was Black or not unlike lots o' folks I know goin' on about the N word an' other hurtful things even my own gran'father

I'm ashamed to say would dress hisself in Klan robes when he was young an' go up by Stone Mountain an' light them crosses I cried and cried when I found out then they go an' carve them three Confederate generals on the side o' the mountain just a few years back as though we was still fightin' the War of Northern Aggression they want to call it an' lots of folks still flyin' that damn flag with them stars and bars an' still thinkin' a man's color means somethin' even my own Uncle Newton made disparagin' remarks when Dr Martin Luther King Jr was shot an' killed an' said well Karma I never unnerstood why your own mother was marchin' in Selma an' Montgom'ry on behalf of them darkies anyway an' I run outside cryin' an' Uncle Newton I hear sayin' Mercy I don't know what's got into that girl Mercy said well the world's done changed that much's for certain so I had sex with that young Black man studyin' to be a doctor but could'n care one way or t'other if'n he was black white yellow or blue an' afterwards I knew what I'd been missin' only I wanted that with someone who wasn't tryin' to impress nobody cause he got a title in front of his name so I tol' him to go on home he was surprised he wanted to stay but I tol' him go on home cuz I got what I wanted an' so he got dressed an' left an' I lay there thinkin' how I wanted that with someone who loved me more'n he loved a title in front of his name then I meet this handsome young man on the bus an' set there talkin' 'bout ev'rything I asked if he liked girls an' how he looked at me made my heart skip two beats we moved on back to the back seat an' played gin me keepin' score all them games some o' which I prob'ly won cause addin' an' subtractin' ain't my strong suits but I'm good with apostrophes an' better with commas then I looked at him in the light an' thought he's an angel for sure only lost that light surroundin' him like he was aglowin' from the inside an' wished he would just kiss me right then an' there an' I could tell he wanted to as well but then he said whose deal now an' I said it's mine an' he says are you sure an' I says sure I'm sure cuz I marked it with my mind which was what I'd done an' he just said it back to me I marked it with my mind with this tone o' voice that was obvious he thought it were the funniest thing he ever heard an' we both broke out laughin' till the tears come to our eyes but we did'n kiss then which was a shame an' we both fell silent in that awkward way when you both are thinkin' the same thing but wantin' him to reach up an' touch my face an' I touch his illuminated as it was by that soft light then he

245

kinda pulls hisself back a bit an' the moment done passed he says you're funny an' pretty smart too he says which I am pretty gen'rally though lots of folks might not think that on account of how I talk which is altogether different than if'n I was writin' a book report requirin' proper English and 'postrophes commas and such but I think even people writin' books don't write the way they think how could you think in words I never could but in pictures like them Egyptian hi'roglyphs an' sounds an' blocks of color light an' darkness ever'thing rolled up into a ball that your mind untangles for you to speak for example when I think of love it ain't no word but somethin' stirrin' in my soul an' spirit that we give a word to love seems so small an' paltry compared to the actual experience of that thing movin' in your spirit an' soul though we say love we unnerstan' the experience of the thing even when we are not in the experience of the moment when that stirrin' is present I think maybe sometimes that stirrin' in my soul an' spirit is God passin' through me or an angel of God if you will not that I'm religious in the least cuz I ain't cuz I have yet to meet the grown man or woman who calls themself religious that I would trust within three foot of my purse all that foolishness about ever'thing in the Bible bein' true cuz it's in the Bible an' tryin' to prove their point by quotin' scripture at you as though it's God or an angel stirrin' in your spirit an' soul which I done felt with that young man on that bus all that day an' into the night headin' to Atlanta then him fallin' asleep in the darkness an' me watchin' him an' that soft light glowin' 'round him I says to myself this here's the one an' I don't even know him but I surely did inside the wordlessness of my spirit I knowed who he was an' knowed he knowed who I was like that story I read one time where man an' woman was once one perfect creation until a god cleaved them in twain for fear this perfect creation might rise up one day an' take away his might an' power creatin' by his action two parts one male an' one female from that moment forward each separated bein' that was created lookin' for the other half of themself in order to once again be made perfect whole an' complete like them Chinese drawins I seen of them things called the yan ying or such which is like some kind o' one eyed carp swimmin' 'round an' 'round each other in a little pond one dark the other light an' each of them with one eye the same color as the body o' the other carp so that each will always have a part o' themself in the other one like some dance of light an' dark spinnin'

246

about each other then we come into Atlanta an' that handsome boy was still asleep 'til I give him a nudge with my elbow an' say well look who's alive when he opened his eyes an' then I see Mercy waitin' outside the bus station an' get off the bus with the young man behind me then waitin' on him to get his bag an' musical instrument from under the bus an' standin' awkward again an' Mercy waitin' on me I says goodbye Charlie an' flung my arms about him an' give him a kiss on the cheek then away to Mercy who says we gots to go we gots to go your uncle done fell an' busted something in his hand so we gots to go an' I say oh shoot I forgot to get his address or phone number or somethin' but Mercy says O honey chile we gots to go right now an' so we left an' that young man stood starin' after me as I sat starin' out the window after him an' ever since then I feel that stirrin' in my soul an' spirit when I think of that young man an' wonder if he feels the same way then the sun begun to set down behind the hills an' I walk aroun' the porch to the front o' the house an' see the last rays o' light playin' upon them Confederate soldiers carved in the stone an' all the light in the clouds went fadin' away until it was full dusk an' the fireflies come out an' blink themself on an' off signalin' each other in the dark an' maybe for them that is the stirrin' in their soul an' spirit that experience o' God an' angels movin' through them an' all creation that hi'roglyph shinin' like a beacon throughout all the darkness an' looking westward I seen the ev'nin' star come out all bright an' lovely an' Saturn close by aglowin' with that soft yellow light of his which was a sign an' a symbol an' that stirrin' come once more like the flutterin' of wings I says to myself that's us right there in the western sky I knowed it in my heart it were a sign he said he was headin' west so it's somethin' ain't it surely an' if I never see that young man never again that'd be okay for I done seen us shinin' together up in the western sky an' so I said right then out loud Karma you best mark that with your mind an' that was what I done so I right then

"'an' looking westward I seen the ev'nin' star come out all bright an' lovely an' Saturn close by aglowin' with that soft yellow light of his which was a sign an' a symbol'"

an' there I made a wish to myself upon them evenin' stars which was actually more like a vow than a wish I done vowed that as soon as I saved myself just a bit more money from my waitressin' job at The Rebel Yell Restaurant I was gonna leave behind DeKalb County I vowed an' fly away west cuz o' the sign and symbol I done seen in the western sky so it warn't hardly a few weeks later I was huggin' my Uncle Newton and Aunt Mercy goodbye and ever'body cryin' then I was on the plane an' in the air headin' to San Diego on account o' the airline givin' special deals since they just started up service to there from Atlanta and I had a whole three seats all to myself but not too long after takin' off there was a man on the plane all dressed in a fancy suit an' necktie wearin' shiny shoes I could tell he was pretty full o' hisself an' his $7 haircut he come by my seat an' asked if he could set nex' to me so I said he could but I kep' a close eye on Mister Fancy Pants cuz there warn't no light shinin' from inside him jus' the light shinin' off his shoes but that warn't nothin' so far as I was concerned an' he starts in on where you from an' where you headed an' what was you gonna do when you got there all o' which was his attempt to seduce ol' Karma though I seen right through ever' bit o' it but still was reg'lar polite to him for the mos' part until I started seein' flashes o' light behin' my eyes an' them squiggly lines which meant I was startin' a migraine so I got up while he was in mid sentence about how much money he made an' went to the lavatory to smoke some pot which kep' the migraine from comin' on then went on back to my seat but the man warn't there no more I could see his $7 haircut up ahead a few rows talkin' with another young woman which was a relief to me so I sat an' stared out the window an' looked down into this deserted lookin' landscape with nothin' there for mile after mile after mile until suddenly there was this kinda an 'X' looking thing way down below me in the middle o' nowhere this little cross carved on the desert floor for the Lord knows what or why an' made me wonder if maybe this there was someone down there lookin' up an' wonderin' about where we was from an' where we was headin' an' what would we do once we got there but then I jus' put it out o' my mind an' then got to thinkin' that this too had to be a sign this 'X' out in the middle o' nowhere like the one I done seen from the porch out in the deepenin' sky west o' them generals carved on the face o' the mountain so that suddenly I knowed beyond the shadow of a shadow of a doubt I would meet my true love an' soulmate when I reached my destination though I can't tell you how I knowed I just accepted it on account of it was jus' too big a mystery the kind that only the Lord can know an' so I headed into the unknown with clear eyes an' humility an' wisdom.

Chapter 33 Gordon Gordon Gordon

"The problem with writing about the past is that you tend to just remember the big things, and all the little details and events that swirled about you at the time are forgotten or their significance is misunderstood or downplayed. The key to understanding the past is often in the details that seem insignificant but are really essential, but I don't mean that in the way Chekhov meant when he said if you have a gun on a table in the first chapter, it's got to go off sometime later in the story, and all the other details are irrelevant. It's precisely the irrelevant details that cause the reader to ask, 'Why is this important?' which is probably the most important question in life one can ask outside of 'Why am I here?' Meaning is what you bring to the table. They are the magic bullets for Chekhov's gun."

Gordon Gordon Gordon stopped talking and stared through the windshield at four lanes of traffic going nowhere on a sultry August evening somewhere between Pasadena and downtown Los Angeles. I had met him at a bookstore in Redlands where he was doing a reading from his latest novel, *Crybaby Angel*, which the New York Times had described as a literary tour de force and a masterwork that redefined the art of fiction. I'd really wanted to meet him when he was supposed to do that reading at Renfield and was disappointed when his visit got canceled. And now, I was sitting in the car of my favorite author, listening to him expound on the intricacies of writing.

After I'd left Benson and Artemis in Kanab, I'd caught a ride to Salt Lake City in a VW van with a Mormon couple with their five kids. Everyone was nice and polite. The kids didn't swear once, not even the oldest son, who was tall and lanky and just a couple of years younger than me. He was going to play basketball at BYU in the fall. The youngest kid was a girl about seven or eight. She was a cute kid with red hair pulled back in a ponytail. She talked the whole ride from Kanab to Salt Lake City. She even had a deck of cards that she used to show me a few magic tricks she'd learned. She was the one who asked me where I was from, where I was heading, what had I seen, whether I'd been to Paris, did I like basketball, who was I going to vote for in the next presidential election, etc, etc.

"She's been this way ever since she could talk," the oldest boy said.

"Prolly got vaccinated with a phonograph needle," the ten-year-old sister said. "I bet you don't even know who said that originally," said the red-haired girl."

"Don't know, and don't care," said her sister.

"Groucho Marx said it," the twelve-year-old brother said.

"Wasn't asking you," said red hair.

"Will you guys please be quiet?" the oldest sister said. "I'm trying to read here."

"I can count to a thousand, Mister, in Spanish," red hair said. "Wanna see me do it?"

"She's been this way ever since she could talk," the oldest boy said.

"I can seriously count to a thousand in Spanish," red hair said.

"I'm not sure I'd like you doing it seriously," I said. "Can you count to a thousand unseriously?"

"Mom! Don't let Brianna count to a thousand in Spanish again! She's annoying!"

"Guys, I'm trying to read!"

"Una, duo, tray, quartro, sinky…."

"She's always been this way."

"I can count to 5000 in Spanish, but who wants to hear that?"

"Nobody cares!"

"Daddy!"

It was a bit exhausting, but kind of refreshing to be with a group of people without the conversation revolving around sex or the consumption of controlled substances. They dropped me off in downtown Salt Lake City. The father got out of the car and shook my hand.

"You survived back there with them," he said good-naturedly. He ran his hand through his sparse hair. "Probably the reason I'm going bald."

He wrote down a number on a piece of paper and handed it to me.

"Give us a call if you run into any problems," he said. Then he got in the van and drove off while Red Hair was trying to get one of her sisters to pick a card.

I wandered around Salt Lake City for most of the day. It was nice there, though the people were maybe just a little too friendly for my taste. I'd discovered long ago that the friendliest people are usually the ones who actually want to get your money or get you to screw their wife, so I was wary the whole time I was in Mormon Mecca. I did enjoy walking around and looking at the big buildings. My favorite building was the Salt Lake Temple with its spires and all. It was pretty impressive for a religion cooked up by some guy in New York who claimed to find some golden plates written in New Egyptian by Native American Israelites and who promoted the religion through family salvation and polygamy.

As I was staring up at the Angel Moroni blowing his trumpet to announce the Second Coming of Jesus Christ, two eighteen-year-old Mormon elders approached me.

"Hello, sir, how are you today?" I turned around to see who they were talking to, but I was the only one there. They both had crew cuts and were wearing short-sleeved white shirts and black ties.

"Pretty good," I said. "Can I help you?"

"I'm Elder Berry, and this is my companion Elder Alder." They extended their hands to me, so I shook them.

"It's nice to meet you," said Elder Alder. "What is your name?"

"Charlie," I said. "Charlie Lord."

"Well, Mr Lord, what we're doing today is conducting a survey." Elder Berry pulled a sheet of paper from a binder that had about ten questions printed on it. "It only takes a few minutes to complete. We'd like to get your opinion on a few things."

"Like what?" I asked warily.

"Well, to begin with, is a close, strong family important to you?

"Sure," I said. I figured it was what they wanted me to say.

Elder Berry wrote down my answer in his binder.

"Do you feel that churches today could do more to strengthen families?" Elder Alder asked.

"Sure," I said. I wasn't sure I believed it, but it seemed like the answer that a decent person should give.

Elder Berry noted my response in his binder.

"Do you believe in God, the Creator of the Universe?" Elder Alder asked.

"You mean like one or the other or both existing at the same time?" I asked. The question seemed to confuse the two elders. They conferred for about ten seconds and then looked at me again.

"We'll just leave that blank," Elder Berry said.

"Do you accept the Bible as the word of God or as a history book?"

"I don't see why or why not," I said. This answer confused the elders again. They conferred once more and skipped down to the last question.

"Would you like to be happier than you are now? What would make you happier?"

"Well," I said. "I've been carrying this duffel bag and my saxophone case all day. I'd probably be happier if someone carried it for me."

So for the next hour and a half, Elder Berry and Elder Alder followed me around Salt Lake City, carrying my gear until I'd seen everything I'd wanted. Then they followed me to the bus station and waited while I purchased a ticket to Boise. They helped the driver load my stuff into the luggage compartment under the bus. Then I shook their hands, thanked them, and boarded the bus while they stood on the pavement staring at me as I waved to them from my seat. From that moment forward, I've always had a soft spot for Mormon missionaries and over the years have had them carry groceries, rake leaves, clean my gutters, and once I even convinced a couple of them to paint my house. I'm not sure they really wanted to, but they did it, and they did a good job, which was a credit to them and to Mormonism in general, although other than supplying me with mainly unskilled labor, I couldn't see much use in joining the church, even though the idea of polygamy had a certain appeal for me. But when I started thinking about how much two wives would cost me to maintain, I vetoed myself from ever participating in their religion other than to have the elders weed my yard when necessary.

The bus to Boise took about five hours; I slept through about half of it. It was a newer bus that didn't smell yet from 100,000 people sitting on the seats and passing gas into the seat cushions and smearing their BO all over the backrests, so I enjoyed the ride. The elders had given me a copy of the Book of Mormon when I got on the bus. I tried reading it, but every time I'd start, I'd fall asleep, so after about the fourth or fifth attempt, I just put the book aside. To be fair, my falling asleep might not have been Joseph Smith's fault for his boring translation of the Book of Mormon from New Egyptian to English. I was pretty beat from all my traveling around since leaving Mythic back in June. I'd slept mostly in cars, trucks, and buses. So I was beginning to look forward to spending a few days in Boise doing nothing. I'd enough money left to be able to get a motel room for three weeks if I wanted, but I figured a few days there would be enough to recharge my batteries before I got back on the road.

Boise was as overwhelmingly white as Salt Lake City, but the city had a lot more breweries and a giant population of Basque folk who had their own festival where everyone danced and drank and ate pintxos and tapas, paella, croquetas made from famous Idaho potatoes, chorizo sandwiches, and all sorts of other great Basque food. So I stayed in Boise for about five or six days and partied with a pretty Basque girl until her father ran me off with what appeared to be threats of mayhem and violence shouted volubly at me in a language I'm not sure even he understood. I got a motel room downtown just a few blocks from the capitol building (which looked nearly identical to the Capitol in Washington, DC, only there was no Smithsonian, so the members of

Idaho's Congress had to entertain themselves in ways that didn't include looking at a giant penis). I spent most of the day wandering up in the hills overlooking the city or walking along the Boise River, where you could look down and see wild trout suspended nearly motionless in the flowing water. While I walked, I encountered wild turkey, deer, otter, and even the occasional mink. I saw a black bear and its cub foraging for blackberries in a big patch of brambles between the river and the trail, although they ignored my presence. There was even one morning when I noticed a mountain lion up on the top of a ridge about fifty yards away, casually stalking me as if my life meant no more in the scheme of things than the life of a rabbit or woodrat. All in all, it was a great place to visit, and I left Idaho feeling a little sad and nostalgic, for the city was a throwback to a different time, as though the 1960s had never happened, and Eisenhower was still president when you could turn on the TV and no one ever said "fuck" or "shit," but it was one of those places I could never live, no matter how nostalgic it made me feel, for the world had changed, and I needed no reminders of how things once were in a mythic America that never really had existed anyway.

From Boise, I went to Wyoming and looked at bubbling pools of mud and watched a fountain of steam water shoot from a hole in the ground up 180 feet into the air. I also witnessed a drunk tourist take off his jacket and wave it at a bison like a matador, which seemed funny until the bison charged, gored him in the ass, and tossed him into a scraggly patch of wild buckwheat about twenty feet away which was better, at least, than getting drunk and trying to pet a grizzly only to find yourself getting mauled or eaten and ending up as a pile of excrement out on the Great Plains, which may or may not be better, at least, than being one of the several million people killed by the initial explosion, subsequent pyroclastic flows, and choking blankets of smoke and ash which will cover most of the country and make vast sections of the continent uninhabitable for decades after the Yellowstone Caldera erupts for the first time in over 640,000 years. I got spooked if I thought about it much, so I tried not to think about it and hitchhiked to Mt Rushmore in South Dakota so I could look at the famous faces of four dead presidents carved on the Black Hills overlooking sacred land stolen from the Sioux and turned into a tourist attraction symbolizing the ideals of freedom and democracy for nearly all Americans, except the ones whose ancestors hunted on the plains for thousands of years before white settlers arrived, or who arrived on slave ships in chains to assist white settlers in the completion of tasks beneficial to humanity everywhere like the planting, growing, and harvesting of cotton, sugar, rice, tobacco, and the leaves of the indigo plant. I hung around Mt Rushmore for a good fifteen or twenty minutes and then got a ride northwest to Billings, Montana, from a rancher with a cattle trailer heading there for a livestock auction. He dropped me off near the turnoff to the Little Bighorn Battlefield, where Custer and his men were all killed by Lakota Sioux, Cheyenne, and Arapaho warriors in less than an hour. The victors called the site of their victory the Battle of Greasy Grass. The battlefield was about a mile from the turnoff, and I walked to where a monument and a bunch of white gravestones marked the scene of Custer's death on another infamous grassy knoll. There were several people wandering about the graves when I arrived, and one man in a suit stood with his back toward me reading the names of fallen US soldiers chiseled into a granite obelisk. As I got closer to him, he turned and put a cigarette to his lips, which he lit with a silver Zippo lighter. It was FBI agent Elijah Vouvray.

"I didn't expect to see you again!" I said. "What are you doing here?" Elijah tilted his head and looked at me.

"Jesus, you're everywhere!" he said. "I'm just paying my respects to the 7th Cav. That idiot Custer got them all killed. Did you know he graduated last in his class at West Point, same as George Pickett? Pickett's Charge and Custer's Last Stand: good men were slaughtered by their stupidity."

While Elijah smoked, he told me that the man who'd shot Cooper Bradley and America had been killed by FBI agents during a shootout north of Belle Fourche, South Dakota.

"He died on the exact spot designated as the geographic center of the United States," Elijah told me. "We still don't know who he was working for, but we're leaning toward Castro, although there might be a mob connection as well."

I'd just passed through Belle Fourche a few hours earlier in the rancher's truck, and for some reason, it gave me great satisfaction to know that the person who'd shot America had been killed in the precise geographic center of the country. Elijah and I spoke for a few more minutes. Then he gave me a ride to Billings, where I hitched a ride to Spokane from the driver of a logging truck.

"Then I took a bus to Portland, Oregon, hitchhiked to Bend, and got a ride to Pasadena from a couple of rock climbers who'd been visiting Smith Rock. I spent the night in Silver Lake and then hitched a ride out here when I heard you were doing a reading!" I said.

I was out of breath by the time I finished telling Gordon Gordon Gordon about my trip through Utah, Idaho, Wyoming, South Dakota, Montana, Washington, Oregon, and California. He just nodded. I expected him to say something like, "Wow, that's really interesting!" or "Yeah, we've done a lot of crappy things in our history," but he just nodded, looked in the rearview mirror, then changed lanes so we could just be stuck in traffic one lane over.

"What I really like about your books, Mr Gordon, is your keen sense of social satire," I said. Gordon Gordon Gordon chuckled softly.

"My keen sense of social satire is bullshit!" he said. "I don't believe any of the crap my characters believe. Why would I? I'm a businessman who writes books for a living. A very good living, I might add, but how many readers do you think I'd have if I actually said or wrote what I really believe about the idiots who buy and read my books?"

The entire drive had been one disappointment after the next. I'd seen an article in the LA Times that someone had left on the counter of a diner in Glendale about Gordon Gordon Gordon reading from his new book out at a bookstore in Redlands that evening. I'd hitchhiked out there to listen to him read, then bought a copy of his book for him to sign. Afterward, I hung around and told him I'd been traveling all around the country and had even just hitchhiked seventy miles to listen to him read.

"Well, I'm heading back to L.A. tonight," he said. "If you'd like, I can give you a lift."

"Wow!" I said. "Sure!"

"Let's grab something to eat first," he said. "My treat!"

"There was an Italian restaurant half a block away from the bookstore and we went there."

There was an Italian restaurant half a block away from the bookstore, and we went there. After we were seated, a waitress brought us our menus. She couldn't have been more than fifteen or sixteen, but Gordon Gordon Gordon eyeballed her pretty hard while she was taking our orders and as she walked away from the table. The same thing happened when a couple walked into the restaurant with their thirteen-year-old daughter. Then, when we left the restaurant and walked to his big black late-model Cadillac, he turned and watched an eight-year-old walk down the street while holding the hand of her mother.

We got into his car. He talked mostly about writing, but by this point, I really wasn't interested in listening to him, though I did tell him about some of my travels and adventures, but mostly it was to hear myself put my own experiences into words in order to make sense of what I'd been through, even if there was no sense at all.

Gordon Gordon Gordon dropped me off somewhere in or around Los Angeles, then he disappeared back into the slow-moving lines of traffic. I threw *Crybaby Angel* into a trash bin outside a restaurant. I found a payphone and called the hospital where they'd taken America after the shooting, but she was no longer a patient there. I called her dormitory in Miami, but the girl who answered the phone said she'd left the university. I even called her parents, but the phone was disconnected. Then I picked up my duffel bag and saxophone case and found a freeway ramp heading south. I stuck my thumb out. After about twenty minutes, a car pulled over, and an older couple from Coronado picked me up in a white Cadillac. While the husband drove, the wife asked me where I was from, and where I was going, and what I was planning to do once I got there. I answered the first question easily enough, but the truth is that I really didn't know where I was going or what my plans for the future were. I pulled out my wallet and counted my money.

"I've got enough cash left for another week or two of travel, then I'll have to pick up a job," I said.

The woman turned around and looked at me. She smiled that smile that everyone smiles when they're about to say something they think you have never heard before in your life.

"Oh, it'll all work out," she said. "The Lord will provide."

Then she turned around and turned on the radio to some station out of Orange County that was broadcasting a sermon from something called the Crystal Cathedral. The man delivering the sermon sounded earnest enough.

"God wants you to dream big," he said. "There's no dream too big that God can't help you achieve. This ministry began with a dream of reaching a million people. Back then I thought it was a powerful big dream, but today, twenty million people around the world are reached through our television and radio ministries! Think of that! We're saving souls all over the world!"

The woman turned around and looked at me. She smiled that smile that everyone smiles when they're about to ask you for something.

"Imagine that, young man. Souls being saved all around the world. A ministry like that takes a lot of money. So many lost souls. So much money! Would you care to donate to Reverend Schuller's ministry?"

"Uh, you mean like money?" I said. "I don't have a lot left."

"Oh, don't worry about that! The Lord will provide! A good tithe is like a single mustard seed sown in a fertile field. In time, the mustard seed becomes a tree where the birds of the sky come to nest in its branches!"

We'd studied mustard plants in biology my junior year of high school. They were more like weeds than trees, and they seldom got more than three or four feet tall. I figured I better not tell the woman this since I was a guest in her car. I'd learned long ago to never disappoint anyone with facts when discussing religion or when you're trying to talk a woman into sleeping with you. Facts just start arguments that are best avoided when you're hitchhiking or trying to get laid. In any event, I opened up my wallet and pulled out a five-dollar bill, which I handed over the seat to the woman. She smiled her smile.

"Well, bless you, young man! I'll see to it that this goes to the Crystal Cathedral's ministry," she said.

She put the money into a thick envelope full of money she must've collected from dozens of other hitchhikers. We passed a sign for La Jolla, and in a short while, we came into San Diego. The car pulled over to the side of the road, and I let myself out by a boardwalk that ran the length of a sandy beach that led down to an ocean filled with glowing neon blue waves. On rare occasions, I had seen carcasses of rotting fish glowing blue on the beaches around Mythic, but I'd never seen anything like this. I stared at the waves as they crashed and painted the sand bright blue. After about ten or fifteen minutes, I walked down the boardwalk and found a bench. I tucked the duffel bag under my head as a pillow and fell asleep cradling my saxophone case in my arms. I was awakened at about 6 am by a cop who tapped me on the leg harder than necessary with his nightstick. I opened my eyes and discovered that the cop held the nightstick in his left hand and a .38 revolver in his right.

"Don't you motherfucking move a motherfucking inch, you motherfucker," he barked. "Now raise your shit-eating hands where I can see them."

I raised my shit-eating hands into the air, and the saxophone case slid off my chest and tumbled onto the ground. It nearly hit the cop's foot. He took a step back and glared at me.

"Hey, you ass-biting dog humper, I was just going to cite you for vagrancy, but now I'm going to charge you and your tittie nipples with attempted assault."

"Attempted assault?"

"Did I stutter? Did I stutter? Stutter, stutter, stutter?"

The officer started to cry. He put his gun into his holster and dropped his nightstick on the ground.

Confused, I looked at the officer's face. Even though his face was a shifting mask of weird tics and spasms, I recognized him! It was Jacoby Rossman, the kid with Tourette's I'd probably had nine or ten wrestling matches against while I was growing up in Mythic. Willy Wetmore wrote a bunch about him in that book he wrote about me. I sat up on the bench.

"Hey, Jacoby," I said. "It's me! Charlie Lord. We wrestled all the time back in Mythic!" Jacoby stopped crying. He wiped his eyes on the sleeve of his uniform.

"I'm not cut out for this butterfucking bullshit, Charlie," he said. "Pissing squid cunts."

"It's okay," I said. "Just take a few deep breaths."

After another minute or two, Jacoby calmed down enough to tell me how he'd become a cop. His mother's brother was a captain in the San Diego police force. A couple of strings had been pulled, and that's how Jacoby had gotten a job that someone with his disability should have never gotten. His tics and scatological vocalizations were always worse during moments of high stress. "I'm going to fucking quit, fucking, fucking, fucking quit and do something else," he said.

"Like what?" I asked.

Jacoby pointed across the street to a billboard where a woman in cowboy boots and some kind of weird combination swimsuit and western wear was riding on the back of a killer whale. Leather fringe hung down from a band that ran about her upper thigh. Above her, these words were written in big block letters: 'OceanWorld™ There's Always Something.'

"I'm going to get a job there, pussy face," Jacoby said. I'll clean the tanks or feed the dolphins. I don't care, as long as I don't have to talk to anyone, duck shit."

We sat on the bench for a good hour or so. By the end of that hour, Jacoby was hardly swearing, and the repetitive tics had vanished completely. We walked down the boardwalk until we found a breakfast place with cheap food and fresh coffee. I bought his meal, and we sat and talked for another hour or so. Then Jacoby looked at his watch and stood up.

"Shift's over," he said. "I'm going to give my notice as soon as I get back to the station."

I stood up and hugged Jacoby. He'd actually been one of my toughest opponents in spite of his Tourette's.

"Good luck," I said.

"Fuck your mother," he said in a voice loud enough for everyone in the restaurant to hear.

After Jacoby left, I picked up my stuff and walked back to the bench on the boardwalk. It was a beautiful morning. The morning sky was deep blue, and the sun was visible through the branches of a lone palm tree on a little hill in the distance. The water was no longer bright blue and beautiful. It looked brown and was covered in patches of yellow foam, but that didn't prevent a small crowd of surfers from paddling out and catching the four-foot waves breaking about one hundred feet from the shore. I sat back down on the bench and looked at the billboard of the woman in the cowboy boots. She was sitting in a saddle on the back of the orca, holding onto a set of reins with one hand. She was blond and beautiful, and something about her seemed familiar. Strafe would've been highly impressed by her un-Japaneseness. I decided to walk a mile or two to see one of the performances. Beyond that, I had no real plans besides hitching a ride north. Then I'd get a job somewhere when my money ran out. Once I'd saved some more money, I figured I'd head up to Seattle, then maybe Alaska.

She was sitting in a saddle on the back of the orca...."

According to a big clock above the entrance to OceanWorld, it was 11:11 am when I got there. I waited in a long line outside the whale enclosure, and then I went in and got a seat down in front of a big tank that had thick plexiglass windows in it so you could see what was going on beneath the surface of the water. While waiting for the show to start, I thought about America Lightshadow. Other than my brief visit with her before the shooting, I hadn't really seen her in over two years, and I was beginning to suspect that, just maybe, she didn't really want to see me. The thought was depressing and liberating at the same time. Unlike most people I knew, the truth was actually beginning to free me from my long-held fantasies and illusions. For the first time since the day I'd met her, I felt unshackled from the lie that America had cared for me as much as I'd cared for her.

I realized that I'd been a victim of and/or hostage to imaginary love. I'd given America my lunches in high school. I'd gone down to the pool in the school's basement and watched her workouts after my own wrestling practice. I'd even given her a ride to New London and back when she'd opted to have an abortion our senior year at Mythic High. In return, I'd gotten nothing but the indifference that I'd mistaken for love and friendship. I was just another member of the adoring public who gave her fawning praise and adulation for her prowess in chlorinated water while wearing a silicone swim cap, goggles, and a red, white, and blue nylon Speedo®. A wave of her hand, to the thousands of mortals who stood and applauded her accomplishments, was supposed to be sufficient acknowledgment from the gold medal Goddess of The American Dream. She was incapable of anything more than that. The gods are capable of anger, jealousy, vengeance, and occasional acts of kindness, but love requires two humans who have nothing but the dim light cast by the other to guide each step of their way.

While I sat ruminating about America, a couple of people sat down in the empty seats beside me. I glanced at them quickly and was startled to see Joey Shapp and Willy Wetmore smirking at me. Willy had an ace bandage wrapped around his left hand, and Joey was still wearing the mirrored sunglasses he'd worn at our high school graduation.

"What are you guys doing here?" I asked.

"I came out here for the summer," said Willy. "I tried to get a writing internship at the studio my uncle works at, but no dice. He got shitcanned for mistaking the mistress of some rich big-shot producer for an escort."

"Wow!" I said.

"Yeah, though the funny thing is that she really was an escort that my uncle had screwed before. He didn't realize she'd gone legit and was seeing the producer in the hope that he'd divorce his wife and marry her."

"A legit gold digger," I said.

"Anyhow, so I got a job for the summer as a stuntman for some movie called 'Tentacles' they're shooting here in San Diego."

"Really? Is that how you hurt your hand?" I asked.

"This?" Willy raised his hand to eye level. "Naw. Some old guy named John Huston got drunk and ran me over in a parking lot. A cop came and gave me a ticket for jaywalking. He tore it up when it turned out we knew each other. You wrestled him in high school."

"Jacoby Rossman!" I exclaimed. "He almost shot me this morning."

"He was a decent wrestler but a shitty cop," said Willy. But the movie's gonna be a blockbuster like 'Jaws.' I'm the stunt double for Henry Fonda. He doesn't even need a stunt double! He doesn't do anything in the movie! They use me just in case ol' Henry gets too hot, or has trouble walking on the beach, or just plain shits himself. Anyway, I'm putting my years of wrestling and pole vaulting to good use."

"Henry Fonda shits himself?"

Willy shrugged.

"Sure. Probably. He's old. Everyone over sixty shits himself."

Joey stood up suddenly, took off his sunglasses, and stared at the sky. I followed his gaze and saw nothing. He looked at me with wide eyes and a toothy grin.

"Trails!" he said. Then he sat down.

"Ignore him," said Willy. "He said he wanted to keep me company, which is why I let him come along, but he's done nothing but eat drugs the whole time we've been here."

"I got plenty left to sell to Hollywood celebrities," Joey said. "Gotta pay for law school somehow."

Joey pulled a joint out from his shirt pocket and put it to his lips. Willy snatched the joint from Joey's mouth.

"Idiot," Willy said. "We're in public."

Joey looked around at the crowd in the bleacher seats around the OceanWorld tank. "Really?" Joey said.

I was rescued from witnessing further acts of Joey's drug-fueled insanity by the sound of rapid-fire music suddenly blaring through about a dozen speakers set up around the tank. Ten or fifteen seconds after the music started, two dolphins raced from a tunnel at the far side of the tank. They leapt out of the water in perfect time to the music, then dove back into the water, resurfaced, and tail-walked from one end of the tank to another while the audience oohed and aahed and applauded like crazy.

While the dolphins were performing, a young woman wearing bikini briefs and a long-sleeved neoprene top came out from behind a curtain near the tunnel where the dolphins had made their entrance. She walked a quarter of the way around the tank carrying a bucket of fish. She was suntanned, and her long blonde hair was windswept and wreathed her face in sun-bleached waves. She sat down on the edge of the tank and dangled her tanned legs in the water while tossing fish to the dolphins as a reward for their performance. A slight breeze rippled over the tank while the dolphins were leaping out of the water to touch a ball suspended twelve feet above the surface. The dolphin girl reached up and pushed her long hair back over her shoulders so that her entire face was visible. It was then that I recognized the girl I'd met on the bus ride from Miami to Atlanta. It was Karma Hamsoak. I was about to look at Willy and tell him that I knew her when one of the dolphins swam over to where she was sitting. The dolphin jumped three-quarters of the way out of the pool and landed between Karma's legs. It tried humping her in time with the music. Karma managed to push the dolphin off to one side, and the dolphin rolled back into the water, but not before I, and everyone else in the OceanWorld crowd, got a good glimpse of the dolphin's long pink prehensile penis.

The music suddenly swelled to a stupendous fanfare, and both dolphins broke the surface of the water, tail-walked in place for ten seconds or so, and then they dove and disappeared back into the tunnel. Willy looked at me slyly.

"Quite the climax," he said.

"I know her," I said. "I met her on a bus. Her name's Karma."

"You know Dolphin Girl, really?"

"Yeah, we talked for about ten hours, but I forgot to get her phone number or address. I can't believe that I just saw her after running into Jacoby Rossman and you two guys."

"Trails," said Joey.

I looked back at the pool. Karma had a broom and was sweeping the deck as the crowd filed out of the bleachers. I glanced toward the exit to the left of the tank where a man in a suit and tie was casually smoking a cigarette. Elijah Vouvray, the first person I'd met when I'd set out from Mythic in search of America, met my gaze and nodded his head. Then he turned, tossed his cigarette to the ground, and exited my life for the last time. I had the sudden realization that everything in my life, each seemingly random moment and incident, my entire history, had led me to this one single moment in time. There were no accidents and no coincidences. There was only this intersection of circumstance and being. Something had tugged upon the invisible threads of destiny and coaxed them into this unlikeliest of possibilities. I opened my mouth and shouted out an acknowledgment to the incomprehensible, unfathomable, and irrational.

"Karma!"

She heard my shout about the noise of the crowd shuffling toward the exits. Our eyes met, and a new intersection of parallel lines, crossing over at some infinite junction, suddenly sprung into being. I moved out of my seat and pushed my way through the crowd to the foot of the deck surrounding the tank. Karma had dropped her broom and raced down a flight of stairs to meet me. We stood in front of the thick plexiglass windows of the tank behind which a solitary orca glided silently past us. Our bodies met, albeit separated by several millimeters of neoprene. She brought her mackerel- and squid-scented hands to my face and pulled me toward her. I drew her face toward mine with my cigarette-scented and nicotine-stained fingers. Then we kissed, which is to say we met each other with lips, tongue, desire, teeth, and tears. It was pretty much a kiss that involved the conscious disregard of our respective, repulsive fragrances, which is pretty much the defining characteristic of love and happiness, anyway. It was one of the many lessons that Karma was to teach me.

Chapter 34 Marriage

Karma and I got married on a chilly morning in March while the rain fell over the North Bay and flooded the roads from Healdsburg to Sebastopol. The ceremony was held in a courtyard inside the Hall of Justice while a witness from the county recorder's office smoked and watched with casual indifference the county deputy marriage commissioner's officiation of our marriage.

The wedding commissioner was a short, stout woman with a mullet and a pair of owlish round spectacles. She looked virtually identical to the woman who'd witnessed my marriage to Karma.

"We're doppelgangers," the witness said when I looked at her curiously after the ceremony. "But we didn't start out that way. I started out male, and I used to be taller. Her eyes were perfect. It wasn't until we'd been working together for three or four years that each of us began changing."

"That's amazing," I said.

"Yes," the commissioner agreed. "Sometimes we forget who we really are and think we're the other person. There were a couple of times when we thought we were each other, and she's performed marriage ceremonies even though she's not certified to do that."

"All rectified in short order," said the witness nonchalantly.

The marriage commissioner and her doppelganger sat down on a bench together beneath a rainbow-colored umbrella. They sat, smoked, and talked while awaiting the next couple to arrive

"The marriage commissioner and her doppelganger sat down on a bench together beneath a rainbow colored umbrella."

and complete their forthcoming nuptials. I didn't, and still don't, pretend to understand anything about them, or about anyone else I've met in my life, but understanding is life's great booby prize. I figured out long ago that the key to happiness is in accepting reality at face value, even when the currency attached to it has irony minted on one side and absurdity on the other.

After the wedding, Karma and I drove home and spent the afternoon in bed while the rain came down, and the hands on the clock revolved from morning to afternoon to evening.

"I think I liked Karma Hamsoak better'n Karma Lord," Karma told me during one of the interludes in our lovemaking.

I propped myself on an elbow and looked at her. She'd hidden half her face under the sheet and was trying not to laugh.

"I love you, Karma Lord," I said simply.

I pulled the sheet down to expose her face, neck, breasts, abdomen, and legs. I moved my eyes across her body as though they were hands and moved my hands across her body as though they were eyes and lips. There was nothing my fingertips did not see and taste. Karma parted her legs, and I entered her with everything that I was, had been, or would ever be, just as I had done half an hour earlier and half an hour earlier than that. Karma arched and pulled me into everything that she was, a burning flame of timelessness, infinite desire, and the irresistible mirror of both our souls united in wordless eternity, the oneness of the lover and the beloved in the presence of the divine. Then the entire universe moved through each of us to be released into the other, where it was to remain and be carried for the remainder of our days.

I pulled myself away, and we lay side by side while the experience of what we had shared began to slowly fade into a pale insubstantial memory of transcendence and luminous splendor.

"Wow!" said Karma. "Wow!" I said.

"I think I'ma gonna keep you 'round for another week or two," she said.

"At least a month," I said.

"Might be a stretch," Karma snickered, but I had already fallen asleep and was dreaming of comets, falling stars, and the angel that hovered over the bed wielding a sword of ice and flame, the one who bore Karma's face and wore her spirit and soul for wings and armor.

I awoke early the next morning. Karma had already gotten out of bed and was out back preparing four or five garden beds to accept the planting of tomatoes, zucchini, cucumbers, lettuce, cabbage, string beans, green peas, and pot. Fortunately, the yard was surrounded by a six-foot redwood fence, and our neighbors were far enough away to prevent them from watching the growth of Karma's migraine medication. As soon as I saw her, an erection began tenting my pajama pants. Karma's back was turned to me, so I snuck up behind her and threw my arms about her waist. Karma turned and looked at me with her bright blue eyes.

"Well, howdy, Mr Sleepyhead. 'Bout time you rose and shone!"

I could feel my erection throbbing in time with my beating heart. I wanted to pick Karma up and carry her, soil-stained and wet from the morning fog, back to the bedroom.

"I see you ain't the only thing that's risin' and shinin' this fine mornin'!" she laughed.

"Are you thinking what I'm thinking?" I asked.

"Well, if y'all ain't thinkin' we need a dog for comfort, security, and as a fit companion for the children we shall bring forth onto this here piece o' God's green earth, then I can't he'p you none."

"A dog?" I said. "Children?"

"Yessir," said Karma, "a dog and a big ol' mess o' kids!"

Karma kissed me, then took my hand and led me into the house and back to the bedroom. "If yesterday's honeymoon sex didn't take, well then, let's fix that today!" she said.

We undressed each other hurriedly. The garden soil on Karma's hands left handprints on my white T-shirt and body. She took me into her mouth, and I felt the head of my penis slip into her throat. I lay on my back and gripped the bedsheets while Karma brought me close to climax. When I could take no more, Karma climbed on top of me and lowered her hips down to meet my body. I entered her, and she shuddered and moaned. She moved her hips, slowly at first, then faster and faster until she was riding my body at full gallop. I began making involuntary grunts and groans that seemed to emanate from the absolute core of all that I was. Then Karma stiffened and flung herself forward to grab my face with her hands to kiss me passionately. I could smell the earth on her fingers and feel the dampness of her hair as it brushed across my face. The scent of the garden brought me over the edge, and I came with leg-shaking spasms and full-body shuddering laughter.

Karma slipped off of me and curled up against my side.

"I wish we could jus' bottle this an' save it for another time," she said.

"Yes," I said. "I love you, Karma. Thank you."

"I love you, Charlie Lord," Karma replied. "Now, let's get dressed an' find us a dog!"

We found us a dog outside a Safeway on Fourth Street. He was a big golden puppy in a box that said 'Puppies $10 $5.' The box contained several of his littermates and lay at the feet of a toothless man wearing a pair of fake leather cowboy boots with two left feet. I picked up the puppy and handed the man five dollars.

"That one's ten dollar, mistah."

"Your sign says five dollars," I said. The man looked at the sign.

"That ain't no puppy," he said. "That there's Gary."

"Gary?"

"Uh-huh, Gary's the reincarnation of James A. Garfield, the twentieth President of the United States.They assinated him six month after being sworn in as president."

"Assinated?"

"Yessir! I can't let Gary go for no five dollar. Wouldn't be fitting to sell him like he was just some sort of common parking lot dog, would it?"

"Pay the man," said Karma.

I gave the man another five-dollar bill. Then I pointed to the left boot on the man's right foot.

"That must hurt," I said.

"Naw! I was born with two left feet," the man said. "It don't hurt none, but I ain't no good at dancing. If'n you want, I can take off my boots an' you can take a photograph of a man with two left feet! Only five dollar!"

Even though Karma dug through her bag and pulled out a camera, I declined the man's offer to photograph his feet only because I'd given the man the last ten dollars I'd had in my wallet. In retrospect, I wish I'd photographed the man's feet, just as I wish I'd taken pictures of the people and things I'd seen on my journey coming across the country. I mean, it's not every day you meet someone with two heads, like Dr Shrewmsberg, or an alligator that coughs up a hairball containing the shoe and wedding ring of a murdered wife, or the near death of America. Sometimes people question the veracity of the accounts I've given of my visit to the world's shortest highway or the cave my uncle lived in overlooking the Grand Canyon. They've even questioned Caliban's gigantic wings that fanned the air of the hospital room as he lay dying, or the man on the bus with two faces and murder in his heart. But the truth is that most people can't see what's right in front of them. They can't see it, because they refuse to see it, and because they refuse to see the wonders in their own lives, they can't admit the miraculous wonders in the lives of others. Not until you hitchhike across the continent of your own heart and journey across the mountains, valleys, plains, and deserts of your own soul will you ever see the reality staring you right between the eyes. That knock at the door is only your life. If you invite yourself in, you finally get to see all the stuff that you've missed.

Chapter 35 Clearlake

Nine months after our marriage, Karma gave birth to our daughter, Destiny. Three years after that, our twin sons, Orion and Argo, were ushered into the world. The bag of waters was still intact about Orion's head, and the amniotic fluid swirling about him resembled tidal oceans flowing across the surface of some distant planet.

Following the birth of the twins, Karma and I moved up to Clearlake, a small town in the poorest county of the Golden State of California. I got a job playing saxophone in a band that played weddings and festivals on the weekends and around the holidays. I did occasional session work at a recording studio in Sausalito. I even toured with a band for a few years that had a couple of hits, so I had more work than I needed to not only pay all the bills but to actually sock money away for the proverbial rainy day. Once the twins were old enough to be in daycare, Karma got hired as a kindergarten teacher in the local school district. Our jobs allowed us to purchase a house on the shore of the second oldest lake in the world, where we raised our children to adulthood, watched them go off to college, marry, and start families of their own. Along the way, Gary, our big golden dog, passed and was replaced by Teller, a morose shepherd, whose intellect was only surpassed by his talent for destroying furniture. He, too, succumbed to the ravages of time, and his spot on the hearth in the lake house was taken by Sufi, then beautiful, soulful boxer, who kept Karma and me company for a dozen years, wanting nothing more than to love and be loved, until the sad day of her passing. But by then, the children were all grown and gone. Karma and I had both retired and were alone, together, for the first time since the early days of our marriage. So we went back to doing what we did several decades earlier, without the fear of pregnancy, the crying of children, the scent of skunk-sprayed dogs, or the demands of jobs to prevent us from reacquainting ourselves with that universe of desire we'd stumbled upon and taken for granted when we were young and first in love.

My only complaint was that the years seemed to rush past us with alarming rapidity. I'd awake in the morning, walk into the bathroom, and wonder where the old man, the one who stared back at me from the mirror, had come from. Internally, I still felt like a young man, one still in the prime of life. I began going to the gym in a vain attempt to reverse time's slow and corrosively etched lines across my brow and around my eyes and mouth. Karma, on the other hand, seemed ageless, like a piece of polished gemstone that was harder, purer, and more beautiful than everything else around her. And so it was that the world spun on its axis, and Karma and I spun with it.

There was a coffee shop close by. I drove there one morning in August and sat at a table outside across from Dwight Markem, a friend who wore a surgical mask to prevent him from having to breathe in the smoke from a 75,000-acre fire raging about 15 miles south of the lake. Every so often Dwight would pull down his mask and take a drag on a cigarette. A piece of star-shaped ash drifted down from the sky and landed in my coffee. From the lakeshore, across the street, came the smell of decomposing algae and thousands of dead fish rotting in the 100-degree mid-August heat. It was the morning of a total solar eclipse. I put on my solar eclipse glasses and looked up at the sky. The sun looked bright red through the thick layer of brown smoke. The eclipse had begun about half an hour earlier, and the sun was about twenty-five percent covered. Dwight Markem was happy to expound on his theories of why catastrophe was becoming the new normal.

"Global warming and chemtrails," said Dwight. "Follow the money, Charlie. This shit is real. NASA is putting lithium in the atmosphere so we won't give a shit what happens to us. Everyone, with the exception of me, are sheep."

"Is…," I said. "Everyone but you is a sheep. Agreement between subject and object."

"Whatever," said Dwight, "but I'm glad you're in agreement, Charlie. For a while there I was beginning to think you were a chemtrail denier. Global warming has killed more Jews than Adolf Hitler could have imagined. How do you think the Cubs and Cavaliers were able to win championships? Does it defy logic? Of course, it defies logic! It flies in the face of reality, man! All this smoke and ash and shit! That's all you need to know about chemtrails!" Dwight stopped talking and pulled a bag of pot out of his pants pocket. He rolled a joint and stuck it in his mouth through the side of his surgical mask.

275

"Medicine," he said. "I have chronic anxiety from all this global warming and chemtrail shit."

"Maybe NASA should put more lithium in the atmosphere," I said.

"The CIA has been seeding the clouds with LSD since the '60s," said Dwight. "You know they killed Kennedy, right?"

"So I've heard," I said. "You don't approve of real acid rain?"

Dwight took a long toke on his joint and then offered it to me.

"I'm cool," I said.

"Cool, Charlie? You should be hot! We're talking CIA. If the government's behind something, no matter how good it might be, then I don't want anything to do with it. Except healthcare. Fuck Trump!"

I left Dwight to continue his discussion of chemtrails and conspiracies with Elder Young, an eighteen-year-old missionary for the LDS church, who had walked up to us and asked if we'd be interested in participating in a brief survey. I laughed and recalled Elder Berry and Elder Alder in Salt Lake City. If I saw Elder Young again, I'd ask him to help Karma with some tree trimming.

I got into my car and drove up Lakeshore, the air ripe with the smell of smoke and dead fish. Across from the hotel, I spotted a dog that someone had shaved and tattooed. It was the sixth or seventh dog or cat I'd personally seen like this in the past month. Each had been tattooed with a scene from the New Testament along with an accompanying Bible verse. The individual responsible for this called himself St John the Tattooist, though no one knew his real identity. After finishing a tattoo, he'd set the animal free to wander the streets of the Avenues east of Highway 53. The unfortunate canine and feline recipients of the tattoos were occasionally rounded up by an officer from the Clearlake Animal Control, but since the city lacked the most basic resources to adequately deal with the problems of drugs, crime, homelessness, and poverty in town, let alone pave streets or even fill potholes, the animals would most often just live feral lives with hundreds of other strays, tattooed or not, on the streets of Clearlake.

I pulled over to the side of the road and called the dog. It may have been a pit bull, although it was difficult for me to tell since it had been freshly shaved down to its bare flesh. The dog came over to me when I knelt down and called to him. He had been tattooed on his ribs with a scene from the Crucifixion. A Bible verse was tattooed above it. "Go ye into all the world and preach the Gospel to every creature."

"He had been tattooed on his ribs with a scene from the Crucifixion."

Apparently, St John the Tattooist wanted the creatures to preach back. I opened the door to my car, and the dog dutifully climbed in. He turned around two or three times on the passenger seat, then lay down with his head on his paws and stared at me. I would take him to the animal shelter when I got the chance later in the day. I slipped on my eclipse glasses and looked up at the sun. The moon covered about half of it now. It was 9:45 in the morning, and the temperature was already 103 degrees. I took off my eclipse glasses and looked at the dog. The tattoo was relatively new. The colors were fresh and vibrant. The details were actually pretty amazing. St John the Tattooist had taken Mantegna's tempera painting of

Calvary as his inspiration. Christ hung from a cross between two thieves. Roman soldiers threw dice at the foot of the cross. Three different women named Mary wept and prayed, and in the distance on a hill, beneath a cloud-filled blue gradient of sky lending perspective to the tattoo, a vast city of stone buildings and towers had been etched on the dog's body in white ink. The overall effect was stunningly beautiful. I put my hand on the dog's head and patted him. He responded by licking my hand. I decided to name the dog 'Cavalry.'

I started my car and headed back up Lakeshore. Just beyond the intersection of Old Highway 53, a shaved cat, tattooed with an image of Christ entering Jerusalem on the back of a donkey, ran in front of my car. I had to slam on the brakes to keep from hitting it. The cat ran behind a Taco Bell and disappeared up an embankment. I pulled over to the shoulder of the road. It occurred to me that "Awake My Soul," a Mumford and Sons song, was just about to come on the radio, but I purposely left the radio off. I no longer needed to actually hear the song to know that it was playing. I just accepted this little prophetic gift as a given. As long as I didn't think about it too much or intentionally try to use it for my own benefit, the gift stayed around, hiding within me in plain sight.

I put my eclipse glasses back on and looked at the sun through them. Two-thirds of the sun was now covered by the moon. I took the glasses off and looked at the evangelical dog. Cavalry was sound asleep and dreaming, apparently, his feet making little spastic running motions, and muted howls and barks came from his throat. I decided to drive back down Lakeshore to the post office on Olympic Drive. I hadn't picked up mail in over a week, and there was probably a residual check or two waiting for me. Back in the 80s, I'd played saxophone for a blues rock band that had a couple of hit singles and one gold album. Stations across the country still played the songs, and you could also hear them on all the streaming music platforms. I'd inherited a little money when my parents passed away, so financially Karma and I were in great shape. I'd reconciled with my parents soon after settling in California, but it took me years to overcome the guilt and grief I'd felt at their passing. I had left Mythic all those years earlier, and other than returning for their funerals, I'd only visited them a couple of times.

278

On the way to the post office, I passed Austin Park Beach. The beach was right next to the roadway, and thousands of dead fish were floating in the water or had washed up onto the shore. The smell was horrendous, but in spite of this, there was a small gathering in the middle of the beach. There seemed to be some type of beauty pageant being held there amid the stinking piles of decaying algae and rotting fish carcasses. I decided to stop and see what was going on. I pulled into the shade beneath a mulberry tree. Cavalry woke up. He yawned and stretched, then hopped out of the car when I opened his door. He followed me down to the beach where a guy sitting in a beach chair wearing a conical braided straw hat was giving instructions to a lineup of exactly one beauty contestant through a bullhorn.

"OK, contestant! I want you to turn around for the judges!" I looked around me. It appeared that he was the only judge of a beauty competition that had one contestant and only about four or five onlookers. Cavalry walked off to sniff the carcass of a carp. I looked at the contestant. She was one of the largest women I'd ever seen: 6-foot-4, at least, blonde hair with silver streaks. She wore a one-piece polka dot bathing suit over a black t-shirt, jeans, and black leather boots with white laces that came midway up her calves. She must've been at least 65 years old, but even at her age, she was breathtaking. Solid bronze direct from the studio of some statue maker in ancient Greece. Over forty years had passed since the last time I'd seen America Lightshadow, but I recognized her the instant I saw her face.

I spent the next hour or so with America. The bullet had nicked her spine, but after extensive physical therapy, she'd been able to walk again, although her days as a competitive swimmer were over. We went across the street away from the park and stood in the shade of a gazebo under some big oak trees. Cavalry lay down by our feet. America regarded the dog with revulsion.

"Only you'd have a dog like this," she said. "It's repellent. The idea of this dog is utterly repellent to me as an American."

America scratched the head of one of the thieves. The sun was nearly fully eclipsed now, and the park was quiet and still. In the growing darkness, you could look across the lake and see the sky to the south painted with fire.

"Back in the eighties I got a job as an assistant swim coach at UCLA," she said. "OOKLA. After a few years, I parlayed that into a head coaching position at Stanford, which didn't pay all that great. I got tired of working for peanuts. That's when I got involved with Ameraway."

"Ameraway? Isn't that a pyramid scheme?"

"That's a common misconception," America said. "It's actually a three-legged, dual-faceted marketing exchange. It's dual-faceted."

"Double-faced," I said.

"Absolutely. Anyway, I make a million per year from Ameraway when you include the influencer bonuses I get from my online motivational speeches. Plus, they gave me a pink motorcycle for being a top producer."

"'Plus, they gave me a pink motorcycle for being a top producer.'"

"You have a motorcycle?"

"Harley," she said. "2020 Road King. I take it on all my long road trips. I'm certified Iron Butt." "Iron Butt?"

"A thousand miles in under 24 hours. My back hurts sometimes when I ride for a long time, but a little ibuprofen, and I'm good to go."

The sun was fully eclipsed now. I looked at it through my dark glasses and watched the bright coronal gases extend out from behind the moon's black disk. I took the glasses off. The stars were out, and everything was eerily still. In the darkness, I could see a fire tornado rising ominously toward the sky from the south. We sat in the gazebo without speaking, now. There was nothing in me resembling desire or passion. America had always been about achievement that she could turn into financial success. She spoke about things, not ideas, and there was nothing of value that I could offer her or that she could offer me. The moon began moving away from the sun, and light began returning to the world. I walked America back to the fish- and algae-covered lakefront. As she was putting on a pink replica WWII German helmet with bolts sticking out of the sides of it, I noticed that she was wearing the ring I'd given her, the one containing the synthetic diamond made out of April Tyler's remains, about her neck on a silver chain. She noticed me looking at it.

"It was the last thing Cooper ever gave me," she said. "When I awoke in the hospital after getting shot, I found it on the nightstand. Oh, that reminds me. Thanks for those ceramic parrot earrings you gave me. I love them so much. One day I'll have to wear them!"

She climbed aboard her pink and white Harley, pushed the bike's starter button, gave me a thumbs up, and wheeled away from me. I watched her go. The fender over the rear tire had a round sticker on it that read "Shapp for President."

The eclipse was long over now. Cavalry sat in my shadow, and together we stared at the bloated bodies of carp rotting beneath the smoky sky. We stayed on the shore of the lake for a few more minutes, and then Cavalry followed me over to my car. On the drive home, we passed the trash-strewn yard of an old mobile home with a sign planted in the front yard: "Elect Joe Shapp." He'd been elected to the US Senate when he was thirty years old. That's where he got rich. He always voted the party line which is how he ended up being selected as the running mate for the current president. Now he was running as the Democratic nominee for president, himself, even though recent allegations of bribery, extortion, and foreign contributions to his campaign were beginning to surface as the election drew closer. I knew too much about Joey to ever vote for him. The America I once loved was gone forever, but I had long suspected that the country I'd believed in, the one of freedom, equality, justice, and unlimited opportunity for all, had never really existed anyway. I still loved the idea of America, for the promise of what it could be, but the levers of power were always in the hands of con artists and grifters like Joey Shapp. Under their leadership, the nation was little more than a shoreline filled with rotting fish and decaying algae.

I got home, opened the door, kicked off my shoes, and invited Cavalry into the house. Karma came into the kitchen while I was giving the dog some food and water. She looked at me, looked at the dog, then looked back at me with light sparkling in her bright blue eyes.

"Jesus," she said. "Ain't that somethin'! You fixin' to keep him?"

"Could," I said.

I ran my hand across the crucified Christ on Cavalry's ribs. The dog turned to face me and licked my hands, my face, and my feet.

"Once a stray dog licks ya, y'all are bound by the immortal rules of the universe to be owner and slaves to one another for the rest of your lives," Karma said.

"Owner and slaves to one another," I said. "Just like us."

Karma flipped a middle finger over her shoulder as she headed out the back door to put an umbrella over the Sour Diesel, Lemon Kush, and Snowcap growing in the sunny planters on the other side of a pair of metallic spheres, one silvery white and one yellowish, that reflected the trees, plants, and vegetables growing riotously in the garden. Cavalry and I followed her out the back door. Karma shaded the pot plants, and then she set about refilling the hummingbird feeders as the little birds hovered, dove, and shimmered the air about her with the frenetic beating of their iridescent wings.

"...she set about refilling the hummingbird feeders as the little birds hovered, dove, and shimmered the air about her with the frenetic beating of their iridescent wings."

I went back into the house with Cavalry. I put him in the tub in the master bathroom and washed all the dirt from him so that the tattoos shone with their original brilliance. I took off my shirt and dried him with it. Then I made a bed for him in the guest room, under a painting by Chagall of a man and woman flying together above the entire world. When I was done with that task, I spent the remainder of the afternoon and evening playing saxophone for the joy and love of playing while everything around me, but Karma and Cavalry, turned to flame and ash.

Epilogue The Final Word

They say the Lord works in mysterious ways which is just another way of sayin' you never know what's gonna happen until it does no matter how much plannin' you do or don't do though I never were one to let things just fly aroun' by the seat of my pants which is why I always carried 'round most ever'thing I ever needed to get by like gum or scissors or them little screwdrivers in case your readin' glasses need fixin' or maybe an extra pencil with a good eraser an' a pocketknife with a leather punch an' nail file the kind that got a corkscrew too or an emergency foil blanket folded up in one of them little squares no bigger than a lady's compact an' a waterproof poncho that comes packaged in plastic an' ain't no bigger than a index card about a quarter inch in thickness an' them yellow squares with the sticky stuff on the back for leaving notes an' such an' a comb an' toothbrush the type that got its own plastic case lined with zinc for killin' germs an' a bottle of ibuprofen or them little one size fits all pair o' gloves etc etc just cause you never know so a body needs to be prepared for any circumstance the same holds true for the things the Lord puts in your path cuz it's better to be prepared for an opportunity an' not have one than it is to have an opportunity an' not be prepared whether its somethin' like a job openin' or findin' your soulmate who I found then lost but found again just two months later an' enterin' into that whirlwind o' passion but then comes the babies an' money stress an' the kids walkin' in on y'all when you're tryin' to be intimate but then the babies grow up an' marry and have their own children an' you're worryin' about gettin' older but findin' ever'thing is better including the sex though some folks might think that ain't the truth but it surely is there ain't no little kids cryin' an' scrappin' out in the hallway you got money an' time to set an' talk an' laugh an' make love slow an' both o' you knowing what you like an' want staring into each other's eyes and seein' them for who they are and who they was when they was young as though you was lookin' not at them but at their soul an' spirit as though they was made of light and star dust mingling with all your light an' star dust in this sorta dance where time just ceases to exist an' both o' y'all are in state o' grace where you an' him are inside each other both body an' mind not knowin' where either o' y'all begin or end in wordless

284

breathless wonder an' miraculous naked amazement where ever'thing you are an' ever was is right there for him to see touch feel taste as it is for you and you together this moment of ecstatic communion passing between y'all for what seems like hours turnin' into eternity filled with passion an' joy at bein' in the moment where it's like you become this body of flame together or the smoke o' candles twistin' up together in the dark o' the room which is more light than the brightest midday cuz your entire bein' is nothin' but a thousand eyes an' those kisses you take are filled with somethin' like the promise o' paradise for as long as you can stand it divine an' holy as angels an' innocent as though it was your very first time no matter how many men you was with before or how many times you receive the gift of his love an' he done received yours this alchemy of the profane distilled into somethin' sacred each second seems forever as though you see the face o' God while you are in that moment you think I remember this I remember this an' how could it be you could ever forget somethin' this extr'ordinary this perfect only it's like there's no way to revisit it in your memory but only through the experience of your light and his dark an' his light an' your dark each cell o' your body a magnet seekin' the iron of hisself an' each cell in him seekin' the iron of who an' what y'all are together makin' somethin' new between the both o' you an' wonderin' how on earth could such love exist as though you found a piece o' heaven or an ancient fossil made o' stars an' comets an' infused with the Lord's breath or when y'all look at each other it's like lookin' in a mirror made of obsidian where you see yourself and all your past an' present an' future through all time this love this endless love this wondrous gift o' the eternal timeless Lord we shall meet again. Love

'...as though you was lookin' not at them but at their soul an' spirit as though they was made of light and star dust mingling with all your light an' star dust in this sorta dance where time just ceases to exist....'"

www.ingramcontent.com/pod-product-compliance
Lightning Source LLC
Chambersburg PA
CBHW070314260626
47160CB00003B/839